www.lostranchbooks.com

WHITE WINTER

To Love Kindness

Laurie Marr Wasmund

The White Winter Trilogy, of which this book is a part, is a work of fiction.
Apart from the well-known actual people, events, and locales that figure in
the narrative, all names, characters, places, and incidents are the products
of the author's imagination or are used fictitiously. Any resemblance
to current events or locales, or to persons living or dead, is entirely
coincidental.

Front cover photograph:
Edith Borland Marr and John Marr, 1919
Wollaston, Massachusetts
Personal Collection of Author
Back cover photograph:'
National Archives
ARC 533111
Troops ready to hold the railway line
Merbille, France

Cover design by Laurie Marr Wasmund

Published in the United States by lost ranch books
www.lostranchbooks.com
ISBN 978-0-9859675-5-0

He has showed you, O man, what is good;
and what does the Lord require of you
but to do justice, and to love kindness,
and to walk humbly with your God?
Micah 6:8

ONE

In the basement typing room of Graves Oil, Mary Jane Grayson pushed the carriage release lever and pulled another document from her typewriter. Reading through it, she searched for mistakes.

Nearly six years now, a voice in her head told her. Nearly six years that she had been coming to work here at 7:30 in the morning on every day but Sunday and sitting for nine hours at this Remington typewriter. Nearly six years that she had been hammering away on the keys, typing leases crowded with details of sections and townships that added up to miles and miles of Wyoming or Texas or eastern Colorado. Oh, it was good money, and her mother and father appreciated the help that she gave the family. But she was nearly twenty-four, and still living at home, and without a suitor in sight.

Miss Crawley came through the door of the typing room, and the metallic chattering of the machines increased, infused with urgency. Standing beside her spotless desk, Miss Crawley rang a silver bell. Mavis Wilson and Annabel Croft, who had worked beside Mary Jane for years, both stopped typing immediately. Edna Dayton, who had replaced Kathleen when she left for France with the Graves Family Foundation Relief Society, was a bit slower, still new enough that she didn't appreciate how infrequently Miss Crawley allowed work breaks. Mary Jane laid her proof-reading aside.

"The afternoon newspapers are here," Miss Crawley announced. "And there are letters from the ladies in France. You may take fifteen minutes to read them."

The other girls leapt up from their chairs and rushed forward, but Mary Jane did not move. Nearly every day, she chided herself for giving up her opportunity with the Graves Family Foundation Relief Society. After that one terrible night in Montdidier, it had taken a month to arrange for her return from France. By the time she had embarked on an ocean liner to America, her homesickness had dried up, like an orange left in the sun, and her aversion to seeing mutilated and limbless men had long been dulled by the familiar sight of them on the streets of Paris.

"Are you coming, Mary Jane?" Mavis asked impatiently.

"Yes, yes, coming."

Reading the letters from the members of the Graves Family Foundation Relief Society had become a regular event, encouraged at the weekly patriotic rallies by Mr. Graves himself. He was certainly proud of the venture. A star-spangled banner that stretched across the front façade of the ornate office building on 17th Street listed not only the names of the men from Graves Oil who were serving in the American Expeditionary Force, but the members of the Relief Society as well: Mrs. Eleanora Brently, who was Mr. Graves' sister, Harriet Mills, Helen Parsons, and Kathleen O'Doherty.

"Read Kathleen's first," Mavis coached Edna, who had the clearest and most exact reading voice.

"It's so fresh you can smell the ink." Edna sniffed the newsprint before she read: "*Dear Employees of Graves Oil, The beginning of January finds us still living in the chateau in Amiens, France, and attached to the British Expeditionary Force. But we celebrated Christmas in good, old American fashion with the American engineers who are stationed nearby. We cut down a Christmas tree from the grounds of the estate, and we decorated it with foil stars and paper nativity scenes. The French women and children who live in the surrounding countryside also came to celebrate the holiday. Because of the shortage of cloth in France, everyone dresses in black, including babies, but their happy faces when they opened our Red Cross gifts of hard candy and socks were anything but mournful.*

The engineers formed a chorus and sang Christmas carols, while the division band played its very loudest and proudest. The chaplain led us in a Christmas prayer, in which we all prayed for a quick end to the war and a lasting peace.

Each of us was given a new fountain pen and a box of writing paper from the British command. In a surprise, Mrs. Brently gave us each a parasol and announced that we will be taking a short leave in Nice soon. We are allowed ten days leave for every four months that we serve with the Red Cross—"

"Where is Nice?" Annabel asked.

"I believe it's pronounced *Neece*," Miss Crawley corrected. "Look at the map. It's somewhere on the coast of France."

Mavis and Annabel ran to the map of the world that hung on the wall. Tracing the coastline of France with one finger, Mavis located Nice. "Here it is," she reported. "On the Med-i-ter—"

"The Mediterranean Ocean," Miss Crawley said. "Let's move on to the other letters. We have only a few minutes."

As Edna read through Hank's and Helen's letters, Mary Jane stared at the spot on the map. *Nice*, she thought. *The Mediterranean Ocean*. Oh, what had she given up?

After work, she hurried from the building before Mavis, Annabel, and Edna—who were still talking about the letters—caught up. Boarding a streetcar, she traveled to City Park, where she consulted a hand-drawn map that led her to a home in Denver's Park Hill neighborhood. The house was a sturdy brick structure, with two columns and a portico of polished granite. Colorado blue spruce trees shaded the front lawn, beautiful sentinels of the property.

Mary Jane straightened her skirt and hat. She wasn't sure why she was here, in this rich and stately part of town that was so unlike her own humble neighborhood, but she was sure of one thing: she had to do something.

The strangest-looking woman she had ever seen answered the door. The woman wore a man's tweed jacket, a shirt and collar, and a pair of wide-legged trousers. Her short white hair was combed straight back from her forehead and looped behind her ears. Her eyes were grayish-green, cool and quick, and her mouth looked as if it might form more easily into a frown than into a smile.

"Good afternoon," she said. "Are you here for the meeting?"

"Yes, ma'am," Mary Jane said.

"Please come in." The woman closed the door behind her. "My name is Julia Reston. And you?"

Mary Jane panicked. She had hoped she could mix into the crowd without being noticed. Her parents would never allow her to attend a lecture called "Peace through True Equality of the Sexes." She had told them that she was attending an organizational meeting of a Ladies' Preparedness Team at Graves Oil.

"My name is Mary Jane"—she searched for a name that she had typed earlier—"Casper."

Miss Reston did not question it. "Welcome, Miss Casper. Come into the parlor."

Mary Jane followed her into a room where twenty or so women were chatting among themselves. Chairs of all sorts, from padded dining room seats to camp stools, formed uneven rows from one side of the room to the other. A grand piano stood in one corner, its wood burnished to a shine, its keys closed away. The remainder of the furniture was old-fashioned and built of heavy wood. Yet the walls were covered by paintings, all in riotous explosions of color—faces highlighted with lavender, hair of orange and rust, hands with green veins standing rigid in the skin. The pure white dome of a cathedral burned against an unnaturally blue sky. A grimy-looking gray-black curtain opened to reveal a cage of sad, drooping birds in magenta and turquoise. A wall sported bricks in every hue but their true color—green, red, orange.

Mary Jane blinked. "Who painted all these pictures?"

"I did," Miss Reston said.

"They're, well"—she struggled to find a compliment—"I've never seen anything like them."

"I would hope not. Please, Miss Casper, have a seat."

Mary Jane sat meekly in a chair, her eyes still on the paintings. In the center of the wall hung a self-portrait—or so Mary Jane believed—of Miss Reston that was as strange as the woman herself. The painted Julia sported midnight black hair pulled severely from her face. Her skin was a pallid, unearthly gray, yet she had stark red slashes of paint on the tender lids above each green-gray eye, just below the eyebrow. Her bottom lip was a rich metallic blue. The paintbrush with which she had just painted her lip was poised in her hand. She was young—decades younger than the trouser-clad woman—and beautiful.

And something more. The only word Mary Jane could think of was audacious.

"Ladies!" A twenty-something woman called from the front. She had rich, dark hair and eyes, and a full-lipped mouth. "Ladies, could we have your attention?" When the chatter did not stop, she repeated, "Ladies, please, let's call our meeting to order!"

The women reluctantly took their seats. Once they were settled, the dark-haired woman said, "Thank you all for coming today. For those who don't know me, I am Mary Reed, Mrs. Verner Z. Reed. I welcome you all."

Mary Jane recognized the name from correspondence she had typed at Graves Oil. Verner Z. Reed was also in oil exploration. Rumor had it that he was far more successful—and far richer—than Mr. Graves. It was also said that Mr. Reed was more than two decades older than his beautiful wife.

Mrs. Reed continued. "In this time of terrible conflict, it is important that we keep the fight for equality in mind, for it is only through true equality of the sexes, through true participation in the government and political mechanisms of the United States and the world that we will achieve peace and full cooperation among nations. Now, let us call this meeting to order and stand for the Pledge of Allegiance."

Mary Jane turned toward a flag that was displayed near the piano. After the Pledge, Mrs. Reed read an ode to Susan B. Anthony that Mary Jane had learned in school: "*Oh, great pioneer in woman's cause! Oh, splendid, loving sister-heart! Oh, noble prophet and preacher! Your name will be revered by countless millions of proud, free women!*"

The ladies clapped heartily, and the call went out for those who had not attended before to stand and give their names and occupations.

Mary Jane's hands grew moist. If she admitted that she worked at Graves Oil, someone might ask her about the Relief Society. They might even recognize her face from the grainy photos that had been published in the newspapers last August. When her turn came, she said: "My name is Mary Jane Casper. I, uh, I work at a quarry."

"Welcome, Miss Casper," the women in the room chimed.

Mary Jane started to sit down, but her eyes caught the savage stare of a woman across the room. Miss Crawley sat on a divan near the far windows.

Mary Jane slumped into her seat, no longer listening as Mrs. Reed dawdled through the minutes of the last meeting and old and new business. Could she simply stand up and walk out? Did it matter if it was rude? With the exception of Miss Crawley, would she ever see any of these women again?

From the front of the room, Mrs. Reed said, "And now, Miss Julia Reston wishes to make an announcement."

Miss Reston rose, holding a sheet of paper in her hands. "I have here a letter from the Equal Suffrage Association of Colorado to the National Woman's Party of Colorado," she said. "Dated December 2, 1917, it states: 'We denounce the methods and actions of the women "picketing" the White House as unpatriotic and not in accord with the principles of this association; we declare they have impugned the good faith of the United States in the eyes of Russia and other foreign nations.'" She paused. "According to this, Mrs. Chapman Catt and the National American Woman Suffrage Association have called for the U.S. Attorney General to investigate the National Woman's Party and its members and donors. Rather than joining hands with us, they are calling for woman to rise up against woman."

The women in the room booed and catcalled.

"The 'Suff Ladies' who signed this letter," Miss Reston continued, "are those who have been led to believe that the strategies used by the National Woman's Party are unladylike. They call them"—she consulted the letter—"'militant.' They denounce those of us who chain ourselves to the Capitol Building. They disdain the watch fires that the National Woman's Party has set up near the White House to demand the right of all American women to vote. They have even endorsed America's involvement in the war—"

Hisses filled the room. Mary Jane glanced toward Miss Crawley. Given Mr. Graves' support of the war, no one at the oil company dared to speak against it. Yet Miss Crawley called out in disapproval.

"But we will not be silenced," Miss Reston said. "We will support our Colorado sisters, Natalie Hoyt Gray, who is a student of law, and Dr. Caroline Spencer from Colorado Springs. Since October, both have been in the Occoquan Workhouse, a place of appalling conditions. They were violently attacked at a rally last year because they carried a banner that men said 'insulted' our President by referring to him as 'Kaiser Wilson.' Yet if President Wilson is insulted by being compared to the Kaiser, why does he not respond to our calls for equality and fairness and drop the idea that the states should decide one by one if women should vote?"

Outrage echoed through the room.

"Enough," Miss Reston ordered, and the room quieted. "The women of the Equal Suffrage Association believe that once a woman is guaranteed the right to vote, our battle will be won. But we know that women will never be equal unless they achieve erotic equality."

The room erupted, the women rising and applauding as one. Mary Jane rose as well, clapping politely, although she did not know what they were talking about. She looked to her left once more, searching for the bruising eyes of Miss Crawley, but she could not see her.

Miss Reston spoke again, and slowly, the women sat down.

"Margaret Sanger knows this," Miss Reston said. "Ethel Byrne knows it. Both have been arrested and jailed because they know it. But the message cannot be kept quiet for long. Any woman who has taken steps to prevent herself from bearing an unwanted child—whether born in wedlock or born illegitimately—will shout it whenever and wherever she can! Parenthood should be voluntary and planned!"

Applause echoed through the room, but Miss Reston held up her hand. "Women cannot allow the church or the state—or a husband or lover or the patriarchy under which we live—to determine when and if they become mothers. They must demand erotic equality in which birth control is available to and practiced by every woman in America."

The women rose to their feet again, chanting in unison: "No God, No Masters! No God, No Masters!"

Once the room calmed down, Miss Reston asked, "What does this have to do with peace? After all, the topic today is 'Peace through True Equality of the Sexes.' In this world that chooses war over peace, that promotes destruction and industrial greed over kindness and love, a mother who bears a son faces the real possibility of losing him in a war such as the one that is killing 20,000 men a day, right now, as we speak."

She paused, letting the silence in the room ache with sorrow. "Am I violating the Espionage Act with my speaking against war? Most likely. Am I violating the Comstock Laws by speaking of birth control? Most definitely. But I contend this: Were all children loved, blessed, wanted by their parents, were all children brought into homes where they were safe and secure, were all children the product of *a woman's choice*"— she waited until the applause died down—"we might not need to endure the brutality, the waste, the slaughter and untimely deaths of our sons, brothers, fathers and husbands. We might better understand that human life is not to be squandered on a foreign battlefield or degraded by conscription or some other device of a government that cares more for its survival than the survival of its people. If all children were the product of a woman's choice, 'cannon fodder' would not be a word in anyone's vocabulary. If all children were the product of a woman's choice, *we might never have war again!*"

There would be no silence after that statement. As the women around her cheered, Mary Jane dashed for the foyer. She had just stepped outside the front door when Miss Crawley caught her arm.

She faced her supervisor. "I'm so sorry. Please, don't fire me. I didn't know what this meeting was really about. I thought it was a peace rally—"

"Calm down, Mary Jane." Miss Crawley used her Christian name for the first time. "I can't fire you for what you do on your free time. Besides, wouldn't I also have to fire myself?"

Mary Jane said nothing. Miss Crawley had just spoken more to her in those three sentences than she had in six years at Graves Oil.

"Let's go inside and talk," Miss Crawley said.

Mary Jane followed her through a narrow gate at the side of the house and into a south-facing room that blazed with light. Part of the room was a standard, old-fashioned, kitchen—black stove, cupboards, a pie safe, with a wooden farm table in the center of it. Yet at the other end, where the light was brightest, oilcloths spread across the floor. Canvases of all shapes and sizes were propped along the walls. An easel with a half-finished picture of bright greens and orange stood near a smaller wooden table that was cluttered with tubes of paint, tins of brushes, and used palettes.

"It's an art studio in the kitchen!" Mary Jane exclaimed.

"Yes, Miss Reston creates her lovely works here." Miss Crawley moved toward the farm table. "Let's have some coffee. Miss Reston usually serves refreshments after the meeting adjourns, but I'm sure she won't mind."

"Are you friends with her?"

"Friends? No." Miss Crawley smiled. "I would like to call myself her friend, for I admire her greatly, but so far, we are only acquaintances. Let's sit down."

Applause echoed from the living room, and Mary Jane wondered what Miss Reston was suggesting now. Erotic equality, birth control—those were words Mary Jane would never hear spoken in her parents' home.

"Why did you come this afternoon, Mary Jane?" Miss Crawley asked.

"I wanted to do something to . . ."

She trailed off, and Miss Crawley said, "I've sensed that you haven't been very happy since your return from France. Perhaps you regret leaving the Society, after you were honored to be chosen?"

Mary Jane swallowed back tears as she nodded.

"Why did you return?"

"I was so scared that first night. Mrs. Brently, Mr. Graves' sister, was very kind to me, and she really wanted me to stay, but—"

Her words fell away, and Miss Crawley did nothing to fill the silence.

"I wish I would have been as brave as the others."

"I see," Miss Crawley said. "I didn't expect you to be the one to return. In truth, I thought it would be Miss O'Doherty. She always struck me as vain and inconsistent, wanting one thing now, another thing as soon as she had her first choice."

"Kathleen? I don't think she would come back."

"Why is that?"

"She's Mr. Graves' favorite. She's always had a love crush on him, and I think he has one on her."

"So that's how she avoided the age requirement," Miss Crawley mused. "Why did you lie earlier about your name and occupation?"

"Because I didn't want anyone to connect me with the Relief Society."

"That might have been a wise move." Miss Crawley plunked two cubes of sugar into her coffee. "As you heard, this faction of the women's movement doesn't support the war."

"This faction?" Mary Jane asked. "Aren't all women for the vote?"

"Not at all," Miss Crawley said. "And there are two ways of viewing women's suffrage. The Equal Suffrage Association, which sent the letter that Miss Reston read, believes that we will win when all American women can vote. But the feminists of the National Woman's Party see that as short-sighted."

"Because women can already vote in Colorado?"

"Not necessarily. But you heard the term erotic equality. You heard Miss Reston speak of birth control."

Despite the warm cup in her hands, Mary Jane shivered.

"I see you are offended by that term," Miss Crawley said.

"I don't know," Mary Jane admitted. "I've just always thought... Isn't it wrong to talk about it?"

"That is what we have been told by our government and the men around us." Miss Crawley said. "How much do you know about what happens between a man and a woman, Mary Jane?"

Mary Jane's mouth went dry. She had spent years ridiculing Miss Crawley with the girls in the typing pool. And now, here they were, in this kitchen where weird and inscrutable paintings leaned against the walls, talking about sex.

"My mother told me about it before I went to France."

"Your mother is a sensible woman," Miss Crawley said. "As you know, women don't always wait until they are married to enjoy the love of a man. At times, there are unintended consequences, usually in the form of a child." She took a sip of coffee. "Some young women try jumping off ledges when they find themselves in that situation. Some try wood grain alcohol or worse, and drink themselves into stupors that leave them witless and slow. Some use bleach as an internal wash, which leaves them damaged and crippled. Some attempt to use sharp objects. Why, only last week, there was an article in the newspaper about a young factory worker who tried to solve her dilemma by using a wire clothes hanger. Did you see it? The police found her and sought medical help, but they also charged her. She is now a criminal."

"But shouldn't she be? She isn't married."

"There are many who feel that way," Miss Crawley acknowledged. "But some young women commit suicide because they are so desperate."

Mary Jane's indignation soared. "Aren't there homes for girls like that?"

"Yes, there are," Miss Crawley acknowledged. "In fact, Miss Reston is a great supporter of the Florence Crittenton Circle that helps young women who stray from the paths of virtue. There is a Crittenton home here in Denver."

"Why didn't the factory worker go there?"

"For many reasons—shame, fear, a lack of education. It might even be a lack of knowledge of the language, for many of the girls are newly-arrived immigrants. Maybe, she didn't know whom to ask for help. And the homes run by the Catholic Church are more bent on oppressing young women than they are on being generous or kindly."

"Kathleen is Catholic," Mary Jane protested. "She always seemed kind, and she wasn't oppressed. After all, she went to France."

"Miss O'Doherty is a peculiar case." Miss Crawley's nose wrinkled as if she had smelled something foul. "She seems quite unperturbed by any type of authority. Do you attend a church, Mary Jane?"

"My family goes to the Methodist church."

"What would your pastor say about these young women?"

"I don't know." Mary Jane considered. "That they will go to Hell?"

"Or that we should help the least among us, as Jesus instructs? Do you think that someone who is driven toward suicide or self-abortion makes that choice lightly? Is it right to punish them for their despair and fear or should we help them?"

"Don't you believe in Hell?"

"I believe in common sense humanitarianism." Miss Crawley's voice grew passionate. "Think about it. If every young woman had erotic equality, none of this would happen. Birth control allows for a woman to make better choices, to live a better life, whether or not she is married. She can decide when she has a baby. She can control her own life."

Somehow, Miss Crawley's words made sense. Every woman wanted to be able to choose her own fate.

"It's unlikely the young woman with the coat hanger will ever have children now, all because the law and the state denied her the right of erotic equality," Miss Crawley said. "Had she been allowed to protect herself with a modern, scientific invention such as the cap, she would not have conceived, and she would still have a bright future ahead. Are you following me?"

Mary Jane shook her head. "The cap?"

"It is properly called a cervical cap, and it can be fitted by a nurse or physician in complete safety and privacy." She shook her head. "But it is illegal, and those who advocate its use—such as Mrs. Sanger—are persecuted and jailed."

Mary Jane said nothing, overwhelmed.

Miss Crawley dug in her handbag. "I have something you may be interested in."

She laid a copy of a newspaper called *The Woman Rebel* on the table. A black square announced the title in hand-written white letters, with the words, "No Gods No Masters" beneath it.

Mary Jane pointed to the slogan. "They were chanting that earlier."

"Yes, they were," Miss Crawley said. "This newspaper was written by Mrs. Sanger. But she ran afoul of the Comstock Laws, which prohibit the sending of obscene materials through the mail—"

"Obscene? I'd better not—"

"According to the law, anything that any postal worker declares 'obscene, lewd or lascivious' can be banned," Miss Crawley said. "Nothing that educates young women about their changing bodies, or teaches them proper hygiene, or addresses relations with their husbands can be sent from one to another. A mother cannot even legally send advice to her married daughter about childbirth. And medical books discussing anatomy cannot be sent through the mail."

She gestured at *The Woman Rebel*. "That is why this newspaper is so rare. It is the reason Margaret Sanger went to prison."

That evening, Mary Jane reads the eight-page *The Woman Rebel* from cover to cover. It's all new to her, strangely exciting and daring. Women are to "look the world in the face with a go-to-hell look in the eyes," and to abandon conventions. On the final page, she comes across a series of statements that resembles the Apostles' Creed that she repeats in church every Sunday:

Because I believe that woman is enslaved by the world machine, by sex conventions, by motherhood and its present necessary child-rearing, by wage-slavery, by middle-class morality, by customs, laws and superstitions.

Because I believe that these things which enslave woman must be fought, openly, fearlessly, consciously.

The next day, she works at her Remington impatiently. Over and over, she types the word, "Casper." She wonders if Miss

Crawley—who acts as if nothing happened yesterday—is assigning the leases to her to shame her for using the town's name as her own.

After the long work day is over, Mary Jane waits for Miss Crawley outside, lurking in the shadows of the stone building, hiding her face when anyone passes. She will be ruined if Mavis and Annabel find out about this.

When Miss Crawley walks around the corner from the side alley and onto 17th Street, she gives Mary Jane a warm smile. "Mary Jane! Are you waiting for me or for someone else?"

"Are you going to another meeting at Miss Reston's?"

"I have another engagement tonight."

"Oh," Mary Jane says, disappointed.

"You read *The Woman Rebel,* then?"

"I did. And then, well, I remembered something last night."

"What is it?"

She draws in a deep breath. "When I was in Paris, I went with my chaperone, Mrs. McLaughlin, to the Scottish Women's Hospital. In one ward were Belgian and French girls—some as young as twelve—who had children who'd been fathered by, well, they'd been born because the Germans—"

"The girls had been raped?"

Mary Jane nods. "The nurses said that no one knew what would happen to the babies after the war. Would they be Belgian or French, because of their mothers? Or would they be German?"

"What a tragic situation for those young women and for the children."

Mary Jane straightens her shoulders. "If there is something that can prevent that from happening, I'm all for it."

Miss Crawley touches Mary Jane's arm. "I'm not sure that anything can prevent the atrocities of war," she says quietly. "But I'm glad you are joining us."

TWO

Coloring first with a blue pencil, then a green, Kathleen tried to capture the colors of the Mediterranean Ocean. Nothing she did seemed real or true enough. The blue of the sky rivaled Colorado's, and the sand along the foaming water was nearly as pure and white as snow. Kathleen sat on a low-slung chair beneath a beach umbrella. Near the shore, Hank and Helen strolled, their faces protected by the parasols that Mrs. Brently had given them after Christmas. Occasionally, one or the other would stoop to pick up something from the sand.

Kathleen sketched quickly, afraid that this perfect seascape might elude her—Hank and Helen, with their skirts steel-blue and salmon-pink, the parasols in delicate shades of dove gray, the indolent fronds of the palm trees along the boardwalk swaying in the breeze. Hank waved at her, and she waved back.

She thought about the letter she was writing to Paul:

It isn't truly warm here, especially when the breeze blows from the ocean. But the sun is so strong during the middle of the day that the sand is hot on the soles of our feet. Then the plein-air *artists come out on the beach in droves, and an equal number of passers-by stop to watch them work. Some of the artists arrive with baskets of food and jugs of wine, and they paint all day. I'm jealous of them—*

Hank and Helen came back to where Kathleen sat. Holding out a pink scallop seashell, Helen said, "Look at the color in this."

Since Kathleen had received a set of colored pencils as a Christmas gift from Paul, Hank and Helen had started to notice the colors around them. The vivid seashells of Nice were treasures for girls from the landlocked state of Colorado. In their room in the hotel, piles of shells were spread across the windowsill to dry in the sun. The entire room smelled of sea salt and raw fish.

"Can we see your drawing?" Hank asked.

"Of course." Kathleen handed the sketchpad to her.

Hank studied it with mock disdain, then announced, *"C'est parfait, mon amour."*

"Merci, ma petite chou."

Laughing, Hank sat down on one of the low chairs beneath the umbrella, while Helen stretched out on a blanket. Digging in a basket at her feet, Hank pulled out her diary. Even though the girls had been in France for only a few months, their adventures had filled up a full leather-bound journal.

"Listen to this," Hank said. "'So much has happened to us that I can hardly remember how we came to be here. The days of preparing for our journey in Denver, our sightseeing trip to New York, and the ocean voyage to Bordeaux seem like a different lifetime—'"

"When did you write that?" Helen asked.

"After two weeks in Montdidier! Boy, I didn't know much, did I?"

"You forgot to mention how many times we sang about the monkey in the zoo on the voyage over here," Helen said.

Kathleen laughed. The song, "Oh, I'd Like to Be a Monkey in the Zoo," which had been performed at a Broadway Revue that they had attended in New York, had become the rallying cry for the Relief Society. Whenever they felt sad, the silly lyrics made them laugh.

She sifted through her own memories: the weeks in Montdidier serving the French soldiers, the Relief Society's move to Amiens, which was under British command, and, last fall, the terrible aftermath of the battle of Cambrai. But Kathleen had a secret life that she hadn't shared with Hank or Helen. In New York, Jim Graves had proposed to her just before she sailed for France. She had said no—a wise choice, for in Montdidier, she had fallen in love with Paul Reston, who drove an ambulance for the French Army.

"'We've heard from Mary Jane that she arrived home safely,'" Hank read. "'She says she is happy to be there—'"

She stopped, and neither Helen nor Kathleen spoke. At last, Kathleen said, "I wish she would have stayed."

No one answered her. Kathleen had not heard from Mary Jane since before Christmas. Perhaps Mary Jane had found other things to make her happy—a husband, maybe, or volunteer work at home. Kathleen hoped that she had found a more fulfilling job than one in the typing pool at Graves Oil.

"Look, here comes Mrs. Brently," Helen said.

Mrs. Brently glided along the boardwalk, wrapped in a full-length fur coat. She wore a cloche hat over her golden-blond hair, and her blue eyes sparkled in the bright day. A smile spread over her face as she joined the girls. "I have news for you," she said. "My brother arrives tonight on the *S.S. Carthage.*"

"Mr. Graves is coming here?" Hank asked.

"It's somewhat of a surprise, even for me," Mrs. Brently said. "I knew that he was destined for Washington near the beginning of the year, but I didn't know he would cross the ocean. I received a cable earlier today."

Kathleen's breath snagged in her throat. She wondered whether Jim would bring up the proposal again. It seemed to her as if it had happened—as Hank had said—in a different lifetime.

"I would like for us to be in our uniforms when he arrives," Mrs. Brently said. "I believe that would be a fine tribute to him."

That evening, the girls waited for him in the hotel lobby in their uniforms, wimples, and capes. On the collars of their capes were jewel-studded brooches in the shape of an American flag, which had been gifts from Jim on their departure from America. Kathleen's hands were clasped in her lap, her shoulders stiff. As Jim came up the steps of the hotel, Mrs. Brently by his side, she saw that he was dressed in a trench coat and tweed hat, which made him appear as European as the British or French gentlemen she had seen in the town. But—

"Look," Hank said. "He's wearing his cowboy boots!"

"I bet no one here has ever seen cowboy boots before!" Helen said.

Hank laughed with delight. There they were—the boots that were famous in Colorado, with their intricate stitching and their brazen designs. Tonight, they had ribbons of red, white, and blue trailing up the seams. Kathleen had forgotten about his great vanity, his need to draw attention to himself, his innate arrogance. She'd forgotten, too, how he outshone everyone and everything near him by the very power of his physical presence.

He swept his hat from his head. "*Bonsoir, Mademoiselles.*"

"*Monsieur.*" Hank dipped in a graceful curtsey.

"Miss Mills, Miss Parsons, Miss O'Doherty."

Blood rushed into Kathleen's cheeks as his gaze lingered on her.

He continued. "Mrs. Brently tells me that you are all healthy. It is nice to see that you are safe as well."

"*Merci,*" Helen said. "*Comment était le voyage?*"

"Oh, I've quite exhausted my knowledge of French," he replied. "But the voyage was pleasant, although we were always on the lookout for German submarines."

The girls laughed, and Jim said, "I believe I've arrived just in time for dinner. Once I've checked into my room and changed, I'll join you here again." He glanced over his shoulder to where a well-dressed gentleman waited. "Harris, go ahead with the luggage."

The man nodded, and Jim pardoned himself to speak with the concierge. Mrs. Brently followed him to the desk.

"He brought his manservant with him!" Helen whispered.

"His what?" Hank asked.

"His manservant. Didn't you read *Oh, Money! Money!* by Eleanor H. Porter? All rich men travel with them. It's very elegant."

"Well, lah-di-dah," Hank said.

The private dining room where their meal was served gleamed with gilt ornamentation, while the bluish green carpets mimicked the color of the sea. Jim sat at the head of the sparkling table, with his sister to his right. He wore a tuxedo with black coat and bow tie. Kathleen sat next to Mrs. Brently, with Hank and Helen across the table. Harris, the manservant, was nowhere to be seen, but a bevy of waiters rushed to attend to their every need.

As they ate, Jim regaled them with stories from America.

"The suffragist movement is gathering strength. And Colorado's plan is being used as a model for giving women the vote throughout the entire country. That doesn't mean much to you two young ladies, who were able to vote in '16, but it means a good deal to the women who haven't yet experienced it." He turned his brilliant gaze toward Kathleen. "And to you, Miss O'Doherty, when you reach the age of twenty-one."

Kathleen bit her lip. No one had mentioned that she was only nineteen for some time, and she had hoped that they had forgotten how young she was.

"What about clothes?" Helen asked. "I've heard fashions aren't very pretty just now."

"You're right, Miss Parsons," he said. "Women's suits are of dark colors such as navy blue and gray. Because of the shortage of fabric, skirts are shorter and the baggy legs of the Oxford suit are no longer fashionable for men. Interestingly enough, hats are becoming larger and grander, because they can be made of scraps."

"My Aunt Maureen has always done that." Kathleen's eyes teared. "She makes the most beautiful hats out of nothing—"

"Oh, don't cry," Hank said. "You'll make us all homesick."

"I hope, Miss O'Doherty, that your aunt has gingham on hand," Jim said. "It's popular right now."

Kathleen wiped her eyes with a handkerchief. "Gingham?"

"The cotton fabric with little square patterns on it. Aprons, curtains, skirts, blouses—you name it, just about anything is made of gingham. I'm afraid they'll start making men's suits out of it, and we'll all walk around looking like checkerboards."

Kathleen smiled. Jim exuded a spark when he spoke, as if words were the wellspring of his power. She looked at the others— Hank, with her toothy grin, and Helen, her eyes rapt upon him. Mrs. Brently sat coolly to one side, but her mouth curved upward in a closed smile. All attention was directed toward him.

He continued, "America is certainly a country to be proud of just now. Every industry in the land is working to win this war. We're building airplanes and automobiles as we never have before. The Navy is recruiting men from every state, including Colorado, to build ships. Carpenters, electricians, welders, plumbers—anyone who has ever picked up a tool, it seems."

"How will they get the ships to the ocean?" Hank asked.

"It's easier to move the men," Jim said. "They'll go to the East Coast to work. There are over a hundred shipyards there now."

"Oh, I guess that makes sense," Hank said.

"Perhaps the best news that I can give you is that President Wilson has just released a plan for peace called The Fourteen Points," Jim said. "It asks for all the warring nations to come together and work toward independence for each and protection of assets and land for all. Under it, war would be forever banned."

"Oh, I'm all for that!" Hank cried.

"So the war might end soon?" Kathleen asked.

"No peace talks have been held yet, but there is hope."

"Oh." Kathleen leaned back, disappointed. Somehow she had expected Jim, with all his glow and smoothness, to know more. Perhaps she even expected him to be part of the peace-making process.

Mrs. Brently cleared her throat. "My brother has come to visit at a convenient time. Your contracts with the Graves Family Foundation Relief Society are up at the end of February. Each of you promised to stay for six months, and you've fulfilled your promise. If you want to go home, Mr. Graves has offered his protection and companionship to you when he sails for New York."

Silence fell over the table, the only sound the clink of waiters carrying away the dishes. Kathleen glanced at the other girls. Hank looked as if she had just been told she was no longer welcome, and Helen's dark eyes glittered with tears. Home, home, Kathleen thought. It had been so long. Jim's eyes were on her, trying to discern her answer. She looked down at her lap.

Finally, Helen asked, "Would you replace us?"

"If you all leave, yes," Jim said. "We would hold another competition to find young women who want to share in this opportunity."

"You have served proudly," Mrs. Brently said. "It won't reflect on you at all if you leave now. Think about it overnight. If you'd like to cable your parents to ask their advice, all you need to do is ask."

"Thank you." Helen pushed back her chair and rose. Kathleen and Hank did the same.

Jim rose as well. "Miss O'Doherty, would you stay behind?"

"Yes, of course." Kathleen avoided Hank's and Helen's gazes.

After the two girls went upstairs, and Mrs. Brently politely excused herself, Jim and Kathleen walked out on the boardwalk. Torches planted in the sand created a fiery and primitive path, and couples strolled in the cool night breeze from the sea.

Kathleen pulled her cape around her shoulders.

"Are you warm enough?" Jim asked.

"I think so."

"Would you be warm enough if you removed your wimple? I'd like to see your hair."

"Oh." She had caught it back in a lazy pony tail this afternoon. When she pulled the wimple away from it, the ribbon holding the pony tail came away as well. Her hair tumbled over her shoulders.

"That's much better." Jim brushed a tendril from her temple. "It's a shame to hide something so beautiful."

She said nothing, struggling with the uncertainty that she felt when he flattered her.

"Listen."

Jim motioned toward the ocean. The waves crashed against the sand and rocks, and the undertow roared. "It's almost ominous when you hear it at night, isn't it?" he asked.

"We've been sleeping with the windows open. I think it's soothing."

"I'm enough of a prairie lubber to find it fairly daunting. We weren't able to see much of the town or beach, coming in as late as we did this afternoon. I'm looking forward to seeing it all tomorrow."

"It's one of the most beautiful places I've been."

"As pretty as Colorado?"

She caught the teasing in his voice. "Of course not."

"I'm glad your loyalties are as they should be. I appreciated the sketch of the ceiling of the chateau that you sent me."

"I didn't have my colored pencils yet. I'll have to draw another for you."

"Colored pencils? Where did you find those?"

"A friend—" She stopped, thankful that the darkness beyond the flaring torches hid her face. "Someone gave them to me."

"Not just the red and blue used by editors and draftsmen, I assume."

"No, eight colors." She named them. "They're especially made for artists in Switzerland. Oh, but the orange doesn't work the way it should."

"If they've excited that much passion in you, I think you'll have to give me a sample of your art to take with me when I leave for Washington."

"Why are you going there?" she asked.

"Oh, it's all very tedious," Jim said. "There's a bill in Congress that concerns leasing for oil exploration on public lands. Do you remember all those leases you typed? Most of them were for land in Wyoming that's owned by the government."

He laughed. "Anyway, our government has a habit of withdrawing public land on which there are proven fields—that's what it's called when oil is found—from the company that discovered them. Most oilmen believe that the government shouldn't have the power to withdraw the land after the discovery, because the royalties are then lost to the individual who has put in the effort to find it. A number of us are set to testify before the Committee on Public Lands, and we've written an alternative proposal. Simply put, it says that if a certain oil company does the discovery work, then that company should be awarded the lease on the land and the money from the royalties."

"That sounds fair to me."

"Perhaps you should go with me and testify. You can be my bulldog."

Kathleen looked away, unsure of how to respond.

"You'll think carefully about your decision, won't you?"

He touched her shoulder, sending sensation down her arm. She hadn't forgotten how his touch affected her. It was as strong as it had always been.

Heat rushed to her face. "I think we all will—"

"Surely, you want to see your Redlands again," he said. "I delivered your sketches to your parents there. The land is as beautiful as you've claimed it is."

His ploy worked. She put a hand on her heart, homesick. "I wish now that I'd brought something from it to remember it. Something I could touch or smell or . . . At night, I think of riding Napoli over the ridge behind the house—"

"If I'd known that, I would have brought something with me. I'll send you something when I get home."

"You might muddy your boots," she teased.

"That is a risk I will have to take. And I will gladly take it for you, Miss O'Doherty. That is, if you don't go home with me."

She looked away. The salty air of the ocean, the gassy smoke from the flaming torches, Jim's nearness and the way he smelled—of freshly-applied aftershave and crisp, woolen clothing—it all made her feel as if she was but one step from falling into or out of something.

"This is all so sudden," she hedged. "I need time to think about it."

"I see." His words were stilted. "Well, then, perhaps we should go inside where you can think in peace."

Upstairs, in their room, the girls undress and wash up in the water from the pitcher on the vanity. It's only when they are ready for bed that Hank asks, "Are either of you thinking of going home?"

Kathleen lies down in her bed, still shaken by her encounter with Jim. She folds her hands under her cheek, as a child might, for comfort.

Helen offers, "When we were still at Amiens in December, I would have said no, because there was so much to do. But now that we're away from it . . ."

"It's so nice to be normal again," she continues. "We know where we'll sleep tonight. We know we'll eat on time. We know we won't be cold, or be kicked out of our beds so a dying man can have them, or be sent somewhere else at a moment's notice."

Helen doesn't mention the worst, but Kathleen senses they are all thinking about it: the blood, the stomach-twisting odor of men who've lived in their own filth for weeks in the trenches, the lice and fleas that feast on tender flesh, the men for whom a tetanus shot comes too late to keep them from the stiffness and agony of lockjaw—

"I wouldn't miss the cold and snow at all," Hank says.

"It will be cold and snowy in Colorado," Helen replies.

"But it's so much wetter here than at home," Hank says. "And my parents had a coal-burning furnace put in our cellar just last winter. It's so warm, even on the second story where our bedrooms are."

To walk away, never to see another wounded man. Never to hear the words trench or mortar or poison gas again. Never to have her hands and skirt spattered with blood, or her hair soaked and freezing around her ears, or her hands chapped and cracked from washing the foreheads and mouths of men who lay in the bitter wind. Never to feel that awful sense that what she does isn't enough—

"I miss my mother and father," Helen says. "And my brothers and sisters. Two of them have had birthdays since I've been gone, and I wasn't there."

Hank sits on the bed and wraps her arm around Helen's shoulders. "But there've been fun things, too. Remember how the Frenchies in Montdidier teased us about how different we were from the French girls? How shocked they were that we were allowed to walk down the street alone, or talk to them without a chaperone? Remember how they called us *les belles bonhommes* and said that we fought the war right along beside them?"

Helen laughs weakly.

"And how many of them asked you to marry them after you sold them cigarettes?"

"It has been fun at times," Helen concedes.

Hank asks, "What about you, Kathleen?"

Oh, to see Papa and Mama and Aunt Maury. To be at Redlands again, and to ride Napoli across the open fields, which would be starting to green. To feel the warmth of spring and to watch the sun go down behind the Rocky Mountains. The cows would be calving now, and the red-coated calves with their pristine white faces would jump and cavort on spindly legs near the banks of the stream. And Mama's flock of sheep would be lambing, the babies' wool nubbly and grayish. They'll shake their tails in glee as they nurse and belch in high, plaintive bleats. And soon, Papa will be hitching up the team of draft horses, Ned and Betsy, behind the plow to plant the wheat, and the wildflowers will bloom in the pastures, creating a carpet of yellow and purple and blue. And—

"I'll stay until Paul leaves," she says.

"Even though Mr. Graves is here?" Helen asks.

Kathleen stammers, and Hank cautions, "You can't deny it, Kathleen. He didn't come here to see us. I don't even think he came to see Mrs. Brently. Why, he barely looked at any of us as we were eating, only you! What did you talk about on the boardwalk?"

"He said that he hoped I would make the right decision."

"Which is the right decision?" Helen asks. "What he wants?"

"I suppose so," Kathleen admits.

"You like him, don't you?" Hank asks.

"I do like him," Kathleen says. "I like to listen to him talk. He knows so much about—well, just about everything."

"We all know that," Helen says.

"But you're still in love with Paul?" Hank asks.

"Yes, I'm still in love with him, and I'll stay in France so I can be with him."

They lapse into silence, and Kathleen feels the old nagging doubt that she felt in New York when she first turned down Jim's proposal. Who wouldn't jump at such a chance? Who wouldn't want such a man?

"If you're staying, I will, too," Hank says.

"So will I," Helen echoes.

Hank offers an arm to Kathleen, and she crawls from her bed and goes over to them. The three embrace, teary-eyed and breathing in gasps.

"It isn't just Paul," Kathleen offers. "I, well, I want to see it through."

"The war?" Helen asks.

She struggles to sort out her thoughts. "If I went home, and then read in the newspapers about the places we've been, I'd wish I were here. I'd feel left out or something."

"I would, too," Helen says. "I'd wonder whether anyone was helping the poor soldiers. And we haven't been assigned to American soldiers yet—I hope that will happen soon! And poor Mrs. Brently. She'd have to teach the new girls what to do and how to behave all over again."

"And even after they were trained, they wouldn't be nearly as good as we are," Hank says. "We are the best, you know."

Hank turns her head first one way and then the other to kiss Helen's and Kathleen's cheeks. Standing smartly and saluting, she trumpets the slogan of the arriving American soldiers: "*Lafayette, nous voici!*"

Kathleen bursts into laughter. Helen joins her, giggling into her hands. Both of them rise with Hank and salute. "*Oui, oui!* We are here!"

And so, the next morning, Kathleen leads Hank and Helen downstairs in a united front. Mrs. Brently and Jim are already in the dining room. As they enter, Jim dashes out his cigarette and rises to greet them.

Once they are all seated and the morning small talk has dried up, Kathleen lifts her chin. "Mrs. Brently, Mr. Graves, we've decided we want to stay for six more months."

Jim leans back, and Mrs. Brently shoots a quick look toward her brother. Hank and Helen watch him, too, their eyes wide with curiosity. Carefully, Mrs. Brently says, "That was a quick decision. Are you sure you don't need to consult with your families?"

"It was a quick decision," Kathleen says. "But it was an easy one."

"All of you are certain about this?"

Their voices sound in chorus. "Yes." "Yes, I am." "Yes, we are."

"Then we'll be going back to Amiens at the end of this week."

Kathleen glances at Hank and Helen for reassurance. Helen's eyes are watery again, but Hank lays a soft hand on Helen's arm.

"When will you go home, Mr. Graves?" Helen asks.

"I'll be in London for a week after I leave here," he says. "Then I'll be on my way to New York and, then, to Washington, D.C."

His gaze meets Kathleen's. It is the first time he has looked at her since the announcement. Fortunately, it is time to say grace. She bows her head, glad to hide the flush on her face.

THREE

As a treat, Jim took Eleanora and the girls to dine at the *Restaurant de la Réserve*, a former lighthouse that straddled the jagged rocks of the cliff near the sea. A pagoda-style private dining club stood on another jutting rock, and an actual sailboat with mast and folded sail perched on a third. The Graves party dined in the curtained pagoda, which they accessed via a set of wooden steps from the beach below the rocks. After a meal of wild sea perch, eggplant, and caviar—which none of the girls had tasted before and which none of them liked—they walked out to the adjoining sailboat over a wooden bridge built between it and the pagoda. Jim stepped into the boat and held out his hand to help Ellie, Hank, Helen and Kathleen across the gap.

"Let's hope the tide doesn't come in and wash us out to sea," Hank said. "The Red Cross doesn't allow swimming for an hour after you eat."

As the girls laughed, Jim winked at Ellie, who presided over them like a contented mother hen. She acted differently here, so stately and settled that he could barely remember the desperate divorcée who had run through a string of men searching for a satisfying love.

From the stationary boat, the choppy Mediterranean Ocean was a deep greenish blue, nearly black where the waves crashed around the rocks. Above their heads, seagulls circled, whining and scolding, hoping for food.

Jim edged over to where Kathleen stood in the bow. "Did you bring your sketchbook?"

"Not today." She laughed. "I thought it might be rude to sketch as we ate."

"It certainly would be."

"Oh, but look at the color of the water! I wish I could capture it."

He restrained himself from laying his hand on hers. Her eyes reflected the aqua of the sea, and the color was high in her cheeks from the cold sea breeze and spray.

He looked out over the waves. "Across this ocean, in the Middle Eastern countries, is the largest oil supply in the world. It's even larger than what we are starting to find in the western United States."

"Those are the countries of the Bible, aren't they?"

"I believe so. Persia, Arabia, Egypt, Lebanon, Mesopotamia, and Palestine."

"To think we're so close to where Jesus walked," she mused. "I imagine camels and deserts and men dressed in flowing robes." Her eyes sparked as she added, "The Bible didn't mention oil. Will you search for it in those places?"

Jim laughed. "Not I. Shell Oil in Britain and the Germans have been vying for years for control over the oil in Persia and Mesopotamia. Some say that is what this war is actually being fought over."

"Oil?"

"And which country will reap the wealth from it."

"But—" She faltered. "But, from what I've seen, the hundreds of wounded and dead—oh, it has to be for more! It has to be for democracy and freedom. Otherwise, my friend Liam is right, and it is a war for the benefit of the rich at the expense of the poor. That makes the tragedy of it even more terrible."

"That's a subject best left untouched, I think."

From the stern of the boat, Eleanora suggested, "Let's walk down on the beach."

Hank and Helen started toward the side of the boat, and Jim went to assist. After he'd helped the women up to the bridge that led back to the pagoda, he turned to Kathleen. "Would you stay here with me for a moment?"

She glanced at Ellie, as if asking for permission. Ellie eyed him with only the vaguest wrinkle of coolness. Jim noted the look that passed between Hank and Helen as well. At last, Ellie said, "We'll meet you below. Don't be long."

Kathleen waved goodbye to Hank and Helen, then turned back toward the ocean. For some time, they watched in silence as the waves crash against the rocks below.

"It's hard to believe there's a war in this country," Kathleen said.

"A war that has taken up the time, attention, and energy of most of the civilized countries in the world while so much else goes unrewarded," Jim said. "President Wilson once said he was afraid that if America went to war, we would never be able to turn back."

"What did he mean?"

"A loss of innocence, I think. A loss of some of our human dignity, maybe even moral decency. Life in America is already faster, more demanding, and, in many ways, coarser."

"Coarser?"

"Everything has been evened out." He reached in his jacket for a cigarette. "The days of great individuality and self-determination are gone. There's an insistence on sameness. In dress, in manner, in entertainment, and even in public opinion. It's considered rude to stand out in any way from the others."

"But you're still wearing your boots."

"So I am." He laughed. "And I will continue to rebel in my own feeble way, too, because I've been stymied in business. Companies such as mine are expected to cooperate with one another rather than compete. Under the new rules, the price for a barrel of oil—or ton of coal or unit of steel—is set by the government, and we all sell our oil at that price. It takes away the glory of it."

"But it sounds fair," she said. "If all the companies are selling at the same price, then the people buying kerosene or gasoline should be paying the same price at every store in town. That's a good thing, isn't it?"

"In one way, but it's much less costly to produce a barrel of oil if the company has the equipment and financial backing of, say, Rockefeller's Standard Oil than it is for a smaller company—"

"Such as yours."

"Such as mine," he agreed. "You have to remember that my company is one of about a hundred thousand, but the three hundred million barrels that are produced each year in America are brought in by only a handful of those entities."

She digested his words. "But if you're—if an oil man is assured of the price, shouldn't he be able to keep his costs below that mark? Isn't it the same as knowing how much money you have to spend on food and planning the meals for the budget?"

"It's not so easily accomplished," he said. "But I doubt that the explanation would interest you."

"Why do you say that?"

The question flared, and he realized he had insulted her. "Let's just say that it doesn't interest me. Not with the waves and the water and the sunset."

She didn't let it go. "It sounds to me as if this is good for people like my parents, who have to work for every penny. It gives them some protection from the dishonest store owner or the businessman who only thinks of how much money he'll make."

"Perhaps," he said. "But I'm not sure it's the government's job to tell a businessman how to manage his own business. Granted, there are some who'll cheat, but the majority of businessmen are honorable. And public opinion would put the dishonest out of business in time."

"Not if there aren't any other businesses of that kind," she said. "Think about people in small towns. They might have no choice but to go to the dishonest businessman. And if you're honest, it doesn't matter if there are hundreds of regulations or laws. You're following them and you don't need to worry."

He took a drag from his cigarette. "Although I resent having to prove that I'm trustworthy. The laws and regulations were put in place for men who have less integrity than I do. Still, it's as if I'm assumed to be dishonest in my business dealings simply because there are some who are."

"Why would you resent it?" she asked. "You should want it, because then you can show everyone just how upstanding you are."

Jim let the ocean swallow the words. "Here we go again, Miss O'Doherty," he said. "Every conversation we have reminds me of a carousel ride."

She did not reply, but looked out at the water, her breast heaving with words that she had not yet spoken. After a moment, he added, "I can assure you that as a businessman, my thoughts are not all about how much money I will make."

"But—"

"Kathleen."

The waves crashed against the rock below. Something hot and glowing rose in Jim's chest, something that needed to be released.

"Since Eleanora's been gone," he said. "I've had no one to talk to. I have a thousand business acquaintances that I speak with—some of them every day—and I belong to all the fashionable clubs in Denver. But I have no one who shares my deepest thoughts. I miss you."

"In New York, you called me naïve and uneducated."

"That's what you remember from New York?" He gave a short laugh. "I also told you I was in love with you. Didn't that stick in your memory?"

A brilliant red rose up from her neck into her cheeks, but she said nothing.

"Let me ask you this," he said. "Did you make the decision to stay independently of Miss Parsons and Miss Mills?"

"What do you mean?"

"You weren't pressured by the other girls to stay, were you? You weren't persuaded by their zeal and commitment?"

"I decided first."

He tossed his cigarette butt over the side of the boat. Why should it surprise him that she had chosen her own fate? Her honesty both hurt and pleased him.

"I haven't given up the hope that you'll be my wife," he said.

"Even though every conversation would be a carousel ride?"

He put his hands on either side of her face. "As long as you, my sweet, are the brass ring."

He kissed her tenderly on her lips, which tasted of salt from the sea breeze. To his surprise, she stepped backward. "What's wrong?" he asked. "Are you worried about being seen?" Then, another thought occurred to him. "You've met someone, haven't you?"

"Yes, and I, well, I have, and I've fallen in love with him."

The words came out in a jumbled pile. Jim looked below to where Eleanora walked on the beach with Helen and Hank. What he had feared had come to pass. Kathleen had grown up.

"I trust he's American." His heart knotted, no longer beating with a precise rhythm. "I'd hate to lose you to a Frenchman."

"He's American," she assured him. "He drives an ambulance for the French. I met him the first night we were in Montdidier."

Jim caught the lift of her chin and glow in her eyes. "He gave you the colored pencils, didn't he?"

"Yes, as a Christmas present. But the fox collar and muff that you gave me are beautiful—"

"You needn't patronize me," he said shortly. "Why didn't you write to me about this? It seems I've come here for nothing."

"I haven't written to anyone about it." She glanced toward the girls on the beach. "Helen's afraid the Red Cross will send us all home because of me."

"I've heard that girls are sent home for far less than falling in love."

"I know, and I, well, I wouldn't do anything to harm either Helen or Hank or the Relief Society." She added, "Or Mrs. Brently. I like her so much."

"Yet you intend to pursue this ambulance driver, don't you? Tell me more about him."

The water shattered like glass against the rock below. "He's twenty-six, and he's been in France now for nearly two years. He went to Yale Law School, and he has a job waiting in Boston for him after—"

"That tells me absolutely nothing," Jim touched her arm. "Is he worthy of you, Kathleen? Can he see the value in a woman like you? Does he realize that you are not only lovely to behold, but that you are intelligent and quick? That you're not the sort of woman to be chained to a household with too little money and too many children, but one who should be treated as precious?"

She opened her mouth as if she would argue or deny his characterization of her. Then, simply, she said, "Yes, he is. He does."

"Then I suppose I shall have to give you up again."

"Will you tell Mrs. Brently?"

"Of course not. What passes between us is our concern. But this is the second time you've disappointed me, you know."

"I'm sorry."

"So am I," he said. "This time is much harder, too. When you turned me down in New York, I could blame your 'naïve and uneducated self,' as you put it. I can't do that now."

She said nothing. On the beach, Eleanora and the two girls were standing in a cluster, all of them looking at something that one held in her hand. He breathed out, trying to regain his equilibrium. "Well," he said. "Let's go down and see what the others have found. Judging by their interest in it, it must be a mythical sea serpent."

Sitting on the porch of the hotel, looking beyond the palms to where the waves washed in and out, Jim pours from a decanter of brandy. He measures his bitterness in the same way as he does the liquor. Kathleen has blossomed with the independence of thought and heart that he had hoped she would possess. Sadly, he can take credit for very little of it.

A movement to his left catches his eye, and Ellie appears at the door of the hotel, wearing her fur coat and no jewelry. In her simplicity and lack of adornment, she seems a stranger to him as well.

He stands and offers her a chair, then motions to the waiter to bring another glass. Opening his cigarette case, he holds it out to her. She takes one and lets him light it.

"What a surprise this has been," she says. "What made you decide to sail the seven seas at this perilous moment?"

He waves the match, killing the flame. "I was quite safe. There were about twelve-hundred Sammies aboard ship, all fully armed, although a few of them showed a distinct lack of understanding of the mechanisms of a loaded weapon."

"So what we're hearing is true? That thousands of American soldiers are arriving every day in France?"

"I have no doubt of it," Jim says. "We sailed in a massive convoy under the protection of French destroyers. Every ship was filled with soldiers."

"Yet there was room for you."

He laughs. "A surprising number of folks are still traveling for leisure on the ocean liners. I think it's mostly out of defiance—a stubborn proof that the free world still exists."

The waiter sets a glass before Ellie and pours brandy into it. After the waiter leaves, she asks, "What's happening at home? Is there any good gossip?"

"None whatsoever," he replies. "Except that Marie Grissom has taken up residence in Denver. I'm hoping Evan doesn't decide to join us as well."

"Oh, dear, Evan and Marie, who make their livings as parasites."

"Fortunately, I didn't see much of her during the fall."

"Well, if that's all the better you can do, I'm quite pleased to be out of the country just now."

As he laughs, he feels a pang, the old sense that he is missing out on something.

"It looks as if you'll keep your flock intact," he says. "Not one of them seems to be the least bit interested in hanging up her wimple and returning to the dreariness of America."

"I'm not surprised."

"Is it so exciting here?"

"I don't think you understand, Jim."

Her words come out too sharply, and she inhales a calming mouthful of smoke, then blows it out before she speaks again. "When we arrived in Montdidier last September, we came into the aftermath of a full-blown battle. From the moment we walked into town, the girls were surrounded by wounded men who were waiting for medical attention and more often than not dying before they received it. It's what drove Mary Jane to go home. And since that night, we've worked eighteen hours a day—even Sunday—and we haven't eaten proper meals, or bathed, or had fresh clothing. During the battle at Cambrai, the girls slept on the floor of the canteen for a week, with mice biting at them." She chokes up. "And still, each one puts her whole heart into her work. Each one willingly sacrifices her own comfort to help others."

"I apologize. I didn't mean to suggest that it wasn't worthwhile."

She leans back. "Will you send a new group of women this coming fall?"

"If the war is still on," he says. "I suppose Mother can help to choose them, and I can find someone from the company to escort them to Bordeaux. But I can't keep sending my employees overseas indefinitely. It's almost as hard to find young women to work as it is to find men, with so many of them taking jobs that were once held by men."

Ellie exhales again. "Think of it. All of that ability and intelligence that has been wasted over garden parties and china painting and babies' diapers is now being put to good use."

Jim laughs. "You sound more like a suffragist every time I see you. You're just as happy over here as the girls are, aren't you?"

"It isn't happiness, it's purpose," she says. "We're living in a way that every woman—that every person—should and few can. We go at a furious pace, with no certainty or security whatsoever of what the next day will bring, and it has made me very aware of finding joy and serenity where we can."

Jim envies her ability to live so fully. Taking another sip of brandy, he asks, "What will you do when you return to your indolent life of tea parties and musicales?"

"I don't know," she admits. "I feel no attraction for that way of life just now." She looks away as she speaks again. "I've met someone here. His name is Thomas Lloyd-Elliot. He's a newly-promoted 'Leftenant'-Colonel with the British Army, but he was in India before the war. He's thirty-eight and was widowed as a young man in his twenties. He has an estate in Surrey and a twelve-year-old son. He won the Distinguished Service Cross at Ypres. We met in passing on our first evening in Montdidier."

"That must have been quite a night."

"What do you mean?"

"Nothing." He waves her away. "I'm assuming the Red Cross rules of non-fraternization apply to you as well as to the girls."

"I suppose they do. But I have to work with Thomas anyway, given that he oversees the facilities near Amiens."

Jim lights a cigarette and flicks the match to the sand below. "It seems backward to ban love in a world that is tearing itself apart, and yet, that's what the Red Cross has done."

Ellie laughs. "That's an oddly romantic comment coming from you."

"Mother will be pleased by the estate. But she certainly wouldn't want to see you living in India."

"Nor would I." She exhales. "But Thomas and I haven't talked about that yet."

"Is there a title other than 'Leftenant' Colonel thrown in as well? You'd make a fine 'Lady.'"

"Mother can't have everything."

Jim laughs, but something aches in him. Both Ellie and Kathleen have found far more in France than could ever be revealed in letters or diaries or casual conversation. They've grown solid and sure, even powerful.

He sets his cigarette aside in the ivory ashtray. "I saw Anneka before Christmas."

"Oh, Jim, not that again."

Her scolding doesn't surprise him. Eleanora had sided with his mother and father about the fate of the young Swedish maid with whom Jim had had an affair nearly eight years ago. It was decided that Anneka Lindstrom would live out her life as a widow in a house provided by Victoria Graves, Jim's mother, and would raise her daughter, Mina, in luxury. Anneka could work in the elder Graves' mansion near Cheesman Park, with all expenses paid, for as long as she did not reveal the name of the father of her child.

Ellie's tone softens. "How is the little girl?"

"She'll turn seven in March," Jim says. "She's a sharp little thing. Her disposition is like her mother's—on the somber side, yet sweet and pleasant."

"Don't grow sentimental over her," Ellie warns. "If that situation somehow became public knowledge, Mother would drop dead from the shame. I nearly finished her off when I divorced Anderson."

"It seems that Anneka has fallen in love with someone and wants to marry."

"Does that surprise you? What she has now is a gilded cage."

"What she has now is security and protection for the rest of her life."

Ellie sips at her brandy. "But wouldn't it be for the best if Anneka did marry? The little girl would be someone else's responsibility. That is, if you believe you can trust Anneka."

The little girl. Neither Ellie nor his mother—and, of course, not his father—have ever called Mina by her proper name. He swallows the urge to snap at Ellie: *That 'little girl' is your niece.* Instead, he assures her, "I can trust her."

"Then, it would be to your benefit."

He does not answer at once. Anneka is only in her early twenties, and Mina is young enough that both of them could lead long lives without many memories of Jim. He thinks of the coat that he gave to Mina after Christmas. It isn't a full-length beaver coat exactly like the one he had given to Anneka, but it is camel-colored wool with a beaver collar. He had given Mina one for her doll, Marta, too, and Anneka hadn't protested. He suspects that she loves Mina too much to say no to her. Certainly he can't.

"Mother would be glad to have Anneka out of the house," he says. "I know that it makes her nervous having her there. It's a terrible burden trying to maintain utter control over everything."

"Dear Mother." Ellie laughs. "There are moments when I would have loved to have had her advice these past few months."

Jim arches his eyebrows. "Now I have proof that you're a completely new person. You wouldn't have asked Mother for the time of day before you left for France."

She laughs, but quickly sobers. "You don't know what a relief it is to move beyond the past. Since I've met Thomas, I can imagine a time when the specter of Anderson isn't standing just behind me and Mother isn't standing just in front of me, both with sour looks on their faces. Only good things could come if Anneka and the little girl were out of your life."

"That has always been the general opinion."

"But not yours?"

"I worry that their way of living will decline."

"That's to be expected. It's not likely that Anneka will marry above her station."

"What if they are poor?" He presses the words out of his chest. "What if the husband is drunk or cruel? What if she and Mina are left destitute?"

"You speak as if you have affection for them."

"I'd be a monster if I didn't, don't you think?"

"I think it's dangerous to have any connection with them," she said. "You could easily be ruined if she became unhappy and chose revenge."

"I don't think Anneka could ever be vengeful."

"I wouldn't be so certain," Ellie warns. "And what about Kathleen? You've created quite a stir among the girls by spending so much time alone with her."

"Well, I'll be sure to remedy that by being highly impartial toward all of them."

"What are you saying to her when you're alone? What are you offering? The only thing you could offer a Catholic girl is marriage, and that would be foolhardy, even for you. She couldn't marry outside her church—unless you're going to surprise us all by becoming a Papist?"

"You don't have to worry."

"Jim." She puts a hand on his. "Don't tangle yourself in another ugly situation, especially with a girl who is even more innocent and hopelessly religious than Anneka was. Surely, you learned some sort of lesson from that."

He inhales on his cigarette. Ellie has always had the power to make him feel small.

"How is it working out, having a Catholic in your group?" he asks sullenly. "I'm sure Miss Crawley and Mr. Hobart would be overjoyed if I went home and reported that she had saddled up like Joan of Arc and caused havoc through France by spreading the word of the Evil Pope."

"I don't believe she's that devout, although she does tend to pray more than the others."

"Don't shrug it off too hastily. There may come a time when you need it."

"Yes, well, if I do, I will reconsider."

"Which one of the girls is your favorite?"

"I couldn't possibly decide," she says. "Hank is always cheerful, always funny, and Helen is so devoted that I believe she could command an army of her own. She's more likely to be Joan of Arc. Kathleen brings a sort of unquestioning determination to everything she attempts."

"I believe that sums it up nicely."

"But you didn't answer my question. What did you offer her, and what did she say?"

"Her decision to stay in France speaks for itself, doesn't it?"

"I suppose it does," Unable to resist needling, Ellie adds, "At least, I'll still have her."

He does not reply, but swallows back his disappointment. Together, he and Ellie watch the waves roll onto the sandy beach until the darkness and the wintry chill drive them inside.

FOUR

Maggie stood behind the counter at Sullivan's Grocery, the store ledger before her. She ran a finger down the neat numbers entered by her mother, who was upstairs in her bed, where she had been since the news came that Donnell MacMahon had died in San Diego from measles. Worried that the next gold star to appear in the neighborhood would be for Seaney, Ma had abandoned the day-to-day management of the store as well as the attic millinery where she made her lovely hats.

The baby moved, and Maggie laid a hand on it. Her stomach had grown into a tight ball that squeezed all her other innards into the nooks and crannies of her body. Her lungs didn't take in enough oxygen, her stomach held only a smidgen of food, and her bladder had a mind of its own. Now that she was standing all day, minding the store, her feet had become great flopping fish attached to swollen ankles.

Still, she thanked Mother Mary every day that nothing had gone wrong.

She picked up a massive list of instructions from the counter in front of her. Newly issued by the U.S. Food Administration, the "home card," as it was called, banned so many foods that Maggie suspected the next version of it would ban food altogether. There were now two wheatless days a week, Monday and Wednesday, and one wheatless meal every day; one meatless day a week, Tuesday, with one meatless meal every day; and two porkless days, Tuesday and Saturday.

The restrictions were even greater for those who sold food. Customers were required to purchase an equal quantity of other grains every time they bought wheat products. With her mother's abdication, it had fallen to Maggie to carefully weigh wheat flour and then balance it with one of the substitutes of corn, oatmeal, or other grains. And sugar—well, if it could be procured, stores such as Sullivan's Grocery had to sell it at a price that allowed for no more than half a cent per pound profit.

She closed the ledger, the burden of regulations swirling in her head, and called, "I'm going to the bank."

No one answered from the dank corner where her father no longer carved meat, as it was illegal to sell it on certain days. In fact, chicken could no longer be offered on the domestic market, leaving the cold storage shed behind the store nearly empty. Pa had nothing to do now but drink.

As she walked to the bank, the voices in her head started up again: *Evelyn had to admit that, even after these many months of marriage, George was a puzzle to her. One day, it seemed she meant everything to him, and the next, she was almost forgotten as he went out to the country club to play golf or to have an evening at the Men's Club with his fellows. She was ashamed that she was jealous of his other connections, and she knew that he loved her, but—*

But—

But she didn't love him. No, of course, she did, but . . . Poor Evelyn, she had just grown weary of trying to figure out what marriage was all about.

Although *The Ladies' Home Journal* had accepted Maggie's second story called "Evelyn's Hope" for publication, Maggie had nothing more to offer. Lately, she had been unable to hear Evelyn's voice. Her head felt at times as if her brain weighed far too much for her skull. Others, it felt too light and breezy to think. And something always interfered—dreadful news from the Front, what she could or couldn't sell that day in the store, Liam's predicament. In the afternoons, after she left the store and before Liam arrived home from work, she sat in front of the mirror of the vanity—that is, when she was not so tired that she had to lie down—and wrote nothing.

"Mrs. Keohane!"

She turned. Mr. Austin, the mailman, was half a block behind her. She waved.

"I have your mail here." He handed her the letters addressed to Liam or her. "Here's yer mother's and father's. Looks like Seaney's written to ya, now."

"Thank you!" Maggie gathered the bunch of letters together and returned to Sullivan's Grocery. Instead of going into the store below, she climbed the exterior steps to the apartments above, one hand supporting the bulge of her stomach.

"Ma!" she called as she went inside. "There's a letter from Seaney!"

No reply came from the darkened bedroom. Ma lay in the bed, propped up by two pillows, her hair in a single braid that coiled over her right shoulder. Her eyes, which had always been a lively blue, were almost colorless in the dim light. Her skin looked shrunken and dull. Yet the room smelled of rose water, her favorite scent.

Maggie sat down on the chair beside the bed and opened the Blue Lady envelope with a kitchen knife. Inside were three letters— one to Ma and Pa, one to Auntie Eileen, and one to Liam and herself. She picked up the one addressed to her parents and read through the greeting to the second paragraph:

"*Christmas Day didn't seem much like Christmas. I missed you and Pa, and I missed Maggie and Liam, and Kathleen and Uncle Irish and Auntie Eileen. But we celebrated the best we could. You'll be glad to hear that the Catholic Church has finally come to France, and on Christmas, Mass was held in the KC tent. The priest is an American, Father Dover, and I've been to confession for the first time in ages—*"

"When was that written?" her mother asked.

Maggie checked the postmark on the envelope. "Four days after Christmas."

"Over a month now," Ma fretted.

"I'm sure he's fine." Maggie returned to the letter. "*On Boxing Day, we went to the new YMCA hall, which was filled with just about every kind of soldier you'd ever see. There were engineers, artillery, medical, pilots, and infantry, all together for the celebration. The whole hall was lit with electric lights, and there was a stage in the center of the building. Bands from both American and French*" *divisions around the area had come in to play for us in a blast of sound that rivaled the horns of Jericho. We stomped our feet and shouted and sang along to the songs we knew—"*

She finished reading the letter, then folded it and placed it on the stack beside Ma's bed, where Ma would read it again and again, until the ink was worn away by the oil of her fingertips. Standing, she leaned over and kissed her mother's forehead.

"I'll be back tomorrow," she said.

At home, Maggie took a crock of pinto bean stew from the cold storage. Because so little meat was available, vegetable stews had become the most common meal in America. As she lit the fire in the black stove, a voice sounded in her head: *A pound of pinto beans is equivalent to 1.63 pounds of sirloin steak or 18.6 eggs.* How did the government figure that out? And who would eat eighteen eggs? She had to start reading Shakespeare and Milton—or even a dime novel or two—again before she forgot how to read anything but facts and figures.

She set the crock on the stove; by the time Liam arrived home, the putrid stuff should be warm.

In the living room, she sat down to read the letter from Seaney. When she was about halfway through it, a knock sounded on the front door. She found Mr. Austin on the stoop.

He offered her a brown-paper wrapped package. "Sorry, I forgot to give ya this when I saw ya earlier."

"Thank you."

The package was from *The Ladies' Home Journal*. Maggie hurried to the sofa. Her heart beating hard, she tore away the paper and found two advance copies of the magazine. She ran a finger down the Table of Contents until she came to the title: "'Evelyn's Joy' by Margaret James." Flipping to the page, she saw on the left-hand side an illustration of a young woman dressed as a bride and holding a bouquet from which petals fell, leaving a dainty trail behind her. The title of the story was written in swirling, cursive letters. On the right-hand page, she read: *Evelyn walked along the path around Seller's Lake. Her step was clipped and brisk, and some might even say it was hasty, but it was all because she was happy. No doubts clouded her thoughts; no petty warnings, dispersed by her mother or Aunt Georgia, niggled their way into her head. She was going to ask George today what he thought of marriage, although she would never be so forward as to ask directly. But with his cousin Arabella's wedding coming up in June, she had a convenient occasion for inquiring—*

Maggie laughed aloud. How had this happened to her? Why was she so lucky? Women all over America would be reading her story and loving Evelyn as she did.

She was still seated on the couch, when Liam came home from work. As he prayed at the font of holy water near the front door, Maggie put the magazines into her sewing basket and closed the lid. She would surprise him after dinner. By the time he had hung up his coat and come from the narrow front hallway, she was slicing war bread, made from potato flour, in the kitchen.

He kissed her temple. "Hello, Mrs. Keohane. How was your day?"

"The same as usual," she said.

"Is your mother any better?"

"I don't think she'll get out of bed until Seaney comes home."

"What a tragedy this is for America's mothers."

Maggie put more effort into sawing the hard bread into slices. Whenever Liam spoke of the war, she was reminded that he still faced charges in the Denver courts for distributing propaganda and refusing to fill out the military Questionnaire. He had been sentenced to nine months in the Denver County Jail in December, but his lawyer from the People's Council of America for Peace and Democracy, Judah Rapp, had filed an appeal on the grounds of freedom of speech and religion. Currently, Liam was out on appeal and awaiting a new court date.

They sat down to eat dinner at the tiny table for two in the kitchen. After Liam said grace, Maggie filled his plate with stew.

"What did you do in the store today?" he asked.

"I spent most of the day trying to figure out what I'm supposed to record and report now, given the new regulations."

"You didn't lift, did you?"

"Pa's doing all the deliveries now," she said. "Although I can't imagine that he talks to anyone. Maybe he just leaves the groceries on the front porch with a ring of the doorbell. Don't worry, I'm just the face behind the counter now."

"And a beautiful one it is."

Maggie reached for Liam's hand. Their fingers touched and twined together. "The baby's moving almost all day now," she said. "I wish you were here to feel him."

"I'll meet him soon enough."

They had set up the nursery just last week. The baby would sleep for the first few months in the cradle in which Seaney and Maggie had slept as infants. Later, he would move into a freshly-painted small bedroom that was next to Liam and Maggie's room, where he would sleep in a proper crib with metal railings. Liam had refinished the wooden rocking chair that Ma had used and put it in a quiet corner of the room. There was also a wicker changing table and a throw rug to warm the floor. Even thinking of the baby and her new role as mother made Maggie's stomach flutter.

"A letter came from Seaney today," she said.

"What does he have to say?"

"He told me all about the food they get. I guess the bread is made from something that makes it grainy and brown. He thinks it's sawdust. Then, there's something called canned bill, which is some kind of meat in a tin that the Americans give them, which is better than monkey meat, which is brought in by the French from Madagascar."

"Is it really the meat of monkeys?"

"I don't know," she said. "I guess it could be. Seaney says they've tried mixing things into it to make it taste better, but that just makes it into 'slumgullion.' It sounds like he's starving."

Liam laughed, and Maggie melted. He still carried the look of the orphaned boy in his tousled hair and plain clothes, but his hazel eyes and high cheekbones spoke of the brilliant scholar that he was.

After she'd cleaned up the kitchen and washed the dishes, she joined Liam in the living room. He had built a fire before stretching out in his chair, his feet on an ottoman, his glasses neatly folded beside him.

He appeared to be dozing in the warmth, but Maggie knew better. Sitting on the sofa next to the electric lamp, she took the magazines from her sewing basket.

"I have a surprise for you," she said.

Liam opened his eyes. "What is it?"

"My story came today." She showed him the front spread of the story. "Look at this! Isn't it pretty?"

"You've done well," he said, but she saw his eyes linger on the name at the top of the page: "Margaret James."

She closed the magazine abruptly, but kept her finger inside as a bookmark. "I'll read it to you, if you want."

Liam smiled wanly. "When will we read the newspaper?"

"Well, we can do that, too, I guess," she said uncertainly. "I don't think it will take long to read—"

"I'm tired," he said. "Maybe another time when I have more pep. I don't think I could follow your story tonight."

"All right." Maggie picked up the newspaper. *"GERMANS MUST REGISTER,"* she read. *"A Letter from Postmaster and Chief Registrar B.F. Stapleton—"*

As she mouthed the words, she agonized. Was Liam ashamed of her? Did he think she was making a fool of herself by writing? Or was it just the name Margaret James that annoyed him? He had never liked it, but Maggie knew that a name as Irish as Margaret Mary Keohane wouldn't do for an author.

Without looking ahead at the next article in the newspaper, she read: "Forty-six are listed . . ."

She stopped as the full headline registered in her head:

46 ARE LISTED AS PROBABLE ENTRIES FOR DRAFT

Men Who Failed to Return Questionnaires Likely to Be Placed in Class 1

Notorious Slacker Liam Keohane Included on List

Heart flaring, Maggie silently skimmed the column: "The local board has now completed its list of those who failed to respond with their answers. These men are to be placed in Class 1, which states that they are 'eligible and liable for military service,' regardless of any claims they may have made in the past to exemption. The only course of action that they may take is to complete and return the Questionnaire immediately. If they do not, the matter will be placed in the hands of the sheriff, who has instructions to seek out these men and to demand that they obey the law."

"What is it?" Liam asked. "Why did you stop reading?"

"No reason, I just . . . I'm sorry, I lost my—"

Liam came to her. Taking the newspaper, his eyes darted up and down the page and settled on the article in the bottom corner.

"I see." He read aloud. "One name on the list, Liam Keohane, is already familiar to the people of Denver. Last fall, on the steps of the State Capitol, he ripped apart the Questionnaire that so many of our brave men have answered without hesitation. Although Mr. Keohane claims that he is a Roman Catholic and a 'Soldier of Peace,' his own church has abandoned him. In October, he was expelled from membership in the Knights of Columbus, a Catholic men's organization, at Blessed Savior Roman Catholic Church, for being guilty of 'creating a public scandal' that is 'unbecoming for a member of the Knights of Columbus.' Mr. Keohane calls himself a 'Conscientious Objector', but we call him a 'slacker.'"

Liam laid down the paper, his face drawn.

Maggie wrapped her hands around her belly. "It's going to start all over again, isn't it?"

Liam looked at the fire. "My appeal hasn't yet been heard. By Rule Thirteen of the Selective Service, I can't be drafted until I am cleared of all civil charges."

"There's still time to fill out the Questionnaire and return it," she begged. "We'll talk to the Draft Board, to Dr. Thorp and Mr. Barry, and see if you can get a deferment. Once the baby is here, I won't be able to work for Pa, and you'll have a valid claim to—"

"You don't understand." Liam's voice rose. "You've never understood! I don't even think you've tried! Where is your faith, Maggie? Where is your devotion to God?"

She leaned back, stunned. "I believe as much as you do—"

"You think I should be like Sean, who just blindly followed along, never questioning, never thinking about what he was doing—"

"He knew what he was doing!" Her voice sounded far too loud in her own ears. "He went to war to serve his country—"

"He went to war because he didn't want to work in the grocery any longer. He wanted to be rid of your father, and maybe even your mother—"

"Ma?"

"She was going to keep him a child forever."

"That's a hateful thing to say!"

"Sean wanted an adventure, like so many of them do. He gave no thought to the laws of God when he signed up. He gave no consideration to his immortal soul."

The baby jumped, and Maggie loosened the grip of her hands.

"And do you know what he's doing in France?" she asked. "He's listening to concerts, and he's watching boxing matches put on by the Knights of Columbus, and he's going to confession. That's the 'wickedness' that he's up to just now! That's how much killing he's done!"

"Undoubtedly he leaves out the things that might upset your mother."

"He'd tell me."

"Would he? He knows you're with child. He knows how I feel. Why else would he write about concerts and monkey meat and bread made from sawdust?"

"He cares more about upsetting us than you do," she charged. "Where is your faith? You're violating the laws of the Church."

"There was no *ex cathedra* ruling on this war," he said. "The Pope hasn't demanded that men of Catholic faith serve in the military. I'm not breaking the Church's laws, I'm only disagreeing with its current position. I'm still at liberty to hold different views from the Church, and we are—for the moment—still living in a free country where I can express my thoughts."

"But we're not! Or—" Maggie stopped, confused.

He ran a hand through his hair. "It's time to go to bed. We can talk about this tomorrow."

"And have the same conversation?"

"This is getting old, Maggie. Now, come on."

When she did not move, Liam asked, "Aren't you going to pray with me?"

"I'll be along in a minute," she said. "Why don't you wash up first?"

Liam left the room, but still she did not move. Why couldn't he just go to France like everyone else and do whatever it was they were doing over there? It didn't sound so bad—at least, it didn't according to Seaney.

She folded the newspaper and left it on the end table. As she laid it down, she noticed the copies of *The Ladies' Home Journal* still resting there. She picked up one of the magazines and ran a finger along the flower petal trail of the illustration. Suddenly angry, she lurched toward the fireplace and started to cast the magazines into the fire. As she was about to drop them, she thought: *No, this is mine, this belongs to just me. No one in the world may want to see it or read it, but it is mine.*

She placed the copies in her sewing basket. When Liam came back in the room, she obediently went to the altar where they said their evening prayers. Kneeling, she folded her hands. Her first prayer was always for the baby: *Please let him be strong and healthy, please don't take him from us.*

Liam began to pray: "My soul proclaims the greatness of the Lord, my spirit rejoices in God my Savior—"

Another prayer crowded into Maggie's mind: *Please, please, don't let Liam cause trouble again. Not for me, but for this baby, and for Ma and Pa. Oh, please, please, please—*

FIVE

Lieutenant Morgan is always looking for volunteers for filthy jobs, whom he names almost immediately after he makes the request. Tonight, Tony Necchi, an Italian from Brooklyn who has recently been promoted to Corporal, and Sean have "volunteered" for night patrol. Their mission is to crawl out beneath the wire in front of the American trenches and scramble through No Man's Land to a pillbox, a concrete fortification near the German lines. The Germans have a machine gun there that has been mowing down the American troops without mercy. It's been heavily bombarded, and for the last few hours, it's been silent, but whether it is empty is another question.

Once darkness has fallen, Sean and Tony smear their faces with burnt cork and shed any clothing that bears insignia. They also leave behind pay books, insurance policies, letters, and even their identity tags—anything that the German Army can collect as a prize. There's an irony to this; if they are killed, no one will be able to prove it.

"Take these." Sergeant Hicks gives them each a set of brass knuckles.

Sean slips them over the swollen knuckles of his right hand. "I wish I'd had these in Denver," he remarks. "They would have saved my hands."

"It woulda saved your hands if you didn't think you could fight," Tony says.

Sean laughs as he straps a belt around his waist. From it hangs a scabbard with a thin-bladed, nine-inch knife known as "M1917." Tucked in another loop is a skull-crushing hatchet. His service pistol is sheathed in a holster on his right hip. In his pack are grenades, and he carries his rifle with bayonet mounted and the required bullet already in the breech.

"Ready?" Sean asks.

"Let's go, Corporal."

"All right, Corporal."

They climb up on the firebay and pull themselves over the top. Ducking under the wire, they move through the viscous mess of No Man's Land. The standing water in the shell holes roils ominously, threatening to spew out the dead whose bodies have been sucked in by the mud. Sometimes, when he has been lying face down in the slop for too long, Sean imagines the corpses rising upward, air bubbling from their mouths in bitter pleas: *Tell my mother, my sister, my wife where I am.*

He crawls forward on his elbows and knees, trying to avoid the sharp sticks of battered tree trunks that can gouge a wrist or thigh. Lengths of wire, left over from previous battles, spring from the mud, and scraps of metal or shrapnel jut upward with flesh-tearing edges. Everywhere, the possibility of a gangrenous wound lurks. Yet what's on No Man's Land doesn't pose near as great a threat as who is on No Man's Land.

At night, the boggy stretch between trenches comes alive with crack troops, and raiders, and patrols all trying to accomplish whatever they've been ordered to do. Sometimes, Sean can hear others squirming through the mud and sinkholes, breathing in gasps that echo through the dead air above the field. Usually, they ignore each other. It's too hard to determine friend from foe, and any sound of confrontation is bound to set off the machine gunners and snipers. If they come face to face, it's hand-to-hand combat with their hatchets or brass knuckles or whatever weapon they can grab, and may the best man win.

Sean and Tony come to the pillbox. Its forward concrete wall is maybe four feet high, a hump in the landscape, with a slit in the front for the machine guns. The pillbox tapers back into the ground, its walls declining in height, until there is just a low embankment at the back. The bombardment has pounded half of the front wall into rubble, but it's still impossible to see what is in the pit of the pillbox.

Tony and Sean slither around to where the back wall stands only a foot or so high. They remain motionless, listening for signs of life. After about ten minutes, Tony looks at Sean and nods, then stands and drops over the wall, his hatchet ready, while Sean covers him with his rifle.

"Gesù Cristo!" Tony says. "It's a shithole down here. Come on."

Sean jumps in and lands on something that gives beneath his weight. The pillbox is an *abattoir*, a slaughterhouse, filled with the dead. They slump over a jumble of trenching tools and supply boxes, their hands and faces and limbs no longer belonging to individuals, but to a mound of slime and putrid water.

"I got it all over my boots and socks," Tony complains. "I'm gonna smell like it."

Sean clicks on a flashlight and points the light toward the concrete floor while shielding it with his other hand. The water around his ankles is the color of rust.

"We have to get rid of this," he says.

At the far end of the pillbox, facing the German trenches, is an underground exit tunnel cut into the concrete. It's around five feet high and only wide enough for the shoulders of a man, but right now, it's blocked by a body—or, at least, pieces of flesh. Tony says, "If we clear up the stuff around this, it'll drain."

Sean picks up a long-handled shovel that leans against the forward wall. He pushes and prods at the flesh that blocks the tunnel, but the dead men are heavier than he expected, melded together as they are.

"Help me out," he says to Tony.

Tony jams another shovel into the pile, and together they lift a limp, dripping body and heave it over the back embankment. They wait, motionless, for the guns to start up, but nothing happens.

They dredge up what they can and heft it out of the pillbox. The water starts to drain, carrying with it a white froth that was once human. With his shovel, Sean flicks at bits of flesh and organs that are splattered against the walls.

Tony sits on a case of medical supplies that stands, untouched and abandoned, in the corner. "How many do you think there were?" he whispers.

Sean shakes his head. "Six, maybe."

"The Heines must have come and taken the gun."

"Too bad they couldn't take their dead, too."

Tony pats the case. "The *Oberarzt* sure as hell didn't do them much good, did he? I wonder why they left all this behind."

"Think they'll come back?"

"For what? Bandages for a bunch of dead men?"

Outside, from the Allied side, a Verey light shoots up into the air and hangs in the blackness before the tendrils fall to earth. In the white phosphorus burst, No Man's Land is a patchwork of blacks and grays, everything colorless and dead. A few guns sound, either snipers or sentries scared by the ghosts of the dead that rise up from the mist. As the light dies away, the night settles back into silence.

Now all they have to do is to keep the pillbox in American hands until the engineers arrive to seal up the tunnel, with its stench and debris of death, and rebuild the pillbox with a window looking toward the German lines.

Tony bends down low and lights a cigarette. "You think you'll ever get the stink out of your hands and feet after we're gone?"

"You mean after tonight?"

"I mean, after we get out of France."

"*If* we get out of France."

From the tunnel comes a noise like a long glide of sandpaper across rough wood. Tony springs from the supply case and moves into the corner to the left of the tunnel entrance. Sean backs into the shadows near the forward wall. He draws up his rifle, bayonet fixed, and waits.

"You think rats?" Tony whispers.

Sean shakes his head. He touches the hatchet and M1917 in his belt. In the corner, Tony cocks his .45.

The sound echoes through the pillbox again—a rustle of rough material against concrete, a slide, and then silence. Sweat runs down Sean's back, and his heart beats hard enough that he strains to hear over it. This isn't the sound of an attack—that would be quick and decisive. Another Verey light flies up, illuminating the walls and floor of the pillbox in stark black and white. Sean sees in Tony's cork-smudged face the realization that there is no way to scale the concrete walls or to hide themselves. They have no escape.

The noise comes again. For whatever reason, the Germans are dragging something up the tunnel. Supplies, maybe, or ammunition. Not the gun itself—it would only weigh about twenty-five pounds.

Sean shrinks back into the corner. If the Huns see him before they exit the tunnel, they will be able to shoot him before they come out in the open.

Rustle, slide, silence. Rustle, slide, silence.

Tony levels the .45.

An illumination rocket bursts in the sky, and snipers from both sides start up in an even rhythm. As the starburst falls earthward, the oval of a face materializes at the edge of the tunnel entrance, looking upward. Sean's whole body jerks, and his rifle wavers up and down. The eyes in the face on the floor widen as the German glimpses Sean.

Tony shoots point blank into his forehead. As the Verey light fades to a glow, the German stares skyward, motionless, the wound in his forehead a third eye.

Both Tony and Sean wait for a response—Germans pouring out from the tunnel, a sniper sighting them, a shell aimed toward the pillbox. Nothing happens.

Sean's stomach heaves upward. "What do we do now?

"I don't want him staring at us."

Together, they wrestle the German, who is soaked through by the filthy water from the pillbox, out of the tunnel. Only his right leg appears, the pant leg stained black by blood. The left is a white bone with a few strings of flesh attached at what was once a knee.

"He must have been pushing himself on his back with his good leg," Tony whispers.

"Where did he think he was going?" Sean asks.

"Maybe he thought the doctor was still in here. Bad luck."

The German's face settles into an expressionless pall of death. Where had he come from? Sean wonders. How long had he been dragging himself along, making that agonizing progression toward what he had hoped was safety? Sean wishes that the German's countrymen would have found him and taken him to the dressing station. There, his leg would have been sawed off and tossed aside, and he would have gone home a hero. He wouldn't have died for nothing.

Tony clips off the insignia on the German's uniform, then says, "We need to put him with the others."

They dump the body over the back wall, with Sean's hands under the German's shoulders and Tony's under the thighs.

Once that's done, Sean says, "Now we wait."

They take up positions in opposite corners, as far from the tunnel as possible. What have they done? Sean wonders. What were they supposed to do? Why is everything in this war so mixed up, unclear? When the relief crew comes, they crawl back through the mud and drop over the side of the American trench without incident. As Sean makes their report, Lieutenant Morgan asks if they encountered any enemies. Tony hands over the insignia.

"We put him out of his misery," Tony says.

Sean winces. He thinks of the animals in the corrals behind Sullivan's Grocery. He had hated slaughtering day—the desperation of the veal calves or the hogs as they sensed what was to happen to them. Once they could smell the spilled blood of those that had already been killed, the animals struggled, and the final blow was not always as merciful as it should be. Sean had always comforted himself afterward by thinking, *At least, they're out of their misery.*

But, my God, to speak of men that way.

"You want some breakfast?" Tony asks.

"No," he says.

He goes to the dugout and throws his gear on an empty bunk. Lying on his back, he closes his eyes. When he finally dozes off, he dreams: Rustle, slide, silence. Rustle, slide, silence.

SIX

Paul shifted from one foot to the other. The day was warm, the sun bright on the greening grass. He stood near the lake of the chateau where Kathleen and the other girls of the Graves Family Foundation Relief Society lived and worked. Beside him, his aide, Latour, held the reins of two saddled horses, a black gelding and a bay mare. The black horse frittered, anxious to move. Latour doubled his hold on the reins, muttering, *"Ce cheval est un diable."*

Paul eyed the gelding. It was said that some horses, like some men, became so accustomed to the noise and movement of war that they were uncomfortable with stillness. They grew increasingly nervous and difficult, and sometimes had to be destroyed.

He spotted Kathleen coming across the lawns, dressed in her gum boots, a dark woolen coat, and trousers. He hadn't seen her since she'd returned from Nice. He hurried forward as she broke into a run. Catching her in his arms, he remembered: the scent of her hair, the firmness of her skin, the feel of her hands around his neck, the sense that her body fit perfectly against his.

She smiled up at him. "I haven't seen you in so long!"

"Forty-three days," he said.

"You counted?"

"Every cursed day." He motioned toward the horses. "Look over here."

"Oh, they're beautiful! Where did you find horses that aren't starving and worked to death?"

"They're borrowed for the day from a French captain and his aide. According to Latour, it's not wise to ask about the details."

She stroked the nose of the bay. *"Merci, Monsieur Latour."*

Latour nodded graciously. *"De rien, Mademoiselle."*

"Are you ready?" Paul asked Kathleen.

"Oui, Monsieur le Conducteur Américain."

Latour spoke. *"Monsieur Reston, le diable est pour vous."*

"Diablo?" Kathleen asked.

"Diable," Paul corrected. "The black is hard to manage. You'd better take the bay."

Kathleen stroked the gelding's nose. "How much riding have you done?"

"I played some polo in college." Paul shrugged. "I managed to stay on the horse's back well enough."

She raised her eyebrows. "I'd better take Diablo."

Latour and Paul exchanged a glance, and Latour said, *"Non, Mademoiselle, vous n'êtes pas—"*

"He won't give me any trouble. Will you, Diablo?"

"C'est Diable," Latour said sourly.

"No," Kathleen said. "Today, he is Diablo. He's a horse of the Wild West, not a war horse in Amiens, France."

Her foot in the stirrup, she swung easily onto the horse's back. Holding the reins in her left hand, she clicked her tongue, and the nerved-up horse tossed his head and side-stepped a few times, threatening to rid himself of his rider. Paul imagined Diablo galloping off, dragging Kathleen behind, her boot caught in one stirrup. But she only laughed at the gelding's antics and patted his neck.

"Oh, it feels so good to be on horseback again!" she said. "But this saddle is different from the one I have at home. There's no pommel."

"What's a pommel?" Paul asked.

Her eyes flashed. "That is why I'm riding the more spirited horse. Where are we going?"

"That way." Paul pulled himself onto the bay mare. "There's a bridge over the stream about a half mile down. Then we'll head south."

With a fluttering wave at Latour, Kathleen clucked again, and the muscles in Diablo's powerful shoulders and haunches launched into motion. The bay followed Diablo easily, as if she were accustomed to being a second horse. Once they had crossed the bridge, Kathleen turned to Paul. "Can I let him run?"

"Are you sure you can handle him?"

"Watch."

She gave an expert prod with her heels to the horse's side, and Diablo broke into a run, then a full-out gallop. Within seconds, the two disappeared over the rolling hillside and reappeared on the next slope. Paul kicked at the mare, but she only managed an uncomfortable trot that left him jiggling back and forth on her back. From what he could see, Kathleen was sitting easily on her horse, leaning forward over his neck. At one point, Diablo gracefully leaped over a low rock wall. After that, Paul lost sight of them, although the bay seemed to know where they were going. He caught up to them again under a broad-canopied tree that grew atop a rounded hillock.

"Good horse, good Diablo." Kathleen dismounted. "Did you feel it?" she asked Paul breathlessly. "How the wind whistles in your ears? And the sun and the smell of spring? Oh, it makes me so happy to ride again!"

Paul climbed without grace from his horse. "I feel like Sancho Panza."

"Who's that?"

"From *Don Quixote*. He's a squire who rides a mule behind his master, always trying to keep up." He stumbled. "My legs have no blood in them. I don't believe my arms do, either."

She helped him to sit on a tree root that protruded from the ground. "It wasn't that bad, was it?"

"It was that bad. Where did you learn to ride that way?"

"I taught myself." With a laugh, Kathleen told Paul of growing up more or less on horseback. As she spoke, her eyes were deep green in the sunlight, and her entire face was lit up with excitement and joy. When she finished, Paul said, "Ah, my girl of the Wild West."

"You should try it."

"The Wild West?"

"You should learn to ride."

"There are a number of things I want to do with my life. Being at the mercy of a beast that could break my neck isn't one of them."

"Diablo wouldn't break anyone's neck unless they didn't understand how he thinks." She spread out her arms. "Oh, look at this tree! I've never seen one this big!"

Paul had to agree. The tree's massive trunk was at least ten feet around and blanketed by green moss, and the sun-craving limbs of the canopy stretched outward in spidery, asymmetrical lines. Ancient roots poked up through the pliable soil, creating table-sized moss-laden humps. Thick beds of leaves carpeted the ground beneath the limbs.

"It must be two hundred years old," he said. "Maybe more."

"Two hundred years," she mused. "Don't you wish it could tell you what it's seen in all that time?"

"It would tell us that this is a good spot for a picnic. It probably told Napoleon the same thing."

With a laugh, she tied the reins of the horses to a root as Paul emptied his rucksack. He had packed a lunch scrounged from the mess at Aumale. After they spread a woolen blanket over the leaves and sat down, Kathleen said, "Hank thought you might take me to a romantic inn for lunch today."

"In your gum boots and trousers?"

"The fine lady." She gestured at Diablo and the tree. "But this is so much better."

Below, in the verdant valley, a village lay near a glittering stream, its church steeple jutting into the sky. People passed along the streets, the women dressed in black, their bony horses pulling overladen carts and wagons. Children played on the banks of the stream, and dogs barked wildly. From somewhere, a rooster crowed.

"A scene like this makes me wonder how we could be at war," Paul said. "Everything is so peaceful."

"I thought the same thing when we were in Nice."

"I've never been that far south in France. What's it like?"

As they ate, Kathleen told him of the Relief Society's trip to Nice and the smell and sound of the Mediterranean Ocean. "I could have stayed there forever, making a living as an artist along *la plage*."

"I'm glad you came back."

"We heard more than once that there was a famous French artist living there," she said. "He's an old man who has been run out of nearly every hotel in town because he has no money to pay his bill. He was supposed to be easy to recognize—wild white hair and a scowl on his face, but I never saw anyone who might be him. His name was Henri Matisse. Do you think your Aunt Julia knew him when she lived in Paris?"

"Who knows? Julia seemed to know everyone, and all I remember is a jumble of strange characters coming through the apartment. It was *la Belle Époque*, you know."

"The Beautiful Era," she mused. "It sounds so fancy in French."

"Speaking of fancy, I have a surprise for you." Paul dug in his rucksack. "Close your eyes and open your mouth." She hesitated, and he added, "I'm not your cousin. You can trust me."

"As long as I don't end up with a mouth full of frog."

"You'd be truly French if you did."

With his knife, he cut into an orange that he'd saved for dessert. Its juice ran down his hand as he pulled off the peel. Cutting a single section in half, he laid it on her tongue.

"Tell me how it tastes."

"Oh!" She covered her mouth with one hand as she chewed. "It's so sweet! We've only had bitter French chocolate for so long—"

"Don't open your eyes. What does it make you think of?"

"I think of blue skies and summer heat, and palm trees, and the ocean near Nice, which is a shade of blue that I've never seen before. Did you know that there are lemon trees and orange trees growing everywhere, and anyone can pick the fruit?" She gave a self-conscious shrug. "Was that enough? Can I open my eyes?"

"That was enough to make me want to catch the first train to *la Côte D'Azur*."

She took the orange from him and tore off a section. "You try it. Eyes closed, now."

He bit from the fruit. Juice trickled down his chin. Her finger glided over the stubble of his beard as she dashed it off, sending a thrill through him, but he did not open his eyes.

"What do you see?"

"I see the most beautiful woman in the world sitting under a giant tree, beckoning, saying 'Come here'—"

"Do I know her?"

"Let me think." He squinted one eye open. "Why, look at that. There she is."

She laughed as she rolled the orange in her hand. "Where did you find this?"

"Latour gave it to me. It's probably wise—"

She finished the sentence. "—not to ask about the details."

With a laugh, she jumped to her feet and disappeared behind the tree. After a few moments, Paul realized he could no longer hear the shuffle of her footsteps through the fallen leaves.

"Where are you?" he called.

No answer came back to him. Standing, he walked around the tree. She stood with her back pressed against the trunk. As he neared, she sprang from her hiding place and ran, laughing as she scurried over the roots that swelled up out of the ground. She balanced precariously on one before she jumped into a pocket of leaves that exploded upward with a crackling sound. Paul chased after her, clumsy and slow. At last, he caught her and swung her around so that she ended up with her back pressed against the trunk. He trapped her with his arms on either side of her, her hands raised above her head, palms open. His chest heaved as he tried to catch his breath, and her whole body shook with the exhilaration of the chase.

"What kind of tree is this?" she asked.

"I believe it's a beech." He worked his hands up her wrists to entwine his fingers with hers.

"I don't think we have them in Colorado."

Paul leaned closer. "Everyone knows that all you have in the Wild West are coyotes"—he yipped near her ear, his lower lip catching on her ear lobe —"and cactus"—a sharp peck to her cheek—"and rattlesnakes." With his lips, he buzzed against the soft side of her neck.

"That's not true!"

He kissed her upper lip, which trembled with laughter, then her lower lip. Her mouth tasted of the orange, of sweetness and softness. He let go of her hands, which hooked around his neck as he pulled her closer. With every kiss, his high spirits deepened into desire. He felt the transformation within her as well. She was no longer the girl who rode wildly, or ate oranges in the sunshine, or played Tag around the tree, but a woman. A moan came from her throat as he parted her lips and touched his tongue to hers.

"Oh, Paul," she whispered.

He ran one hand along the curves of her side and ribs and hips. Unbuttoning her blouse, he slipped a hand inside. Beads lay on her chest under the collar, concealed by the fabric. She reached up and moved them aside. "My rosary," she said.

He nipped at her lips. "Have you ever been kissed before?"

She took his face in her hands. "Not this way."

"So, who did you kiss in the Wild West?"

"Does it matter?"

"Who was it?" He punctuated the question by kissing near her left ear. "A boy on the school playground?" A kiss to her jawbone. "A farm kid from your hometown?" He found her lips again, catching the sensitive corner of her mouth. "A wee lad from the ol' parish?"

"At church? Never!"

"Who, then? Tell me."

"No, let's keep doing this."

"Would I be shocked?" he teased. "Was it your cousin?"

"Seaney? Of course not! I would never—"

Her final words were lost beneath a steady thrum. A shadow passed over the beech, blocking the sun that shone through the budding branches. It was a German biplane, grayish-brown in color, the Iron Cross on its fuselage. The pilot and gunner sat in open cockpits, visible from the ground. Behind it were three olive green escort Fokkers.

From the left, above open field, four French fighters with tri-colored tails darted toward the German planes, then danced away, tantalizing and quick.

Paul pulled Kathleen as close to the trunk as he could.

"What's happening?" she asked.

"I hope nothing," Paul said. "The French are scouts, I think. Reconnaissance. I don't know what the Germans are doing here."

The French planes wheeled upward and pivoted toward the Germans. One of the Fokkers broke away, moving out toward the French, its engine roaring. Diablo spooked, and Paul ran to make sure that the horses were securely tied to the tree root. He pulled his hat from his rucksack and clapped it on his head.

"Do you have your tin hat?" he called to Kathleen.

"It's in my bag."

Paul found it and handed it to her. "We'd better find some shelter."

She tightened the strap around her chin. "They can't see us here, can they?"

"If they see the horses, they might strafe us."

"Where can we go?"

"The village."

Riding ahead of her, Paul sought out the shadows of the trees along the hill. All three of the Fokkers had joined in the pursuit of the French, who were circling and spinning just above the magnificent beech tree.

Machine gun fire ripped through the air, and the bay mare side-stepped frantically. "Whoa, easy," Paul said. Near the bottom of the hill, the copse of trees broke, leaving the horses and riders unprotected.

"Come on!" He yelled as he coaxed the bay into the open.

The horses' hooves clattered onto the cobblestones of the road through the village.

"*Ici! Là!*"A priest in a black cassock stood in the middle of the street. The bell in the church steeple swung back and forth in deafening peals. As a woman and child darted across the street, Paul slid from his horse and led it along at a run, his other hand urging Kathleen and Diablo forward. The airplanes had come east now, so that the French SPADs were just above the village.

"*Laissez les chevaux,*" the priest shouted, indicating a set of iron rings attached to the side of the church. "*Ici, vite!*"

Kathleen turned to Paul. "We can't just leave them. It's too cruel—"

"We can't afford to lose them either."

"*Vite, vite!*"

Paul tied up the mare and helped Kathleen secure Diablo's reins. With the priest behind them, they clattered down uneven, stone steps into the *abri* beneath the church. As Paul's eyes adjusted to the dark, he saw sandbags lining the walls of the cellar and supporting the center. The woman and child who had come in ahead of them forged their way toward the back, where a conversation sprang up with others that Paul could not yet see. Along the nearest wall, a mother and four children sat in silence, while a second woman kept track of a toddler and a young girl. Seated on sandbags along the opposite wall, two gnarled old men passed a bottle of wine between them.

Everyone stared at Paul and Kathleen.

"*Bonjour, bonjour,*" Paul said, and a few replied.

Kathleen said nothing, and Paul took her hand as they sat down on the dirt floor, their backs against the sandbags. "You're all right?" he asked.

She removed her hat. "The horses. I'm worried—"

"We'll just have to hope they're still there when we leave."

The priest began to pray, and Kathleen pulled her rosary from beneath her shirt, bent her head, and folded her hands. Paul clasped his hands in imitation, but he couldn't remember any of the prayers he'd learned as a boy, and he wasn't even sure he understood what the priest was saying. After the prayer ended, Kathleen and the villagers made the sign of the cross over their bodies.

"I'm afraid I'll be late getting back," she whispered. "Mrs. Brently will be so upset—"

"We'll talk to her."

She buried her head in his chest. He put his arms around her. "It'll be all right," he said. "Don't you think she would rather you were safe than on time?"

"It isn't that. We shouldn't be in a place where this happens. We shouldn't be hiding and hoping that we aren't hit by a bullet. We should be—"

"But we aren't," Paul said. "We're here, and—my God—we've managed to fall in love despite it all."

She started to weep, everything within her, it seemed, breaking apart and flowing out in tears. The villagers watched her, dry-eyed and curious, as if they had long ago forgotten how to cry.

From outside, the oscillating whine of the plane engines and the tapping of the guns grew louder, as if the dog fight were taking place over the church. Kathleen burrowed her head deeper into the hollow of Paul's shoulder. He stroked her hair with one hand.

"It was Jim Graves," she said suddenly.

"What?"

"You asked me who I had kissed before I, well, before. It was Jim. We kissed in New York, in Central Park, and in Nice."

Paul's mind worked slowly, as if he couldn't understand what she was saying. "In Nice?" he asked. "He was there?"

"Yes, he was on his way to London—or Washington, I guess—and decided to meet us in Nice."

"That's quite a detour," he said. "He's in love with you?"

"He says he is. He asked me to marry him when we were in New York."

"Why didn't you tell me?"

"Why would I? I didn't ask him to kiss me, and I said no when he proposed."

"I had no idea." The blood drained from Paul's arms and legs. "I would never have interfered with . . . Can you truly say you never felt anything for him, even after he kissed you? Even after he proposed?"

"No, I—" She stopped. "Oh, I shouldn't have said anything."

"How old is he? Isn't he older than his sister?"

"No, he's probably thirty or so."

Another shock. "I'd imagined a gray-haired man with a wife and children," Paul said. "I don't know why. Perhaps because he's so wealthy, I thought it would take a lifetime to accumulate—"

He stopped, aware of the USAAS uniform he wore. Even though it was fairly new, it already had oil and blood stains that could not be scrubbed out even with ether. He thought, too, of the paltry pay that he earned as an ambulance driver and of the money that Julia sent him each month, as if he were a boy earning an allowance. "How did you . . . what happened in New York?"

"He had taken me to Mass at St. Patrick's Cathedral, and we went to the Park, and the others weren't there yet. He had brought lunch, and so we had a picnic . . ."

"Why were you at church with him?" Paul asked. "Is he Catholic?"

"No, but we were in New York on Sunday, and I'm the only Catholic in the group. Mrs. Brently took the other girls to Protestant services, while Jim escorted me to Mass. Afterwards, we went to the Park to wait for the others. And, well, I drew his portrait—he asked me to—and I think it was just the moment or something, but he asked me to marry him."

He shook his head, disbelieving. "Why did you say no? A man with that kind of wealth and power—my God, the whole world would be open to you. You could travel, you could live wherever you want—anything!"

"I don't care about that—"

"But I have nothing to offer you."

"Offer me? What do you mean?"

"I don't even have a job in America."

"You're a lawyer, you told me so, and you have a job in Boston—"

"I have a law degree that's never been used," he said. "It's a piece of paper, that's it. And the job was just an offer—who knows if they'll hold it for me until the war ends."

"Why does that matter?" she asked. "Jim asked me if you were worthy of me. That was the word he used—worthy. And when I told him you were, he said I should love you."

"You told him about me?"

"In Nice, when he . . ."

Her words faltered, and Paul filled them in. "When he asked you a second time to marry him?"

"Yes."

"But you came back to me."

"Yes, I did."

The enormity of her decision struck him. To pass up a life of endless luxury, to turn down a man who was so wealthy that he could send his own Relief Society to France, a man whom President Wilson would not allow to serve as a foot soldier because his contributions in the States were so important—

Jim Graves was eminently worthy of Kathleen. And yet—

"Then I had better be worthy of you," Paul said. "And I will be, Kathleen. I promise. Everything changed for me the night I met you in Montdidier. I had put away all my feelings—I'd forgotten them in all the mess and hardship. But you . . . I want things now, you've made me want them. I want the war to end, I want to go home, I want a job and a house, and I want to be a father. I want to love my wife and children without thinking about—"

The priest came toward them, and Kathleen straightened up, moving quickly away from Paul.

"*S'il vous plaît, Monsieur,*" the priest said. "*Iriez-vous avec moi?*"

"*Oui, Monsieur.*" Paul touched Kathleen's shoulder. "He wants me to go with him to see what's happening."

"Why you?" she cried.

He strapped on his tin hat. "I'm the only able-bodied man here."

Outside, Paul stood with his back against the protective stone wall of the church as he waited for the priest. Above their heads, the bomber and the Fokkers were flying to the north, while the French circled eastward. On the hill beyond the village, in the clearing just to the west of the beech tree, a French SPAD had crashed in a fiery heap.

Paul ran toward the plane, the priest following him over the footbridge that forded the stream at the bottom of the valley. The

SPAD, built of canvas and wicker, roared with flame, an acrid, oily smoke rising from it. The pilot lay on the ground, writhing, his skin charred into blackness.

Paul knelt down beside him. The man groped at the air, as if trying to claw his way out of his body. A sound like the wail of wind in a chimney came from his mouth.

Paul turned toward the priest. *"Est-ce que un médicin ici?"*

"Non, pas encore."

"We need water, wet blankets to wrap him in—"

In his head, he begged: Anything, anything that will stop that sound!

The pilot's body began to jerk, rocking from one side to the other, foam bubbling at his lips. The priest crossed himself and intoned last rites.

The other French pilots had landed their planes on the flat grassy bottom near the stream. Running up the hill, they shouted, "Maurice! Maurice!" Behind them were the women and children who had been in the *abri*.

"Kathleen!" Paul shouted. "Keep the children away!"

Kathleen turned to the women. *"S'il vous plaît, les enfants—!"*

The oily plane smoldered, the fuel that had flared up so quickly and with so much heat spent, the flimsy materials charred into paper-thin ash that fluttered away in the breeze. The three pilots, the priest, and Paul stood in silent despair.

There was nothing to be done.

After the fire smoldered out, one of the pilots retrieved a tarp from his SPAD, and the three of them wrapped the body of the pilot in it. Solemnly, and with Paul as the fourth, they lifted the body and followed the priest down the hillock and across the footbridge into the village.

Behind the church was a cemetery. Many of the headstones were ancient, some uprooted or crooked from shifting in the fertile soil. Yet, beyond, the lawn had been churned up for a rash of new graves, all of them marked by crosses with names carefully written by hand, all of them bearing the names of men.

And here was another. As Maurice Pierre Bernard was laid to rest, with only the three pilots and a handful of strangers as witnesses, Paul thought of the family that would never truly know what had happened to their young man, who might not even know how he had died or where his body lay. And for what? The dogfight had yielded nothing—it probably hadn't even been planned. Numb, Paul stood silently beside Kathleen while the priest intoned, *"Pater Noster, qui es in caelis, sanctificétur nomen tuum—"*

She mouthed the words, her voice not even a whisper.

The remaining French pilots shook Paul's hand, thanking him for his help. Beside Paul, Kathleen wept silently. He put an arm around her waist, and they left the cemetery to find their horses.

"I wish I could have helped," she said.

"We did what we could. We saw him honorably and respectfully buried. His family may never know, but if they did, they would find comfort in that."

The horses were still tied to the iron rings outside the church.

"Oh, they're all right!" Kathleen cried.

She climbed on Diablo as Paul mounted the bay. Without speaking, they rode back to the beech tree to collect their things. The SPAD still smoldered, a black stain on the green of the hillside. A few villagers poked around the debris, scavenging what they could use. Even though they were in a hurry, Kathleen did not urge Diablo to gallop on the return jaunt, and Paul let the little mare take her own time. After they came over the bridge to the grounds of the chateau, Kathleen reined in Diablo and faced Paul.

"Let's go home," she said. "I'll leave the Relief Society. I only agreed to spend six months here, and I could say I've changed my mind—"

"I'm with the American Expeditionary Force now." He leaned forward and wiped away a tear that rolled down her cheek with his knuckle. "I'm no longer a volunteer in the French Army with a year-long commitment to a private ambulance service."

She looked toward the chateau. "Of course," she said at last. "You can't leave."

"No, I can't." He reached for her hand. "If I could, though, you would never have gotten out of that church cellar until that priest had married us. Even if I couldn't understand a word he was saying, even if he gave the ceremony in Swahili, I would have said, 'I do,' loud and clear."

She managed a tepid laugh.

Paul sobered. "You will let me know if I am not worthy of you, won't you? You'll let me know if you think of him again or if he asks you again—you'll give me a chance to make it right? I could not bear to lose you."

"You won't need a chance," she said. "I will always love you."

He kissed her. "Come on, then. Let's go face our fate."

Latour was waiting for them on the gravel drive outside the chateau.

"Je suis désolé." Speaking in French, Paul launched into an explanation.

Latour muttered something unrepeatable. Immediately, he mounted Diablo, the reins of the bay in his hands. Without another word, he kicked the horse into a gallop. Kathleen said softly, "Goodbye, Diablo."

Paul took her arm. "We'd better go inside."

They went into the canteen by the back door.

"It's closed," Kathleen said.

Mrs. Brently sat at one of the tables beside a man with soft, brown eyes and graying hair at his temples. He was dressed in a British military uniform with a Colonel's insignia. Paul recognized him from the sketch Kathleen had drawn of him on horseback in Montdidier. He promptly saluted.

"At ease, Private." The Colonel returned the salute.

"Kathleen!" Mrs. Brently said. "Where have you been? We've been so worried—"

"I'm so sorry. We went for a ride, and we were caught by a dogfight—"

"A ride?"

"On horses. They were borrowed for the day."

"Where were you?"

Kathleen looked at Paul. "I don't know the name of the town. Somewhere south of here—"

"Southeast." Paul stepped forward. "Mrs. Brently, I'm Private Paul Reston—"

She turned toward him. "May I speak with Kathleen alone?"

"Yes, ma'am."

Paul left, with the British officer following.

In the graveled drive of the chateau, the Brit said, "I'm Lieutenant Colonel Thomas Lloyd-Elliot. I don't believe we've met."

"I'm Private Paul Reston, of the U.S. Army Ambulance Service, sir."

"You're a former Harjes man, aren't you? How long have you been here?"

"Since June of 1916, just before the Somme."

"I see you've won the *Croix de Guerre*."

"Yes, sir, for service at Verdun."

"What are you doing here today?"

"I'm *en repos* just now, sir."

"Isn't that 'on leave,' now that you're with the Americans?" The Colonel did not wait for a reply. "You understand that your young American friend will face consequences for this lark, don't you? The American Red Cross follows the same rules as the American military. It is under its aegis."

"I understand that, but Kathleen—Miss O'Doherty—had a day off, just as I did, and all we did was to go for a ride in the country. We were late because we were caught in an *abri* during a dogfight." Paul went on to describe the downed SPAD and the pilot's funeral. "I don't believe we broke any rules, except that we were late in returning."

"You were alone with her," Colonel Lloyd-Elliot said. "I believe that's quite against the rules. Whose idea was this poorly-conceived escapade?"

"It was mine, sir. I borrowed two horses for the day—"

"Aren't you aware that in less than a month, the war will start up again?" the Colonel demanded. "The Germans weren't just winging across the plain for their own amusement. They were trying to cause trouble. They could have bombed the village where you were, if they'd seen a uniformed man in it. You imperiled the people there as well as Miss O'Doherty."

"I kept Miss O'Doherty safe, sir," Paul said fiercely. "She was never in more danger than she was in Montdidier or she is here. As for being alone, we had a picnic under a tree within sight of the village—"

He stopped speaking as the side door to the chateau opened, and Kathleen and Mrs. Brently came from the canteen. Kathleen still wore her dirty trousers, and her hair was in a messy bunch at the nape of her neck, with loose tendrils floating here and there. A black smudge marred her left cheek—oil from the reins, grease, mud, something else. Beneath her eyes were two trails washed clean by tears.

"Kathleen wishes to speak with you in private," Mrs. Brently said.

With Colonel Lloyd-Elliot and Mrs. Brently following, Kathleen and Paul walked toward the spot near the lake where they had met that morning.

"What happened?" he asked.

"I'm no longer allowed to see you, at any time, alone," she said. "You can come to the canteen—inside the canteen—if you want to talk to me, and Mrs. Brently must know about it."

Paul breathed in relief. "You aren't being sent home, then?"

"No," Kathleen said. "But that has more to do with our Relief Society being so few and Jim—and Mr. Graves—having already sailed from London than it does with my deserving it."

"You don't deserve it," Paul said. "We did nothing wrong. Kathleen, you acted bravely and decently. You kept the children from witnessing the worst of it, and we honored and mourned a soldier who died far from his home and family. That can never be wrong."

"But we . . . she asked me what we had done together."

"What did you tell her?"

"That we had kissed, that's all," she said. "Oh, Paul, she threatened to punish Hank, too. Hank told her that I was sketching at the cathedral today."

"What will she do to Hank?"

"I think I talked her out of it. Oh, if we don't see each other again—"

He took her face in his hands. "Don't fret, my girl of the Wild West. We can still send *les lettres d'amour, n'est-ce pas*?"

"Oui," she managed through tears. "Every day."

"And I will find you after the war, even if I have to ride a horse from here to Colorado," he promised. "All the way across the ocean—I'll just have to hope it can swim. Then I'll show up at your door, saddle sores and all, and you'll have to help me to walk again, just as you did today."

She laughed weakly. "I'll be waiting for you."

"Je t'aime, Kathleen," he whispered. "I know you know what that means."

He kissed her forehead—neither the Colonel nor Mrs. Brently scolded him for it—then watched as the two women and the Colonel walked toward the chateau. Kathleen glanced back at him, and Paul touched his lips with his fingers.

In return, she mouthed the words, *I love you.*

SEVEN

Kathleen lay on her bed in the chateau. Handkerchiefs piled on the pillow beside her, and still the tears came. She had turned her face to the wall, unwilling to meet the gazes of Hank or Helen or Mrs. Brently or whoever else might come into the room. She didn't want to hear more about how wrong she had been, or how irresponsible, or how young she was.

The conversation with Mrs. Brently had not gone well. Through tears, Kathleen had told her everything—from meeting Paul in Montdidier to the decision to go for a horseback ride. Afterward, Mrs. Brently had asked, "What have you done with this man, Kathleen?"

"We kissed, and he, we—"

She stopped, but her hand went to her breast as she recalled the warmth of Paul's palm against it. Mrs. Brently's sharp eyes caught the gesture, and Kathleen knew it was as good as a confession.

Mrs. Brently warned, "You realize that there are punishments for women who are not of decent moral character—"

"It was never indecent!" Kathleen cried. "We were sitting beneath a tree—"

"You signed a contract that made it clear you were not to engage in any sort of off-hours fraternization with the opposite sex—"

"I know I did. But it's no different than you and Colonel Lloyd-Elliot—"

Mrs. Brently had balked. "I beg your pardon. That is not appropriate. Has Private Reston asked you to marry him?"

"Yes, he has," Kathleen said boldly. "This isn't just a love crush or a French fling—"

"It's very easy for an experienced man to promise something to a girl in order to have what he wants." Softening, Mrs. Brently had taken Kathleen's hand. "It isn't just the Red Cross rules that you should consider. You're still very young, and you must think beyond this moment. Your life, your marriage—one day—to a man who loves you, a man at home, who you'll meet through your church, in all likelihood. Is Private Reston a Catholic?"

Kathleen shook her head. "No, ma'am."

"Then, isn't your relationship against everything your church teaches?"

"Yes, but I . . ." Another fear came into Kathleen's head. "Will you write to my parents? My mother will never let me stay if she thinks that I—"

"I don't know," she said. "I haven't decided on that yet. This is a serious breach of your contract and of the Red Cross rules. I'm very disappointed in you. And certainly, my brother will be upset by this."

"He knows."

"I beg your pardon?"

"I told him about Paul in Nice."

At that, Mrs. Brently's barely concealed anger had erupted. "He said nothing about it to me. When did you tell him?"

"The night we stayed behind on the boat, outside the restaurant—"

Too late, Kathleen realized what she had done. Not only was Mrs. Brently furious with her, but with Jim as well. Oh, how she wished she could relive today! She wouldn't have gone for a ride, and Paul wouldn't have known about Jim, and she would still be in Mrs. Brently's good graces—

Except . . . she would never have refused to go with Paul. Of that, she was sure.

She rolled onto her back and pushed her wet hair out of the sticky tears on her face. In the end, Mrs. Brently had decided that she would not write to Kathleen's parents, for she believed that Kathleen had learned her lesson. She also declined to report it to her Red Cross supervisor unless there was another infraction. "Now, go upstairs and take a bath and change your clothes," she had said. "There's a strong smell of horse about you."

Hank and Helen tiptoed into the room. Kathleen kept her face turned toward the wall, but she knew their evening routine well enough that she could envision their actions: folding their uniforms neatly over the foot of the bed; washing up in the basins of water; sharing the communal can of tooth powder before they brushed their teeth. Helen would sit on her bed to read the chapter of scripture that she assigned herself every night, while Hank knelt beside hers to pray.

At last, Hank asked, "Should I put the candle out?"

Helen said nothing, and Hank asked again, "Kathleen, are you ready for bed?"

No longer able to keep her feelings inside, Kathleen said, "Oh, Hank, it was so terrible."

Helen answered. "Terrible! You went out with a man who you aren't supposed to be seeing in the first place, and you nearly got Hank sent home. And we couldn't open the canteen tonight because Mrs. Brently was so worried, and there wasn't enough help, and we just had to send the men away. So no one was able to do what they needed to do."

"You don't know what we saw today—"

"And all because you're selfish, and you think that you don't have to follow the rules. You think that because you're Mr. Graves' pet you can do what you want. We all know you did something to make him like you more than he likes us. Are you doing the same with Paul?"

"Are you accusing me of—?"

"Why aren't you being sent home? You've broken so many of the rules. I'm ashamed to be part of the same Relief Society as you are."

"Helen!" Hank intervened.

Kathleen burst into fresh tears. "A plane crashed, and the pilot died. It was the most horrible thing I've ever seen, and there was nothing we could do."

"We've seen that before," Helen said harshly, but Hank came to Kathleen and sat beside her. "Don't think about it," she said.

"But it was so terrible! The smell, and the way he looked—"

"What happened?" Hank asked.

Kathleen told the full story of the pilot's death. "One minute, he was alive, and flying his airplane, and he probably thought he was quick enough to get out of it, and the next he was—"

Her words trailed away, and Hank asked, "Did you tell Mrs. Brently about it?"

"We didn't get that far—"

"Well, maybe if you tell her in the morning, she'll be more forgiving." Hank took her hand. "But it was supposed to be a fun day. What did you and Paul do?"

"We rode horses to a village a few miles away. I rode a horse named—well, I named him—Diablo, and he was fast and strong. Then, we had a picnic under the most beautiful tree that had mounds of leaves beneath it—"

"It sounds romantic," Hank said.

"But then it was spoiled by the dogfight." Kathleen frowned, not entirely sure that all had been lost. How could an afternoon that ended with mutual declarations of love be ruined? "We wouldn't have been late if the plane wouldn't have crashed," she said. "We weren't that far from here. If it wouldn't have happened, no one would have known, and Mrs. Brently wouldn't—"

"We would have known," Helen said. "We would have known that you lied."

The first shot of the spring offensive was fired near Saint Quentin, some fifty miles from Amiens, by the Germans. Within hours, the entire Hindenburg Line was under siege. The ground-shaking, percussive booms from the Front could be felt within the chateau, its lead-glass windows rattling in their ancient frames. British troops marched in and out of the gates by the thousands, and long-range Howitzers were dragged in by straining teams of horses to a hill just beyond the chateau. At night, search lights swept across the trees, lake, and grassy expanses. Everywhere, smoke drifted in the air, carrying the burnt, bitter smell of devastated land and dying men.

On a cold day in March, Kathleen knelt before the altar in the chapel in the west wing of the chateau. The chapel had been built for the family, with only four rows of pews. A white marble statue of the Virgin Mary stood within an arch on the altarpiece. To her left hung a portrait of Christ, and to her right was a painting of the Pietà. On the outer wall of the chapel, a vibrant stained glass window glowed in the sun. Votive candles burned along the inner wall, one of them lit by Kathleen for the pilot, Maurice.

She bowed her head: *O my God, I am heartily sorry for having offended Thee and I detest all my sins . . .*

But I haven't sinned.

Of course, you have. We are all sinners, we are all wicked—

But all we did was to go on a picnic—

He touched you, and you wanted him to—

She lifted her head. How could she pray when she couldn't constrain her own thoughts? How could she atone for her sins when she couldn't convince herself that she had done anything wrong?

She would be twenty in July—an age at which her mother had been married for nearly four years. Without the war, she would be home, undoubtedly wed by now to a young man from the parish, although she couldn't remember even one who had attracted her, and—with God's blessing—she might be a mother. Without the war, she would never have met Paul or known the way his lips felt on hers or the caress of his hands over—

She readjusted her rosary in both hands. Starting over, she made the sign of the cross as she prayed, "In the name of the Father, and of the Son, and of the Holy Spirit—"

A clanging sounded outside the chapel. Kathleen rose from her knees and hurried to the Great Hall. Already, the room was filled with stretcher bearers carrying the wounded between them. They wore gas masks, which made them appear to be insects with goggle eyes and snouts, and which hindered their ability to see. One stretcher bearer rammed into a column in the Great Hall, and the wounded man dropped onto the tile of the chateau floor. The stretcher bearer ripped his gas mask from his face and cursed as he scrambled to pick up the patient.

"Kathleen!"

Hank stood across the room, gas masks in her hands. Kathleen zigged through the line of stretcher bearers.

Hank handed her the gas mask, then strapped on her own. "We have to move the patients into the cellar."

"All of them?"

"That's what we were told. I guess there aren't enough gas masks for everyone. I don't know what they'll do with the ones with broken bones who are trussed up to their beds."

Kathleen slung the bag with the filter around her neck and brought the rubber mask over her head. She closed her lips around the tubing that guided purified air from the filter into her mouth. The whole thing sagged on her face, weighing against her skin. She jostled the cloudy goggles, which were set wider than her eyes, and squinted to see.

Helen arrived, her gas mask securely strapped on her head.

"Where were you?" she demanded of Kathleen, her words muffled as they issued from her mask. "We looked everywhere, and we couldn't find you. You weren't with him again, were you?"

"I was in the chapel," Kathleen said.

"Oh." Helen looked away.

Mrs. Brently appeared with her gas mask over her face. "We are to help upstairs with those who can't move on their own," she said.

The girls followed her to a ward designated as "Head Wounds." Some patients were conscious, and some lay in comas, their eyes open and glazed. Nurses in gas masks bustled about, fixing oxygen tubes in the boys' mouths. The air had taken on a white sheen that made the light seem too bright.

"All right," a British nurse said. "Your job is to keep the tube in their mouths while they're being moved into the gas-proof chambers below. Don't let them breathe anything but what comes from the tube."

Kathleen found herself assisting at the bed of a young Scot. As the stretcher-bearers jostled him out of the ward to the cellar, she held the tube in the boy's mouth, with the cylinder of oxygen and pressure regulator laid out on the stretcher beside him.

It was no easy task. The stretcher bearers had to jimmy the stretcher down the narrow steps leading to the cellar. Sandbags were piled high around each doorway, making it nearly impossible for Kathleen to squeeze through beside the stretcher. Her gas mask slipped, and she could see out of only one goggle. All the while, the air clouded to the color of milk.

"This has all been set on us by our own lads." One of the stretcher bearers—Kathleen couldn't tell which—spoke from behind his mask. "They decide to gas the Germans, but no one checks to see which way the wind is blowing. So we get it."

"The British did this?" Kathleen asked.

The stretcher bearers turned their insect heads toward her, as if they hadn't realized she was with them. "Don't worry about it," one said. "It's just the latest in a long string in this comedy of errors."

Kathleen said no more. Once the Scot was settled in the basement, she returned upstairs to help with another patient. Soon she was panting from climbing the spiraling stairs to the wards and descending back down into the cellar. The tubing of the mask would not stay put unless she bit on it, which blocked the air flow, and the stale, charcoal-smell of the filtered air made her stomach turn. On her eighth trip to the cellar, she vomited into the gas mask, making it useless.

"Kathleen, don't!" Hank, who was just behind her with another patient, cried, as Kathleen unhooked the mask and thrust it from her face.

The contents of her lunch dripped from the mask on to the floor of the dank cellar. She wiped the back of her hand across her lips, but her cheeks and chin had a wet film of vomit.

"Orderly!" the stretcher bearer shouted.

A doctor appeared from out of the dim depths of the cellar. "Here," he said, offering her the patient's oxygen tube.

"Oh, no, I couldn't take it from him."

"Only a whiff," he said. "And sit down. Once you feel better, you can breathe down here without a mask."

She collapsed, exhausted. The cellar—or *la cave*, as the French called it—was filled with dust. Rough benches had been haphazardly nailed together and placed along the walls. At the very back of the dirt-floored expanse, wine casks and racks of bottles were guarded by a British soldier. At Kathleen's feet, the stretchers were laid in the dirt with almost no room between them, the patients without blankets or other protection from the damp cold.

She leaned against the wall and closed her eyes. Her head swirled, and she had a sense that the unnaturally white light upstairs had burned into her eyes and affected her vision. She wondered if the gas had infiltrated the cellar after all. It was said to linger for days in valleys and near bodies of water.

Someone said her name, and she blinked more than once before she could see clearly.

"I brought you this."

It was Helen, carrying a shallow pan of water and a clean cloth.

"Mrs. Brently told me to bring it to you," she said. "It isn't very warm. The fire has been out for a while, and I wasn't allowed to build a new one because of the gas."

"Thank you." Kathleen dipped the cloth in the water and scrubbed at her face.

They sat side by side without speaking. Kathleen had not yet forgiven Helen for the rift over Paul a few days before.

"What do you have in your hand?" Helen asked.

She looked down at her left hand. She had wrapped her rosary around her wrist when she left the chapel, unable to slide it over her wimple to her neck. Now she found that she had clenched the crucifix against her palm. "It's my rosary," she said.

Helen unfurled Kathleen's fingers. "It left a mark."

On her hand was the cross, with deeper indentations where the knees and hanging head of Christ had pressed against her skin.

Kathleen burst into tears. "Oh, Helen," she cried. "I'm so tired of this—"

Helen pointed to the imprint in her skin. "You should take this as a sign. Does your church believe in signs?"

"I think so."

"Then, this is telling you that you need to behave better. You need to do what you're supposed to do. And you need to stop thinking that you're better than we are."

Kathleen said contritely, "Paul asked me to marry him."

"Before or after?"

"Before or after what?" Her mind moved slowly, trying to determine Helen's meaning. At last, she said, "We kissed, that's all."

"But you would have, wouldn't you?"

She was right, Kathleen knew. If Paul had asked her to make love, she would not have refused.

"Yes," she whispered.

Helen said nothing, and Kathleen straightened up and dried her tears. As she rinsed the soiled cloth in the pan of water, the orderly who had taken her gas mask appeared. "'Ere, love," he said. "Can't get yours clean, so you can 'ave this one. The bloke who 'ad it don't need it where 'e's goin'."

EIGHT

The long night in the cellar ends, and the phosgene gas dissipates. After the all clear is given, the back-breaking work of moving the patients upstairs begins with the same rickety and rough ride. A few—too jounced about by their travel to the cellar, or perhaps banged on the hard floor, or chilled by the damp air in the cellar—do not return to the wards, but are carried away for burial. Almost everyone emerges from the cellar with coughs, and the doctors warn that the true effects of the gas might not appear for another two days.

Kathleen comes back to the world of light and fresh air with a pounding headache and an inability to eat anything more than toast and tea. All the same, the girls open the canteen for the troops who pass through the chateau grounds.

Late in the afternoon, a bulletin from Colonel Lloyd-Elliot is posted in the Great Hall and the wards. It arrives in the canteen in the hands of a British runner.

Hank reads it aloud. "On March 21, the German Spring Offensive opened along an active 40 mile Front from Ypres to St. Quentin. Forces from all Allied armies are involved, including the French near Verdun and the Americans near Mont Blanc. As of today, the British command reports that the city of Cambrai has fallen into German hands."

"Cambrai!" Helen gasps. "After so many died to take it last fall."

"I heard someone say that the British don't have any reserve soldiers left to hold on to it," Hank says in a low voice. "Too many were hurt or died last November."

And so the Germans simply took it back? Kathleen's indignation burns up through her stomach, into her heart and head. After all the misery and death last fall, the British simply walked away from it?

Of course, they hadn't, she chides herself. They had undoubtedly fought as bravely as they ever had. That means they will have wounded.

As the girls serve sandwiches of eggs and jam, they listen for the ambulances to start their dreary drill of pulling into the front courtyard of the chateau to unload their tragic cargo.

But the ambulances don't arrive.

"What's happening?" Kathleen asks a Tommie as she fills his tin cup with soup. "Why aren't they bringing the wounded here?"

"We're comin' back."

"Coming back? What do you mean?"

"It's a full-on retreat," he says. "The Germans are marchin' hard on our heels, over the Hindenburg Line—"

"Where are they taking the wounded?"

"Someplace called Royal Mont or something, as far as I know."

"Where's that?"

"South of Paris."

"So far!" Kathleen says. "Why so far?"

"Because the Germans are headed for Amiens."

Kathleen glances at Helen, then at Hank. As if they have no thoughts on the matter, they go back to work. Kathleen's hands shake as she ladles soup, sloshing it on the counter and down the sides of the tin cups. Helen cuts the bread for sandwiches, the knife blade precariously close to her fingers, but even Hank doesn't offer a warning to be careful.

Late that night, ambulances and lorries arrive in a pack in the courtyard. As the chateau springs to life, Helen climbs from her bed and looks outside. "The wounded are finally here!" she exclaims. "They're bringing in . . ."

Kathleen reaches for her dress, but Helen falls silent.

"What is it?" she asks at last.

"They aren't bringing them in," Helen reports. "They're carrying them out and loading them on the ambulances."

As she speaks, the door opens, and Mrs. Brently enters.

"We're leaving," she says. "It's expected that everything and everyone be neat and orderly, in a proper military fashion. Once you've finished packing your own belongings, bring them down to the canteen. We'll have to pack our supplies and take them with us."

"Yes, ma'am," Hank acknowledges.

Putting their things in order doesn't take long—they learned well on their departure from Montdidier in the fall. In the canteen, Mrs. Brently is already packing up the supplies and equipment in crates.

"We're taking everything?" Helen asks as she dons her apron.

"Yes," Mrs. Brently says.

"We didn't when we left Montdidier."

"Montdidier wasn't about to fall into German hands."

As the day dawns foggy and cold, they carry the supplies, the equipment, and their trunks to the lorry assigned to them. Once everything is hefted on board by two British soldiers, Mrs. Brently starts to climb into the tarped bed.

"I'm sorry, ma'am," one of the soldiers says. "The lorries are for military personnel only."

"We are military personnel," Mrs. Brently says. "We are with the American Red Cross, attached to the American Expeditionary Force, and temporarily assigned to the British."

The soldier, who is probably as young as Kathleen, repeats, "I'm sorry. We have to keep this lorry available for military purposes."

The two soldiers slip into the cab, and the driver revs the motor once before the lorry rolls away, the gravel of the courtyard crunching beneath the tires.

"What should we do?" Hank asks.

"We shall have to walk," Mrs. Brently says.

They walk beside the lorry, which is one of hundreds that crawl along the main road from Amiens to Paris. Ahead and behind them, the ditches and fields are packed with refugees: French farmers in rickety wagons pulled by oxen whose ribs and spines bore outward through their skins; Belgians who had lost everything nearly four years earlier and now carry nothing but a few rags of bedding or a bucket of bread; women dressed all in black, their cheeks sunken and their eyes squinted in the morning light, their babies silent from malnutrition. Kathleen thinks of the gardens that are sheltered by the walls of the great cathedral of Amiens, the precious food now lost to those who tended it so carefully. She hopes it does not fall into German hands.

The passage of heavy artillery has hollowed out deep ruts in the road, and some of the lorries have become stuck or stranded. Beyond the maze of traffic, British troops flank the wagon train. The men move in sloppy lines, their military precision and order gone. Some help those with bandaged heads or arms; others stagger along until they fall and are either prodded into walking by their comrades or loaded on a stretcher and taken away.

More than once, Kathleen sees soldiers drink the brackish water from puddles along the road. Her own lips are cracked and numb from the bitter west wind. Freezing drizzle coats her cloak and wimple and turns the mud under her feet into a slick, icy mess. She longs for her fur collar and muff, but they are packed in her trunk. The lorry that carries it has long since disappeared.

After a while, she realizes that she can't see Mrs. Brently and Hank. Helen limps, favoring her left foot.

"What's wrong?" Kathleen asks.

"My gum boot has a hole in it. The water's coming in. My sock's soaked through, and it's causing a blister."

"I didn't even think to keep my bag with me. I should have packed extra supplies."

"We were to ride on the lorry!"

Kathleen casts a wary look toward her. It is unlike Helen to complain. "Don't cry," she says. "Maybe we'll stop soon."

"How long have we been walking?"

"I don't know."

They slog forward. Kathleen can't recall how the day began, or how they ended up trudging along this soggy stretch. Her right cheek feels stiff and stone-like, and needles of cold stab through her fingers. Helen's limp grows worse, and at times, she lifts her heel and pokes at the sock inside her boot.

Kathleen asks, "Should we wait for Hank and Mrs. Brently?"

Helen nods, her jaw clenched, her bottom lip trembling. Kathleen guides her off the road and through the ditch to where a log lies on the muddy ground.

"You're so cold." Kathleen flings her own cape over Helen's shoulders and draws it around both of them. "Here, share with me."

Helen shivers uncontrollably, sending tremors through Kathleen's body. She falls almost at once into a doze. Kathleen rocks back and forth, keeping a protective hand on the side of Helen's head to shield her from the wind. She watches the road for Mrs. Brently and Hank—how far behind could they have gotten? She sees no one that she knows from Amiens in the faces of approaching soldiers, refugees, lorries, and strings of horse and mule-drawn wagons.

Her wimple weighs on her head, wet and cold. How long has she been here? Minutes? Hours? The wind swirls around her, and she tries to wrap the cloak more tightly around the two of them, but there is not enough cloth. She fights the urge to fall asleep with Helen. One of them has to watch for Hank and Mrs. Brently.

Her father's voice speaks in her head: *Never sit still during a snowstorm. Keep moving, don't stop. If you can't find shelter, walk, jump, do anything, but keep moving!*

But this isn't a snowstorm, Papa. It is fog and rain. We don't have that in Colorado, where it's so sunny and—

Caitlin, me love, don't sit. Get up and move.

Kathleen shakes Helen. "We need to go on," she says, her mouth stiff. "We need to get our blood percolating, as Hank says during morning exercise."

Helen mumbles something that Kathleen doesn't catch.

Kathleen jostles her again. "We need to keep moving. Now, we need to go now."

"Just a few more minutes, I'm so tired—"

A stark thunder cuts through Kathleen's stupor. A mortar? An explosion? Unable to focus at first, she struggles to track the sound. It is familiar, comforting in some way, but she just can't place it. Then, from the dense fog, a rider on horseback emerges, galloping toward her from the opposite direction of the evacuation train.

I will find you, even if I have to ride a horse from here to Colorado.

Paul, she thinks. He's come for me. Oh, Paul, let's go home, let's go back—

As Kathleen twists to see the rider's face, Helen slumps. Kathleen catches her just before she slides to the ground. Colonel Lloyd-Elliot reins in beside the girls.

"I've been searching for you," he says.

"Where's Mrs. Brently?" Kathleen asks, aware of how slow and slurred the words sound.

"She and Miss Mills are up ahead on the lorry that you were assigned to. Come on."

"I don't think she can walk," Kathleen says of Helen, whose eyes are glazed and uncomprehending. Her face is a ghostly white.

Colonel Lloyd-Elliot shouts. "Sergeant, I need help over here."

Four British soldiers—who look as exhausted as Kathleen feels—stagger from the line. One of them lifts Helen into his arms, while the others flank Kathleen, ready to lift her as well.

"I can walk," she says.

"Are you sure?" Colonel Lloyd-Elliot asks.

"Yes, thank you."

But she stumbles, and one of the soldiers sweeps her up in his arms. He follows the man who carries Helen while Colonel Lloyd-Elliot carves a path through the traffic with terse orders and his horse's body. The other two soldiers accompany them, sloshing through puddles and over the deepening ruts of the road. About half a mile beyond where Kathleen and Helen sat down, the Colonel halts beside a tarped lorry. "Here we are."

Mrs. Brently and Hank appear from behind the tarp at the back of the lorry. "Helen! Kathleen!" Mrs. Brently cries. "Oh, what happened?"

"We got so cold." Everything revolves around Kathleen. "I don't know how we were separated—"

"Put the ladies in the lorry," Colonel Lloyd-Elliot orders.

The soldier who carries Helen hops up on the bed of the lorry and gently lays her on the floor. The other soldier follows with Kathleen. She sits, stunned, on her sleeping bag.

Mrs. Brently lays a hand on Colonel Lloyd-Elliot's arm. "Thank you, Thomas." She acknowledges the soldiers as well. "Thank you all."

"Yes, ma'am."

"Thank you!" Kathleen calls belatedly. No one replies.

"Hank, take off Helen's wet clothes and find something dry for her," Mrs. Brently says. "I'll take care of you, Kathleen."

As if she is a child, Kathleen lets Mrs. Brently remove her cape and her uniform. Her arms and legs are limp and unbending. "I'm sorry," she says. "I'm trying to help you, but—"

"Just sit still. It's fine."

Kathleen puts a hand behind her to keep from toppling over. Nothing looks right; the fog that was cloaking the ground outside has seeped into her head. Mrs. Brently lowers Kathleen's nightdress over her head and helps her to find the armholes. She puts dry socks on Kathleen's feet. Together, Hank and Mrs. Brently place Helen inside her sleeping bag. While Hank buttons it up, Mrs. Brently wraps Kathleen's sleeping bag around her.

Hank takes a hot water bottle from her trunk. "I wish we had water and a fire."

"I'll see if I can find some." Mrs. Brently opens the tarp that divides the cab of the lorry from the bed. "Private Parks, we need hot water."

"Go to sleep," Hank croons to Kathleen. "You're safe now."

Kathleen closes her eyes and gives in to the wooziness in her head. Now that she is out of the wind and cold, blood surges through her arms and legs. Her ears and fingers and toes sting, as if a flame has touched them. She closes her eyes and swallows the urge to vomit. Almost at once, she drifts into sleep.

She wakes in a cocoon of warmth and darkness. She moves, and a hot water bottle sloshes next to her. Clutching it against her, she sits up, but the world is still topsy-turvy as the blood rushes through her veins. Her heart flutters unevenly in her ribcage. A lamp hangs from a nail pounded into the frame of the tarped bed.

Helen stirs from her sleeping bag, her face drained of color. "What happened to me? I don't remember—"

"You were too cold," Hank says. "I'm so glad you're all right."

No one speaks, and Kathleen senses they are all thinking the same thing: they could have died in the cold and freezing drizzle.

"I'm just glad we're all together again," Hank says. "We were so scared you'd been lost."

"We thought the same thing," Kathleen says.

"Remember the soldier who told us we couldn't ride?" Hank asks. "Colonel Lloyd-Elliot was so angry that he ordered him off the lorry. He's walking now!"

"Oh, he shouldn't have done that," Helen says. "Not for me."

"He didn't do it for you. He did it for Mrs. Brently. He called her Ellie."

"That's such a pretty name."

"Where is she now?" Kathleen asks.

"She went to a military briefing," Hank says. "She'll be back soon. We've put her sleeping bag behind the boxes, there, where she can have a little privacy."

Someone knocks on the side of the lorry. The girls eye one another for a moment before Hank opens the tarp. A young soldier hands her a sheet of paper that reeks of eye-stinging mimeograph fluid. "Official dispatch," he reports in a curt, English accent.

"Thank you."

Hank waves the sheet a couple of times to dry it, then reads: "After three days of battle, with each night spent on the march or in reorganization of troops, the British are tired almost to the limits of endurance. Our troops continue to fall back. Positions lost: Jussy, Aubigny, Brouchy, Cugny, Eaucourt, and Clery—"

"That's a long list," Helen frets.

"There's something written on the edge here." Hank squints. "Oh, it says, 'Recently reported, the British line at the Somme has been broken.'"

"The Somme!" Helen says.

"To all evacuees from Amiens," Hank reads. "Be warned that there is to be absolutely no noise or light from the fall of darkness to reveille that might alert the Germans and allow them to set up artillery that could reach this position. Anyone caught making unnecessary noise will be punished."

Hank's voice fades into silence, then resumes in a whisper. "It is estimated that the Germans are no more than five miles behind the evacuation train."

As the caravan moves southward, the members of the Graves Family Foundation Relief Society go back to work. During the day, the girls move from lorry to lorry, offering their aid to the wounded. They pilfer supplies where they can: a load of bandages from a female ambulance driver; a crate of cigarettes and chocolate from an abandoned YMCA hut; a kerosene hot plate on which they can boil water for tea to serve to the thirsty troops. In another of her seemingly miraculous acts, Mrs. Brently finds enough loaves of bread and cans of rancid-smelling meat to make about a hundred sandwiches.

Every evening, the girls retire to the bed of the lorry where they sleep, and every evening, a dispatch arrives to inform them of the fate of the British army. None of the news is good.

On their fourth night in the lorry, Kathleen takes the dispatch from the soldier who delivers it. Mrs. Brently has not yet returned from her evening meeting with Colonel Lloyd-Elliot and the other British officers who are trying to keep the hundreds in the evacuation train fed and safe.

"What does it say?" Hank asks.

Kathleen reads. "Albert has fallen—"

"Where's that?"

"Up near . . . Arras, I think. And, oh"—Kathleen breathes out—"oh, Montdidier has fallen."

"Montdidier?" Helen says. "Oh, no!"

Kathleen's heart aches as she reads, "The attack on Montdidier has opened a vulnerable gap between British and French forces—"

"Do they say how much damage was done to the town?"

"No, it only says that it was 'lost by the French.'"

"Like a spare key or a handkerchief," Hank says.

"Oh, I hope, oh, it can't be gone," Kathleen says. "We were so happy there."

They say no more, but prepare for bed. Hank sits on her sleeping bag, braiding her hair, while Helen opens her prayer book for her nightly reading. Kathleen puts away the dispatch and kneels near her sleeping bag, her rosary in her hands. No words of comfort come to her even after she repeats all the prayers she knows. Yet, a voice in her head begs: *Oh, please God, not Montdidier, not that beautiful town, those wonderful people—*

After Kathleen makes the sign of the cross, Helen looks up. "What do you think happened to the girls who took over for us in Montdidier?"

"Let's hope the Germans didn't find them," Hank says.

Kathleen climbs into her sleeping bag, unwilling to follow Hank's train of thought further. It is common knowledge among women—whether French or Belgian refugees, or British ambulance drivers, or American Red Cross workers—that the Germans use rape just as they do their bayonets, as a weapon.

"Did you ever think you might die here?" Helen whispers.

The silence outside the lorry rings until Kathleen answers in a low voice, "No, I didn't even think about it. I just thought about how much I wanted to come." ˙

"Do you think Mrs. Brently or Mr. Graves thought about it when they planned this?"

"I don't think they did," Hank says. "No one asks someone to take a job where they might be killed."

"The AEF does," Kathleen reminds them. "President Wilson does."

Silence falls again, and Kathleen wishes she had not spoken. She hears both Hank and Helen breathing, one of them at a quickened pace that might be a sob.

Kathleen speaks again, mostly to silence her own thoughts. "I don't think we'll die here. I think we'll all go home and get married and have families. I think we'll tell our children and grandchildren about the War to End All Wars, and how we helped our country, and they'll be so proud of us."

"And we'll all stay friends, because of what we've done here," Hank says.

Helen asks, "Even with Mrs. Brently and Mr. Graves?"

"Even with them," Kathleen assures her.

No one questions how or why she can speak for them, and Kathleen's eyes tear suddenly. She thinks of Jim, of his competence— so much like his sister's—and command over seemingly any situation. She knows that it is just fear, that she is just tired, but something within her wishes she could speak to him right now and hear him tell her that no matter how dire the problem, there is a way to solve it.

Dear Paul,

Oh, I wish I knew where you are. We have arrived in Chantilly after the evacuation of Amiens. If you are still in Aumale, you are more than a hundred miles from me. I'm so scared that we won't see each other again.

I don't know how long we'll be here, because we aren't really stationed here. For a while, we were living and sleeping in the back of a British lorry, but Mrs. Brently demanded that we be given a Red Cross billet. So we are now sharing a small room at a private home, our trunks stacked to the ceiling. It's warmer than the lorry, of course, but we step on each other whenever we move.

We have no canteen here. We go wherever we are needed, but we don't work as a group as we have in the past. One day might see me at the Scottish Women's Hospital in Creil, while Helen goes to the "Cantine des Deux Drapeaux," which is a large white canteen tent run by the Red Cross, and Hank is at the civilian hospital helping the refugees. Sometimes, we're called to work twenty-four hour shifts, which is confusing for all of us. We don't know where the others are or if they are in danger.

We learned only a few days ago that an American Red Cross worker by the name of Ruth Landon had been killed. She was a canteener, just as we are, and she died when a shell from the "Paris Gun" hit the Church she was attending on Good Friday. I don't know if you've heard of the gun, but it has killed hundreds in Paris and none of our Allied armies can seem to locate it. It's thought to be nearly eighty miles from the city, and the very thought of something so evil and deadly scares us all. I pray every night that God allows me to live and to be your wife and the mother of your children someday.

I wish I could write more, but I have to go. I want to see you so badly, just to hear your voice and see your face. I miss you so. I love you so.

Forever yours,
Kathleen

NINE

At the Graysons' home in south Denver, Mary Jane set plates and silverware on the table. The kitchen was steamy and warm, the windows dripping with condensation. On the gas range, pots bubbled over the open flames. Mary Jane's mother, Lanita, stirred stew in a Dutch oven. Born in Alabama, she was soft-spoken and proper, a member of the Woman's Christian Temperance Union and the Methodist Ladies.

The door opened, and Mary Jane's father and brothers came inside. They stripped off their dust-laden coats and boots in the enclosed back porch that had been tacked on to the house years ago. As her father, Amos, passed by Mary Jane, he gave her right shoulder an affectionate squeeze. Her brother, Matthew, followed him. At twenty-one, he took after their mother, quiet and deeply religious, with the brown-sugar hair and hazel eyes that all the Grayson siblings shared. Nineteen-year-old Avery, the baby of the family—who still acted like one, in Mary Jane's opinion—had dimples and a boyish cleft in his chin that had more than once helped him to escape punishment for some prank. Passing behind Mary Jane, he plucked at the pins in her hair above her left ear. As she swatted at his hand, he asked, "What's wrong, dodo head? You have to pin your brain inside so it won't fall out?"

The last to enter the kitchen was Mary Jane's favorite brother, Ross, who was twenty-seven. Since he had received his draft notice two weeks ago, he had been quieter than usual, almost secretive. Tonight, his mouth was drawn up in a frown.

"Are you all right?" she asked.

"Fine," he said brusquely.

Work at the gravel quarry was hard and heavy, and all the Grayson men came home exhausted from grinding and loading rock. As the boys washed up in the sink, Mary Jane heard Matt and Avery talking.

"Yeah, but they don't even belong in this country," Avery said.

"But who else is left?" Matt asked.

In the kitchen, Mary Jane's mother turned to her husband. "What's this about?"

"We had a Negro apply at the quarry today," he said. "It caused a stir about whether we should allow those kinds to work for us. We're pretty short-handed just now—"

"A Negro!" Mary Jane's mother said. "Oh, Amos, you wouldn't want to do that. I wouldn't feel safe bringing you and the boys your lunch if you hired him. And I certainly wouldn't let Mary Jane go to the quarry alone."

"This isn't Alabama, Lanita."

"Mr. Graves hires them," Mary Jane offered. "The attendant in the Ladies' Employee Washroom is colored. Her name is Raynelle."

"That's a woman," her mother said. "That's a far different cry from the men."

"His chauffeur is a colored man, too," Mary Jane said. "I'm sure Mr. Graves wouldn't hire anyone bad."

Ross, Matt, and Avery came into the kitchen, and her mother said, "This is a conversation for later. It's not fit for the dinner table."

As the men shoveled stew into their mouths, Mary Jane fumed. Compared to the women at Miss Reston's house, her parents were so dull. Sometimes she wanted to blurt out something just to stir things up, but she had already disappointed them enough by returning from France rather than doing God's work to help the American soldiers, as her mother called it. She ate in silence.

After dinner, she helped her mother with the dishes before she joined Ross on the back porch. He sat on the step, whittling on a stick of pine with a small knife. Peels of wood fell onto the grassy lawn.

"What's wrong?" she asked.

He looked at her with hazel eyes. "I guess I've got the wind up—isn't that what they call it?—about going off to France."

Mary Jane looked away. Only Ross knew the story of her one terrible night in Montdidier: the men bleeding to death before her eyes on the train platform; the terrible cries of the wounded; the coal shed behind the railroad station where the bodies were piled. The others believed she had come home because of homesickness.

"You shouldn't listen to me," she said. "The other girls write about dances with the officers and visiting the great cathedrals and men who propose to them in French. They seem to be having plenty of jolly times. You'll see, it will work out."

Ross patted her knee. "Good old M.J." He called her by her childhood nickname. "It'll be up to you to keep this family straight after I'm gone. You're the next one in line."

"Lucky me."

"So, it's up to you to keep Matt from praying himself to death—"

She laughed.

"—and Avery from acting like a complete—what is it he calls you?—dodo head."

"I can't promise that—"

"And all this fuss about hiring a Negro." Ross sobered. "If he can do the work, what difference does it make? He seemed all right by me. But you should have heard Avery go on about it."

"More than Mom did? I think it's silly—"

"He brought up all those lynchings that have been happening in Georgia and Tennessee. He said he figured they were justified."

"As Dad said, this isn't Alabama."

Ross jettisoned another strip of wood to the ground. "It makes me feel guilty."

"Guilty? You didn't enlist. You were drafted."

"I just wish I could do more for Dad," he said. "What if Matt and Avery get called up, too?"

"Surely, the Draft Board wouldn't send all of you to France."

Ross turned toward her. "M.J., there's something—"

The screen door creaked open and closed behind her. Avery poked his bare toes into her back. "Wish it was you going back to France?"

Mary Jane ignored him. "I'm going inside," she said. "We'll talk later." As she rose, she patted Ross' shoulder. He made no reply.

On the day that Ross left for war, the crowds on 16th Street were smaller than they had been when the Graves Family Foundation Relief Society had left Denver the previous fall. Only a dozen or so people gathered on each corner, most of them family members of a departing soldier. No confetti wafted from the windows of the buildings on either side of the street, and a motley collection of musicians serenaded the travelers with patriotic songs. Mary Jane supposed that the lack of enthusiasm was because the war had lasted almost a year now, rather than the month or two that had been expected. And by all accounts, France was still losing.

As Ross marched by in his unit, Avery put two fingers in his mouth and whistled. Mary Jane clapped her hand over her ear, deafened by the shrillness. Ross looked handsome and strong in his new khaki uniform and campaign hat, with a glistening bayonet spiking upward from his rifle on his right shoulder. Regret flashed through her. She might have been in France to greet him when he arrived.

As he embraced her at Union Station, he slipped her a letter.

"Is this what you wanted to talk about?" she asked. Between her demanding days at Graves Oil and Ross' long hours at the quarry, they had not had the opportunity to talk privately again.

"Yes, and I'm sorry I didn't get to tell you myself." His voice had a tremor of desperation about it. "Listen, I don't want Avery or Matt to know about this. Or Mom. She wouldn't understand. But you will."

"Oh, don't be gone long!" Mary Jane thrust the letter into her coat pocket. "Take good care of yourself!"

"I will," he said. "And promise me you'll see to this."

"I promise."

It wasn't until after dinner, when she was in the privacy of her own room, that Mary Jane read the letter.

Dear M.J.,

I know I haven't been gone long enough for you to miss me, but I already miss you and Mom and Dad and Matt and even Avery, that stinker. Take good care of them all for me. You're the only other one of us who sees things in a true fashion, apart from Dad, but this isn't something I can tell him. But since you've been to France, you know what happens in war. It's none of the heroics of the serials in the newspapers or moving pictures. I know, too, and I just hope that I'm one of the lucky ones who comes home.

Mary Jane looked up from the letter. Outside the window of her bedroom, the trees had leafed out, and the flowers bloomed in the gardens. He was wrong: she missed him already.

Blinking away tears, she read again: *You've probably noticed that I've been out most evenings. It's because I have fallen in love with the most wonderful woman. I haven't told anyone. But I need someone to keep an eye on her while I'm gone and to be a friend to her so that she doesn't forget me.*

Her name is Anneka Lindstrom. She lives at 707 Corona Street. The two of you already have something in common in that she works for the parents of Mr. Graves, your employer. She's been a maid in their house since she came to America from Sweden.

I know you'll like her. She is a widow with a little girl named Mina. I know that Mom wouldn't approve of me marrying a woman who already has a child, but I intend to marry Anneka as soon as I am home, if I come home. If I don't, I want you to be there to comfort her. She is the most beautiful woman I've ever met, and I love her dearly. Promise me that you'll write to me about everything that the two of you do and say to each other. Promise me, too, that you'll let me know if she needs anything. She has no family in Denver. I trust you to do the best for her and for me.

All my love,

Ross

P.S. Anneka doesn't read or write well in English. Ask her if you can read my letters to her so that I am sure that she understands just how much I love her.

Ross in love! No wonder he had grown so solemn and solitary. Mary Jane folded the letter and hid it in her underwear drawer, beneath the copy of *The Woman Rebel*.

Two days later, when she arrived on Corona Street, she found that Anneka Lindstrom's house was in far better condition than its neighbors. The yard had a picket fence and flawlessly weeded flower beds. The brick walkway led to a pristine, oak door that stood between symmetrical, floor-to-ceiling arched windows. The house was painted white, and the gable above the front door was delicately scalloped with gingerbread shingles and painted in a soft reddish-pink.

It was a full-sized doll's house—the kind that every little girl dreamed of. Even more unsettling, a child with picture-perfect white blond hair and bright blue eyes answered the door.

"Hello," Mary Jane said. "You must be Mina. Is your mother here?"

"Yes, Miss." A great gap showed in Mina's mouth where she had lost her two front teeth. She was, after all, just a normal child.

From within the house, someone called, "Who is it, Mina?"

Anneka appeared from the back of the house, and Mary Jane blinked, awed by her beauty. She had curling, dark blond hair and the same blue eyes as her daughter. Her features were lovely, even though her teeth pushed forward to give her a slight overbite. She wore a finely-stitched pink day dress that brought out the color in her cheeks.

"Hello, Mrs. Lindstrom," Mary Jane said. "I'm Ross Grayson's sister, Mary Jane."

Anneka smiled brightly. "Oh, he said that you would come!" She spoke with a heavy accent. "Oh, I'm so happy you did. Please, come in. And please, call me Anneka."

In the living room, Mary Jane shed her coat. "This is very nice."

"Please, sit down," Anneka said. "I'm so happy you've come." She motioned toward the kitchen. "Let me go and start the tea."

Alone with Mary Jane, Mina asked, "Do you want to meet Marta?"

"Of course," Mary Jane said.

As Mina bounded toward the back of the house, Mary Jane studied the room. The window curtains were of a breezy taffeta, and plush pillows lay on the divan. The coffee and end tables were of heavy, dark wood. On the floor was a finely-woven Chinese rug. Old Mr. Graves must pay his household staff much better than young Mr. Graves paid his workers, which was generous enough.

Mina came into the room carrying a doll in her arms. She had changed into a yellow dress frilled with chiffon and lace that was identical to the doll's. The doll had white blond hair and a fragile china face. Her blue, glassy eyes opened and closed under lashes that were carefully inserted into the lids.

"This is Marta," Mina said.

"May I see her?" The doll looked uncannily like the child, as if it had been fashioned after her. Mary Jane lifted the doll to her face. "Hello, Martha."

"It is Marta." Mina corrected. "It is a Swedish name. Like Mother's."

"And your own name? Is Mina a Swedish name?"

"No, I was born in America. It's American."

Mary Jane stroked the doll's soft hair. "She's so different from any doll I've ever seen, so much prettier, I guess. She even looks a little like you. Where did you get her?"

"She was a present from Mr. Yeem," Mina said.

"Mr. who?"

"Mr. Yeem," she repeated with stubborn certainty.

"I've never heard that name. Who is—?"

From the doorway leading to the kitchen, Anneka spoke in Swedish to Mina. The girl looked down at her lap, her lips pressing into a thin line. Confused, Mary Jane handed the doll back to her.

"She speaks of a family friend," Anneka assured Mary Jane.

"Oh, I see," Mary Jane said.

As Anneka set the tea tray on the coffee table, she said, "I am so glad you came. I am so happy that Ross sent you."

"How did you meet him?" Mary Jane asked.

"At a concert at City Park last August," Anneka said. "There were two lady musicians with a violin and a cello, and four dancers. I wanted Mina to see it, because I used to pretend to be a ballet dancer when I was a little girl."

"I can't imagine Ross watching ballet dancers!"

"He wasn't. He was just passing through the park. But he told me"—she grew shy—"he told me that he saw me, and that he couldn't leave without speaking to me. Then he saw an empty chair next to Mina. So he paid his twenty-five cents to sit there, and Mina spilled her lemonade on his leg."

"I didn't mean to do it," Mina said.

"But how lucky that you did," Mary Jane said.

"Ross was very polite about it all," Anneka said. "Very much a gentleman. He walked us home, and told Mina that he would bring her another lemonade. And he did, a few days later."

"Mr. Ross brought me ice, too," Mina said. "I'd never had it."

Mary Jane laughed. "I've been told that we have more in common than just Ross. We both work for the Graves family."

"Oh, yes." Anneka poured the tea. "What do you do at the oil company?"

"I'm a typist," Mary Jane said. "And I was—I suppose Ross told you—I was one of the members of the Graves Family Foundation Relief Society."

"The group that is in France? No, he didn't tell me."

At once, Mary Jane wished she had not admitted to her failed trip to France. "I came home," she said. "I'm not sure why. Sometimes I'm sorry I did."

"You should have asked Mr. Graves if you could go back," Anneka said. "He went to France in January."

"He did?" Mary Jane asked. "We heard in the typing pool that he's in Washington, D.C. to meet with some Congressmen about oil exploration."

Anneka quickly retreated. "I have only heard he went to France from the others at his parents' house. Perhaps I am wrong."

"I wonder if he went to see Kathleen."

"Kathleen?"

"One of the girls in the Relief Society," Mary Jane said. "I'm sure there's something romantic between them. When we were in New York, he spent all his time with her. You've seen her sketches in the newspapers, haven't you? She's the one who draws."

"Yes, I have. She's very good."

"I think so, too. Kathleen caused quite a stir when she was chosen. She was only nineteen, and the age restriction was twenty-one, but Mr. Graves didn't care." Mary Jane caught herself. "But my mother would say that it's sinful to pass on stories about others. I'm sorry. I hope you don't think I'm a gossip."

"That's all right. Does Kathleen work at the oil company?"

"She's a typist just like me."

"And she is only nineteen? She is younger than I am."

Mary Jane hesitated, puzzled that Anneka had compared herself to Kathleen. Before she could speak, Mina announced, "I am teaching Mother to read."

Anneka issued another correction in her native tongue, and Mina said, "I am teaching her to read in *English*."

"I can read and write very well in my own language," Anneka said. "I did not leave Sweden until I was sixteen, and I was given a good education there. But I can only read what a six year old can read in English."

"You must have married so young! How old were you?"

"What? No, I—"

"I'm sorry, that was impolite." Embarrassed, Mary Jane volunteered, "I can teach you to read English. I'll help Mina with her school work, too, if you like."

"Yes, I would like that." Anneka smiled tenderly at Mina. "You must know that there is nothing wrong with Mina's teaching. She is very patient and good to her stupid mother—"

"You aren't stupid, Mother," Mina scolded.

"Just slow, then." Anneka laughed. "But I would so like to be able to read the newspapers in English the way Ross does."

"Then, I'll be back with books," Mary Jane said. "He asked me to help you read his letters, too, in case there are words you don't know."

"How kind of him."

"Oh!" Mary Jane said. "This will be fun!"

From her own library, Mary Jane chose *Rebecca of Sunnybrook Farm* and the Glad Books, including *Pollyanna*. From Ross, she borrowed a volume of *Black Beauty* that had been a birthday present from their mother. She knew Ross treasured it. She expected Anneka would, too.

It wasn't Anneka who paged through the books until the bindings creased, however, but Mina, who could read almost anything that was handed to her. Mary Jane realized that her offer to help Mina with her schoolwork was unnecessary. The girl picked up on everything in the blink of an eye. To offset Mina's curiosity, Mary Jane brought her mother's magazines, *McCall's* and *The Ladies' Home Journal*, for Anneka. Mina didn't like the magazines as well.

"There's the most wonderful story in this one," she told Anneka as she flipped through a copy of *The Ladies' Home Journal*. "It's called 'Evelyn's Joy.' Want to read it together?"

Anneka trundled through the words, using a ruler to guide her and consulting Mary Jane when she stumbled. The story ended as Evelyn and George stood at the altar, about to become husband and wife.

"Oh," Mary Jane breathed. "Wouldn't you love to be married to someone like that?"

"I will be."

Mary Jane laughed, happy for Ross. Mina began to waltz with Marta, the two dressed in matching pink dresses. Both Anneka and Mary Jane stopped reading to praise Mina's graceful steps and beautiful face.

TEN

Maggie dipped her hand into a sack and pulled out a handful of something that ran like water through her fingers. Last year, the governor of Colorado, Julius Gunter, had encouraged the people of the state to eat pinto beans. Now, he was pushing Coloradans to eat rice, which Maggie had never seen before.

Carefully, she measured out a pound of rice to take home. Although she hadn't the least idea how to cook it, she should be able to tell her customers what to do with it.

That is, if there were any customers.

One by one, the families that Sullivan's Grocery had served for years were disappearing. Maggie had said nothing about it to her mother or father, who must surely know by now, stationed as he was behind the meat counter. She knew that she—or rather, Liam—was to blame: ever since the newspaper article in the *Denver Post* had blackballed Liam, business at the store had more or less dried up.

The bell that hung over Maggie's head rang. She wiped the grainy dust of rice from her hands and called to her father, "I'm going upstairs."

There was, of course, no answer. If a customer came inside while she was gone, he would probably be able to loot the entire store before her father deigned to talk to him. With any luck, the crook would carry away the bag of rice so she wouldn't have to deal with it.

She found her mother sitting up in bed. Beside Ma was a pile of Seaney's letters. Maggie knew that she had read through them again.

"Is there any mail?" Ma asked.

"Not yet," Maggie said. "Do you want me to make you some tea?"

"Would you? I know that you're wantin' to get home to Liam—"

Tenderly, Maggie smoothed back the hair from her mother's eyes. "He won't be home for a while," she said. "I'm in no hurry."

She drank a cup of tea with her mother before she walked home. At the front door of her own house, she dipped her fingers in the font of holy water and made the sign of the cross over her body. Rounding the corner from the foyer to the parlor, she found Liam on the couch, his face in his hands.

"Liam!" She ran to him. "What's wrong? What's happened?"

He made no reply. Brendan came from the kitchen with two glasses of whiskey in his hands. Liam immediately took a swallow from the one Brendan handed him.

"What are you doing here?" she asked. "What's happened?"

"I got a draft notice." Liam picked up a sheet of paper from the table. "It came today by special delivery to the railroad office. I'm to report in three days to the Induction Center."

"But you've never filled out the Questionnaire!" Maggie cried. "They can't draft you—"

"I've called Judah," Brendan said. "He's on his way."

"But—"

All at once, the day was too hot, and the smell of the ripening spring too strong. She stumbled toward the armchair.

Brendan grabbed her elbow. "Maggie, be careful."

She plopped into a chair, her belly pulling her downward. She felt as if she would vomit up everything she had eaten for the past six months.

"How did this happen?" she asked. "You said you couldn't be drafted as long as you were to stand trial for—"

"Liam," Brendan said. "For Maggie's sake, you have to search your heart. Isn't it possible that you're resisting this out of your own stubbornness? Don't you think it's time to quit?"

"You know better," Liam snapped. "I am following my conscience. If it weren't for this war and the law of conscription, I would be, as I've always been, a law-abiding citizen."

"But you have a tendency to challenge authority. You have since we were boys. Remember when Father Joseph used to—?"

"Tell me this," Liam demanded. "What's the difference between the Conscientious Objector of 1918 and the Northern abolitionists of 1860 who refused to return slaves to their owners? They objected to one law—the law that required them to send fellow humans into bondage—not to the government in general. In 1860, they refused to obey that one law, and today we think of them as the best of American citizens."

"Stop it!" Maggie cried. "All you do when you're asked about this is to come up with some theory or philosophy or something. You never answer the question!"

"I'm not doing this because I'm trying to cause trouble. I'm doing this because I must."

"But it's wrong. All of this is wrong. It hurts too many people. Ma and Pa, and the store, and Brendan, and me and the baby—"

"It is never wrong to honor God's will."

"Yet every letter or speech you make just antagonizes them!"

"Antagonizes who?"

"The Draft Board. Or the Knights of Columbus, or the *Denver Post*, or President Wilson—"

"I have no antagonism toward any of them," Liam said. "My objection to war springs from my great love of God, and, more so, from my quarrel against conscription, which forces men who would never pick up a weapon against their neighbors to do so."

Brendan spoke again. "Liam, think of Sean, and Frank, and—may he rest in peace—Donnell. They've all gone. You can't keep asking people to choose between supporting you or supporting their loved ones—"

"I don't ask anyone to do that—"

"You ask Maggie to choose between Sean and you every day that you refuse."

"I've never asked her to choose between us. Maggie knows that."

The thought echoed in her head: *Do I know that? Do I believe it?*

She pulled herself out of the chair, wobbling as she stood. She needed silence, a chance to think.

"Are you all right?" Brendan asked.

"I'm going upstairs."

In the bedroom, she knelt beside the bed and laid her head against the quilt. Oh, God, how would she survive this?

"Maggie."

Liam had come into the room. He helped her up to sit on the bed.

"This can't be good for the baby," she said. "I'm in tears half the time and scared to death the other half. When he's born, how do we raise him when we're always fighting over this?"

"I don't fight with you, Maggie," Liam said. "You try to do battle with me."

"I would never do that! I only want you to hear what I'm saying. You can't keep this up—it doesn't help anyone, it doesn't do anything."

"And yet I can't give in without turning my back on God. No one can ask that of me. Not you or Brendan or even the Catholic Church."

"The Church is God," she protested. "It has always been our way to Him. And the Church supports the war—"

"You're too upset. We can't talk when—"

"No, Liam, no," she said. "You can't keep pushing me aside as if I can't think for myself. You can't keep assuming that I haven't thought it through enough to have something to say about it. Every time I try to talk about it, it's time to pray, or time for bed, or—"

Her words failed, and she bit back a sob. "You're right," she went on. "I don't understand what you're doing. I don't see why you can't be like the others and do your duty."

"Do you remember the first time Brendan and I came from the orphanage to your house for Sunday dinner?" Liam asked. "It was in the spring, I think."

"What does this have to do—?"

"Hear me out."

She remembered how excited she had been to meet the new orphan boys, whom she'd only seen from afar. Yet when Liam had actually been seated at the table, she had been too shy to meet his gaze. "All right," she said.

"You and Sean were dressed for church. And Kathleen was there, and she was just so pretty with her fiery curls and snow-white stockings. And there Brendan and I were in our tan overalls and cardboard shoes that were all that we—that any orphan from Mount St. Vincent's—owned."

"They squeaked."

Liam smiled wanly. "I used to think about how wonderful your life was—"

"Wonderful?" Maggie snorted. "It wasn't at all, with Pa always drunk and going on a tear, and Ma crying over—"

"But you had a mother and father," Liam insisted. "You had a home, a place you went to every night after school, where you knew that you would find your parents. You had bedrooms. I used to look at Sean's room and think, he has everything. Toys, and a door he can close, and a kitchen where he could just walk in and take whatever he wanted. A sausage from the pan or a hunk of bread for a sandwich. My mouth would water when I thought of how fortunate he was. And you had such pretty furniture and rugs—"

"It's my grandmother's furniture—"

"I knew that was what I wanted," Liam said. "To live in a house with parents, to have enough to eat, and to wear clothes that weren't made or meant for someone else." When he spoke again, his voice was pained. "And I resented Brendan. I always needed to protect him. His eyesight was so bad—and no one figured that out for so long. Everyone just thought he was stupid. He was always crying because he was afraid of being left behind, and he was whipped for being lazy when he didn't do his schoolwork. But it was just that he was nearly blind."

"I'm sorry that happened to him. He's such a gentle person."

Liam said nothing, caught up in memories. At last, he continued. "Finally, I realized that I couldn't go through life being envious of Sean and angry at Brendan. And so, rather than having to confess my sins again and again, I made peace with God. I knew He wasn't going to give me a home and parents who lived by the word of God, or a brother who was strong and handsome, or a pretty cousin. I knew that he had given me Himself, and that He would be enough."

"But you have a home now, and you have me, and I will always be here—"

"But don't you see? God has always been there, even when I didn't want to understand or recognize Him." His eyes were orange in the fading light of the day. "Maggie, my life has always been dedicated to Him."

Maggie rocked back and forth, soothing both the baby and herself. Liam rarely talked about his time at Mount St. Vincent's, but she had always known that he loved Brendan with a fierceness that came from being the guardian of his younger brother.

"If there wasn't a war—" She stopped, then started again, "If America hadn't gone to war, then you would have what you wanted. A home, a wife, children, the Church, and you'd be just like every other Catholic father and husband who goes to Mass and confession and lives out his life without any trouble."

In the silence, voices floated upward from downstairs, Brendan's and another man's. A dog barked somewhere in the neighborhood, and children shouted. A horse clopped by on the street below.

"Yes, that's true," Liam said at last.

"Then we were just born at the wrong time."

"There is no wrong time in God's plan."

Then, the wrong time is in my life.

She put her hands over her face.

Liam wrapped his arms around her.

"Liam?" Brendan called from downstairs. "Judah is here."

"We'll talk later," Liam said. "Rest now, my beloved."

Maggie lay down on the bed. Tenderly, Liam removed her shoes and brought her a glass of water. He stroked her hair from her face and covered her with a light blanket. "There," he said. "You'll feel better soon."

After he left, she cried herself to sleep.

****

That night the two men slept at the house, Brendan stretched along the couch and Judah in an armchair in front of the fire.

The day after the draft notice arrived, a flurry of messengers came to the door. Every time the doorbell rang, Maggie cringed, sure that it would be the police. But the deliveries were missives from the People's Council of America for Peace and Democracy, letters from legal experts that Judah had contacted, and other documents. A telegram came from the U.S. Attorney General's office in response to a cable from Judah.

"The U.S. Attorney General has noted the irregularities of your case, meaning the charges in the Denver County court," Judah told Liam. "But he is allowing the Draft Board to go ahead with the summons to induction—"

"So they're ignoring Rule Thirteen of their own Selective Service regulations," Liam said. "What other laws will be ignored?"

Late in the afternoon, a telegram arrived. Judah ripped it open with the words, "At last, here is our answer."

He read it slowly, silently, then lowered the slip of paper.

"What is it?" Liam asked.

"It's from the National Civil Liberties Union," he said. "I sent a telegram in the hope that it would pick up your cause." He looked again at the telegram and read, "'The Supreme Court has upheld conscription as constitutional. Do not fight it.'"

The night before Liam was to report for induction, Maggie stood by the window of the bedroom. Outside, the night was quiet and dark, a normal night for most folks. When Liam came in from washing up, he stood behind her and put his arms around her, his hands resting on the baby. She covered his hands with hers and leaned back against him.

"You have to go tomorrow," she said.

"You know I won't."

"But the baby—"

"Either way it goes, I would be away from you."

"But if you go to the Induction Center, you could apply for—"

"I have to know that you will be—if I am away for a long time, I have to know that you will always care for our baby and stay true to our love."

"Of course, I will. You know I will. I've always loved you."

"That's all I ask," he said. "I could not bear to face this if you weren't by my side."

Maggie gave a choked sob. "What if something happens to the baby? My mother couldn't—"

"But this baby has grown from our love, which is strong and whole. It's as near to perfect as human love can be. The baby will be that way, too."

"I love you."

"Let's go to bed," Liam said. "Tomorrow will be another long day."

"Would you, will you—?"

"What? What do you want?"

"Make love to me," she whispered. "Please, just let me—"

She lowered her face, ashamed. She had never asked him to touch her before—she had never had to. But right now, she needed him to quiet her thoughts and subsume her senses, to make her forget who she was and what awaited them both.

He turned her so that she faced him and kissed her, his lips full and warm against hers. "Come to bed."

That night, she lay in his arms, but she didn't sleep. Long after midnight, she could still feel both their hearts beating hard, as if in fear.

On the morning of the day after Liam was to report to the Induction Center, two Denver policemen appear at the door of the Keohane house. Brendan and Judah are both there, ready to argue.

"It won't do you any good," one of the officers says. "We're to escort Mr. Keohane to Fort Logan."

"Fort Logan?" Judah demands. "That's a military installation. This man has never been inducted into the Army. He's only just received his notice. He's a civilian."

"We're to take him to Fort Logan, where he'll be turned over to military authorities."

"What does that mean?" Brendan asks.

"He may have slipped his way through the civil courts, but no longer," the officer says. "He's to be held at Fort Logan until the time of his court-martial under the Sedition Act of 1918."

"Court-martial?" Judah says. "He can't be court-martialed if he's never been inducted—"

"It's all right." Liam speaks. "God's will be done."

Without further argument, he slips his arms into his coat. His face glows with a sheen of sweat in the early morning light. The officers flank him as they go out through the front door of the house.

"No," Maggie cries. "Oh, no, Liam! Please, you can't—"

The door closes in her face.

ELEVEN

My darling brother,

We are now in Chantilly. We came here in a harrowing fright, evacuated from Amiens and plagued by faulty communications with our British hosts. Suffice it to say that we are all well at the present time, although this letter sounds much calmer than I feel. Please believe me when I say we have been through the worst we've seen so far.

We are in a much different situation in Chantilly than we were in Montdidier or Amiens. The business of war is in full swing here. The station-yard is a completely functional transportation center and is well-guarded by five "saucisses" or sausages, as they're called by the English. These are observation balloons that ascend into the sky as far as the guy wires will allow. From the baskets below, soldiers with far-ranging binoculars and rigged-up telephones report what they see.

We serve in the hospitals in Creil, where every type of wound is seen to and every sort of operation is attempted. Trains full of wounded arrive every day, and convoys of ambulances crawl through the streets. Barges of wounded float down the Oise to the pier, where ambulances wait to carry them away. The military hospitals will not tend to the refugees, of whom there are thousands in and around the city, so there is always confusion at the hospital doors, with civilians—some of them near death—being turned away, while soldiers are being rushed inside. I have never seen so much human suffering and unfulfilled need. I hope I will never see it again.

Helen has been unable to walk well since the evacuation because of chilblains on her feet. It was suggested to me that she visit the "Ambrine" hospital, which is run by the Baroness de Rothschild, and is dedicated solely to those who have been burned by gas, flamethrowers, or in other explosions.

The doctors here are perfecting a system that involves the application of a mixture of heated paraffin and other resins, which the French call Ambrine, to form a sort of patch over the burned skin. Before the paraffin cools, a layer of gauze is applied. The process is then repeated with further layers of wax and cotton, and then the wound is wrapped with a gauze bandage that holds it all together. The French claim that this method allows the natural secretions of the body to rebuild the skin, leaving behind no scars or permanent disablement. As you can imagine, Helen's chilblains were no challenge for the doctors, and she is well.

On a more personal note, I have no intention of chastising you from afar, but you should have told me of Kathleen's involvement with the American ambulance driver. The discovery of it caused us much embarrassment and turmoil, which ended only with the evacuation and the urgency of our situation. While I can't condone your secrecy in this matter, I will tell you that I won't allow Kathleen more latitude than I've already given her. My comfort is that, according to Colonel Lloyd-Elliot, the young man's intentions toward Kathleen seemed honorable.

Love to you and to Mother and Father,
Ellie

In his office at Graves Oil, Jim read the letter, then laid it aside for a few minutes before reading it again. He could sense Ellie's raw emotion: fear, worry, indignation. He had caught only glimpses of the war in his travels through France and England: the limbless or blind men at the French train stations; the shattered bodies in the rehabilitation hospital that he had toured in Kent; the submarine hunters of the English Channel. Now, Ellie's anxiety rooted in him, making him feel off kilter.

He heard the clock in the Daniels & Fisher Tower strike one and gathered his coat and hat. After walking the distance between 17th Street and Colfax, he arrived at the Capitol Building. The second meeting of the Committee to Americanize Colorado, to which he had been named by Governor Julius Gunter, was to be held in a third floor meeting room. The first meeting had taken place while he was in Washington.

The Committee consisted of five women and ten men. Professor George Norlin, whom Jim had met in December, stood near the head of the polished, mahogany table speaking with Governor Gunter. Postmaster Ben Stapleton, a long-time friend of Jim's parents, spoke with two well-dressed women. Jim greeted him, then took a seat next to an officious-looking gentleman dressed in a simple dun-colored suit.

Jim introduced himself, and the gentleman replied, "I'm Ernest Morris."

"It's a pleasure to meet you," Jim said. "I'm afraid I'm somewhat behind. I missed the last meeting because of business in the east. Can you fill me in on what happened?"

Mr. Morris gave a quick, derisive snort. "All we did was argue about Alma Gluck."

"Alma Gluck? The opera singer?"

"The prima donna of the Metropolitan Opera Company in New York, yes." He eyed Jim through thick-lensed glasses. "Were you at her concert at the Auditorium in December?

"No, I believe I was out of town when she performed."

"Well, she sang a number of songs in German, and she was booed by those who found it unpatriotic. It caused some uproar that she would dare to sing 'Stille Nacht' rather than 'Silent Night.'"

"Isn't the original carol in German?"

"It is. Written by Franz Gruber. But that sort of thing isn't allowed any more. It's believed that we have enough good American music without singing German songs, and that there is more music in 'The Star Spangled Banner' than in any German oratorio. Poor Wagner."

Jim chuckled. "And this is what was discussed?"

"In large part. In her defense, Mrs. Gluck has donated more than $20,000 to the American Red Cross since her concert. However, I don't believe she will ever be forgiven for 'Stille Nacht.' The newspapers—and our Committee here—have called not only for a ban on any production written in German, but also the advertising or promotion of such a performance, until the barbarous Hun has been humbled to dust."

Jim laughed aloud at Morris' sarcasm as Professor Norlin called the meeting to order. Old business was covered, then the members—including Jim—who hadn't been at the initial meeting were introduced. Soon after, Ben Stapleton, was asked to speak.

"The registration of German alien enemies has gone well," he reported. "As you know, registration was held during one six-day period in February. All districts are reporting only a few who did not follow the law and are now liable to be interned until the end of the war."

"What was entailed in the registration process?" someone asked.

"Each citizen of Germany was to fill out a registration card, giving name, residence, place of business, and length of time in this country. He was also expected to furnish four photographs of himself, one of which is to be attached to the registration card, which he is required to carry at all times, and a set of fingerprints. He also signed an oath not to take up arms against our country at any time."

Beside Jim, Mr. Morris stirred. "May I ask, sir, how well the registration process went in the rural parts of the state? There was some concern that residents were put in straits because they had to travel many miles to find a photographer and that some were hard-pressed to pay for the photographs. In fact, I heard that some German citizens who work in the mines near Oak Creek had to travel as far as Steamboat Springs to find a photography studio."

"I believe there's some truth to that," Ben said. "However, it's long been known that the registration process was required of all German alien enemies, and it was their responsibility to complete it by February 9. Distance was not a valid reason for failure to comply. And who can't afford a five-cent postcard photo?"

Jim shifted. He knew plenty of workers in the oil fields for whom five cents was a day's worth of food.

A woman by the name of Abigail Lake raised her hand. "Are there plans to register female German aliens as well?"

"Yes," Mr. Stapleton replied. "I believe that will happen in the next few months. On a side note, we've not yet had any reports of alien enemies moving from one address to another, which they cannot do unless it is reviewed by the Postmaster."

"So they can't move from one part of the city to another if, let's say, a new job opportunity comes along?" Jim asked.

"Not unless it is approved."

Jim leaned back in his chair. A memory of the woman he had met last year in the small town on the eastern plains—he couldn't remember her name, Dahlia? Delilah?—came into his head. She had accused the German residents of treason simply because they were German.

"Thank you, Mr. Stapleton." Professor Norlin said. "Mrs. Bradford, would you give the report for the Department of Public Instruction?"

Jim doubted that there was anyone in the room who did not recognize the middle-aged woman or her florid hat. Mary C.C. Bradford had long been a fixture in Colorado—the first woman in America to be a delegate to the Democratic National Convention; the first woman in the country to sit on the Superintendent's Committee of the National Education Association; and more recently, the first female president of the National Education Association.

"In the Department of Public Instruction, we are currently writing a *War-Modified Course of Study* for use in Colorado's public schools," she said. "We are framing events from the past few years in ways that will guide discussion of and learning about the war. A sample question is why Germany invaded Belgium first rather than directly attacking France. In pointing out the geographical features such as the steep foothills that divide Germany from France and the openness of the land between Belgium and Germany, we have incorporated military history with social science."

Mrs. Lake posed another question. "Hasn't it been largely accepted that nothing having to do with Germany is to be taught in the public schools? My understanding is that teaching the German language is no longer allowed, and that German texts are being removed from libraries."

"To a large extent, yes," Mrs. Bradford agreed. "But geography is still a required subject, and what better way to educate our young people about the unscrupulous behavior of the enemy? After all, Belgium had no quarrel with Germany."

"Are the colleges following in the footsteps of the Department of Public Instruction?"

"The University of Denver's chancellor, Mr. Buchtel, has refused to ban instruction in German." James Stephens, the chairman of the Americanization Department of the National Council of Defense, spoke. "However, students there are showing much more patriotism by banning the 'Merry German Club.' They've even turned in their dachshund-shaped lapel pins."

A titter of laughter went round the room.

"And the University of Colorado?" Mrs. Lake asked. "So many of the professors there have been educated in German universities that they must still have some ties to them, such as friendships or professional relationships. One fears that their loyalty to the United States may be tainted."

"I believe I can speak to that," Professor Norlin said. "The staff at the University is fully committed not only to the education of our students but to the cultivation of upstanding, patriotic, and productive American citizens. In fact, recently, the University sponsored the burning of several German texts."

Jim shifted again. He recalled reading Nietzsche and Engels during his own college education. Goethe, Mann, Rilke—he had enjoyed them all.

Ralph Smith, who was the representative from the American Protective League, took the floor. "By spring, we hope to have a chapter of the America First Society in every small town in Colorado."

"That's a worthy goal," Governor Gunter said.

Mr. Smith continued. "To that end, the National Council of Defense has created a pledge card for the American Protective League that reads: 'I pledge myself to be first of all an American, to promote with all my power knowledge of the language, the government, and the ideals of this country; and to support her by my every word and act in her struggle for the freedom of mankind.' It further states, 'He that is not for America is against America.'"

Jim could no longer ignore his concerns. "So much of what I've heard here today seems to be in favor of erasing or stripping anything German from American culture," he said. "Yet in the past, Germans have always been fairly desirable as immigrants to our state—much more so than the Italians or Greeks whose socialist and anarchist views are found in the southern coal fields. And I haven't heard any evidence that the majority of Germans who live in Colorado are loyal to Germany and not the United States. In fact, many of the men with whom I have business—such as Mr. Godfrey Schirmer of the German-American Trust Company—are true patriots."

Governor Gunter spoke. "I believe this was covered at our last meeting. I have already publicly vowed that any German-American who is loyal to our country will not suffer from abuse or intimidation. Colorado welcomes loyal German citizens into our state and hopes to protect them."

"I'm sorry, I was absent," Jim said. "But these actions—burning German texts, banning the teaching of German, requiring the signing of a pledge card—seem contrary to that aim."

The governor glared. "In addition, Senator Shafroth read a statement into the Congressional Record in Washington attesting to the patriotism of most German-Americans in the Western states. I believe your insinuation of a widespread persecution is wholly without basis."

"I wasn't insinuating anything of the sort," Jim said. "But I think that we must proceed with caution. Isn't our goal to assimilate foreigners?"

Mr. Smith resumed his speech after a sour look at Jim. "Today, Governor Gunter, Professor Norlin and I are asking for all of you to sign the pledge card as a show of good faith. We don't feel that we can ask the public to sign unless we have set the example."

As the cards were passed along the table, newspaper reporters were allowed into the room. While the others waited patiently for the pen and ink to pass from the head of the table, Jim read the card again and again. Why should he sign it? Why should anyone? He felt the same resentment at having to prove his intentions and character as he did with the newly-created regulations on drilling for oil.

"Mr. Graves?" Mr. Smith asked.

"Remember the President's words, Mr. Graves," Mrs. Lake taunted. "'Proud to Prove.'"

Jim reached for the pen.

After a group photo, which would appear in the newspapers, and handshakes all around, Jim left the Capitol. Two hours still remained in the workday, but he felt too restless to return to the office. He walked along Broadway, fingering the newly-signed card in his pocket, until he came to Corona Street.

He could hear Mina sobbing from outside the gingerbread cottage. When he rapped on the door, Anneka answered, her hair tangled around her face, her mouth pursed with frustration.

"What's going on?" He entered the house. "It sounds dreadful."

She closed the door behind him and motioned toward Mina, who lay face down on the sofa, crying into the cushion. "She has a fever, and I want her to go to bed, but she is being . . ."

"Bull-headed?"

"If that means that she will not do as she is told, then, yes, she is being a bull-head."

Jim stifled his laugh. "Let's see what I can do." He removed his coat, gloves, and hat and handed them to Anneka. Sitting on the sofa, he said, "Mina, Mina, what's this all about?"

She raised her head, her cheeks tear-stained. "I want to play, Mr. Yeem."

"Little girls who are sick should be asleep in bed," Jim said gently. "Don't you think?"

He placed his hand on her forehead, which was clammy beneath his palm. Mina broke into a low wail as she rocked back and forth.

"Have you called a doctor?" he asked Anneka. "Her temperature seems high—"

"I think she only has a cold—"

Mina's cries grew louder.

"A doctor should see her. It could be more serious—"

"If she isn't well in a few days—"

"A few days could be too late, if it's scarlet fever or polio."

"Why must you say that?" Anneka charged. "Why must you frighten us?"

"I don't intend to frighten you—"

"She doesn't have scarlet fever. She doesn't have"—her English failed—"the other thing. She just needs to go to bed!"

Jim had never heard Anneka speak so harshly, especially to Mina, who now cried so loudly that he nearly had to shout to be heard over her.

"Bring out her pillow and her favorite blanket," Jim said. "She can sleep here, on the sofa. And bring her doll as well."

"She does not need such spoiling! She needs to go to her room—"

"Mina," he asked. "Would you sleep here, with my lap as a pillow?"

Mina nodded, still moaning and rocking. Without objecting again, Anneka went toward the back of the house to fetch the bedding and the doll. Jim said to Mina, "Let me take off your shoes."

He removed them, then untied the bow at the back of her pinafore. Anneka returned with her nightdress. As Mina changed clothes, he fluffed the pillow and laid it on his lap, then spread out the blanket on the sofa. He laid the doll's head in his lap and covered her with the blanket. "Here," he said. "Your bed is waiting. See? Your dolly—what is her name?"

"Marta," Mina said.

"Marta is already asleep."

Mina stretched out, her head on the pillow, Marta in her arms. Anneka laid a blanket over her. Jim stroked Mina's hair—white-blond, the color his was when he was a child.

Mina grabbed his hand. "Your hand is funny."

Anneka spoke sharply in Swedish, but Jim turned his hand palm upward.

"You have a bump in the middle of it," Mina said.

With one finger, she traced the scar. Jim had gotten it from clinging to the runner of the sleigh after the accident in the frozen lake at Inglesfield, his parents' castle in the mountains.

He opened his other palm. "I have bumps on both my hands."

Mina ran curious fingers over the scars. "They're ugly."

"Mina!" Anneka said. "You will not speak like that again to Mr. Jim. Please apologize."

Mina's face soured. "I'm sorry, Mr. Yeem."

"I don't like them much either." Jim ran his hand over her hair again. "It makes it hard to feel how soft your hair is. Here, lie down."

Mina obeyed, but her fascination with his hands did not abate. With her index finger, she traced zigzags across the scar on his left hand. The repetition of the motion calmed her, and within a minute or two, she had fallen asleep.

"Her tears were of true exhaustion," he said in a low voice.

"She has been fighting me for the whole afternoon," Anneka said. "I don't like it when she does not listen to me."

"The complaint of all parents, I suspect."

"You should not let her always have her way. She needs to do as she is told. And you cannot let her be rude to you. You should not have let her say what she said without scolding her."

"Why are you so upset? She does what you want most of the time, doesn't she?"

"*Ja,*" Anneka admitted. "Most of the time, she is a good girl."

Jim rubbed Mina's back. She snored slightly from the congestion in her lungs.

"Where is your fiancé?" he asked Anneka. "You aren't expecting him, are you?"

"He is in North Carolina with the Army now."

"Did he enlist?"

"He was called up to go," she said. "I heard that you went to France."

"I was in Nice for a few days, then London for another week. After that I was in Washington for nearly a month."

"You saw Miss Eleanora in France?"

"Yes, she and the girls of the Relief Society were in Nice for a few days. It was a welcome break for them."

"The one that sketches," Anneka said. "She's very good, yes?"

Jim puzzled at her curiosity. "She has a passable amount of talent," he said. "I don't believe it will ever be anything more than the ability to capture what she sees in an orderly and realistic way."

"She is very young, isn't she? Too young to be with the Relief Society?"

"Where did you hear that?" he asked.

"There are rumors," Anneka said vaguely.

"Have you been listening to the gossip at my parents' house?" he teased. "Shame on you, Anneka. You know it's mostly tripe."

She shrugged, and he did not press it. Since his return from France, he had wasted hours dwelling on the details that Kathleen had given him about her young suitor—a lawyer, younger by a few years than he was, a Yalie from Boston, undoubtedly well-heeled. He couldn't help but feel some satisfaction at Ellie's revelation that the two had been separated by distance and circumstance.

"How easily you travel to these places," Anneka said. "I remember the voyage across the ocean as so tiring. I thought the train trip across America would never be over. How much longer could we go? How big can this country be? It was so confusing."

"How did you come to be here, Anneka?"

"My father wanted to come to America because the land was all gone in Sweden. So we came here to homestead, but there was no good land left. Then my *Mor*—my mother—became sick. When she died, my father went to work on the railroad. He died, and my brothers all went to Minnesota to be with my uncle."

"How many brothers do you have?"

"Five."

"Are any of them in the AEF?"

"Three of them. The two youngest are still in Minnesota."

"Why didn't you go to Minnesota with them?"

"They left the summer I met you. I didn't want to go." She shrugged. "And I had a good job here already."

Jim shifted, longing for a cigarette. He had never before asked Anneka about her past. He had never cared before, he supposed. Yet he wished now that they had talked of it as they lay in bed, thrilled to be breaking the rules, or as they walked near the South Platte River, or as they picnicked at Inglesfield. He wished he had known her better.

"I had to sign a pledge card today to uphold American values," he said.

"What do you mean?"

"It's in my coat pocket."

She rummaged in the coat, then handed it to him.

He read the card to her and told her of the meeting of the Committee. "I believe they plan to make everything that is German disappear from this country."

"I hope it isn't suggested that all foreigners leave—"

"You have nothing to worry about as long as Sweden stays neutral."

"And if it does not? I have no reason to hate it here. People come—we come—to America because we want something better than what we had, not so we can cause trouble for others."

Ve vant sum-ting better tan vut vee had.

"Do you have something better than what you had in Sweden?"

"I have Mina," she said simply.

Jim stroked Mina's hair again, but the girl did not move. His leg beneath the solid weight of her head had started to fall asleep, and he longed to stretch his back or shift his position. Yet chances such as this—to hold Mina, to touch her, to see her as she was when she wasn't moving and talking—came rarely.

"Do you remember when I read Goethe's 'Prometheus' to you?" he asked Anneka.

"It was when we met. Why do you think of it now?"

"I thought of it today when Professor Norlin spoke of burning books by Germans. What foolishness, to belittle the substance and beauty of a work just because it was written by someone who is currently unpopular."

"You told me that poem was how you felt toward God."

"So it is," Jim said. *"Here sit I, forming mortals After my image; A race resembling me, To suffer, to weep, To enjoy, to be glad, And thee to scorn, as I!"*

Anneka glanced at Mina, that mortal formed in Jim's and her own image. Jim touched Mina's hair, although he could feel nothing against his deadened palm.

"She should go to her bedroom," Anneka said gently.

"I might be able to carry her in without waking her."

He gathered Mina in his arms. She was light, a feather. He had picked her up before, to hug her or kiss her, but he had never realized how delicate and fine she was.

Laying her in the bed, he helped Anneka to pull the covers around her. Together, they stood over her.

"She seems peaceful," Jim said. "Have you eaten? I could call over my cook—"

"I am fine."

He reached out and touched her hair. To his surprise, she didn't move or pull away. "Let me take care of you, at least until your soldier friend is back."

She straightened her shoulders. "I am learning to read and write in English so I will know it when he comes back."

"Your husband will be proud of you."

"Yes, I think he will."

As he followed her down the hallway to the parlor, he remembered Ellie's assessment of Anneka's situation: a gilded cage in which—at least as Anneka saw it—she was alone. Yet Anneka seemed to have become harder, wiser, more independent, perhaps, in the time that he had been in France. Somehow, she had changed.

"I'll send Dr. Erickson over in the morning," he said.

"Thank you."

He kissed her forehead, then let himself out into the night.

TWELVE

After more days in the trenches and more night patrols than he can remember, Sean applied for a pass to Langres, south of Verdun, with Tony, Kevin and Nicola. The town was surrounded by a Medieval wall with towers and battlements, which overlooked the nearby French countryside and the Marne. Sean half-expected knights on steeds to be patrolling the streets, but all he saw were French officers, drinking at cafés and standing in line before music halls. Wandering through the streets, his gaze lingered on the townswomen, who were especially young and pretty—or maybe, he thought, they just seemed that way because he hadn't seen a woman dressed in anything but a tart's *lingerie*, as they called it here, for a long time. The four Doughboys bought a hodgepodge of things, spending their francs on any trinket that struck their fancy: maps, postcards, hats, gooey marzipan. At the city center, they came across the great cathedral.

"Wanna go in?" Tony asked.

"Sure," Sean said.

Inside, the four dipped their fingers in the holy water, made the sign of the cross, and genuflected as they passed into the nave. Sean marveled at the vaulted ceilings and the great columns that reached up and out into beautiful arches. In the apse, the altar was fitted out in velvet and gold. A silver figure of Christ on the Cross hung directly over it, lit from behind by stained glass windows.

He had never seen anything like it—nothing as large, or as rich, or as beautifully decorated. Every detail—the Angel Gabriel, the Raising of Lazarus from the dead, the great organ at the back of the sanctuary—was perfectly wrought and lovingly kept. It was such a contrast to the world that lay around it, where buildings and men were so ruthlessly knocked down and destroyed.

Sean moved into one of the rows of wicker chairs, and the others followed him. Throughout the Church, old women in black prayed, their rosaries wrapped around their claw-like fingers. Sean reached beneath his collar for his rosary. He hadn't prayed for so long, he doubted he remembered any prayers.

But, in a great flood, the words came back to him. The Our Father, the Hail Mary, the Doxology, the Divine Blessings: *"Blessed be God. Blessed be His holy name. Blessed be Jesus Christ, true God and true man. Blessed be the name of Jesus. Blessed be His most Sacred Heart. Blessed be His most precious Blood—"*

Yet another voice spoke in his head as well: *Forgive me, God, for what I am doing. For sneaking up on men as they sleep, and for killing them for no other reason than the place of their birth. I came here with a good heart, with the aim of serving my country. I came here to do my best, not—*

He heard the scraping of the chairs on the tile floor as the others moved, yet he stayed where he was. Their footsteps echoed as they left the Church, and he breathed out, relieved to be alone. Another prayer came to him: *"O my God, trusting in Your promises and because You are faithful, powerful, and merciful, I hope, through the merits of Jesus Christ, for the pardon of my sins . . ."*

He did not lift his head when someone sat down behind him.

At last, Tony whispered, "We're gonna find something to eat."

Sean murmured Amen, made the sign of the cross, and raised his head. Outside, in the gathering evening, he said to Tony, "I've never seen a church like that."

"You don't have churches where you are?"

Sean laughed, although his heart still felt too full. "No, that's not it. But our church in Denver is small, and brick, and even though it has a couple of stained glass windows, it's just a building."

Tony glanced up at the great spires of the cathedral. "In Italy, there's one like this every place you go. Always right in the middle of town. You don't even think about them after a while."

"Are they all so old?"

"I guess so, I don't know. You ever thought about being a priest?"

"Maybe," Sean said.

"My brother in Italy, he's a priest."

"What about you?"

"I won't give up the whores."

"Just don't get caught."

"Jesus, he forgives," Tony said. "Blackjack, he don't."

Sean laughed. Recently, General Pershing had made the punishment for visiting the French-controlled brothels much stricter. The restriction hadn't slowed down the men much, although the result was often a spell in the base hospital with venereal disease. A joke had started to circulate: "Three hours with Venus, three years with Mercury."

The streets swarmed with men in khaki and blue. Langres, it seemed, had attracted every Doughboy and every French soldier who had a pass for an evening out. Around the square, peddlers sold food, from pork cooked over open fires to sweets and cakes served by sweeter-faced girls. After Sean had eaten and had a few cups of the dark, red wine that flowed so freely in France, he began to watch the women who promenaded around the square. Maybe he wouldn't give up the whores either.

From a side street, a Frenchman approached.

"*Vous êtes à la recherche d'un hôtel pour passer la nuit?*"

The words, spoken so quickly, went past Sean, but he caught the last one: night.

"*Oui*," he said. "*Une salle de—*"

"*Une chambre à coucher*," the Frenchman said. "A room for the night."

"Good job, Sean," Kevin said in his ear. "You speak French so well that he just gives up and speaks English in return."

"You speak it, then," Sean growled. "See where it takes you."

The Frenchman beckoned them to follow. Almost at once, Sean regretted the decision. They left the brightly lit public square for winding alleys and narrow, cobblestone streets where the shadows of the buildings on either side loomed opaque and indecipherable. The smell of manure and sewage grew stronger. After a few minutes, Sean became convinced that they would never find their way back to the cathedral, much less to the train station outside of the town. At last, their French guide stopped in front of a hulking, brick edifice that might have served as a fifteenth-century prison. The guide rang the bell twice, then, impatient, banged with his fist on the heavy wooden door. Tony glanced at Sean, and Sean scuffled his feet a couple of times, unsure whether they should stay or run.

The door opened, and a boy no more than four feet tall with the blackest skin that Sean had ever seen appeared, a candle in his hands. After a few testy exchanges, the guide turned to Sean.

"There's only two beds left," he said. "Eight francs—you, you, you—"

"From each of us," Sean supplied.

"—*pour la nuit et pour le petit déjeuner, n'est'ce pas?*"

Sean looked at the others. "Eight francs for bed and breakfast. That's a dollar sixty. What do you think?"

Tony shrugged, a look of amused curiosity on his face, and Nicola—whose English was as limited as his French—said nothing. "That's rich," Kevin said.

"Four francs," Sean ventured.

"*Quatre? Non, non, non—*"

"Five."

"*Ce n'est pas assez pour payer le pain—*"

"Six, *c'est tout.*"

"*D'accord,*" the guide said, then grumbled something in French that Sean doubted he wanted to understand.

"It's probably a sack of straw filled with fleas," Kevin commented.

The little boy stuck out his hand, carefully counting the money as each man passed and dropping it into a leather pouch that hung around his neck. The Frenchman loitered in the doorway, waiting for his cut.

The boy led them up an imposing wooden staircase, walking before them with his candle lifted. Sean and the others stumbled along behind. In the corridor of the third floor, the stained wallpaper drooped where it had been torn from the plaster, and the carpets buckled. Kevin was right—they'd all have to have another sulfur bath after their night here.

"*Voilà.*" At the end of a dark hallway, the boy opened the door and went into a room. Without speaking further, he lit the candles in the candelabras from his own, then poked a smoldering fire in the open fireplace into a flame. As the room flickered with light, Sean saw two wide beds spanning the floor, their coverings white and— it seemed to him—clean. Two rocking chairs sat near the window, and a washstand complete with two pitchers of water stood beside a full-length mirror.

"Look at this." Kevin gawked at the room. "It's the Taj Mahal inside Frankenstein's castle."

"*Merci.*" Sean tossed the boy another franc as he left the room.

"A bed," Kevin said. "I haven't slept in a bed since I left Brookings last summer."

They stripped down to their underwear—the first time Sean had done so since he left America. He'd slept in his trousers for so long that his naked legs prickled even in the warmth of the room. After washing up, the men blew out the candles and laid down, Tony and Nicola in one bed, and Kevin and Sean in the other.

Sean listened to Kevin drop off into a full, snoring sleep. He shouldn't waste—he couldn't afford to waste—this luxury of sleeping in a bed, among sheets that smelled of some kind of potpourri. Yet the comfort seemed to have the opposite effect on him. Who would have ever thought that he'd be lying in a bed in Langres, France, with a pile of men he'd never have met if he'd been born a decade earlier or a decade later? Who would have thought that Kathleen, whom he had never imagined far from Redlands, would be only a few hundred miles away? Or that Maggie, whom he still thought of as a little girl, was soon to be—if she wasn't already—a mother? He wondered about Liam and Brendan, and Frank and Donnell MacMahon, and the McKenna boys. Where were they now? He supposed they were all spread across France, wondering the same about him.

A movement alerted him. Tony rose from the bed to use the chamber pot in the corner of the room. After he finished, he sat on the window ledge and lit a cigarette. Sean crawled from beneath the heavy covers and joined him.

"We should be sleeping like them." Tony pointed his chin at the others. "But I don't sleep so good on something so soft."

"You don't have a mattress at home?"

Tony scoffed. "In *Italia*, Mamma puts us boys—there are nine of us—all in the shed without no beds, no blankets, nothin', just whatever we find or steal from each other. She keeps the mule in the house so it don't get stolen. Nobody in Italy wants more kids, but the mule—everybody wants him."

Sean laughed. "Don't you have a bed in Brooklyn?"

Tony eyed the two beds. "Stuffed with straw, not what's in there—"

"Goose down, I think."

As if the words conjured up something distasteful, Tony puffed a couple of times on his cigarette.

"What about you?" he asked. "You talk about your sister. Don't you have more brothers and sisters? I got eleven of them."

"My mother always wanted more, but it didn't happen."

"In Italy, it happens no matter what. You look at a girl, and next thing, she comes to you and says you gotta marry because she's gonna have a kid."

"That's usually how it goes for the Irish, too."

"What will you do when you go back to Colorado?"

"I guess I'll go back to working in my father's store. I don't know. What about you?"

"I'm goin' back to stringing wires for the telephone company. Everybody in New York City wants a telephone, so we put wires everywhere. The whole sky—you look up and all you see is wires. You gonna get married when you get home?"

"Sure," Sean said. "As soon as I find somebody who wants me."

Tony laughed. "You gonna be waiting a long time."

He snorted. "What about you?"

"Naw, no girl," Tony said. "But I'm gonna find me a good Italian *ragazza* who says, Whatchu want me to do for you?"

"Women aren't like that in America," Sean teased. "You better catch a ride back to the Old Country."

"Not your mother? Your sister?"

"My mother pretends to do what Pa wants," Sean admitted. "But she really does what she thinks is best, especially with running the store. Mag—well, I haven't seen her since she and Liam got married, but she probably stands up for herself pretty well. She always did with me. And she writes—"

"What's that?"

"Writes." Sean pantomimed the action. "Stories and, I don't know, maybe even books. And Kathleen—"

"The nun?" Tony teased, referring back to the photo Sean had of Kathleen in a wimple.

"She did whatever she wanted when she was a kid. Uncle Irish never told her no, although Auntie Eileen fussed at her. But it didn't make any difference. She didn't listen."

He looked out into the street, quelling a wave of homesickness. He didn't remember streets this dark and quiet in Berkeley Park. It was as if no one really lived in this French town, as if no one spoke or sang or prayed or talked behind any of the black-windowed buildings along the way.

He asked, "What do you think of what we're doing? The night raids and all that. What do you think of it?"

After taking a long inhale on his cigarette, Tony breathed out the words with smoke. "You just don't know, you just don't know."

You chust a-doh-noe, you chust a-doh-noe.

"You do what you're told," Tony continued. "And the Germans would kill us, if they caught us. They say they don't have no food over there in Germany, so why would they want prisoners?"

But when does doing what you're told become something else? Sean wondered. When does it—when does even witnessing it—start to stick in your soul and rot there? When do the sins of others become yours as well?

"Do you go to confession?" Sean asked.

"What am I gonna tell an American priest that he don't already know?"

"What do you mean?"

"In America, you walk down the street and the girls whistle at *you*, and you drink too much but you don't lose your job, and you get in a fight and nobody stops you. There's no priest watching you in America, saying he's gonna tell your mamma or God."

Sean laughed. He thought of Father Devlin, never sober enough to report back to anyone's parents, and now soft-spoken, serious Brendan, who seemed more interested in studying the spiritual mysteries of the church than in scolding parishioners.

From the bed nearest them, Nicola muttered something in Italian.

"He says, 'Shut up.'" Tony dashed out his cigarette. *"La Bella Addormentata."*

"What's that?"

"I don't know what you call it. It's a story about a princess who falls asleep when a, uh, *strega—*"

"Sleeping Beauty?"

"Yeah, that's it." Tony moved toward the bed. "Goodnight."

Sean lay down next to his own Sleeping Beauty—Kevin—who never moved throughout the night. Kevin's snoring never quieted, either. In the morning, breakfast consisted of omelets, with bread and butter, coffee, milk and sugar, which none of them had seen since leaving America. They all—except for Sean, who never did fall asleep—agreed that the night's restful slumber was worth every *centime* of the six francs.

THIRTEEN

The Germans failed to reach Amiens, but the refugees who flooded into the south of France breathed no sigh of relief. The Fifth British Army, already limping, had been nearly annihilated, with more than a hundred and seventy-five thousand casualties.

In Chantilly, percussions from the bombs at the Front rattled the windows. In the *Cantine des Deux Drapeaux,* pots and pans clattered on hooks suspended from the ceiling, and the supplies on the shelves slipped to the floor. At night, the town fell silent. The streets emptied at the curfew, and automobiles and trains sat motionless. Light of any kind was prohibited, except for the searchlights and observation balloons that surrounded the city. Overhead, scores of American and French fliers sortied from the Aerodrome in Issoudun to the Front on bombing missions, and the noise of the Front was amplified into a drone-like roar.

Mrs. Brently made a trip to Paris to speak with Mrs. W.K. Vanderbilt, who was in charge of the American Red Cross canteen system, about finding another assignment for the Graves Family Foundation Relief Society. While the two women met, Helen, Hank, and Kathleen visited the American Red Cross Studio for Portrait Masks. The studio was located in a graceful mansion that was nearly hidden from the street by overgrown, climbing vines.

A serious-looking woman dressed in a white artist's smock with a Peter Pan collar and neatly cuffed sleeves answered the door.

"*Bienvenue,*" she said. "*Je m'appelle Jeannette.* Please, come in."

The airy, sun-filled foyer was tiled in checkerboard black and white. Small tables and potted plants gave the entryway the feel of an outdoor café. Around the tables, uniformed men smoked or played cards or chess. Kathleen quickly glanced away from them. Many had at least one feature missing from their faces: a nose, an eye, lips, an ear.

Jeannette led the girls toward the back of the house. On one wall of the hallway hung a row of plaster casts of faces posed in horrible, grimacing agony. Their mouths were skewed, their chins wrinkled and lopsided. Some had only holes for noses. Beneath them, casts of the same faces were displayed with all the parts perfectly symmetrical.

"This is Mrs. Ladd's work," Jeannette said with only a trace of French accent. "You can see, the top row is how the men look when they come to us. Their faces have been lost or injured by explosions, bullets, or flamethrowers." She pointed to the bottom row. "These are the molds that Mrs. Ladd creates to make a mask for *les bonhommes* so that they can go out into the city streets again. Many are afraid or ashamed to do so when their faces are so ugly."

"Oh, they shouldn't be ashamed," Helen said. "Not after they've done so much for France."

"You saw them out there, *oui?*" Jeannette said. "For them, it does not matter what they've done, it matters how they look. Some people think they are monsters and think that they should not be allowed in public. They spend their days here because they feel safe with others like them. Come now."

She led them into a spacious room that had all the messiness and clutter of an artist's studio. Pots of paint and jars of brushes lined the shelves, pallets with dried paint lay amid piles of rags, and splattered oil cloths covered the floors. Kathleen breathed in the smells of linseed oil and turpentine, as jealous of this place as she had been of the *plein-air* artists in Nice.

In the middle of the room, beyond an imposing artist's work table, a man sat in a wooden-framed chair with his back to the girls. A plain-looking woman in her late thirties bent over him. She was dressed in a formal suit and crisp, white blouse. Her dark hair was pulled away from her face, although a number of tendrils had escaped near the nape of her neck.

"Come in," she called. "I'm Anna Coleman Ladd. And you are?"

After the girls introduced themselves, Mrs. Ladd said, "I'm so glad that so many young American women have volunteered their time and services to come over here. Mrs. Vanderbilt tells me that you are the new '400'—the most respected and eligible girls in America."

"Eligible?" Hank asked.

"Without a doubt," Mrs. Ladd said. "What man wouldn't appreciate a wife who knows how to bandage a broken arm and change a tire on an automobile while brewing cocoa on the stove?"

As the girls laughed, Kathleen said, "We're proud to be here. We just signed up for six more months in February."

"Bully for you." Mrs. Ladd wiped her hands on a towel. "You've come at a splendid time. We're just fitting Henri with his final mask. If all goes well, he'll take it home with him today."

The man before them was in his early twenties. His lush, brown hair was parted far on the left side and swept over the crown of his head, and he wore wire-rimmed spectacles over dark, liquid eyes. His high cheekbones gave his face a regal air. Yet it wasn't skin on his cheeks and chin, but a thin covering of some kind. His mustache was made of thick bristles of hair.

Mrs. Ladd examined the wires of the spectacles. "I need to adjust this," she said. "Are we ready to see?"

"Yes," Helen said.

Mrs. Ladd pulled away the spectacles. With them, most of Henri's face came away, leaving a blunted, half nose with flaring holes for nostrils and a jagged gash across his face for a mouth. His left cheekbone was partially gone, and the skin beneath it had healed in a shriveled, sunken crater. Kathleen felt a rush of sorrow at the broken and misshapen face. She hated to think of the pain and fear that he had endured.

"Henri was wounded at Verdun in 1915," Mrs. Ladd said. "The doctors did a number of surgeries to repair his face with plastic surgery, but the damage was too great."

As she spoke, she worried with the wire earpiece of the spectacles, holding it over a small flame, bending it, then holding it over the flame again.

"So, the French Army sent Henri to me. I made a plaster cast of his face. Jeannette showed you those, didn't she?"

"Yes, she did," Hank said.

"Using photographs, Henri and I worked together—*toujours ensemble, n'est-ce pas, Henri?*—to rebuild his face in plaster until it looked just as it had before the war. Then we made a gutta percha mask from the mold. This"—she laid down the mask and picked up a piece of rigid tan material—"is gutta percha. It is made from the sap of a tree in Malaysia."

Mrs. Ladd handed it to Hank, who asked, "Where is Malaysia?"

"It's a tropical island near the Equator, near China."

"China," Hank breathed as she handed the mask to the others. "That's so far!"

Mrs. Ladd laughed. "After I sculpt the gutta percha, I put it in this copper bath for two days." She motioned toward a gas hot plate, where a heavy, cast iron cauldron sat above a flame, occasionally bubbling. "Look inside."

Kathleen peered into the cauldron, which was filled with a swirling orange-yellow liquid.

"That is molten copper," Mrs. Ladd explained. "I suspend the mask from wires and leave it in here for two days to allow the copper to adhere to the gutta percha. After the copper cools, I paint it as nearly as I can to match the young man's skin. Henri's mask is the finished product, which has taken hours and hours to complete."

"May I touch it?" Helen asked.

"If Henri doesn't mind." She spoke in French to the young man.

He nodded graciously at Helen. "*Bien sûr, Mademoiselle,*" he said, his deformed mouth moving in an agonizing, toothless grimace.

Helen handled the mask lovingly, turning it over and over in her hands. "It's so real," she said. "And it hardly weighs anything."

"That's because the continual movement in the copper bath

allows for just a thin sheath of metal to cling to the gutta percha. The mask is as thin as I can make it and still have a form that will hold."

Helen handed the mask back to Mrs. Ladd.

"Now, Henri," Mrs. Ladd said. "We're going to put this back on you, and you'll be a new man." She hooked the spectacle wires around his ears and stepped back, eyeing it critically. "Is that comfortable?"

Henri's voice was muffled by the voluminous mustache that hid his missing lips. "*Oui, Madame.*"

"There's a glare just beneath the left eye that I'd like to touch up."

She reached for her brush, which was sitting in a pot of flesh-colored paint. Kathleen leaned forward, holding her breath. Oh, to have the talent to do something like this! With only the lightest of touches, Mrs. Ladd brushed beneath the left eye of the mask.

"*Voilà!*" she said.

The girls applauded as Henri moved his face from side to side, while Mrs. Ladd made one final inspection. "It looks wonderful," Hank said.

"No," Helen said. "*He* looks wonderful."

"Oh, yes," Hank said quickly. "*Très beau.*"

"I have pamphlets that you can take with you," Mrs. Ladd said. "Please show them to anyone who is interested. Although the American Red Cross is generous, we are forever hoping for more funds to keep us going."

"May I have an extra?" Kathleen asked. "I'd like to send it to Mr. Graves, who sponsors our Relief Society. I think he would consider this a worthwhile cause."

"Of course," Mrs. Ladd said.

For another hour, they watched Mrs. Ladd work on faces: another complete mask, one that was only a nose, and one that had a bristling, black goatee made from horse hair attached to it. At one point, Mrs. Ladd produced an ear, its curves and folds perfectly formed in copper.

"How will you tie it on?" Helen asked. "You used spectacles for Henri, which looked natural, but if there is no ear—"

"I use thin wires or sheer ribbons that can be pinned into the hair. When a man has thick hair, no one can see the wire. If there is no hair—and for many of them, hair doesn't grow where the skin has been so damaged—I make a wig and affix the ear. A man can always wear a hat as well."

After the girls bid Mrs. Ladd goodbye, they waited outside in the warm, spring sun for Mrs. Brently to arrive in a smoke-spewing taxi cab. As Mrs. Brently paid the driver, she asked, "How was your morning?"

"Oh, you should see Mrs. Ladd's work," Helen said. "It's almost like magic."

"Magic?" Mrs. Brently laughed in her silvery way. "That's quite a recommendation."

"What did Mrs. Vanderbilt say?" Kathleen asked.

Mrs. Brently smiled widely. "Oh, it was all good news. We're to be assigned to Chaumont, where the American Expeditionary Force is headquartered, and we are to leave as soon as our orders are written."

Later, Kathleen writes a private message to Jim:

We visited the studio of Mrs. Anna Coleman Ladd, who is the wife of a doctor from Harvard College. Last year, she came to Paris and started a studio to help the soldiers whose faces have been damaged in battle.

Her story is very interesting. Her husband is with the Red Cross Children's Bureau, but Mrs. Ladd wasn't allowed to come because the United States won't allow women whose husbands are with the AEF to travel to France. So she went to London and enlisted as a volunteer ambulance driver. Once in France, she quit the ambulance service and opened the American Red Cross Studio for Portrait Masks.

I wish you could see the work she is doing. The men look very much like they did before the war after they're given a mask. Mrs. Ladd leaves holes large enough so that the men don't have to take off the masks to smoke or—if it's possible—to eat and drink, so they can live normal lives. The masks cost $18 each, which is a large sum, but that's only for the copper and paints. Mrs. Ladd charges nothing for her work.

Hank, Helen, and I are starting a "kitty" with the hope that we can send enough money to Mrs. Ladd to buy a mask for some unfortunate soldier, but I would like to ask a favor of you. I've sent you the pamphlet that shows the results of Mrs. Ladd's work. Would you be willing to donate to her studio? I know you have a generous heart, and your donation could make a difference for so many.

We will be moving to Chaumont soon. I'm so excited that we'll be helping our own soldiers at last—

Yet, as she writes the words, she scolds herself. To wish that the American soldiers would soon be in battle, especially after what she had seen today! But she remembers something that Paul had said long ago: *Don't think about what has happened here. You can't change it. Think about what you can do.*

She finishes the letter to Jim and seals it in an envelope. When Hank and Helen come into the room, Hank begins to empty her drawer of the one dresser they share.

"What are you doing?" Kathleen asks.

"I'm packing." Hank says. "Mrs. Brently said that the Red Cross near Chaumont is in an awful state, because the American soldiers are arriving so much faster than the aid organizations can set up canteens and the like. If there's so much to be done, they should let us leave immediately."

"I suppose that's a good idea," Kathleen says. "It will be nice to leave in a peaceful and orderly way, not in a hurry or in an evacuation."

Helen takes some of her clothing from her drawer, but before she folds it, she sits on the bed.

"What did you really feel about what we saw today at Mrs. Ladd's?" she asks.

"You called it magic earlier," Hank reminds her.

"To give those men back some chance of happiness," Helen mused. "That does seem magical to me."

"I wonder, though," Kathleen adds. "What will happen when he falls in love? When he removes his mask, will the woman still love him? It would be so hard to overlook—"

"That's a vain and selfish thing to say," Helen scolds. "You fall in love with what's in someone's heart, not the way he looks."

Kathleen says nothing more, but she wants to tell Helen that she knows better. She has not heard from Paul since the evacuation from Amiens, which was more than a month ago, but at night, she dreams that she is once more beneath the beech tree, his lips on hers, his hands touching her. The feel of his jawbone, the way that she ran her fingers over his lips, the beauty of his eyes—oh, it makes a difference.

Within ten days, orders come through for the Graves Family Foundation Relief Society to move to the American Sector. The night before they leave, Mrs. Brently gathers the girls together in the dining room of the boarding house.

"Helen has asked to be released from her contract," she says. "And Mr. Graves and I have agreed. I received a cable from him last night." She reaches across the table and takes Helen's hand. "She is not going to Chaumont with us."

"No!" Hank cries.

"You're going home?" Kathleen asks, shocked.

Helen shakes her head. "Not home."

"In the past few days," Mrs. Brently continues, "Helen has been corresponding with Mrs. Ladd at the Portrait Studio in Paris. Mrs. Ladd's assistant, Jeannette, is leaving the studio, and Mrs. Ladd has asked if Helen would like to come and take the position."

"Oh, Helen!" Hank says. "Is that what you want to do?"

Helen's smile widens into a full-mouthed grin. "It is."

Kathleen remembers how gently Helen had handled Henri's mask. She had seemed to treasure it not only for its beauty, but for its purpose.

Mrs. Brently speaks again. "As much as I hate to have Helen leave us, I've been helping her with the paperwork and the letters of credit that will allow her to stay in the French war zone and live in Paris. She'll still be a part of the American Red Cross, but she will no longer be a member of the Graves Family Foundation Relief Society."

Kathleen swallows her pride. "I will miss you."

Half crying, Helen reaches for Hank's and Kathleen's hands. "I will miss you both so much! But I can't give up this chance. It's fate,

I think, that Jeannette is getting married, right now, while we're still near Paris, and I . . ."

"I can't imagine how we'll stay organized without you," Hank says.

Helen laughs through her tears.

"Is someone coming to replace you?" Kathleen asks.

"Not at this time." Mrs. Brently answers.

Kathleen eyes Hank. "So it will be just the two of us."

"I guess you're stuck with me," Hank says. "I'm not leaving."

"Neither am I."

Hank squeezes both Kathleen's and Helen's hands as she sings, "*Gee, I'd like to be a monkey in the zoo—*"

"*Why, you'll never find a monkey feeling blue!*" Helen adds.

Kathleen joins in through tears. "*You've got no one to please, All you do is look for fleas, Oh, I'd like to be a monkey in the zoo.*"

"That's our song," Hank says. "The anthem of the Graves Family Foundation Relief Society. Whenever we hear it, we'll remember everything we've done, and—"

Hank's words end in a sob. Mrs. Brently lays a comforting hand on her shoulder.

"Don't cry," Helen says. "When we're home, we can teach it to our kids when we tell them what we did here in France."

"I'll sing it to them every single night for a lullaby," Hank promises.

FOURTEEN

April 20, 1918

Dearest Aunt Julia,

I am sorry that it's been so long since I last wrote. I can only offer the excuses that I've stated here, which are pretty feeble, considering that you've always been my source of strength and intellect. I wish you were in Paris, where I could see you again.

My life and activities—always dependent on the war—have become more complicated with my new assignment with the U.S. Army. It's changed the way that I'm accustomed to operating, and in some ways, it's changed my view of myself. I'm no longer a volunteer here, but a soldier, no better or worse than the nearest conscript.

My time is spent in undergoing inspections and drills in the bitter air of the morning and on K.P., which is the Army's abbreviation for cooking meals and cleaning the kitchen. While drivers who've been in France for only a matter of weeks are sent to the Front, I stay behind and wash the windows of the barracks. All my knowledge of the roads, the battlefields, and the terrain of France is wasted.

Our Harjes ambulances have been painted, which means that the old Field Service Section numbers have been covered over with the number of the USAAS section. It's silly, I know, but I've found that it has taken something from me—

"Private Reston."

Paul flipped over the sheet of paper before he stood and saluted his superior, Sergeant Terrell. A young recruit stood at the Sergeant's side. He was thin, with a freckled face, and his hair was stiff with pomade. He looked no more than eighteen.

Sergeant Terrell spoke. "There's a call to go up to Beauvais to pick up wounded and take them to, um, Saint Dennis."

"Yes, sir. That's Saint Denis."

The sergeant cast Paul a sour look. "San-Denee, it is, then. Same Frenchie place, if you ask me. Private Coggins here needs some experience. I thought you could teach him a thing or two."

Paul glanced at Coggins. "Yes, sir."

"Coggins drives a Tin Lizzie, Private Reston. Can you handle it? I've heard that you boys who drove Packards for Harjes have a rough time of it with the Fords."

The insult brushed past Paul. "I'm sure I can, sir."

He followed Coggins to the stables that had once sheltered horses, but now housed the automobiles, all parked facing forward. After Coggins cranked the Model T to start it, he headed for the passenger's side of the car.

"Aren't you to be driving?" Paul asked.

Without a word, the boy came around the car and took his place behind the steering wheel. For a moment, he looked helplessly at the hand lever.

"Push it forward." Paul said, as he secured his driving goggles. "Then lift your foot off the right foot pedal."

Coggins did so, bouncing the Model T out of the stable. His driving showed no improvement once they were on the torn up roads. Although he managed to keep the car into low speed on the hilly terrain, every time he let up on the left pedal, the car lurched into high speed, making Paul wish for the simple H gearbox of the Packard.

"How did you learn to drive?" Paul asked, as the boy once again struggled with the lever and pedals in order to shift the car into high gear.

"I was at Camp Crane for three weeks," he said.

"Where is that?"

"Allentown, Pennsylvania."

"Had you driven before you went to Allentown?"

"Naw." Rather than skirting around a muddy hole in the road, Coggins went through it. The car bounced roughly, and mud splashed up into the open cab. "I didn't drive there either, but two times. We learned how to shoot and stuff there. That's all."

"Did you learn to speak French?"

"They don't teach that no more. With so many Americans comin' to France, they say the Frogs better learn English."

Paul looked out the passenger's side. The wind blew on his face, cold and damp. When Richard Norton had recruited drivers from Yale, he had referred to them as "gentlemen volunteers." Paul had taken an oath to "behave like gentlemen and be a credit to the cause of the Allies and the American flag and to the civilization that the brave French soldiers have been defending for so many years in the trenches."

Obviously, that was not the sentiment among the American recruits.

As they neared Clermont, Paul began to watch the passers-by on the streets. Whenever he saw a woman, he would try to catch a glimpse of her hair, searching for Kathleen. With every disappointment, he settled back in his seat as a physical pain overtook him. He hadn't heard from her since Amiens was evacuated, and a letter he had sent to her in Amiens had been returned to him. Why had he let her go? Why hadn't he run away with her when she suggested it—to Switzerland, to the south of Italy, to England, Ireland, even?

Now, Coggins asked, "Where do I go?"

Opening the map, Paul said, "The battalion aid station should be over there."

Three patients were waiting for transport, the most that the Model T could carry. Paul checked out the wounds. Two had blood-stained rags wrapped around their heads. The third looked to have lost a leg. It would need to be a smoother trip back to the base hospital than it had been coming to Beauvais.

Paul motioned to Coggins to draw back the tarps on the back of the Model T, but the boy took a step back, his face twisted in disgust and fear. Paul secured the tarps, one on each side. As the bulky stretchers were loaded, he wished again for his Packard. It had been equipped with tracks and a pulley system that allowed for a smooth movement into the cargo bed. With the Model T, the stretcher bearers jostled and pushed, shoving the metal legs of the gurneys against the wooden floor. As one of the stretchers jammed, one of the injured called out, "Oh, God, it hurts!"

Paul gritted his teeth as the Model T jerked out of the drive of the battalion aid station. Once on the open road, Coggins pushed the lever into high speed. The car rumbled down the road, its tires jouncing.

"Slow down," Paul said. "You could cause more injury to the men in the back. Sometimes the wounds start to bleed again if they're roughed up too much."

Coggins made no reply, but shifted the Ford into low speed. The car roared as it climbed up a rolling hill. As it crested the top, Paul saw a mule train traveling up the opposite side of the hill, headed directly for them.

The Model T careened down the slope.

"Right pedal!" Paul ordered. "Pull the lever back!"

"I got it back!" Coggins shouted.

Paul heard a snap as one of the transmission brake belts broke. No matter what they did now, they had no brakes. The wind rushed over the screen into the cab.

"Put it in reverse," Paul said. "Center pedal!"

The first mules in the train shied to the right, and the Model T flew by them, but the second wagon moved too slowly. The car crashed into the wagon, and the animals jammed up against each other, trying to escape. Splinters from the wagon frame flew through the air. Breaking through the team of mules, the car skidded into a ditch, its front end smashing against the embankment.

Someone shouted, "What're you doing? Whoa, there, whoa!"

For a moment, neither Paul nor Coggins spoke. One of the patients in the back was moaning or crying. The injured mules brayed miserably. Behind the car, the rest of the mules and wagons halted.

"Are you all right?" Paul asked.

"I think so," Coggins said.

"We have to see to our wounded." Paul slid from the car and parted the canvas flaps of the bed. Hoisting himself up, he saw that one of the men was unconscious. The amputee moaned, his face slicked by sweat. The third stared straight ahead, seemingly in shock.

As Paul hurried around to the front of the car, his stomach sank. The right front wheel was deflated. "We have a flat."

Coggins left the cab and came to stand behind Paul.

"Open the tool box and find the jack and spare," Paul said.

The boy handed the pieces of the jack to Paul, who assembled it. "Did they teach you how to do this at Camp Crane?" he asked.

"No."

Paul knelt down and frantically worked the jack. It squealed and nearly slipped, taxed by the fully loaded back of the Model T. Once he managed to raise the car a few inches off the ground, he began to peel the tire off the clincher rim. But the rubber kept twisting back on itself and sticking in the mud that had caked on the tread. "Private Coggins," Paul said. "Help me with this."

There was no answer. Gripping the tire tightly to keep it from coiling back around the rim, Paul looked over his shoulder. Coggins was gone. Paul pried at the rubber until he heard the roar of a motor and honk of a horn. A truck with an American flag on its doors dodged in and out of the mules. Finding himself stuck behind the mess of the accident, the driver turned off the engine and came to where Paul squatted next to the Model T.

"What's going on?" he asked.

"Help me to lift it."

The driver grabbed beneath the chassis and lifted, and Paul quickly pulled the rubber tire out.

The driver picked it up and turned it in his hands. "Huh, horseshoe nail." He cast a look at the mule train. "Damned things better not blow my tires or I'll run a few of them down."

Paul glanced to where the suffering mules had been taken from their traces and shot. "We've already done that."

He took a new rubber tire from the box in the back. Again, the truck driver lifted the chassis as Paul forced the new tire onto the rim, then grabbed the air pump and began to inflate the tire.

"You'd better hurry," the truck driver said. "The line up north has broken. The Heines are moving south like a swarm of locusts."

"I don't know where my other driver has gone," Paul said.

"There's a shelter about fifty yards that way. Saw them poking their fool heads out."

Coggins came from the *abri* when Paul appeared at the top of the steps. Without speaking to him, Paul walked back to the Model T and took the wheel. The delay for these men had been long enough. He was not about to let Coggins shake them to death.

He wound his way through the last of the mules. When they reached open road, he asked Coggins, "Why did you leave the car?"

The boy did not answer.

"Never leave your car," Paul continued. "Never leave the wounded. They're helpless, and it's your responsibility to see them to wherever they're going. Would you just leave them to die?"

Coggins looked out the passenger's side.

"Answer me."

The boy turned back toward Paul. "You been tellin' me what to do all day," he said. "But you ain't an officer. You got no right."

Paul said nothing. The rest of the trip to Saint Denis passed in silence.

At the USAAS barracks at Sandricourt, Paul eats a late supper before going outside into the glowing evening. The sunset spreads across open sky in the west, orange and purple above the green hills. He takes his pipe from his pocket, tamps tobacco into it, and lights it. It's a foolish habit, picked up at Yale as an undergraduate. Breathing out smoke, he looks south. He is close enough to Paris that he could almost walk the distance. If only he hadn't stayed. If only he'd gone home, like so many of the Harjes men had when the ambulance corps was inducted into the U.S. military. His stomach burns, the consequences of his decision eating away at his insides.

Sergeant Terrell comes around the corner of the shed. "I heard you and Coggins had a rough ride today."

Paul's muscles seize up. "Yes, sir. A nail from a horseshoe punctured the tire."

"Private Coggins was pretty shaken," Sergeant Terrell says. "Not the introduction to the USAAS that I'd hoped for. He told me you drove back."

"We'd lost a good deal of time in changing the tire. I thought it best that a more experienced hand take over."

Sergeant Terrell mulls it over. "How long have you been here?"

"Since July of '16."

"You win the *Croix de Guerre*?"

Paul hesitates. "Yes, sir."

"Well, then, you got what you came for," Sergeant Terrell says. "Because you ain't getting a promotion here. General Pershing doesn't appreciate you boys who came over here on your own, and he's said that promotions are to go to the true American soldiers, those who joined up to fight for America. You'll be a Private for the rest of the war. You hear me?"

"Yes, sir."

"And the next time you go out with one of our boys—if you go out—they drive, you coach. You don't take the wheel again."

A few days later, Paul finds a letter stuck beneath the pillow of his bunk. Sent from within France, it has a military return address beneath the name, "Lt. A.B. MacKenzie." Paul's heart lifts. Alexander Bruce MacKenzie, or Kenny, as he preferred to be called, had been his roommate at Yale. More than once, the two of them had flown in Kenny's airplane to the wealthy shores of Long Island, where the MacKenzies lived in a veritable palace. Kenny had been a daredevil, flying inverted or twisting in the air, laughing as Paul heaved the contents of his stomach.

Paul rips open the letter and smiles at the salutation. Kenny had never called him by his first name.

Dear Reston,

You're probably surprised to hear from me. How many years has it been since we lived together in that stuffy room at Pierson

Hall? But I'm hoping to catch you before you flee France with the other Harjes boys who are going home because they can't stand the heat. Don't do it—you'll only get a draft notice and a one-way ticket to the trenches.

I'm trying to recruit you in to the Observation School for the U.S. Army Air Service. As you've guessed, I'm already here at the French Camp D'Instruction de Cazaux, *near the French Riviera. I was recruited by Artemus Gates—do you remember him? He and most of the others from the Lafayette Escadrille are now flying with the First Yale Unit. But we are desperate for observers.*

Be warned, it's a terrible job. You'd have to fly with me again, and that's no safe bet, especially for someone who throws up if the plane even heaves an inch (I haven't forgiven you). We train under the French, who sometimes treat us like simpletons, and there aren't enough planes or parts or trained mechanics or just about anything but danger to go around. But listen here, Reston, it's a way to do something that not many can, if you've got the courage. We can make history here, and we can make something out of our own miserable lives as well.

So, are you in?

If you complete the training, you'll be a full lieutenant, and you'll be one of the few to win the honor of flying in this war. Write me back, soon, with your answer.

Paul lays the letter aside. He and Kenny had become good friends at Yale, and had stuck together through exams and college pranks and other folderol. The memory of the pilot's burned body near Amiens looms up in his head. He wants so much, he hopes for so much, mostly to keep himself alive and to be with Kathleen at the end of all this. Yet, to be as useful and proud as he had been with the Harjes Formation, to make history, to know that he is doing his best—how can he refuse?

Paul writes back to Kenny that night. Within a week, he transfers to the United States Army Air Service.

FIFTEEN

Maggie shivered as she sat in the guardhouse at Fort Logan, a squat stone building on a treeless plain. Across the room, Brendan smoked a cigarette, and Judah Rapp looked out of one of the narrow windows. Young men, so newly-conscripted that they did not yet have uniforms, drilled on the parade grounds beyond.

She laid her hand on her stomach. The baby rolled, and a snake-like bulge pressed out of her belly. She imagined an arm, the elbow poking outward, or a leg, the foot trying to kick. Every day, the tiny one within her grew more restless with the urge to come into the world.

She, Brendan, and Judah had been coming to Fort Logan nearly every day since Liam's arrest with the demand to see him. And every day, they had been left to sit in this room at the guardhouse with a single table and four chairs until some junior officer came to tell them they could not speak with him.

Oh, it was all such a mess. Only last week, Maggie had moved in with her parents, like a shamed daughter who had run away with a cad and found herself abandoned. At night, she slept in the little girl's bed that she had always occupied. In the morning, she woke to the same faded curtains that she and Ma had sewed when she was in sixth grade, the same tattered rug on the floor, the same linoleum that had worn away in spots to a crumbling black. She ate at the same table where she always had and attended Holy Mass with her mother in the evenings as if she were still a parochial school girl.

The only thing that separated her from that girl was this child that tumbled around in her abdomen.

The door opened, and the aide to Colonel Parton, Captain Lowell, entered the room. "Good afternoon, Mrs. Keohane, Father Keohane, Mr. Rapp. As you have been told, Liam Keohane is not allowed visitors."

"Please," Maggie begged again. "Please, sir, we've been here every day this week—"

Brendan spoke at nearly the same time. "Mrs. Keohane has not seen her husband since his arrest three weeks ago, and soon she won't be able to travel as easily, with the birth of their child—"

Captain Lowell's eyes skiffed over Maggie's stomach, but he said nothing.

"I only ask that I see my husband before our child is born," she said. "Please, may I just talk to Colonel Parton? If he saw me, perhaps he would—"

Captain Lowell wavered. "I will ask."

He left the room, and Brendan, Maggie, and Judah looked at each other in surprise.

"Progress," Judah said.

Maggie straightened her dress over her bulging stomach and smoothed the lace on the cuffs and around the neck. Surely Liam would be surprised by how much she'd changed. The sharpness of her face had filled out into soft curve with the weight of pregnancy, and her breasts were full and round beneath the wool of her dress. She had grown from a skinny girl into a woman in this past month.

Colonel Parton came into the room. Maggie rose as the Colonel introduced himself to Brendan and Judah and shook their hands.

"Good afternoon, Mrs. Keohane," he said. "Please sit down."

She stayed on her feet. "Colonel Parton, please. I haven't seen my husband since March 16."

Judah spoke. "Might I remind you, Colonel, that Liam Keohane is a civilian who has never been inducted into the Army. Holding him as a military prisoner is illegal—"

"I won't discuss it," Colonel Parton said shortly. "I came here because Captain Lowell made an impassioned plea on behalf of Mrs. Keohane. I intend to speak only to her."

He motioned toward the chair where Maggie had been sitting. "Please, Mrs. Keohane, sit down. A woman in your condition should be resting."

Maggie obeyed. Colonel Parton sat in the chair next to her, shifting so that he could look directly into her face. "Do you know what we have offered to your husband?" he asked.

"Offered him?"

"Yes, Mrs. Keohane, offered him. We have offered him a job on the grounds work crew. It's a paid job, since we are aware that he has a wife and, soon, a child to support. But he has refused, saying that mowing the lawns and keeping the gravel walks aids the military, and therefore supports the war."

He waited for a reply. Weakly, Maggie said, "I didn't know—"

"We've also offered him a place in our kitchens, cooking for our incoming soldiers, those who are willing to do their jobs in France, but he's refused that, too. He considers that to be assisting in the war effort."

Maggie's lungs felt squeezed of air, not only by the baby, but by the enormity of Liam's refusal. Why was he doing this? Why wouldn't he agree—if Colonel Parton was telling the truth—to such a generous offer?

"Your husband prefers to sit in his cell, alone, and to write letters to President Wilson and the newspapers," Colonel Parton said. "He chooses to spout anti-war propaganda whenever we make an attempt to better his situation here." He laid a stack of papers on the table. "Feel free to look at these."

Maggie picked up the top sheet. Liam's meticulous handwriting greeted her: "Dear President Wilson and Members of the United States Congress—"

"Read a little of it for us," Colonel Parton urged.

She read aloud: "The Conscientious Objector cannot engage in any participation in the war. Alternative service promotes the cause of the war just as completely and unutterably as military service. The man who refuses to fight at the Front, but who will work behind the lines at home to assist others to kill and be killed, is the true coward. The government may or may not grant the Conscientious Objector an exemption, but the Conscientious Objector is ultimately indifferent to what the government may do because he follows the principles of his own conscience, which are informed by God's—"

Sickened, Maggie laid the papers upon the table and pushed them away from her. Judah immediately snatched at them. "These are the private writings of my client," he said. "They are his property, and he has the right to send them to whomever he wishes. You can't impede upon his right to free speech—"

Colonel Parton let Judah sputter into silence, then turned back to Maggie. "Mrs. Keohane, what influence do you have over your husband?"

"I . . . I don't—" She started again, her voice nearly a whisper, "I love him very much."

"Does he listen to you when you talk to him? Let's say, when you need more money for the weekly groceries or something of the kind."

"Yes, he does."

"And does he agree to give you more? Can you persuade him to do so?" Colonel Parton leaned forward. "You're pretty enough. Does he do what you ask?"

Maggie glanced up at Judah, unsure what to answer. Her gaze slipped to Brendan, who nodded almost imperceptibly.

"Yes," she said, with more conviction. "He does."

"Well, then, if you have that much influence over him, I will let you see him."

The offer, so contrary to past experiences, echoed in the room. At last, Judah asked, "By saying that you will let Mrs. Keohane 'see' her husband, are you offering to allow her to meet and talk with him? Or is this some sort of trick—?"

"If she can persuade him to end his campaign against our great country and its Army and serve out the war quietly, working in our facilities—then, yes, she can meet and talk with him."

"Oh, I'll try!" Maggie said. "I'll do everything I—!"

"I don't want you to try," Colonel Parton said. "You must promise me that you'll succeed."

Brendan interceded. "That isn't fair—"

"I promise," Maggie said. "I will!"

"Very well."

Colonel Parton left the room, and Maggie cupped her hands over her face in joy. She was going to see Liam! Everything in her was churning—her heart, her breath, even the baby, who somersaulted in her womb. Immediately, Brendan and Judah began talking to her.

"Maggie," Brendan said. "You have to convince him that this is the only way—"

At the same time, Judah said, "For his own good, you must make him see—"

The door opened, and Liam entered the room. His hands and feet were shackled, the chain between his ankles only five inches at most. A chain ran from his hands around his waist, so that he did not have full use of his arms. He wore the black and white striped shirt and trousers of the prisoner, the fabric grayed by stains. Grayer yet was his face, stripped of its natural color, and his hair, which had lost its thickness and sheen. Only his eyes burned, although they seemed slightly crossed. His glasses were missing.

"Liam!" Maggie cried. "What have they done to you?"

His bleary gaze settled on her. "Maggie, oh, my love."

She embraced him, but he could not separate his hands to return her hug. The thin wings of his shoulders and the vertebrae in his spine jutted through the fabric of his shirt. Beneath Maggie's cheek, his collarbone poked sharply.

He kissed the top of her head. She stepped back, and Brendan came forward to greet his brother. "Where are your glasses?" he asked.

Liam blinked. "Am I not wearing them?"

Brendan glanced at Judah. "No, you aren't."

"I don't know," Liam said. "I've been in the dark for so long that I hadn't noticed they were gone—"

"You didn't notice?" Maggie asked, just as Judah said, "They're keeping you in the dark?"

"Hello, Judah," Liam said. "I didn't see you."

Liam's body quivered. He shuffled his feet, as if he were no longer sure how to take a step. He looked at them all with his cross-wise gaze in a way that made Maggie fear that he couldn't think of why they had come to see him.

"Sit down." She helped him into the chair where Colonel Parton had sat. Sitting in her own seat, she caught his jittery hands in hers.

"Tell us how you've been treated," Judah said.

Liam cleared his throat, a hoarse, ratcheting sound. "I am in a cell that has no light except for a narrow slit of window at the very top of the wall. I can't see out of it—it's too high—and by afternoon, the sun has moved to the other side of the building."

"You must write your letters when there's sun," Judah said.

"Yes," Liam said vaguely. "It's so good of you to come. I have been in solitary confinement since I've been here."

"Solitary?" Brendan asked. "For what reason?"

"Because I won't work in their gardens or their kitchen. To punish me, I've had companionship, daylight, and food taken from me. I only get bread and water to eat."

No one replied, until Brendan said at last, "We'll leave the two of you. I don't know how much time Colonel Parton will give you." He touched Liam's shoulder as he walked toward the door. "I will at least demand that your glasses are returned to you. If they're lost, I'll bring another pair."

"Pray for me, brother," Liam said.

"We'll try to negotiate better conditions, too," Judah said.

The two left, the door of the room clanking behind them.

"Oh, Maggie, Maggie," Liam said. "I have thought of you, dreamed of you. And the baby—"

"Here, you can feel him moving."

But Liam couldn't reach that far. Maggie stood in front of him so that he could lay his twitchy hands in a splayed fashion on her stomach. The baby kicked, and Liam smiled. "He seems healthy," he said.

Maggie knelt in front of him. "The baby will be here any day now, and I need you—"

"I can't be with you," he said. "I would be released only on the condition that I join the Army."

"Then, at least cooperate with them!" she cried. "Work with them! Do what they want you to do! They'll let you outside, Liam, where there's sunshine and air. Or go to work in the kitchen. They'll let you eat there—"

"You can't ask me to abandon my conscience. No matter what becomes of me."

"What about me? I'm living with Ma and Pa now, because the Erwins wouldn't let me stay in the house. It's like I've never left, as if we never married. Ma treats me like I'm a little girl who can't take care of herself—"

Liam's lips curved in a shaking smile. "Your mother loves you. You know that."

"—and Pa won't even talk to me. He pretends that I'm not even in the same room as he is! I can't go anywhere, I can't do anything—" Breathless, she stopped. "At church, no one will speak to us. No one comes into the store anymore, either, because of all this—"

She tried to draw in a breath, but her throat felt flayed. "I'm sorry," she said. "I didn't mean to nag at you—"

"I didn't realize this would be such a burden for you," Liam said. "Or for your parents. I'm sorry this is happening. I never wanted to hurt you."

For the first time, he seemed less than adamant. Maggie sat down and looked into his eyes. "Listen to me," she said. "I promised Colonel Parton that I would convince you to take a job here at the camp—"

"Why did you do that?"

"I gave him my word."

"You can't speak for me—"

"But I can speak for myself. I'm lonely, Liam, and I cry every night." She stopped herself. "And I can't stand to see you like this, your face all gaunt and cold and your arms so thin. You're shaking— did you know that? Your whole body is shaking like you're sick! Please, please, I can't live knowing that this is happening to you—"

"Get a rope! Get a rope!"

Maggie twisted around toward the window. Four young men stood outside, peering into the room, their hands visored against the glass for a better view. Maggie jumped from her seat and rushed toward the window, grabbing for the cords to draw down the blinds. She could not reach them. The recruits laughed at her, imitating her clumsiness by stumbling around with their cheeks inflated and their bodies bumping against each other.

The door opened, and Judah and Brendan rushed in with Captain Lowell. Striding to the window, Captain Lowell shouted at the recruits, "Get away from here! Get back to your patrol! You'll be punished for this."

Colonel Parton stalked into the room and stood near the door, his fisted hands on his hips, his lips tight as he sized up the situation. After Captain Lowell left to re-establish control, the Colonel moved forward and addressed Maggie. "Do you see, Mrs. Keohane, the disruption that your husband's presence here is causing? Do you see how dangerous it is for all concerned that he is refusing to do his duty?"

Maggie's body crumpled, as if it had no muscle or bone.

"So, tell me, Mrs. Keohane," Colonel Parton continued. "What is your husband's answer?"

A sob caught in Maggie's throat, and she put her hand over her mouth.

"I will not aid in the killing machine that is this war," Liam declared. "I will not cooperate with an institution that is antithetical to my faith and God's—"

"I am speaking to your wife," Colonel Parton said. "Did you keep your promise to me, Mrs. Keohane? Did you persuade your husband to work in our camp?"

Her hand still over her mouth, Maggie shook her head.

"I beg your pardon, Mrs. Keohane? I didn't hear you."

"No!" A wail came from deep within her. "No!"

Liam jumped up from his chair, his bound hands fumbling in the air in front of him. "Maggie! Don't, my love, don't cry so—"

"Take him back to his cell," Colonel Parton snapped at an MP who had come into the room.

As the MP hauled Liam out of the chair, Maggie screamed, "Liam, please, oh, please—!"

Liam shouted as he was dragged from the room: "The eye is the lamp of the body. So, if your eye is sound, your whole body will be full of light—'" From the hallway, he called, "Matthew 6:22, Maggie! The eye—'"

The door closed behind him. Colonel Parton glowered. "This is a warning to the three of you," he said. "Do not come here again or I will have you brought up on charges of interference with the Armed Forces under the Espionage Act—"

Judah spoke. "We are well within our rights as citizens. You are the one who is breaking the law by holding a civilian for court-martial—"

"Shut up, you officious little kike," Colonel Parton said. "And you, Father, one word of sympathy for your brother in any of your sermons, and I will see your Popish church locked up as a place of sedition. Do you understand me?"

Neither Judah nor Brendan spoke.

Colonel Parton turned to Maggie. "And Mrs. Keohane, I wish you well with the baby. It appears you'll be raising it alone."

As Maggie sobbed, he left the room.

Judah dropped Maggie off in front of Sullivan's Grocery. Brendan slid out of the Model T as well. "I'll walk to the church," he said. "Thank you, Judah."

Maggie grabbed onto the handrail of the outside stairs to go up to the apartments, but stopped after two steps. "What did he mean?" she asked.

"I'm sorry?" Brendan said.

"What was Liam calling to me? 'The eye is the lamp—'"

"'The eye is the lamp of the body. So, if your eye is sound, your whole body will be full of light; but if your eye is not sound, your whole body will be full of darkness. If then the light in you is darkness, how great is the darkness!'" Brendan said. "It's St. Matthew."

"But why did he want me to read it? What does it mean?"

"The eye is usually interpreted as the conscience." Brendan sounded like the Catechism teacher he was. "If the judgment of the conscience is sound—that is, if a man chooses to live by the moral truth that God has set forward for us—then 'the body is full of light.'" He paused. "He meant it to comfort you, Maggie. To tell you that whatever happens to him physically, his faith will sustain him."

When she didn't reply, Brendan added, "Truly, Maggie, he wants you to know he is at peace with himself and his purpose."

"Thank you, Father," she said, from habit.

"Want me to walk you inside?"

"No, I think I'll stay outside for a while. I need to think."

After Brendan bid her goodnight, Maggie walked toward Berkeley Lake. She came to the edge of the water as the sun was setting in the west, etching the snowy slopes of the Rocky Mountains in pink. High clouds burned red in the deep blue, darkening sky.

She crossed her arms over her breasts, her right hand pressed against her throat. She could not bear to think of him without his glasses. Liam, who loved to read and write, whose whole existence was caught up in words. She closed her eyes: *Please, God, give him my eyesight so that he can see in the darkness, and give me his. I don't need it. I don't want it. Please, do that for me.*

She opened her eyes. The sunset was just as lovely, just as clear and brilliant.

She turned toward home. It was sinful, stupid to try to bargain with God. He never responded, anyway.

In the apartments, her mother was sitting up in bed. "Anything new?" she asked as Maggie came into the bedroom.

Maggie sat in the chair next to the bed. Without speaking, she put her hands over her face and laid her forehead on the bed. Tears poured from her eyes. Her mother stroked her hair.

"They let me see him this time," Maggie sobbed. "But they asked me to try to talk him out of it, and I couldn't. He wouldn't agree to—"

"*Is mór an trua é,*" Ma said.

Maggie knew enough Irish to understand: *It's a shame.*

"I'm sorry, Ma," Maggie said.

"Did you tell him that we're havin' to borrow more to keep the store in business and—?"

"Yes, Ma," she said, suddenly exhausted. "I did all I could."

She went to her room and changed for bed. Lying down, she closed her eyes. *Darkness, darkness, darkness. If then the light in you is darkness, how great is the darkness!* The words kept going through her mind until she couldn't stand it. Creeping through the apartments to the store, she went to the attic and fetched the kerosene lantern that she used when she wrote at Ma's vanity. Returning to her room, she turned the flame up to a soft flicker. She watched it until she could no longer stay awake.

The baby is born on April 30, 1918. Ma and Auntie Eileen help with the birth, at home and without the aid of a doctor. Maggie suspects that Dr. Thorp, a proper Knight of Columbus and pillar of the parish, has refused to come.

Auntie Eileen sits on the bed beside her, supporting Maggie's shoulders. "Scream if you need to," she hisses in Maggie's ear. "'Tis your turn."

Maggie grits her teeth. Tears stream down her face, but she holds in every sound but the weakest whimper. If Liam can stand to be jailed and starved, then she should be able to endure this. If God is going to separate her from her husband so cruelly, then she will refuse to give in to the bitter, brutal pain that God gave to woman after Eve took a bite of apple. Mercifully, the birth goes smoothly for Maggie, who falls back on the pillows, exhausted as her mother swaddles the baby in a towel and whisks her away. "'Tis a girl," her mother announces.

"Is she alive?" Maggie asks.

Her mother does not reply, and Auntie Eileen's hand tightens around Maggie's.

The baby lets out a screech.

"Aye, there she goes." Auntie Eileen relaxes. "A powerful set of lungs on that one, all right."

Maggie closes her eyes. Liam, she thinks. Why aren't you here? Why aren't you with me to meet your daughter, the one we will name after your own mother. Ailis, Ailis Colleen. Alice.

She feels another press in her belly and a flood between her legs. Auntie Eileen says, "There's the end of it now." She collects another towel from beneath Maggie and carries it out of the room.

Ma brings Alice Colleen to Maggie, bundled in a flannel blanket. She has a fuzz of red hair, newly-washed and smelling of rosewater, and her hands clench in waving fists. She looks at Maggie with squinty, unfocused eyes that have not yet adjusted to the light of the world.

Her mother lays Alice Colleen on Maggie's breast.

"She'll suckle, if you offer it," Ma says. "You may not have much to give her yet, but 'tis best that you both start learnin' the way it is."

Maggie lifts her breast to the baby, and the baby mouths it. And, from that moment on, Alice Colleen is adored. Maggie cannot hold her tenderly enough, or listen to her breathe for long enough, or touch her tiny fingers and toes often enough. She won't allow the baby to sleep in the low cradle on the floor beside the bed that Ma once used for both Seaney and for her. Instead, Alice Colleen sleeps in bed beside her mother. Maggie cannot bear to have her daughter so far from her. She cannot bear to think of Alice Colleen alone in the darkness, as Liam is.

Brendan comes to see Alice Colleen, holding her in his arms with the same gentle care that he has shown to the children he has baptized. He tells Maggie that Judah will carry a message to Fort Logan and demand that it reach Liam.

"Isn't he worried that he'll be arrested?" she asks.

"Perhaps." Brendan shrugs. "But he's willing to do it for you and for Liam."

Pa will not come in to see the baby, but Uncle Irish does, arriving with a giant teddy bear that wears a tartan vest and Teddy Roosevelt glasses. He tucks the bear in beside Maggie, who is sitting in the rocking chair with Alice Colleen in her arms.

Maggie laughs. "It's bigger than she is!"

"She'll grow into it," Irish says in his careless way. "Look at you, Muffin. You grew up."

His kindness makes her cry. "Thank you, Uncle Irish."

"Let me see her." He bends over to peer at the baby. He smells of peppermint, tractor grease, and tobacco. "Well, she's a pretty thing, isn't she?"

Maggie tucks the blankets around Alice Colleen again as Uncle Irish walks to the window and lights a cigarette.

"Whatever she needs, Muffin, just ask me," he says. "I can't say I agree with Liam. If he were my son, I'd knock him up alongside the head for what he's done to you. But, on the other hand, I have to respect him for believing so deeply and being so sure that he's right."

"It's my fault!" Maggie blurts. "He's still in prison because of me!"

"What do you mean?" Uncle Irish asks.

The story, which has been running through her head since the day at Fort Logan, spills from her. She hasn't dared talk to Ma about it, or to bring it up with Brendan, who surely must blame her for failing to talk Liam into joining the work crew. Yet Maggie readily tells Uncle Irish about her promise to Colonel Parton and Liam's refusal.

When she's finished, he shakes his head. "That was a cruel thing to do to you."

"Liam wouldn't be cruel—"

"No, this Parton fellow," Uncle Irish says. "To ask you, alone, scared, expecting a baby, to do what no one else has been able to do—what starvation and ill treatment couldn't even do—is cowardly. He asked you to do the impossible, then shamed you for it."

Maggie starts to cry. How many nights has she asked God to forgive her for failing Liam? How many nights has she sat in front of the mirror in Ma's attic and stared at her face, hating herself because she can't save him? During grace, when Pa asks God to bless Seaney and Kathleen—neither of whom are half as devoted to their beliefs as Liam is—Maggie presses her tongue against the roof of her mouth to keep from lashing out, from demanding that they spit in the face of a God who would allow his faithful servant to be so humiliated.

"Why is he doing this, Uncle Irish?" she asks.

"I can't answer that, Muffin."

"I wish he would just come home and be a regular husband and father." The admission feels like betrayal. She quickly adds, "I can't think about this in any way that makes sense to me."

"That's because it doesn't make sense." Uncle Irish's voice is harsh. "It's a terrible thing that's happening to our country just now. A war devised by the rich, conscription, the persecution of people just for speaking their minds—and the Church is doing nothing to stop any of it, although it claims to be a moral institution. It's all madness and waste." He touches her hand. "I'm sorry, I didn't mean to make you cry."

"I cry all the time," she says. "It doesn't matter."

"Well, if you need money, come to me," Uncle Irish says. "I know you aren't getting any from your mother and father."

"It isn't their fault. The store's doing so badly—"

"Well, I'll help you however I can. Do you need clothes for her? Toys?"

"But Redlands isn't doing that well, either—"

"That's not for you to worry about," he says. "There, now, no more tears. As long as I'm alive, Muffin, you and Alice Colleen can count on me."

A few days later, Maggie lies in bed on a warm afternoon. Alice Colleen has been fussy lately. Ma claims it is just a bit of colic, but it has kept Maggie awake all night, terrified that she will lose her baby as her mother lost so many of hers. In the darkness, Maggie listens for Alice Colleen's breathing, holding her own breath until she hears her daughter exhale.

Now, exhausted, Alice Colleen rests easily. Maggie dozes off into the warm, milky smell of the baby's body next to hers, sleeping soundly for the first time since Alice Colleen's birth. Yet, through the sweetness of slumber, she hears the telephone ringing in the parlor.

Someone answer it.

Ma, the telephone is ringing. Seaney, answer it—

Maggie sits up. The telephone falls silent, and she forgets about it almost immediately. She lies down and reaches for Alice Colleen. Pulling back the blanket, Maggie touches her tiny fingers, with their slivers of nails. How can a human being be as delicately perfect as this one?

Contented, she drifts back to sleep.

She wakes again to a pounding on the door that leads to the outdoor landing. Again, she hopes for someone else to bother with it, but no one does. Maggie pulls herself from her bed and fastens a calico housecoat over her nightdress. She tucks a pillow on either side of Alice Colleen, who sleeps peacefully, and goes to the door.

Brendan stands outside.

"Maggie, get dressed. You need to come with me. Liam's being transferred by train to another location—"

She runs a hand through her tangled, unwashed hair. "Another location? Not Fort Logan?"

"He called me. I've been trying to call you, I think something's wrong with your phone—"

"No, I heard—"

"We have to go now. He told me he had only a few minutes before the train left."

Maggie runs to the bedroom and puts on a frock, stockings, and shoes. She snatches Alice Colleen from the bed, and the baby begins to wail. Maggie grabs an extra blanket to wrap around her.

As she hurries back to the parlor, she hears her mother arguing with Brendan. "She can't go with you," Ma says staunchly. "She's not to be out of bed yet—"

"Mrs. Sullivan, I understand," Brendan says. "But this might be her last chance to see Liam, and for him to see the baby—"

Ma faces Maggie. "You're not to be goin' out."

Maggie jiggles Alice Colleen, trying to quiet her. "I have to. I'll be all right. I'll be careful."

Outside, the parish car is parked at the curb. Brendan drives to Union Station while Maggie cranes her head, surveying the men on the sidewalks, as if Liam will be among them. He will be able to meet his daughter, she thinks. Able to see Alice Colleen and to kiss her. *And to kiss me.* She cuddles Alice Colleen against her and kisses the baby's head, nearly giddy with hope.

Union Station teems with soldiers and regular passengers, rushing in and out of the gates, onto the platforms, their baggage heaped here and there. With Maggie beside him, his hand holding tightly to her arm, Brendan threads his way through families bidding young soldiers farewell, businessmen striding toward their train, and women with baskets and shopping.

"Wait here."

Maggie sits on a high-backed bench. Alice Colleen is calm now but wide awake. Rocking the baby in her arms, Maggie whispers, "You'll meet your daddy. And he will love you. He will love you as much as I do, as we all do." Glancing up, she searches for Brendan, who has disappeared into the crowd heading for the platforms. What will Liam look like now? The last time she saw him, his face was so starved—

More than half an hour passes. Maggie's high spirits falter as train after train is called for boarding. At last, Brendan returns, alone.

"He's gone," he reports to Maggie. "The conductor said that a man in a civilian's suit was taken on the train to Lincoln, guarded by about nine military men. He was put on a private car with the shades pulled down—"

"No," Maggie lurches off the bench. "No, he can't be gone!"

She whips around in a circle. He must be here, somewhere among the hundreds of people around them. They haven't looked hard enough yet, they just haven't found him yet—

She clutches Alice Colleen, unaware of the baby's shrieking until Brendan orders, "Maggie, give her to me."

He wrests the baby from her arms. Pain stabs through Maggie's chest as she is separated from her daughter. Her breasts release their milk in a flood, and her belly, still loose and flaccid, roils as if her tender insides will slip from her and pool on the floor.

Her knees buckle, and she falls onto them, clutching at her stomach. Brendan grabs her arm and tries to lift her upward with his right hand while holding Alice Colleen in the crook of his left elbow. Maggie tries to wriggle out of his grip. She wants to lie on the floor, to feel the cold tile against her feverish forehead, to close her eyes and forget.

She hears Brendan say, "Her husband's just gone."

Someone replies, "Poor girl. Here, Father, let me help—"

No one can help, Maggie says—or doesn't say, for she hears no response. No one can do anything, but him, but Liam. He could do something, but he won't, he won't! He doesn't love us enough, he doesn't care—!

A soldier and a worker in a flannel shirt pick her up from the floor. Securing her between them, they escort her to the car outside the station. Brendan delivers her home, and Maggie returns to her bed without speaking again to him or to her mother.

Yet, their voices float down the hallway from the parlor to her bedroom.

"We were too late," Brendan tells her mother. "Liam told me over the phone that he had begged Colonel Parton to let him call before they left Fort Logan, so we would have time to meet them, but they didn't let him call until he was at Union Station and the train was already on the track."

"Where were they takin' him?"

"I don't know. I hope it isn't far. If it is, how will any of us know what's become of him?" Brendan pauses. "Mrs. Sullivan, please watch her carefully. She isn't taking this well—

Maggie rolls to her side, her knees as close to her chest as she can bring them, her arms wrapped around Alice Colleen. Closing her eyes, she hopes that they will not open again.

SIXTEEN

In eastern Colorado once again, Jim sat at the round table in his suite at the one hotel in town. By the light of the kerosene lamp, he waded through a pile of documents in front of him. They were contracts with the railroads for shipment of oil, crude, and refined gasoline. Now that the railroads were under government control and dedicated mostly to the movement of troops, it had become difficult to secure transport for the millions of barrels of petroleum products that fueled the war effort. Recently, a court order had been filed by Judge Robert Scott Lovett to ensure that petroleum found its way to the great seaports of the nation and on to the Allied Forces in France. Tank cars that had been sidetracked for weeks were traveling the rails once more.

But now, oil barrels were in short supply, for the steel industry, too, was under government control. Jim supposed it would take another court order before barrels would be manufactured again.

A knock sounded at the door. Without looking up from his work, he called, "Come in."

"Hello, Mr. Graves."

A woman entered, carrying the dinner he had ordered from the dining room. The timbre of her voice was tremulous, coy.

A memory rolled through his mind. Night, this hotel, this suite of rooms, a woman. He could not think of why he would have slept with her. She wore a white apron over a dowdy brown dress, and she carried a good deal of weight in her hips and thighs, although her lips were berry-colored and full. Her brownish hair was parted in the middle and drawn severely away from her face.

"Is that all this time?" she asked.

He recalled her name in another flash: Daisy.

"Yes, thank you, Daisy." He reached in his pocket for a tip.

"You don't need to do that," she said. "You left me plenty the last time you was here."

He handed her the money. "That was last time."

She rolled it carefully in her fingers. "I won't be able to do that again. I'm gettin' married."

"That's good news," Jim replied. "Is he a soldier?"

"Naw, he's the sheriff right here in town. Henry Waring."

"You have a son, don't you?"

"Yes, sir, my Jesse, he's my Kewpie doll. He's lookin' forward to havin' a daddy again."

"I'm happy for you."

"Thank you, Mr. Graves."

After she left, Jim removed an envelope of Kathleen's sketches from his elephant skin briefcase. They had all been drawn with the precious colored pencils given to her by ambulance driver lover—a rosette sprouting from the dirt between cobblestones, entitled "Spring Is Coming;" a mounted cavalry officer identified as "Private MacGregor of the Royal Scots;" and a picture of Hank with her feet in a tub of steaming water, called "Long Day."

He laid down the sketches and took a letter from Ellie from his briefcase. After pouring himself another brandy, he read:

Troops are always coming and going here in a hodgepodge of nationalities. Of course, there are the French, British, and Italian, but there are also soldiers from the Foreign Legion. There are large numbers of African troops who sport red fezzes and whose skin is darker than any I've ever seen, and hundreds of Indian troops with thick beards and their heads wrapped in turbans. Kathleen recently tended to an Arab patient who called out to Allah whenever she applied Dakin's solution. He knew no English whatsoever.

The men of these various nationalities coexist side by side, with the exception of the Americans. It's disheartening to see the sign at the Knights of Columbus tent that reads, "Everyone Welcome, Everything Free," beside one that reads: "No Coloreds Allowed." The YMCA has the same restrictions, as does the Red Cross. Perhaps it is because the Europeans have grown so war-weary that they no longer care who does what, but I feel a hint of shame that my country bars its own citizens. The Negro troops in the trenches are under the command of the French, because American officers will not—

An insistent knock on the door interrupted his reading. Daisy stood in the corridor.

"Come quick, Mr. Graves," she said. "There's somethin' you better see."

He reached for his coat. "What's happening?"

"There's a Heine man in town," she said as Jim followed her down the stairs and into the street. "His name is Emil Reutter, and everyone says he's been makin' all sorts of insults against America."

"What kind of insults?"

"He's been sayin' things like, well, a lady shouldn't say it—"

"Then you needn't—"

"Well, he said 'To hell with the Army' and that the Kaiser has licked Russia, and America will be next. He says we'll be beggin' for peace come three months from now."

"Where did he say all this?"

"Down in our dining room!" she exploded. "He's been stayin' for a week at our place, and now look at it! We find out he's a traitor!"

Three blocks from the hotel, about thirty men had gathered near an abandoned storefront where a sign read, "Joe Tyler Clothing," just above a "For Lease" notice. Flaming torches and kerosene lanterns, lifted to shoulder-height, illuminated the night.

"People are really mad." Daisy's breath rose in a cloud above her head. "They say they're goin' to tar and feather him and then hang him—"

Daisy pushed her way through the crowd toward a lanky man wearing a cowboy hat. On the boardwalk in front of the store, a rough-looking man in a wool coat and trousers held a rope that encircled another man's throat. The bound man's coat and shirt had been stripped away and dumped in the street, and he shivered in the bitter wind. Down his spine was a painted yellow stripe.

"Henry," Daisy said. "This is Mr. Graves, the big oil man from Denver."

"Pleased to meet you." Henry shook Jim's hand. "This man is Emil Reutter. He was talking down the U.S. Army earlier."

"So Mrs. Ellington told me. Who is the man with the rope?"

"That's Joe Tyler," Daisy offered. "He used to run this store here."

Jim sized up the restless crowd. A few of the men carried shotguns or rifles. A low, angry buzz collected in the air above their heads along with the steam from their breath. Jim caught the gaze of a burly man, who glared at him.

"What are you planning to do?" he asked Henry. "This much agitation could lead to violence."

"No laws have been broken yet." Henry stepped forward. "Listen, folks, we've got a special guest staying here in town, Mr. Jim Graves from Denver, one of our state's most successful businessmen and a patriot like no other. He's been doing everything he can to see that the Heines lose this war, including drilling for oil up north of town. Some of you even work for him."

Some of the men applauded, and someone called out, "Yes, sir, Mr. Graves!"

"We need to show Mr. Graves that we're behind America all the way, just like him and the members of the America First Society, and that we know how to deal with men like this one, this Emil Reutter, this foreigner and maybe even a spy—"

"A spy!" Daisy exclaimed.

"—who wants America to be beaten and done in. We need to show him that this man isn't one of us—"

Shouts drowned out the rest of Henry's speech. "Go back to Germany!" someone screamed. "Get out of my country!" Another yelled, "Let's take him out to Jensen's farm. There's hanging trees out there!"

Mr. Tyler yanked the rope hard, and Reutter's head jerked, his face darkening and his cheeks distending. Jim looked over his shoulder. More people were arriving, as word evidently spread. A few horses galloped up the street, their riders fully armed with rifles and rope, and an automobile pulled in close to the boardwalk, its acetylene headlamps casting elongated shadows down the street.

"I got the tar!" someone shouted.

The burly man dashed toward Tyler and Reutter, an American flag cradled in his arms. Men doffed their hats, whistling and saluting, and a woman cried out, "God bless America! Thank you, Walter!"

Walter shook the flag in front of Reutter's face. "Swear allegiance, Heine," he said. "Swear allegiance and kiss the flag."

Reutter struggled, raising his hands to push the flag away, but a third man pinned his arms to his sides as Tyler tightened the noose. Walter shoved the flag into Reutter's face.

"Kiss the flag," Walter ordered. "Kiss it!"

"Kiss it!" Tyler demanded. "Kiss it or you'll be tarred and feathered!"

Grabbing Reutter by the hair, Walter shoved his face into the cloth, then pulled Reutter's head upright. "There, see? That ain't so hard," he said. "Now, kiss it of your own free will, so everybody here can see."

Reutter spat. Tyler jerked the rope so hard that Reutter's tongue lolled from his mouth. Walter smashed a fist into Reutter's gut, and Reutter's knees buckled. Only the rope around his neck kept him from falling face down into the street. It caught just under his chin, the knot of the noose near his ear, his head tipped to the left.

"By God, you're asking to be hanged!" Tyler shouted. "Say you love America! Say it!"

When Reutter did not respond, Tyler jerked the rope again. A foamy drool ran from Reutter's open mouth. "Say it," Tyler repeated. "Swear on the Bible that you love America!"

"Aren't you going to stop this?" Jim asked Henry.

"Mr. Tyler is the head of the America First Society," Daisy said. "Ain't that the organization you're in? The one with the card that says, 'If you ain't with America, you're against her'?"

"Kiss the flag!" Tyler screamed. "Kiss it and swear allegiance—"

Unable to be still any longer, Jim stepped forward. "Gentlemen, ladies," he called. "Listen to me, please—"

He waited until the threats stopped. "Loosen the noose," he said quietly to Tyler. "Let the man breathe."

Tyler glanced at Henry, who gave Jim a sour look, but nodded.

Jim continued. "We all love our country, we all love America and believe her to be the greatest nation on this earth. But part of America's greatness is because she is a country where the law is upheld. America isn't a place of barbarism and cruelty as Germany is, where the Kaiser rules according to his whims. No, America is a country where we practice justice for all. There are laws that will bring this man, Mr. Reutter, his just punishment and sentence. The Espionage Act was put in place to protect our country from hateful and unpatriotic behavior such as this. So, as citizens who treasure freedom, we cannot allow ourselves to give in to raw emotion, but must trust in our great judicial system, and preserve the laws and dignity of our society."

He stopped, out of breath. No one moved or replied, and he turned toward Henry. "Sheriff?"

Henry's face screwed up in a tight knot. "Mr. Graves is right," he said. "I'll escort Mr. Reutter to the jail."

Tyler interjected. "If Mr. Graves is right, then this Hun should be in the hands of federal authorities. Ain't that true?"

"Yes," Jim said. "This falls to the office of the U.S. District Attorney, Mr. Harry Tedrow, with whom I'm well-acquainted. Mr. Reutter will most likely be charged with sedition based on what we've all witnessed here tonight."

"We'll take him to the depot." Tyler gave the rope another jerk. "And there he can buy himself a ticket to Denver—"

"I'll escort him to Denver myself," Henry said self-importantly. "I'll send a message for the U.S. District Attorney to meet us at Union Station." Turning to Jim, he added, "Since you know the D.A., I'd like you to go with me and tell him what you've seen here tonight."

"I'll take responsibility with you for seeing Mr. Reutter into the right hands," Jim said. "Now, Sheriff, remove the noose from his neck. Give him back his clothes."

Henry gave a nod to Tyler, who begrudgingly complied. Once the rope was loosened, Reutter coughed violently and massaged his neck. Henry wrapped the shirt and coat around Reutter and cuffed his hands. Jim opened his mouth to ask if it was necessary, but the crowd cheered as Walter and the other man lifted Reutter to his feet and started to drag him down the street.

"I'll need to collect my luggage," Jim told Henry.

"We'll be at the depot."

At the hotel, Jim packed quickly, anxious to be free of this place. If he hadn't been here tonight, Reutter would undoubtedly have been lynched, as others had been. As he shoved papers into his briefcase, Daisy appeared at the door of his room.

Without asking if she could come in, she strode to the table. "Why did you defend him? He should be hanged."

"Perhaps he will be," Jim replied. "He seems to have no regrets about his sentiments—"

"Then why did you stop it?"

He faced her. "If the good people of this town had done it— no matter how true their intentions—it would have been murder. Surely your beau Sheriff Waring is aware of that."

"That ain't the way I see it," she fumed. "We were standin' up for our boys who're gone to war. Just about every family here has one, and Pete Tyler's already been killed—"

"Mr. Tyler's son?"

"Yes."

"Then I'm sorry for him, but his grief doesn't countermand the laws of this country."

She said nothing, but watched as he latched the valise and briefcase. He gathered his coat and hat, ready to leave. When she did not move, he asked, "What is it, Daisy?"

"My dad says you don't need to pay your bill," she said. "He says he's proud to give free room and board to a true patriot. But I don't think you're a patriot. I think you just done this so you can have the glory of bein' a big shot in Denver."

Jim moved past her to the door of the room. "I'll pay my room and board. Your father can then make the offer to someone who is, in your opinion, more worthy of it."

She folded her arms over her breasts. "We're doin' what we should here. Most of us are members of the America First Society now, and we run a German shoe repairman named Schneider out of town just last week. You told me the last time I saw you that I was a good patriot. Now you need to be."

She ran down the stairs to the lobby, and Jim followed warily. At the desk, he paid his bill.

When he arrived at the train station, the townspeople mobbed him, exacting promises that he would see Reutter tried for his treason. The crowd had doubled in size, with wagons and cars parked helter-skelter in the street. Armed men spilled from them.

"It isn't my decision," Jim said. "But I will pass on whatever I can to the U.S. District Attorney."

When he finally pushed his way inside, he found Reutter sitting on a bench in a corner. Henry, Tyler, Walter, and two others stood near the doors that led to the platform, smoking and talking.

Jim walked to where Reutter sat. Reutter's neck was swollen and bruised. His left eye was swelling, and his lower lip was cut. The American flag that he had been forced to kiss was draped around the brim of his hat, so that he appeared to be wearing a red, white and blue turban. Around his neck hung a scrawled placard that read "Bound for Berlin."

"Who hit you?" Jim asked.

Reutter said nothing.

Jim lit a cigarette. "Where are you from? What are you doing here?"

"I am from Austria." Reutter wheezed in a heavy accent. "I sell the lightning rods to the farmers."

So Reutter was a flimflam man as well as a traitor. With a laugh, Jim asked, "Do you want a cigarette?"

Reutter took it with his right hand, the chain on his handcuffs clanking. Jim lit the cigarette for him. Reutter took a drag, but coughed violently. Sputtering, he croaked, "Who are you that you can say what happens in this"—*dis*—"town?" Mockingly, he added, "I know this, I know that, I know the District Attorney."

"Would you rather I let them hang you?"

Without waiting for a reply, Jim walked away. The door to the depot opened, and Daisy came inside, carrying a wicker basket. The smell of sausage and biscuits wafted through the station.

She set the basket on a table and called, "I have breakfast for you all. I wasn't sure how many of you are goin' to Denver, so I brought plenty."

She dished up plates as the men moved toward her. With each one, she said, "There you go, Henry, Joe, Walter, you got a long day ahead."

When Jim approached her, she fell silent. He took two plates from the pile. She stared at them.

"I'll take one to Mr. Reutter," Jim said.

"I don't have enough for him."

Jim nodded at the ample supplies in the picnic basket. "Even a condemned man receives a last meal."

"You gave him a cigarette," she said. "I wouldn't even do that." Jim touched her hand. "Daisy—"

She glanced toward Henry, who was watching them closely. Without speaking again, she dished up a second plate for Reutter.

Jim set the plate on the bench beside Reutter. After a moment, Reutter ground out his cigarette in the eggs.

At the State Capitol Building, Jim sat in the office of Governor Gunter, who had generously agreed to see him. He held a glass of fine Scotch in his hand that the Governor had offered from his private stock, purchased long before Prohibition took effect in Denver. Between the two men, the Governor's desk shone, polished into a mirror-like sheen.

"What brings you here today, Mr. Graves?" Governor Gunter asked.

"I've just come back from one of our small towns on the Eastern Plains, near the Kansas state line," Jim said. "I experienced a disturbing incident there."

He told the story of Emil Reutter's near lynching. "I'm afraid that we might be headed toward another incident such as the one involving Robert Praeger in Illinois."

Governor Gunter took a swallow of whiskey. "I believe there were other circumstances surrounding that situation."

"From what I've read in the newspapers," Jim said, "Praeger's clothes were stripped from him, as Mr. Reutter's were, and he was paraded down the street. He was made to kiss the flag before he was hanged to death. It's even said, sir, that a young boy tied the rope to the tree and that a number of children were encouraged to pull him up to his death."

"I read the newspapers, Mr. Graves," Governor Gunter said coldly. "It's also said that the lynch mob was made up of a number of drunks. Was alcohol involved in the incident that you witnessed?"

"No, I believe the men involved were sober." Jim flicked aside his annoyance. "Which might make the incident more frightening rather than less."

"People have the right to protect their town."

"As long as it is within the law—"

"Of course."

"But every day I read about some kind of action taken against those of German heritage," Jim said. "The school superintendent in Grand Junction was relieved of his job and nearly hanged for recommending a book that had a favorable approach to Germany, and in Delta County, residents have had yellow crosses painted on their homes. I strongly believe that Emil Reutter would have met the same fate as Robert Praeger had I not persuaded Sheriff Waring to calm the crowd."

"What do you suggest, Mr. Graves?"

Jim spoke cautiously. "When I joined the Committee to Americanize Colorado, I believed it would be a way to encourage foreigners to adopt our ways, while speaking out against the fears that can drive persecution. I thought it would be for unity and understanding. But it seems that the recent registration of enemy aliens has done nothing more than to point out where they live."

"That was a federal mandate over which I have no power." Governor Gunter leaned forward. "Do you know that I personally write letters to the families of those who've lost soldiers in battle? What am I to tell them about the Germans who live in this state? That we have more sympathy for their plight than for those who've lost sons and fathers?"

"Of course not, sir. I simply believe that we must lead by example. What good is fighting for democracy in Europe if we are taking away guaranteed rights at home? We need to be certain that the patriotic zeal of some citizens doesn't overshadow the good—"

"Mr. Graves," Governor Gunter interrupted. "As someone who pushed Preparedness long before it was popular, you must know that Colorado was the first state to appropriate funds through the Legislature for mobilizing its National Guard troops in January of 1917—long before America went to war. It was also the first in the nation to pledge loyalty to President Wilson when he declared war in April. Our patriotic zeal, as you call it, sets us apart from other states."

"I'm aware that Colorado has been a leader in many things, and I'm proud that it is my home," Jim said. "I always will be."

"I am glad to hear that." Governor Gunter stood. "Thank you for coming here today, but I have a meeting—"

"Of course."

The two shook hands, but as Jim walked out the door into the echoing, marble-floored hallway of the State Capitol Building, he swallowed back the knowledge that he—once again—had been dismissed.

SEVENTEEN

At Julia Reston's house for another meeting of the National Woman's Party, Mary Jane sat with her gloved hands folded in her lap. To her right, Miss Crawley listened attentively as Miss Reston spoke. To Mary Jane's left, Anneka's gaze was glued to Miss Reston, her lips slightly parted.

Dressed in men's trousers and jacket, Miss Reston held up a copy of a Denver newspaper. "I have here an article that asks the question: 'Should Women Wear the Gold Star and Abandon Crepe?' It says here that, as the list of American casualties in France grows, we must reconsider our approach to mourning and how we shall dress for it." Her lips turned downward. "The article includes the quote: 'Men must die that nations may live, and women must lose those men.'"

The attendees, who perched on every possible seat or stood along the walls, hissed and murmured in disapproval.

"How far we have strayed from our cause," Miss Reston continued. "How much we have resigned ourselves to. We are no longer discussing how to establish the peace, or preserve it, or guarantee it, but how we must dress for the lack of it."

Mary Jane leaned toward Anneka. "Isn't she odd?"

"But she is very sure of herself. I like that."

Miss Reston spoke again. "And what has become of the discussion of Woman's Suffrage and, more importantly, Equal Rights? It has been forgotten in the past year of war. What will become of the Susan B. Anthony bill that has been languishing since 1870—before the turn of the century, before Colorado was a state, and before anyone in this room had the right to vote? Nothing. Why? Because not all suffragists are feminists!"

Catcalls echoed through the room.

"The Suffragists are fighting for the vote, but the feminists of the National Woman's Party are fighting for Equal Rights. We want to end the disenfranchisement of women from the world of business and politics and international diplomacy to end. We want domestic and federal laws that don't discriminate against women. We want the right of self-determination, and we want emancipation from the conventional attitudes and systems in this country that bind women to the household, and child rearing, and toiling in the factory, and other work that ruins their health and pays only pennies on the dollar. That is what the National Woman's Party wants."

Beside Mary Jane, Miss Crawley jumped to her feet, as did most of the women in the room. Anneka followed, and Mary Jane rose as well.

"Equal Rights includes the freedom of reproduction!" Miss Reston raised her voice to be heard above the clamor. "My words may cause some of you to blush—and I do not apologize if they do—but our soldiers have recently been issued condoms to protect them from impregnating the women of France, while we—their sisters, mothers, and wives in America—are not allowed to talk about or write about protecting ourselves because of the Comstock laws. Nor are we free to buy birth control or be equal partners with our husbands in the decisions made about our lives. Why is it that a woman—who can best judge her desire and ability to have and rear a child—is denied this basic tool of health and decency while the men in France casually indulge in encounters in the brothels of Paris that have no emotional or social meaning?"

The women broke into a chant: "No Gods, No Masters!"

"What does that mean?" Anneka asked Mary Jane.

Miss Crawley answered. "It is the slogan that Mrs. Margaret Sanger uses in her writings about birth control."

"Oh," Anneka said.

The usual rose color in Anneka's cheeks had darkened to mauve, and she grew somber and quiet. Mary Jane wondered if it had been a mistake to bring Anneka here where the talk was so unfettered. She didn't want to offend her future sister-in-law.

After the meeting ended, refreshments were served. Women gathered in groups to talk about what they had just heard, or what they believed, or what they wanted. As Mary Jane ate finger sandwiches and tiny cakes and drank lemon water, Anneka gazed at Miss Reston's wild and colorful paintings.

"What do you think of them?" Mary Jane asked.

"They are very modern-looking," Anneka said. "I like that they are not all the same, I mean, that they are different from the real thing. Look at the flowers there—how they look almost like teardrops in the way they droop."

Frowning, Mary Jane studied a design that looked like a piece of meat wound round with thorns and stuck through with a spear. "Give me a good landscape," she said. "That's art."

"Such as your friend Kathleen draws?"

"Exactly. There is no guessing what it's supposed to be."

"Look behind you."

Mary Jane turned toward the opposite wall of the room. A sprawling portrait of a young man had been placed above the fireplace mantel. Miss Reston hadn't used any fanciful colors or weird shapes in this painting, but had drawn the likeness as if the soldier had sat for it in a studio. Wearing a tan uniform and officer's cap, he had green-gray eyes that mirrored Miss Reston's and a face that she had lovingly detailed, with a strong chin and cheekbones.

Miss Reston came to stand beside Mary Jane and Anneka. "That is my nephew, Paul. He is with the U.S. Army Air Service in France."

"He is very handsome," Anneka said. "And the painting is beautiful."

"You have an interesting accent," Miss Reston said. "Where are you from?"

"Sweden."

"Ah, a long way from home," Miss Reston said wistfully. "As am I, for I consider Paris, where I lived the happiest days of my life, to be my home." Her eyes returned to the portrait. "And Paul's. He came to live with me when he was only six years old."

"Your eyes are the same," Mary Jane commented.

"Oh, yes, our eyes." Julia laid a hand on the mantel, as if she longed to reach up and stroke the portrait's cheek. "Our eyes brought us together. After Paul lost his parents in a tragic accident, it took me some time to arrange to come back to the States from Paris for him. He was left for months in the hands of a Mrs. Arbuckle, who was a good enough person, I suppose. But he grew shy, inward, difficult— and who could blame him? He had lost everything. When we met, he was terribly afraid of me, an aunt he had never met, and perhaps never even heard of, come to take him away to a foreign country, away from all he had ever known. So he hid behind the couch."

"Poor little boy," Anneka said.

"Yes, poor child," Miss Reston agreed. "We did all we could to coax him out. Mrs. Arbuckle even threatened to give him a sound whipping. I pleaded and flattered, offering candy and toys. But he just ground his fists into his eyes and vowed never to open them again."

Mary Jane laughed. "I can imagine one of my brothers doing that."

A tender smile lingered on Miss Reston's lips, and the weathered crow's feet of her eyes were soft and moist. "I knelt and said, 'Open your eyes and look into mine. They are the same color and shape as yours. We can see together what no one else can, because our eyes are the same.' Then I waited—and I must admit, I was very close to accepting Mrs. Arbuckle's offer of a birch switch. But, at last, curiosity won out. One little eye popped open. Then the other. And he came out from behind the couch."

As Anneka and Mary Jane laughed, Miss Crawley, who had joined them, spoke. "He was fortunate that you took him in."

"No, I was fortunate he came to me." Miss Reston said. "Paul sees more than others see. In Notre Dame, he studied the fall of rose-colored light on the hand of a statue. In Montmartre, he looked beyond the antics of the street actors at the feathers falling from the ragged, torn costume. The chapped, chalky hands of the potter who tries so hard to mold clay to greater beauty, the faults in a wall from which weeds grow—these are the things Paul saw." Her voice grew thick with emotion. "He often senses the detail that defines the whole."

A woman touched Miss Reston's arm to say farewell, and Miss Reston excused herself to walk her guest to the door.

Miss Crawley nodded at the portrait of Paul. "He's a nice-looking boy. I hope he comes home safely."

"Yes," Anneka said softly. "As I hope my Ross comes home."

Mary Jane reached for Anneka's hand and squeezed it. Linking arms with her, she said, "We should be going. It's getting dark."

Outside, Mary Jane asked Anneka, "What did you think of this afternoon?"

"What intelligent women!" Anneka said. "What an exciting day. What Miss Reston said, it is the first thing I have believed in for a long time."

The two women chatted about the afternoon as they took the streetcar to Corona Street. It was only when they reached the privacy of Anneka's home that Mary Jane asked, "What did you think about, well, the talk of birth control?"

"I think all women should have it," Anneka said fiercely. "Not just married, but all women. They should be able to decide if they want a child. That is worth fighting for as much as the vote."

Mary Jane looked down at her hands. "Wouldn't it just mean that more girls would . . . well, you know? They'd no longer have to marry because they'd be able to . . . and then, we'd have a whole country full of people who don't want to get married because they don't have to."

"I don't think any woman would trade the love of a man and the joy of children for a life alone, no matter how free that life might be," Anneka said. "I think more women would marry, in fact, because they and their husbands would be able to have children when they wanted them. They would be what Miss Reston called 'equal partners' with their husbands."

"Miss Crawley told me about a girl who tried to take care of it all by using a coat hanger," Mary Jane said. "She hurt herself badly, and she was arrested, too."

"There are others like her," Anneka said. "Women who find themselves with a child and alone and fearful."

Mary Jane opened her mouth to ask Anneka if she knew of anyone who needed help, but Mina came through the front door with the neighbor.

"Oh, there she is!" Anneka rose from her chair and hugged her daughter. "Thank you so much for keeping her, Mrs. Stroop."

"Where have you been, Mother?" Mina looked up from where she still clung to Anneka's legs.

"I have been at a meeting," Anneka said. "I heard the most exciting things about girls who grow up to vote and work and do all sorts of wonderful things. A girl doesn't have to be a maid because her mother was one."

"I want to be a maid," Mina said. "You have to wear a uniform like a soldier."

"Are you talkin' about the women who want the vote?" Mrs. Stroop asked. "That's not all they're goin' after. They don't want to be mothers or wives, but want free love and divorce, mind you. They want to be better than men and take up politics and smoking and drinking in bars, too. Shameful, I call it, sinful and against what St. Paul said in the Bible."

Mary Jane opened her mouth to argue, but Anneka said gently, "We didn't talk about any of that. Here is your payment. Thank you for seeing to Mina."

After Mrs. Stroop dropped the coins in her pocket and left, Mary Jane said, "Well, I guess we won't invite that sour old puss to go with us next time."

Anneka spoke to Mina in Swedish. The little girl ran down the hallway toward the bedrooms.

"You shouldn't say such things in front of Mina." Anneka sat in the arm chair across from Mary Jane. "I have no one to rely on when I need help with Mina but Mrs. Stroop. I don't want Mina to think poorly of her."

"I'm sorry." Chastened, Mary Jane added, "That will change when you marry Ross. He'll be a good father, and he'll help you with her. He helps—he helped—my mother all the time at home." She paused. "What was Mina's father like?"

"He is—was—a good man. Sometimes not always the wisest, not always thinking about what might be best. He never had to—he was handsome and rich. He was always a little, I don't know the word—"

"Rash?"

"What does that mean?"

"That he acted without thinking about what might happen later."

"Yes, that is the word. But still a nice man."

"What was his name?"

"Jakob."

"Do you have any portraits of him?"

"No, it was all lost on the ocean voyage."

"Oh, no!" Mary Jane said. "Were you shipwrecked?"

"No, nothing like that. I lost them, that's all."

She shrugged. Mina came from the bedroom, carrying her school books, and Anneka said, "Since Miss Mary Jane is here, you may sit on the floor and do your work at the coffee table."

That night, Mary Jane sits at the girlish desk in her bedroom, a sheet of paper with a half-written letter to Ross before her. Something has been bothering her since she came home from Miss Reston's and Anneka's houses. The stories that Miss Reston told of Paul echo in her mind. Why doesn't Anneka ever share detailed stories about Mr. Lindstrom? Not once has she volunteered how she met him or where they lived in Sweden or what he did for a living. Or how he died. She doesn't even seem to be particularly sorry that he passed away at such an early age.

She chews on her pen before she continues writing:

I don't want to stir up trouble, but certain things about Anneka seem odd. Please don't think I'm being petty, but how does she have the money to buy such nice clothes and furniture? I'm sure you've noticed that she has a full-length beaver coat, and that Mina has one that looks almost like it. No one I work with could afford such nice things, and surely we make more as typists at Graves Oil than a foreign maid makes working for old Mr. and Mrs. Graves.

That isn't all. Anneka told me she came from Sweden with her family when she was sixteen. Mina was born when she was seventeen, almost eighteen, but Jacob Lindstrom died in Sweden, and she has no photographs of him. Mina talks about someone named Mr. Yeem, who gave her the lovely doll. I don't know what kind of name "Yeem" is, but he sounds like a Chinaman to me.

How well do you really know Anneka? I worry that she hasn't told you everything about herself—

Mary Jane lifts her pen and skims over her words. Why would she express such misgivings about Anneka, of whom she is truly fond? Why raise such doubts for Ross, who is now aboard a ship bound for France? She isn't even sure that there is anything amiss in what Anneka has told her. Perhaps it is only, as her mother calls it, her own "snoopy, trouble-making way." Perhaps she misunderstood when Anneka explained her past or perhaps Anneka misspoke in English. Perhaps it is simply Anneka's cool Swedish nature that makes her so unsentimental.

Mary Jane wads up the letter and begins anew on a fresh sheet of paper: *Today, Anneka and I went to a meeting of the National Woman's Party . . .*

EIGHTEEN

It doesn't take long for the members of the Graves Family Foundation Relief Society to fall in love with Chaumont. Located atop a gentle hill, the walled and turreted town overlooks the verdant valleys of the Suize and Marne rivers. Beyond, leafy sycamores and blackish pines grow on the rolling hills. The town's spires and mansard roofs are so pristine and picturesque that the village could be the setting of a fairy tale.

Yet Chaumont is the most modern of towns. Trains spill thousands of khaki-clad American men onto the platforms each day, and more march into town over the roads that come from the south and west. American Negroes unload tons of supplies at the rail yards and haul them by mule train to the headquarters and beyond. Red Cross trains deliver a more delicate cargo in the form of soldiers bound for the wards of Base Hospital #15, where the iron beds measure only inches between them. Automobiles jam into the ancient, cobblestone streets, zipping past buildings with inches to spare.

The girls are billeted on the top floor of a spacious apartment house whose floor-to-ceiling windows overlook the Suize. From their room, they can see the former barracks of the French Army that now serve as the Headquarters of the American Expeditionary Force. The barracks form three sides of a sprawling square and are surrounded by an iron fence and a massive, ornamental gate. Hundreds of officers, aides, and support staff rush in and out of the barracks every day, and the Hello Girls of the Army Signal Corps also have offices there.

The most impressive sight in Chaumont is *Le Viaduc*, a graceful railway bridge of grayish-white stone that spans more than 2000 feet. Mrs. Brently takes the girls to see the bridge on the first Sunday of their stay in Chaumont. She translates from a French pamphlet: "'The bridge rises nearly 600 meters—'"

"Almost 200 feet," Kathleen supplies.

"'—into the sky in three tiers of arches. On the first or bottom tier, twenty-five arches set a solid base for the second and third tiers, which have forty-nine and fifty arches respectively. The viaduct was started in 1855. For fifteen months, more than 2,500 men and three-hundred horses working day and night—'"

Kathleen sketches the climbing arches as a train trundles across the bridge.

"Look at that," Hank says. "I don't think I've seen anything so lovely. It's so graceful."

As they reach the base of the bridge, it becomes apparent that the American soldiers have discovered that the lovely archways allow for a certain amount of privacy. In more than one cubby, the girls surprise a soldier and his young woman, kissing in one of the most romantic spots outside of Paris.

Mrs. Brently affects a haughty stance when they pass the couples, but Hank giggles and elbows Kathleen, who wishes that she could stand in the shadows with Paul, their arms around each other. A flight of stairs leads up to the first tier walkway. Looking down the length of it, the interior arches frame one another in a never-ending display.

Mrs. Brently pauses, seemingly taken in by the architecture.

"What is it?" Hank asks.

"My parents' house in Denver has a series of arches, very similar to this," she says. "I was reminded for a moment of home."

"Your house looks like this?"

Mrs. Brently laughs. "It isn't a bridge, if that's what you are imagining. And I am talking about, perhaps, eight or nine arches, not nearly fifty."

As Hank and Kathleen lean over the railing to look at the ground below, Mrs. Brently describes her parents' house in Cheesman Park, with its large rooms, Persian carpets, and art-laden walls. It is the first time she has revealed details of her personal life, and Hank laps up her words, her eyes bright with devotion.

"When we were young," Mrs. Brently says, "we used to hide behind the arches and jump out at one another."

"You and Mr. Graves?" Hank asks.

"Yes, and—"

Mrs. Brently stops, and Hank urges, "Your friends?"

"Yes, of course."

Mrs. Brently's eyes meet Kathleen's, and Kathleen knows that she is thinking of her brother and sister, Stephen and Elizabeth, who were lost in the mountain lake near the family's castle. Kathleen looks away, reminded of the drawing she did of Jim so long ago in Central Park. She had sensed then that his haunted memories of the accident would never subside. She wonders if Mrs. Brently—who was rescued by Stephen after plummeting into the water—has the same, or even more, darkness in her.

As if she's intuited Kathleen's thoughts, Mrs. Brently commands a little too sharply, "Come, we should be going back."

Hank and Kathleen were assigned to work as nurses' aides at Base Hospital #15. Many of the hospitalized suffered from disease or illness, but soon, wounded began to arrive from American-led battles at Cantigny, Seicheprey, and Xivray. The wards filled at an alarming rate, and the corridors and storage areas were cleared so that more cots could be set up. Kathleen wrote to her father:

I arrive in my ward, which has room for eight patients with stomach injuries, at 8:45 every morning. The first thing I do is to count my patients. Sometimes, the beds that were filled the night before are empty because someone has died. I start my day by waking all my patients and taking their temperatures and pulses. If I have a new patient, I pull off the dirty bandages that were applied at the Front and give him a sponge bath so that the doctor can examine the wound.

When the doctor arrives, I help with checking for infections and re-wrapping bandages. We use the Carrel-Dakin method of treating wounds. A glass bottle of Dakin's Solution, which is a scientifically-balanced mixture of bleach, baking soda, and purified water, is attached to a portable tree-like stand next to the bed. A rubber tube runs from its base into the open wound of the injured man. The flow of the solution can be regulated by a clamp and measured into a cup attached to the tubing. My job is to release the right amount of Dakin's Solution into the cup and then into the wound. I do this for all my patients every two hours from 10 in the morning until 6 at night.

It's a painful process, because the wounds have to be left open and the Dakin's Solution stings. Some of my patients close their eyes, or groan, and some of them can't keep tears from coming. I tell them that it will all be worth it, that they won't have an infection or gangrene, and that they'll be good as new, but I still feel sorry for them. Some of them have as many as six rubber tubes running into their bodies. For these boys, the Dakin's is agony.

After I take my noon meal in the Mess downstairs, I feed my patients. Quite a few of them can't cut their meat or even spoon food into their mouths, so I do it for them. In the afternoons, I take temperatures and pulses again, then close the drapes so that everyone can sleep. For an hour or so, I'm free to visit with Hank or the other Red Cross girls or to sketch and write letters. At four, I am back on the ward, waking my patients again for their sponge baths and a rubbing of aromatic vinegar scented with lavender or peppermint and talcum powder. At five, I serve the evening meal. After another round of Dakin's, I'm finished at 7 or so.

It sounds exhausting, and I suppose it is, but I don't notice, because we are here at last in the American sector, where everyone speaks English and we see the Stars and Stripes flying proudly from every building. I feel in a way as if I've come home.

Kathleen quickly learned that the Americans managed their wounded soldiers much differently than the French. Rather than evacuating the wounded from the *postes de secours* at the Front with only minimal treatment, the American medical personnel performed necessary surgeries and care at mobile units, then delivered patients to the base hospitals in convoys of trucks. As the stretchers arrived, orderlies examined the "ticket" affixed to each wounded man by the medical staff at the Front. The injuries were sorted, with similar types going to the same ward. Those with non-urgent wounds were put directly to bed with the belief that sleep was more important than immediate care for men who had been in the trenches for months.

The American hospital, too, was run much differently than those of the French or British. Rather than nuns or wealthy volunteers or refugee girls from Belgium or France, the American Army Nurses in the wards had practiced together as a team at Roosevelt Hospital in New York.

"It's been a big fight in the States," Hank told Kathleen. "Only women with college degrees who have worked as nurses can be sent to France. I guess President Wilson and the Army wanted to send just about anyone who volunteered as a nurse. "

"Who told you that?" Kathleen asked.

"Mrs. Brently," Hank said. "In fact, it was Mrs. Delano of the American Red Cross who insisted on it."

On a bright day in June, Kathleen found a Private named Arlington Davies in her ward. The nurse on duty warned her that he refused to talk to anyone, including the doctor. After Kathleen saw to his care, she offered him an assortment of magazines. He said nothing.

She tried again. "Is there something I can do for you, Arlington? Would you like me to write to your family? I'm sure they'd be happy to hear from you."

He made no reply.

"Do you have a girlfriend or wife who would want to hear from you? I can write a letter, if you don't feel up to it."

When he made no reply, she gave up. "I'll be back in a while to check on you."

She had already turned away when he exploded, "Tell them to go ahead and kill me!"

She started, and the cups on her tray clanked against one another. "Tell who to kill you?"

He pointed at a white bow tied to the end railing of his bed. "That means I'm done for, doesn't it?"

Kathleen swallowed her laughter. "It means you're restricted to a milk diet until your stomach is better. You aren't done for at all. You'll be the same as you always were in just a few days. I promise."

"Cross your heart and hope to die?"

"What?" Kathleen asked.

"It's an old country rhyme that you use when you want somebody to swear that it's so."

"All right," she agreed. "So, yes, cross my heart and hope to die."

"Stick a needle in your eye?"

She laughed. "That, too."

Arlington's face relaxed into a craggy grin. "You're an angel, ma'am! A real live angel!"

"Where are you from?"

"Odessa, Texas," he replied. "At home, I sell wage insurance, so that if somethin' like this"—he beckoned toward his bandage-wrapped torso—"happens to you, you get paid the same as you did when you was workin'."

"Is there anything you'd like me to get for you?"

"Some regular old Wrigley's chewin' gum, please, if you would, ma'am. This stuff they have here, I think it's made from old tires or somethin'."

The next day, Kathleen returned with chewing gum that she had found at a YMCA canteen in the center of Chaumont.

Yet, even though Kathleen had crossed her heart and hoped to die, and promised to stick a needle in her eye, the Texan was gone, his bed occupied by a ragged, unwashed sleeper.

NINETEEN

From the second seat of a bi-place Salmson, Paul scoured the ground. He lowered the binoculars and shouted at Kenny to descend to 600 meters altitude.

Kenny brought the plane into a sideslip, banking the wings while pointing the nose downward. Paul braced his feet against the movement and reached for a long-nosed pistol attached to the side of the plane. Cocking it, he fired a rocket that burst into a six-star pattern as it fell earthward. He peered through the binoculars again. Below, a white panel unfurled, pulsing in the wind, each corner held by a member of the infantry near the forward-most trench.

Catching movement to the left of the panel, Paul signaled to Kenny to fly in a tight figure-eight. Through the binoculars, he sighted a supply wagon and a number of troops on a slight knoll to the east of where the panel was fluttering. Beyond, more troops were moving forward along a road.

He reported on the wireless by speaking through the microphone around his neck: "Time: 15:17, Panel of 1st Division: 329.8-214.9. Wagon: 330.7-229.6. Approximately 150 troops on road: 332.3-233.7." There was no reply, for the transmission went only one way, due to the instability at the Front. Paul wrote out the same words on a form that had the heading: "*URGENT: Hand to Nearest Officer.*" He wrapped the paper around a metal weight. "I need to drop," he called.

Kenny swept the plane into an elongated circle. Paul's gaze alternated between the coordinates on the map and the ground below until he saw a stand of trees near a wide road. As Kenny brought the plane just over the treetops, Paul dropped the weighted message and someone ran from the trees to fetch it. The man disappeared into the cover of the wood again, and Paul called to Kenny, "Drop successful!" He had just delivered to the U.S. artillery the location of the front lines. Now, the Division and Corps Commanders would be able to stage the rolling barrage in the best way to protect the infantry.

As he glanced toward the Front again, he noticed a feeble two-star explosion well over the German lines. He grabbed his binoculars. A panel wallowed in a shell hole, barely visible from above.

"We have advanced troops!" he yelled to Kenny. "Give me another pass!"

Kenny banked the plane over the lake and flew back toward the battlefield, dropping in altitude for a better look. Paul recorded the coordinates of the panel that he had seen and then reported them through the wireless.

"Enemy planes!" Kenny shouted over his shoulder. "Ten o'clock!"

Paul braced the back of his thighs against the wall of the fuselage and grabbed one of the dual Lewis machine guns that were mounted on a tourelle near the tail of the plane. He pointed at the higher of the two enemy planes. As Kenny beat a hasty retreat, the enemies dodged and swept through the sky. Paul struggled to keep them in the gun's sight. At the same time, Kenny did a series of maneuvers— racing toward the ground, climbing upward again, banking first left and then right, entering a "vrille" or tail spin. At last, the enemy planes stole away, leaving Kenny and Paul in wide, open sky.

Paul relaxed as the wind rushed into his face. His eyes watered even beneath the heavy goggles, and the bitter cold bit at his ears through his leather cap. His neck prickled under the fur collar of the leather flight jacket, partly from the chill, partly from the exhilaration of the flight.

Kenny jogged the plane up and down as they came in toward the runway at Cazaux. Paul smiled. True to his flying style, Kenny fearlessly tested the capabilities of the Salmson in the air, doing vertical loops that barely cleared the treetops of the heavily forested hills, or flying inverted, or spinning downward in lazy spirals, all the while singing to himself "Oh, Oh, Oh, It's a Lovely War."

So far, Paul had not vomited.

Now, Kenny brought the biplane in smoothly on the ground. The two "enemy planes" landed just behind him.

The French flier from the first, Captain Renault, came to Paul as soon as he had rolled to a stop. "I think you would have taken me down," he said in accented English. "But you needed to watch what Monsieur Étienne"—he gestured toward the second enemy plane—"was doing. He could have come up underneath you."

"Yes, sir."

"And remember, there aren't always just *les deux avions*. There might be five or fifteen. You will not know until you are there, so you need to keep a 360 degree watch. It is never as clean or as easy as it was today."

"Yes, sir."

"Otherwise, that was a fine bit of observation, Lieutenant Reston. You found all the objectives. I will deliver a full recommendation as soon as I write the report."

Paul saluted. "Thank you, sir."

The Captain left, and Kenny went to get an assessment of his flying from Lieutenant Étienne. Paul headed toward the Mess Hall at Cazaux Aerodrome. Swanky, confident men filled the room—some in the sky blue uniforms of the French, some in the green-gray of the Italians, some in the drab of the British RAF. The men of the U.S. Army Air Service wore tan gabardine jackets with stand-up collars and sleeves. On each side where the collar closed were the letters "US." Nearly all of the aviators sported a Sam Browne belt over their uniforms and an officer's hat with the Army Eagle insignia center-front.

The Mess was usually boisterous with fliers comparing their flying skills or lobbing false criticism at one another, but today, it was louder than usual. Paul sat with Kenny, who had come in behind him. A former Yale student turned flier named Owen Chancellor sat down next to Kenny. His observer, Hugh Evans, took a seat next to Paul.

"What's going on?" Paul asked.

"It's the news from the Front," Hugh said. "The First Division has taken the town of Cantigny for itself, and we're fighting one hell of a battle at Chateau-Thierry and Belleau Woods. Maybe we'll win this goddamned war for the Frenchies!"

"Well, we all know we're going to do that," Kenny said. "It's just a matter of how fast we can do it."

"Lieutenant Reston!" someone called.

Paul raised a hand. A Corporal spotted him from across the room and brought him a handful of mail.

"What's all this?" Kenny asked.

At last, *la Poste Française* had caught up to Paul. Five letters had arrived—all of them with "Private Paul Reston" crossed out and rewritten as "Lieutenant Paul Reston." Further confusion had reigned about which branch of the service he was with; the letters had "United States Army Ambulance Service" and "United States Army Air Service"—both abbreviated USAAS—scratched out and rewritten at least once. Three of the letters were from Julia in Denver, but two precious letters came from Kathleen.

"You have a girl?" Kenny asked. "In France, no less?"

"She's with the Red Cross," Paul said. "She was in Amiens when it was evacuated."

"The Red Cross?" Owen laughed. "They can't even look at a man without getting in trouble."

"We learned that," Paul said, much to the amusement of the others.

He shoveled in his food as quickly as he could. After he finished, he went outside into the warmth of May on the Mediterranean. Behind the look-alike buildings of the Cazaux Aviation Instruction Camp were the rolling foothills of the Pyrenees and France's border with Spain. The Lac de Cazaux lapped right up to the steps of the aviators' housing. Trees grew on the hills, along the roads, and between some of the buildings—trees that had not been splintered into stumps, that harbored the nests of birds, and that offered miles of shade beneath their canopies.

He took a seat on a bench beneath an oak and opened the first letter from Kathleen.

Dear Paul,

Oh, I wish I knew where you are. We have arrived in Chantilly after the evacuation of Amiens. If you are still in Aumale, you are more than a hundred miles from me. If you receive this, please, please, write back to me as soon as you can. I have been so scared that we won't see each other again—

Anxious, he opened the second letter, which had been sent from Chaumont.

When we walk down the streets in Chaumont, we don't hear French spoken, but English, and we have yet to meet a man who is not wearing the khaki of the United States. Chaumont is called the "nerve of the Army," because it is at the center of all the American training camps and bases in the Toul area.

The place is full of officers from every branch of the military, including the Navy, which seems odd since we are near the eastern border of France. General Pershing lives in a chateau about five miles away. He arrives in the barracks where we work in a long, olive drab car that shines like a mirror and has a flag flying from it. In town, all the hotels and homes with spare rooms have been taken over by the thousands of Americans who are billeted here.

The funny thing is, now that we are among our own kind, I realize how much I miss home. I was fine, as long as I heard French or British English spoken around me. Yet when I hear our soldiers talking, I close my eyes and imagine I am on 17th Street in Denver, about to enter the alley near Graves Oil, ready to spend a day in the typing room.

I must be very homesick if I'm longing for Miss Crawley and her ridiculous ruler—

Paul skimmed through to her parting sentiments: *I miss you so. I want to live every day we had together again. I would do so much more, and I would say so much more, and you wouldn't be able to stop me from kissing you. I'd tell you every minute how much I love you—*

"Moi aussi, mon amour, moi aussi," he whispered to himself.

With relief, he folded the letter. She was safe; she was no longer on the move through this strife-ridden country. Longing came over him: to see her, to talk to her, to hold her against him, to kiss her again. His desire brought a tingling to his palms, dryness to his mouth. Taking paper and pen from his rucksack, he wrote:

Dearest Kathleen,

You'll see my new address on the envelope. You may be surprised by what I've done, but my long story has what I consider to be a happy ending. I've signed up for a "second act" by volunteering for the AEF's Aerial Observer program. More than 300 observers are needed, but so far, only 80 men have come to the French Camp d'Instruction de Cazaux. We're supposed to be getting more from the States, but because of the lack of training facilities there, they'll be inexperienced and nowhere near ready to face the Germans.

We take classes here that remind me of my college days in that there is so much to learn. I've learned about the construction and operation of the airplane and machine gun, and the theory of radio transmission, and the nature of poison gas, and that's just the beginning. I believe I will be a fine observer. I seem to have exceptionally good recall of terrain and landmarks, and I read maps well. Other skills, such as staying cool in the face of danger, having plenty of nerve, and being able to make decisions quickly, I learned from being an ambulance driver.

The best part is that I am content again—at least, as content as someone at war and separated from his beloved can be. I am among men that I went to college with, and I am again using my wits and knowledge in my work. My day starts before dawn when I report to the mess, where my pilot Kenny McKenzie, who roomed with me at Yale, and I receive our orders for the day. Next, I go to the Observers' Room to collect my maps. Sometimes I have to create them myself. We have a store of ink, pencils (although none are colored, as yours are) and pens, glue, paste, thumb tacks, paints for coloring terrain, and magnifying glasses for our art that you would envy. We've found that the maps designed by the French in the middle of the last century are either too crowded or have been worked over so many times that they are useless, so we've devised our own system of grids that we lay over the map. Each square is one kilometer, and we assign our own system of coordinates to the points.

My maps ready, I join Kenny at the plane, which the enlisted crew has rolled from the hangar. They've also filled the fuel tanks, greased up every joint with castor oil, and started the engine by twisting the propeller by hand. While Kenny checks over all the parts and the engine, I make sure that the mounted machine guns are calibrated and loaded with one of the six magazines that are carried on board. Once the plane is ready, we do a short flight, during which I test my sights and the wireless set. If we don't have any problems with engine or communication, we're ready to go.

I am hoping to get leave and come to Chaumont to see you. You don't know how relieved I am that you're safe and away from the Front. You would love Cazaux. It is probably as pretty as Nice, but it will never be as beautiful to me as the beech tree on the hill in Amiens. I relive that day almost every night, wishing I was kissing you still.

À toi, pour toujours,

Paul

As he finished the letter, a voice niggled at him. In mentioning the beech tree, he would undoubtedly raise the specter of Maurice, the pilot in Amiens. Taking up the pen again, he added:

P.S. Please don't worry about me now that I am a birdman, as we're called. Kenny is an excellent flier, and we have done well when "huffing" or practicing dogfight maneuvers. The real change is my role in this war. I have given up my neutral stance, the one that I held proudly when I drove for Harjes, but I am, at last, fighting for America, my own country. Of that, I am equally proud.

TWENTY

Seated at the letter writing station at a YMCA canteen in Choloy, Sean opened the plain black book that was now his diary. The soft-leather journal that Brendan had given him when he left America had long since been filled. This one, a "Daily Reminder" book purchased at the Y, had faint lines on its inner pages, and the edges weren't trimmed in gilt, as the first had been. It was ugly, but so was much of what he'd written in it. He shook his cuff back from his wrist and wrote:

We came into town yesterday, after hitching a ride in a convoy of trucks, which our sore and blistered feet were happy to see. Once here, we were turned out to go to the delousing station. We all had a good bath, and were given new underclothes, socks and uniforms. We've been in the trenches so long that just about everyone and everything is worn thin. Mules, men, socks and shoes—all of it. Rumor says that we're to go on to the Front near Rheims next week, but who knows? It's all wait and guess in this war.

On our way here, we marched through the Belleau Woods, where a terrible battle between our Marines and the Germans was fought. I'd heard about it—we all have—because the woods were conquered foot by foot, at great cost to both the Marines and the civilians in the area. Lucy, Bouresches, Torcy, and some of the other towns are now nothing more than heaps of stone, and the railroad tracks have been torn apart into twists of steel and wood.

We could smell the woods long before we came to them. You would never believe it, the way this country smells. It's the smell of meat that has been left too long in sun, of the maggoty rabbit kits that Mag and I used to find in the garden. It's the smell that drives the cattle wild when they reach the slaughterhouse, that stench of guts and blood. In the railway cuts, German soldiers had crawled between the high banks to die. One after another, they lay near the wrenched-up steel of the tracks. The flies rose in great black clouds, their buzzing like the sound of an approaching vehicle. We could see bodies from where we stood all the way to the horizon. All in their beloved feld-grau, all in the agonies of death.

Wheat fields rolled off on the other side of the tracks. From a distance, they were beautiful, stretching for miles in the bright sun. But as we came closer, we saw that the wheat was dug through by lines of gun-pits. Here, then a few feet further, then a few feet more, until the luckless soldier met his end. Hundreds of men lay where they had fallen, the bayonets of their guns thrust into their bodies and their identification tags wound around the triggers until the time when the area is cleaned up and they're buried.

"They're us," Tony said, and I haven't been able to forget those words. They're us, Americans, men that we may have seen marching past us, or billeted in a village a few miles away, or in the YMCA canteen on Saturday night. The Marines had to advance just a mile from Lucy, I've heard, just a mile, and more than half of them fell in that time. It's enough to break your heart.

Just beyond the wheat fields, the woods began. The trees in Belleau grew dense and black, but they're shattered now, the tops blown off by the shells. Bodies and equipment were caught up on the leafless limbs, and horses and mules were bloating in the heat. Where the Germans had been, soldiers lay where they had died, left behind in the quick retreat. They sprawled over their wrecked machine guns or lay on their back in gun-pits, gaping up at the sky, looking as if they were watching birds or clouds. We marched on, the bodies multiplying the deeper we moved into the woods. At some point, we came to a sheltered clearing where the dressing station must have stood. Blood had stained the ground a rusty black, and amputated limbs had been pitched between the stumps of trees. The *flies feasted there by the thousands. They swarmed around us, too, sweaty and filthy as we were, as if we were next meal.*

Then, we came to a scene that could only be found in the darkest nightmare. Germans who had died early in the fight, maybe as much as three weeks ago, had been piled in heaps but not buried. Their faces and features were gone, and only their uniforms and boots marked them as men. Otherwise, they were melting piles of raw meat. Against one tree, a soldier sat, his skull shot away, and his head broken and hollow, brains and eyes gone, the flies so thick that the skull was black—

Sean looked up unsteadily from the page. At a table across the room from him, four men were playing poker, their heads wreathed in smoke from cigars. A soldier in a heavy woolen American cap played the piano, while two others sang in what was supposed to be harmony, but which sounded flat even to Sean's tin ear.

Yesterday, as they were about to leave the woods and the carnage behind, Tony had stumbled and fallen onto one knee. Sean had caught his arm and lifted him up, but Tony had seemed unable to gain his balance again. Michael and Sean had flanked him until they had come to a clearing, which—thank God—was free of bodies. There, the unit halted, the men simply staring, silent, unable to speak, maybe, or to put words to what they had just seen.

"Are you okay?" Sean had asked Tony.

"What did I trip over?" Tony asked. "What the hell did I trip over?"

"I don't know."

For the rest of the march, Tony had avoided Sean and the others, and he had not spoken to any of them since. Sean understood. To fall in that carnage, to be on the ground among the corpses and maggots, the pieces that were once men, how could a man ever stand again, be able to walk and breathe and eat again? In being so surrounded by death, how did he know he was still living?

He writes again: *I thought when I came over here that I'd feel some sense of pride or satisfaction of something. I thought I was doing what was right. But there's no such thing. You tear up a man so he won't tear you up first. You kill him, and then you search his pockets and pack for tobacco and food, because you're hungry or want a smoke, or you want a souvenir to send home. But regardless of what you find to eat or smoke or sell or take home with you, it doesn't matter. You're rotten, stinking, might as well be dead yourself. Your mind is filthy, your body, your entire soul is dead just because you've been here and you've seen what you've seen and done what you've done.*

Sean closed his diary, unwilling to think about it any longer. Scooting back his chair, he went outside. The air was still warm and humid, the summer in its fullness. Choloy was beautiful, surrounded by fields and low hills. In the west, the sunset spread yellow-orange across the azure sky.

He walked along the main street, which was crowded with American soldiers and wagon trains, toward the fields where the troops trained. He found Tony seated in a grandstand that had been erected next to the parade ground. The field beyond had been plowed over into a baseball diamond.

Sean climbed up the steps and sat next to Tony. He did not recognize anyone on the field; the players must be from one of the other battalions or from the ranks of the engineers, who followed the troops, rebuilding the wreckage as best they could.

At the break in the inning, Sean asked, "Do you play this game?"

"We played it in Brooklyn," Tony said. "In the street, not on any place like this. What about you?"

"Not much," Sean said. "With the Irish, it's boxing."

Tony exhaled smoke. "They said I could be an American citizen if I went to war," he said bitterly. "That's all it would take. I wouldn't be Italian no more, I'd be American if I went and killed two Germans. So I did what they said."

Sean watched as a soldier struck out on the field.

"How many have I killed now?" Tony asked. "I don't know. I don't count. But I done my two. I better be an American now."

"Have you gotten your papers?"

"Nobody says nothing about it now, over here. Maybe it's not still true."

On the field, the batter hit the ball in a straight shot into the outfield. The runner sprinted around the bases and stopped at third.

"Why are you here?" Tony challenged. "You're already an American. You don't need it."

"I don't know. I didn't want to work with my father anymore, and there wasn't much else I could do. It's hard to find a job when you have an Irish name. I wanted to make something of myself, I guess."

"When I come to Brooklyn from Italy, I was seventeen," Tony said. "My father had gone to *l'America* ten years before, and he promised to come back for us, but he didn't. He sent one letter, that's it. He said, 'It snows in New York.' That's the only thing I remember from it. 'It snows in New York.' Then, he's gone, like he's not there no more, and we never hear from him again."

A crack of the bat resounded, and the ball flew up, was caught and thrown to first base. A few of the spectators applauded.

"In Italy, we walked three hours to our fields, every day, to work there. We had this orchard there, with pears and cherries and fig trees, and some pigs and chickens, and the grapes on the hillsides, and we would eat what we found on the ground, as long as Mamma don't catch us. That was our meals every day—whatever we could get in our mouths before we got beaten."

Sean laughed, but Tony shrugged. "In the summer," he said, "snakes crawled all over the ground because it was so hot. I hated them. So I thought it would be better in America, because my Papà never talks of snakes. Only snow. So me and my brothers Guarino and Pietro go to New York to see snow."

"What did you think of it?"

Tony flipped his cigarette butt onto the ground. "Papino didn't tell us it was cold, so now, I hate snow."

"Is it worse than the snakes?"

A batter hit a ball high up in the air. Tony watched as it came down into the mitt of the shortstop, ending the inning. "Maybe," he said. "I don't know. I have forgotten what it's like. The snakes, the snow. Everything, I have forgotten everything."

Sean understood that, too. Men forgot who they were here. They did stupid things, things they would never do at home. Lutheran boys from Minneapolis drank, Mormon farm boys from Utah brawled over cigarettes. They were brutal to the French whores and to each other. And to themselves. They walked into battle without their tin hats, or rushed over the top during bombardments or gas attacks, asking for death. More than one Doughboy came out of the jump-off trench laughing or singing with his fellow soldiers, ignoring the bullets and shrapnel that split open the air.

Because in the end, they could all end up in a place as foul and dark as the Belleau Woods.

"Did you find your father in New York?" he asked Tony.

"No," Tony said. "Somebody tells us he's in Montana at the copper mines. Maybe when I get back, I can see if I can find him."

"Montana's not far from Colorado. Come find me in Denver, and we'll go together—"

Tony straightened up, and Sean saw that Lieutenant Morgan was headed their way.

"*Merda*," Tony muttered. "Now what?"

Both men stood and saluted the Lieutenant. After a quick return, Lieutenant Morgan addressed Sean. "Corporal Sullivan, Major Buell wants to see you."

"What?" Sean said.

Lieutenant Morgan made no effort to reprimand him. "I'm to escort you to his office now."

Sean glanced at Tony, who shrugged his shoulders. Some of the other men in the grandstands murmured as Sean followed Lieutenant Morgan down the steps.

As they left the parade ground for the administration building— once a hotel—on the main street, Lieutenant Morgan said, "I have no idea what this is about. Do you?"

"No, sir," Sean said.

"You didn't write a complaint of some kind about how your easily-insulted Irish temperament is always being tested, did you?"

"No, sir. I did not."

Two American captains, including Sean's own, Captain Decker, met them in the lobby of the hotel. After a round of salutes, Captain Decker said, "Major Buell is in the dining room."

The dining room had been turned into a war room. Desks formed neat rows near the swinging kitchen doors, while the dining tables were laid out with maps and instruments. Armchairs and a sofa clustered near a central fireplace. Major Buell signaled to Sean to take a seat in the armchair next to him. Lieutenant Morgan and Captain Decker sat on the couch, while the third captain bustled away, charged with fetching coffee and tea.

As soon as the tray arrived, Major Buell offered a drink to Sean.

"No, thank you, sir," Sean said tightly. What had he done wrong? He hadn't tangled with Danhour or anyone else, lately, and as far as he knew, he hadn't been disobedient in any way. At least, he didn't think he had been. Certainly not enough to attract the attention of a Major.

"You're Sean Sullivan of Denver, Colorado," Major Buell said. "That's correct, isn't it?"

"Yes, sir."

"Tell us about growing up in Denver."

Sean shot a questioning look toward Lieutenant Morgan, but his face was rigid and blank. "I grew up in Berkeley Park, just west of the city—"

"You're Catholic, correct?"

He shifted nervously. "Yes, sir."

"Do you know Mr. Liam Hennessey Keohane?"

"Liam?" Sean asked, bewildered. "Yes, sir, he's my brother-in-law, married to my sister, Maggie—that is, Margaret Mary."

"Did you see Mr. Keohane often when you were in Denver?"

"Yes, sir, nearly every day. He was usually at our house in the evenings to see Maggie."

"He's a friend?"

"Yes, sir, he and his brother, Brendan, were—"

"When was the last time you saw him?"

"He and Maggie saw me off at the train station—Union Station—in Denver, when I left for Camp Funston at Fort Riley. They weren't married yet, because she hadn't graduated—"

"Did he say anything at that time that made you think he was not wholly supportive of the war?"

Sean faltered, remembering how annoyed he had been by Liam's posturing. "He spoke out against the war, he always has. He thought conscription was unfair to the working man who just wanted to stay with his family and earn a decent wage." He paused, afraid he had said too much. "What's this all about, if I may ask, sir?"

Major Buell eyed Captain Decker.

"You'll know in a moment," Captain Decker said.

"Has Mr. Keohane written to you?" Major Buell asked.

"Yes, sir," Sean said. "He's not only my brother-in-law, but we've been friends since we were boys at Church together—"

"Do you have those letters? We need to see them."

"Yes, sir, but I don't think I've received any from him lately."

Major Buell nodded. "In his letters, did he mention anything about supporting the German war effort?"

"What?" Sean blurted. "Never!"

"Perhaps you should see this."

Captain Decker laid a copy of the *New York Times* in front of him. The front page headline declared: AMERICA'S YELLOWEST SLACKER SENT TO CAMP DODGE FOR COURT-MARTIAL

As Sean read the first paragraph, his stomach twisted. The article claimed that Liam had been removed from Fort Logan, Colorado, where he had been held since March, to Camp Dodge, Iowa, for his own safety. "The number of lynch mobs and vigilantes that have plagued Fort Logan while Mr. Keohane was being held there," it read, "necessitated his removal. It has long been known that Mr. Keohane has been writing letters to President Wilson,

Henry Ford, the Pope and others that express his objections to the war from the confines of his prison cell. He refuses to stop these unpatriotic activities even though he has been treated fairly and even leniently by the United States Army, which has offered him a number of—"

The article continued in the next column at the top of the page, but when Sean shifted his gaze, he realized that all of the eyes in the room were on him. An itchy sweat broke out on his forehead and back. Surely this wasn't true—it must be a mistake or a trick of Lieutenant Morgan's or Danhour's. Neither Ma nor Maggie had written a word to him about it.

"This is the first I've seen of this," he said weakly. "I . . . I didn't know."

"There's some speculation that this man is a German spy," Major Buell said. "Think carefully, son. Did he ever ask you to send him information about where troops were located or what maneuvers or action might be taken?"

"No, sir . . . I . . . No."

"You realize, Corporal, that this man's defiance threatens our entire country and our success in this war. Anyone connected with him is bound to be suspect."

The words rattled around in Sean's brain before he realized their import. "Me?" he asked. "Sir, I serve the best I know how—"

"Have you ever expressed any opinions that are sympathetic with the German cause?"

"No. Absolutely not. Never."

"Have you ever spoken about being discouraged by the war or about wanting to go home?"

"I want to go home, sir," Sean said. "Of course, I want to go home—"

"Major, if I may speak." Lieutenant Morgan addressed Major Buell. "Corporal Sullivan is a dutiful soldier. He often volunteers for extra details and—"

The Major cast Lieutenant Morgan a look that silenced him. "You and Captain Decker will escort Corporal Sullivan to his quarters"—the Major eyed Sean again—"where you will turn over any letters you have received from Liam Keohane since you enlisted and any other correspondence that Captain Decker feels should be examined."

"Yes, sir."

Dismissed, Sean walked back to the thrown-together barracks between Captain Decker and Lieutenant Morgan. Beside the bunk that he shared with Kevin, he dug through his pack for the bundle of letters that he had faithfully kept since he had left America.

Handing the bundle to Captain Decker, he said, "These are from my mother and sister, and from Liam, and from other folks in the parish, and my aunt and uncle, too. Some of them are from my cousin, Kathleen, who is here in France."

"Your cousin?" Captain Decker said. "What's she doing here?"

"She's with the Red Cross. She's—well, they move around some, but the last letter I got, she was in Chaumont. She may have moved, for all I know."

"Surely you know that Chaumont is the Headquarters of the American Expeditionary Force," Captain Decker said. "Has she ever spoken out against the war?"

"I don't know. I can't think that she did if she's willing to come over here."

"How did she come to be with the Red Cross?"

"I don't know. I had already left for Fort Riley, I, I think she just wanted to get away from home and her job, so she applied."

Captain Decker turned the bundle of letters over in his hands.

"Surely you don't need them all?" Sean protested. "They're important to me. I look through them sometimes when I miss—"

"We'll see." The Captain straightened up. "What is your cousin's name?"

With a sinking feeling, Sean gave Kathleen's name and the information about the Graves Family Foundation Relief Society. "Sir," he asked. "Will I get my letters back once they've been approved?"

"That will be up to Major Buell."

The officers left, and Sean set about putting his things in order. As he did, his diary spilled out of the pocket of his coat where he'd stashed it earlier. Thank God he wasn't foolish enough to tell them that he kept a record. He found the pages he had just written about Belleau Woods. Remembering Major Buell's question about discouraging thoughts, he tore them from the book and wadded them up. He would burn them later.

Tony appeared in the aisle at the end of the bunk, Kevin behind him.

"What was that about?" Tony asked.

Sean's heart pounded, in shame, in fear. "Nothing."

"You weren't promoted or anything?" Kevin asked.

"No."

Across the room, he caught sight of Danhour, who smirked. At once, Sean knew that Lieutenant Morgan had told him.

He lay down on his bunk and covered his face with his arm. What was happening? Little Liam, as Ma used to call him, who loved to read and to work with his hands in the garden or building birdhouses, who prayed twice as hard as any other boy Sean knew, except for Brendan, and who served as altar boy twice as often as the rest of them. Liam, who grew up to be the man Maggie loved with the kind of bright-eyed, unwavering devotion that every man longed for.

Homesickness rampaged through his gut, hurting so badly that he rolled to one side and doubled up.

TWENTY-ONE

After a brief stint at Base Hospital #15, the Graves Family Foundation Relief Society was assigned to the canteen at the AEF Headquarters in Chaumont. Every soldier in the American Expeditionary Force seemed to march into, out of, or through Chaumont. Most of them were new to France, having landed in Bordeaux only days before, but some were on leave from the trenches.

"You've heard what's happening up at Xivray, haven't you?" a bright-eyed soldier asked Kathleen. "The Americans are givin' the Heines the dickens. We're just here for a few days before we go up for the big battle."

"They won't last another month," another American assured her. "You just watch. It's gonna be big."

In July, the mail from Amiens caught up to them.

Hank sorted through it at the girls' third floor apartment. "Oh, there's a letter from my mother and my sister, and one from your father, and, oh, there's a package here for you, too."

Kathleen rose from the chair beside the window, where she had been sketching. "Is it from Paul?" she asked.

"No, it's from Mr. Graves."

"I'm not expecting—"

"What do you think it is? Shake it."

"It might be breakable."

"A diamond ring isn't breakable."

"It isn't a diamond ring," Kathleen protested.

She was surprised that Mrs. Brently had given the box to Hank. Usually, she delivered Jim's correspondence to Kathleen in private.

But after Nice, perhaps Mrs. Brently felt that there wasn't anything to hide. To appease Hank, Kathleen held the package to her ear and shook it, but there was only a muffled thump.

She removed the brown paper wrapping. On top of a simple wooden box lay a note that read: *As promised, Jim*

Hank snatched the note. "What did he promise you? Oh, Kathleen—"

When she lifted the lid of the box, the smell of pine wafted from it. She picked up two large lumps wrapped in fine paper. Inside were pine cones still attached to twigs of bristling Ponderosa pine needles.

"He sent you pine cones?" Hank scoffed.

Kathleen said nothing. She remembered telling Jim in Nice that she wished she had something to remind her of Redlands. She had teased him that he might muddy his boots, and he'd said, "That's a risk I'll have to take."

She smiled at the memory. For some reason, tears formed in her eyes as well.

"Why would he send you pine cones?" Hank asked.

"Because I"—Kathleen's throat tightened—"I asked for them."

"Why?" Hank peered into the box. "What else is in there?"

Kathleen picked up a fine linen handkerchief with its corners neatly tied. It held an assortment of small rocks: petrified wood, white quartz, a few flakes of mica, bluish feldspar, others she couldn't name.

"Did you ask for those too?" Hank asked.

"Yes, I wanted something that reminded me of home."

"So, what's in the pouch?"

She tugged at the leather drawstrings and poured reddish sand into her palm.

"He sent your dirt?" Hank's incredulity spilled over. "All that money, and he sends you rocks and dirt."

Redlands. Kathleen could smell it in the grainy sand that was sprinkled with specks of quartz, mica and feldspar, in the dust that lifted up from it in a tiny cloud. A dot of mica stuck to her skin, and memories washed over her: the smell of the fall leaves beneath the scrub oak, the black grease on Papa's hands, the strong soap that Mama used in the ringer washer, the hay in the barn loft.

"Maybe that was the diamond ring," Hank suggested. "But just like all the other packages we've gotten, it didn't survive *La Poste Française.*"

Kathleen didn't laugh. She might cry if she did.

She wondered if Jim had known how much receiving this package would mean to her, or how deeply it would affect her. How it would make her want to tell him how much, how dear, how warmly she appreciated him and his thoughtfulness.

As Hank continued to tease, she poured the sand back into the pouch and folded the handkerchief over the rocks. After she closed the box, the smell of pine lingered. She set the box next to the head of her bed, where it could find its way into her dreams.

On a sweltering day in July, Mrs. Brently and Kathleen stood at the cutting block, making sandwiches for the troops. Sweat collected beneath Kathleen's wimple and in the pits of her arms. Without Helen, canteening had become strenuous work. All day, nearly every day, Mrs. Brently rolled dough for donuts and Hank made sandwiches, while Kathleen served coffee and lemonade. On busy days, Hank and Kathleen served hundreds of meals to the incoming American soldiers, who were overjoyed to find American girls in the canteen.

Hank came from the back of the canteen. "There's a soldier to see you," she said to Kathleen. "He just knocked at the door and asked if you could meet him outside."

Kathleen's heart tattooed. "Is it—?"

"No," Hank said. "It's an American Doughboy, and he's *ooh-la-la!* You have to introduce me to him."

Kathleen looked to Mrs. Brently for permission.

"I had better go with you," Mrs. Brently said.

Hank followed them outside.

The courtyard of the barracks was filled with American men leaning against the walls, sitting on the gravel, gathered around trucks or cars, smoking, eating, or drinking from their canteens. Rucksacks and rifles were piled in khaki mountains, and equipment, sheddite bombs, sandbags, and lumber were assembled in carefully-guarded mounds. In the bright light of the day, the soldiers all looked the same.

"Kathleen! Over here!"

She searched for a moment, then flew across the courtyard. "Seaney, oh, Seaney!"

He wrapped his arms around her and held her close.

"Oh, how are you?" she cried. "I'm so glad you're here. How did you find me? Are you in Chaumont for long—?"

"May I ask who this is?" Mrs. Brently's voice cut through Kathleen's questions.

Kathleen stepped away from Seaney. "This is my cousin, Private Seaney Sullivan—"

"It's Corporal Sean Sullivan, ma'am," Seaney said.

"Corporal!" Kathleen said. "This is Mrs. Brently, and Hank—Harriet Mills."

As Seaney shook their hands, Kathleen became aware of three dark-complexioned men standing nearby. With them was a raw-boned, freckled, strawberry blond boy. Seaney turned to them. "This is Corporal Necchi," he said. "And Private Giordano and Private—"

"Tony." The most handsome of the three men spoke. His curly black hair was combed back from his forehead, and his eyes were a rich brown in the sunlight. His skin was the color of rye bread. "This place," he said. "It's like America in France. I'm Tony from Brooklyn, right over there past them buildings."

Kathleen and Hank laughed, and Seaney gestured toward the boy. "This is Private Kevin O'Neal."

Kevin grabbed Kathleen's hand. "I've heard about you since I met Sean in Kansas."

"That long!" Kathleen laughed. "You must be bored by now!"

"Not by a long shot. I—"

"Can you come with me?" Seaney asked impatiently. "Just for a while?"

Kathleen looked toward Mrs. Brently, who nodded. "But we must be getting back to the canteen," she said. "We probably have men clamoring for coffee and donuts by now. Come along, Hank. Gentlemen, feel free to join the line."

Reluctantly, Hank followed Mrs. Brently back to the building, while Seaney and Kathleen started toward the gates of the compound. Kevin and the three Italian men sauntered toward the canteen, evidently intent on going inside.

Seaney watched them go. "Weren't there four of you?"

"We've had a thinning of the ranks."

"So have we."

"I hope your friends like to flirt. Hank excels at it."

"Tony does, too," he said. "The other two don't speak that much English. But Tony will have your friend singing 'O Sole Mio' like a true Italian before the evening is over. He's done it with all the French girls. And Kevin has enough 'How Are You Going To Keep 'Em Down on the Farm' stories to last until midnight."

Kathleen laughed. "Oh, I'm so glad to see you. You'll have to let me sketch you for Aunt Maury. She'll be so happy that I've seen you!"

"Just about every letter, she asks me if I've seen you. She thinks France is like a neighborhood—the Eiffel Tower in the middle and the trenches on either side."

Kathleen laughed. "She asks me the same about you. I sometimes think that she thinks you're the only American soldier in France."

Outside the gates of the compound, they walked along the cobblestone streets, barely glancing at the quaint, mansard-roofed homes and picturesque gardens of the town. They talked of home, of their parents and the Church, of gossip that had been passed along in letters.

Seaney walked with a pounding stride, as if he needed to get somewhere quickly. Kathleen worried. She had read of soldiers who grew tense and nervous, and who could not return to normal living. She hoped he hadn't changed; oh, how she hoped he was the same, old hot-headed Seaney.

Suddenly, he said, "There's something I need to talk to you about."

Kathleen felt a stab of panic. "What is it? Nothing's gone wrong at home, has it?"

"Well, sort of," he hedged. "Liam is in trouble."

"Liam!" Kathleen said. "How could he be in trouble? He's the best—"

"I was called in a few weeks ago, before our last trip up to the trenches, to talk with a Major Buell," he said. "It's all unbelievable."

As they walked toward the river, Seaney told her about Liam's refusal to serve in the military and his imprisonment. "It was on the front page of the *New York Times*." Seaney fished in his pocket. "I brought it to you. Read it for yourself."

Breathless, she sat on a stone bench and read: "'Mr. Keohane's resistance is an embarrassment and insult to American patriotism in the eyes of Russia and America's wartime allies. In the opinion of the editors of this newspaper, Mr. Keohane deserves the punishment for all traitors, which is death by firing squad—'"

She covered her mouth. "Oh, no, Seaney!"

"I sent a cable home to Ma," he said. "But I didn't hear a word back. She was probably scared to death when she got it and hasn't forgiven me yet, but Uncle Irish wrote me a letter."

"Papa?"

"He said it's all true," Seaney said. "Liam was arrested a few days before Easter and sent to Fort Dodge in Iowa in May, only a couple of weeks after Alice Colleen was born. They're planning to court-martial him, even though he is a civilian—"

"Why didn't anyone tell us?"

"Uncle Irish said it's because Ma and Auntie Eileen didn't want us to worry, seeing as how we're so far from home—"

"But, now, we've found out from a newspaper that's two months old and have no idea what's happening today!"

"I doubt they thought it would be in the *New York Times*."

"But Liam, oh, I still can't believe it. Poor Maggie. And the baby!—oh, poor thing!"

"I don't know what to write to her," he admitted. "Do I tell her what I think about it?"

"What do you think?"

He looked toward the river, where colorful houseboats were moored. Children bounced on and off the docks, and dogs—neither starved nor vicious—chased ducks or lapped up the river water.

"I don't know," he said haltingly. "How can I forgive him when I see our own soldiers shot down one after another before they've—"

He stopped, and Kathleen said nothing.

"He should just do what he's supposed to do," Seaney said. "Just like the rest of us are. There are plenty of us who don't want to be here."

"I wonder what Mrs. Brently would say about it."

"I'm afraid it might catch up to you," Seaney warned. "I told Major Buell about you. I had to. They took my letters, every last one that I'd gotten since I left home. I never got them back, and now Captain Decker is gone and we've moved again, and there's no one to ask."

"Then I'll write to you twice as often," she said. "Or will you have to turn those over, too?"

"Lieutenant Morgan has taken to opening my letters for me," Seaney said bitterly. "It's been great fun for everyone but me. They know things about me that I'd never want them to."

"Such as?"

"That I'm called 'Seaney.' They've had a field day with that."

"I'm sorry."

"It doesn't matter. I'm not well-liked anyway."

"But your friends—"

"We're all Catholic," he said bluntly. "Sometimes, Lieutenant Morgan sends us all out on raids together. I think he's hoping we won't come back." He shrugged. "What about you? You're looking well."

She turned toward him. "Oh, Seaney, I've met the most wonderful man. Oh, I wish you could meet him. You'd like him so much. He came here to drive an ambulance for the French—"

"He's French?"

"He's American. He went to Yale University, and his aunt lives in Denver—"

"I thought all those types went home when the AEF arrived because they were afraid they'd have to fight."

"That's not true!" Kathleen protested. "And they're not afraid of fighting. They've been on the front lines for years, and they've seen just about everything."

"Huh," Seaney said skeptically. "Better tell me about him then."

As they walked along the banks of the Suize River, she told him about Paul. Near the end, her worries overcame her. "I haven't heard from him for a while. I don't know where he is."

"Well, you know how the mail is," Seaney said. "There's nothing for weeks, and then you get *beaucoup* letters. Everything in this country is either *beaucoup* or *rien*. Cold, food, marching."

"Not for us. It's always *beaucoup de travail*."

"You must have learned pretty good French by now."

"Not as much as you'd think." She laughed. "Paul loves to tease me about my accent. He grew up in Paris and sounds right at home."

"You really love him, don't you? I can tell by your face."

"You aren't going to tease me about blushing, are you?"

"You're not blushing," Seaney said. "You're . . . well, I'd call it sparkling. Like water."

"Sparkling!" Kathleen laughed. "I love him more than I've ever loved anyone."

"Well, if that's so, you'd better go for it. Is he Catholic?"

"No," she said, then ventured tentatively, "Do you care that he isn't?"

"I don't know. For Mag, yes, I can't see her with anyone but Liam. For me, there's nothing but a Catholic girl. But for you, well, you've never been one to—"

He let a shrug fill in the words for him.

She wrapped her hands around his arm and hugged him against her. "Thank you, Seaney."

He motioned toward the west. "It's getting dark. We should go back."

When they returned to the canteen, they found that Kevin and the others had taken a table close to the counter. Tony stood nearby, a concertina in his hands, singing "O Sole Mio" as Hank watched dreamily. Even Mrs. Brently had paused in her work to listen.

Seaney smirked at Kathleen. "What did I tell you?"

She laughed as she went back to the counter and donned her apron.

Throughout the evening, Kathleen kept watch on Seaney. As Tony made Hank flutter around him and the other Italians soaked up coffee and donuts, Seaney sat at the edge of the group, quiet, almost wary. He held himself tightly, stiffly, with a granite-like shell that Kathleen had never seen before.

She asked Mrs. Brently if she could be excused to talk to Seaney. Mrs. Brently agreed, and Kathleen ran to her apartment to fetch the box that Jim had sent her. Seated at the table in the canteen, she showed it to Seaney. "This all came from Redlands."

He fingered the items. "Why did he send you this?"

"He wanted to send me something that reminded me of home." She undid the drawstrings of the pouch. "Look, it's dirt from Redlands. He must have gotten it up by the big rocks on the hill where you and I used to play cowboys and Indians."

"I thought you were in love with the ambulance driver."

"Paul?" Kathleen asked. "I am."

"You seem as thrilled by this as you did when you were telling me about him."

"Well, I think it's nice." Kathleen defended herself. "Jim must have gone out to Redlands and picked this up himself—"

"Jim? You're that friendly with him?"

She looked down at the treasures. "He asked me to marry him. In New York and again in Nice."

"Why would he want to marry you?"

"We've been, well, we've been friends since I met him, and—"

Her voice trailed away. She wished she hadn't shown Seaney the box. It seemed spoiled now, a reminder of her tangled feelings for Jim. She wondered if he had sent it to her just to make her homesick. She shut it abruptly. "I'd better get back to work."

The men stayed until the canteen closed for the night at 9:30. As Seaney hugged Kathleen before he left, he whispered, "Don't marry him here—either one. Make him come home and prove himself."

"I will," she promised. "But you need to come home, too."

He kissed her cheek. "I miss you so."

After they left, the girls started to clean the canteen.

"Corporal Necchi's singing voice is quite good," Mrs. Brently remarked.

"And he uses words in the funniest way," Hank added. "When I'd say, 'That's not right,' he'd say, 'It's right enough for *un uomo bello* from Brooklyn.'"

"What does that mean?" Kathleen asked.

"He wouldn't tell me," Hank said. "But it sounds an awful lot like *un bel homme* in French."

"A handsome man?" Kathleen laughed. "He must think well of himself."

Hank beamed. "Well, it's true. He is handsome."

"It's good to see our American boys so cheerful and hardy," Mrs. Brently remarked. "Your cousin and his outfit seem like a nice group of fellows."

The words caught at Kathleen's heart, and she burst into sobs. Oh, God, what if Seaney died? What if she never saw him again? Mrs. Brently put her arm around her shoulders.

"I'm sorry," Kathleen said through her hands. "I'm so sorry. I don't know what . . . I meant to laugh or . . . Oh, I miss home so much, I want to go home—"

"It's all right. It's completely understandable." Mrs. Brently turned. "Hank," she called. "Take Kathleen up to bed. I'll finish up down here."

TWENTY-TWO

The Committee to Americanize Colorado gathered around the mahogany table at the State Capitol. As Jim settled into his seat, Mrs. Lake, whom he had met at the last meeting, spoke to him.

"I hear you were quite courageous on the Eastern Plains last month," she said.

The story of the near tar and feathering in the little prairie town had been shared in more than one Denver newspaper, with an abundance of details both real and embellished. Jim had even been asked by a reporter for his comments on the incident, which were then printed on the front page.

"I wouldn't call my actions courageous," he replied. "I was simply doing what needed to be done, as anyone in this room would."

From the end of the table, Governor Gunter said, "Your modesty isn't warranted, Mr. Graves. According to the eyewitness accounts, your words delivered Mr. Emil Reutter into the hands of the proper authorities. I believe you saved his life."

Jim said nothing. His last meeting with the Governor certainly hadn't been this cordial. In fact, he remembered a warning that he was exhibiting too much sympathy for Reutter.

"Perhaps we should nominate Mr. Graves for Governor," Mrs. Lake said.

Governor Gunter's face twitched. "I believe there is already a Republican candidate, although I have no doubt that Mr. Graves would like to sit in the Governor's chair one day."

Mrs. Lake laughed at the Governor's feigned calm. Recently, hounded by reports of statewide discrimination against Colorado's

German-Americans—including the incident Jim had witnessed—
Governor Gunter had appointed Ernest Morris, who sat on this
Committee, to the State Council of Defense, in order to prove there
was nothing to fear. But the move had been a powder keg for the
Governor. The *Denver Post* immediately dubbed Morris, who had
been born in Prussia, "the Prussian Rat," and insinuated that he
would hand Denver over to Germany. His "comrade," Governor
Gunter, had been labeled "pro-German." There was now talk that
the Democratic Party had refused to nominate the Governor as its
candidate for governor for the fall election.

"I have no such plans, sir," Jim said. "The oil industry keeps
me fairly busy."

Governor Gunter smirked. "I see."

The proceedings were called to order by Professor Norlin
from the University of Colorado. After the minutes of the previous
meeting were read and old business covered, the discussion moved
to the recalcitrance of certain residents of the state to sign the
pledge of loyalty.

"Mr. Stephens, who is here with us today, has come across a lack
of cooperation from the Jugo-Slav, Pole and Czecho-Slovak miners
of Leadville," Professor Norlin said. "Most of the men have refused
to sign the pledge card because they are afraid to offend the Austrian
sympathizers who work in the mine. We suspect that certain foreign
elements are engaging in a campaign of intimidation."

Mr. Stephens, who chaired the Americanization Department
of the National Council of Defense, added, "I took along reels of
moving pictures of fine quality to show in Leadville, but even that
failed to draw a crowd."

"What were the movies?" Mrs. Lake asked.

"I beg your pardon?"

"Perhaps they weren't to the liking of the miners."

"I believe one was *Kicking the Germ Out of Germany.*"

"Oh, my," Mrs. Lake lamented. "If they don't like Harold Lloyd,
then they truly are anti-American."

The room filled with laughter, and Professor Norlin waited for it to subside before he called on Ralph Smith of the American First Society to speak.

"I'm pleased to report that our campaign is going better in other parts of the state," Mr. Smith said. "The Greeks in Pueblo have organized a chapter of the America First Society, and I believe the residents of Globeville—many of whom are Austrian or Slavic—will soon have a chapter. Those are two of the most unassimilated groups in our state."

Professor Norlin spoke again. "I recommend that anyone born outside the U.S. should be required to take citizenship classes."

A murmur of assent rounded the table, but Jim offered, "Wouldn't that mean your own parents would need to take classes? I understand they are of Scandinavian descent."

"Why, yes, they, too, would need to take classes," the Professor admitted.

"What about those born in England or Scotland? Or in France? I can't imagine that we would doubt our Allies."

"I believe it's wise to question everyone's loyalty, Mr. Graves," the Professor said. "A Frenchman could be against this country for his own selfish reasons, as could a British subject."

"We've all read about the Conscientious Objector from Denver whose sedition trial is taking place at Fort Dodge in Iowa," Governor Gunter supplied. "His last name is Keohane, if I recall correctly, and he is of Irish descent."

"That's no surprise," Mr. Smith said. "It's long been known that the Catholics in Ireland will fight for Germany rather than fight on the side of the British. I doubt it's any different here."

Governor Gunter continued. "And, Mr. Graves, wasn't Emil Reutter, the Austrian whom you had the privilege of saving from the noose, exactly what he appeared to be to the people of the town?"

"Yes, sir, he was," Jim acknowledged.

"Well, he is now enjoying a diet of bread and water in the Denver County Jail while he awaits trial. There are enough German-

Americans whose loyalty isn't known for us to be cautious, Mr. Graves. The last I heard, there were nearly three thousand German belligerents interned at Fort Douglas in Utah."

"But we aren't talking only about German-Americans here," Jim protested. "We're talking about thousands of peaceful and productive citizens whose only fault is that they weren't born here. Certainly every one of us in this room has an ancestor who was born in another country. Perhaps even a mother or father or sister or brother."

No one spoke, but Jim did not back down. At last, Mrs. Lake said, "I believe that Mr. Graves is using the same common sense approach on us that he used on the lynch mob in eastern Colorado."

"We are hardly a lynch mob," Professor Norlin snapped. "But I propose that we table the discussion for now. May I have a motion?"

Someone motioned so; someone seconded; a vote was taken. But Jim's objections ran on in his head: When did self-preservation turn to persecution? And where would this Committee—with its ambitious and politically-connected members—draw the line?

After the meeting was adjourned, Jim shook hands all around, including with Mrs. Lake, who seemed to be a new admirer. As he walked through the echoing halls of the Capitol Building, he swallowed back an underlying aversion to the Committee's suggestions and purpose and, even, to its very existence. How easily the rights of others could be tramped down and transmuted into something else. How comfortably they talked of "others" and of what was best for them.

On the ground floor of the building, a group of school children stared open-mouthed upward into the dome. Jim glanced up to where the square walls of the lower floors transitioned into a circular pattern. Light descended nearly two hundred feet from the top of the gold-plated dome to blaze in splendor on the white marble floor of the Rotunda.

Governor Gunter was right.

He would like to sit in the Governor's chair someday.

****

A few days later, at his house in Cheesman Park, Jim wrote to Kathleen:

I've heard from my sister recently, but very little from you. I'm glad that you received the box from Redlands. It was my pleasure to find those things for you. Your parents were well when I saw them, and your father walked with me and added to the collection. I enjoyed his company and his knowledge of the land.

According to Eleanora's letter, our Relief Society has lost yet another member. I believe that soon it will be my responsibility to send relief for the Relief Society. I heard from Miss Parsons that she has reached Paris and is now working in the Studio with Mrs. Ladd. She intends to continue sending letters for publication in the Denver newspapers so that Americans are aware of the plight of the men in France. As you requested, I have arranged for a letter of credit for $1000 to be sent to Mrs. Ladd in Paris. I hope that will please you.

Last night I attended a farewell gala that reminded me of the morning I said goodbye to you. It was for the Red Cross Base Hospital #29 unit, which is made up of doctors and nurses from the University of Colorado's School of Medicine and Denver University. The unit is sailing to England, where it will serve at the North Eastern Fever Hospital in Tottenham. They will be working with the men who have been evacuated from France because of illness.

Since I've returned home, I've thought of you more rather than less than I did before I saw you in Nice—

The telephone rang. He glanced at the clock. Seven-thirty—far too late for a business acquaintance or his mother to call. He heard rushed footsteps in the hallway as Harris went to answer it. As he waited, he finished the brandy in the glass beside him.

Moments later, Harris knocked on the door of the study. He carried Jim's greatcoat, hat, and gloves.

Jim folded away the letter to Kathleen. "What is it?"

"Sir, it was Mrs. Lindstrom. She asked that you come to her home right away."

Jim spun out of his chair, and rolled down his shirt sleeves. Harris rushed to help him attach the cuff links and put on his suit coat. For Anneka to call here—rather than his mother's home— meant that something was terribly wrong.

He parked his Mercer in front of the house on Corona Street. The warmth of the July day lingered in the air. The flowers in front of Anneka's cottage shimmered white and gray in the light of the full moon.

Anneka answered, still dressed in the uniform that she wore at his mother's house.

"Have you been working late?"

"No, I just haven't changed yet," she said. "Come in."

He entered the house, and Anneka quickly closed the door behind him.

"Where's Mina?" he asked. "Is she all right?"

"She's all right." Anneka motioned toward the couch. "She is in her room. I'll call her in a few minutes. Sit down."

Jim sat, and Anneka poured tea. He picked up his cup, but made no move to drink it.

"I called because two ladies came here yesterday," she said. "They asked me to sign a card to pledge that I would have one meatless and one wheatless day in this house every week. I said that I am doing that now, but they said they needed the card signed to know for sure—"

Foreboding twitched in him. "Did they tell you their names?"

"No, but they said they were from the Colorado 100% American Club. They said I was un-American unless I signed it."

"Did you sign it?"

"I did not want to," Anneka fumed. "I was scared that they were trying to trick me somehow, that they thought because I have an accent, that I am stupid —"

"You aren't stupid—"

She cut off his words. "Then, today, two men came, and they said I must register. I asked why, and they said that all German women should have registered with the Postmaster by June 26. I said, I am not German, and they said, then, why didn't you sign the pledge card yesterday? I told them I did not want to, and they said, you must be a German sympathizer. You speak like you are. You look like it. I told them that I am from Håga, in Sweden, but they don't know where that is. They said that if they don't know about it, then I must be lying."

"What idiocy," Jim said. "Did these men wear uniforms? Did they give you their names—?"

She seemed not to hear. "And they asked me if I have bought a Liberty Bond, and I said, no, I have my daughter to take care of, and I make only six dollars a week, and they said others are buying bonds who make less than this, and that I should do so to show my patriotism—"

"Why did you call so late?" Jim asked. "I would have come over earlier—"

"Because I had not seen this." She picked up a newspaper. "Look at it. They have published all the names and addresses of the women who are German in the newspaper, and they say they will publish more. I am so afraid my name will be there because of those men. They wrote it down in a notebook!"

Jim looked at the front page of the *Denver Post*. Listed there were the names of all enemy alien German women in Denver who either lived alone or in boarding houses. *Louisa Ficht, 1177 Lipan Street; Mata Duppman, Rosina Ploen; Gretchen Froeb, Mrs. Ehrlich's Boarding House, 896 S. Bellaire Street—*

"This is not the right thing to do!" Anneka said. "To make people afraid in their own houses! I worry for Mina. What if they ask to register the children of those who are foreigners in this country? She will be on a list, and her name might be put in the newspaper. No one knows she is an American citizen!"

Jim steadied himself against the criticism. Since the true identity of her father had not been acknowledged, Mina was known as the daughter of a Swedish immigrant. At last, he said, "I haven't the power to stop this—"

"You have all the power!" Anneka protested. "You are an American, you are a man. They have listened to you for years—telling them we should go to war or that we should buy the bonds for the war. You saved a German man from being tarred and feathered. You are on the Governor's Committee. You should be able to help me!"

"I'm on the Committee, but I have no special privilege."

"You cannot protect your own child?"

"Do you want me to find you another place to stay until you feel safer?"

She pinned him with a steely gaze. "Your mother has given me this house. It is Mina's home. I won't leave it because of them."

"I would gladly help you in whatever way I can—"

"Then you will do what is best for Mina."

The words hung in the air. At last, Jim said, "You've told me you're marrying a man who will give you and Mina his name, and who will—"

"If he comes home. If he lives through this terrible war. But if he does not—"

"Mr. Yeem!" Mina bounded from the hallway that led to the bedrooms.

"Come here, my darling." Jim took her on his lap. "Tell me how you are."

As Mina described her day at school, Jim eyed Anneka. The words that Ellie had spoken in Nice—warnings of a vengeful lower, the risk of public exposure—echoed in his head. Yes, he had kept Emil Reutter out of the hands of a vengeful mob, but he already knew what the reaction of the Governor and the Committee would be if he mentioned that a Swedish maid in his mother's household felt threatened. He could feel all the righteous indignation that he wanted, but, truthfully, there was little he could do.

TWENTY-THREE

Maggie sat on a high-backed bench at Union Station. She was dressed for Church: a goldenrod frock with cuffed, three-quarter length sleeves, a lace inset on the bodice, and a violet grosgrain ribbon that she had taken from her mother's millinery supplies and tied around her waist, its ends reaching nearly to her knees. On her hands were spotless white gloves.

Around her, the crowd seesawed in a blur of khaki uniforms— sweethearts sharing one last kiss before the train departed; mothers foisting heavy picnic baskets into the hands of their sons; fathers patting their boys' backs as they made their way to the platform. The ebb and flow of war, Maggie thought. The new vocation of the nation.

She clutched at a telegram that she held in her hand. It read, simply, "Sentence twenty-five years. Will be in Denver noon Tuesday. Brendan."

Why she had brought it with her, she didn't know. Maybe she intended to confront Brendan with it, as if he had played a cruel prank on her. Maybe she hoped that the letters would magically reconfigure themselves to say: "Liam will be in Denver noon Tuesday." Maybe she believed that Brendan would say, No, this is a mistake. It should say "2 to 5 years," not twenty-five.

Twenty-five years. In twenty-five years, Alice Colleen would be a woman, perhaps married and a mother, and she would never have met her father. Maggie herself would be an old woman, in her forties—Ma's age—and no longer attractive. Would she still be living in the apartments above the store, fighting for every dime against the government regulations? Would she still be hiding away at night—

dried up and long past her child-bearing years—to write stories about newlyweds whose worst problem was a misunderstanding about who should see to the monthly bills?

Brendan stepped off the train from Chicago, dressed in his Roman collar and black suit, his valise in his hands. He moved as if he were an old man, nearly stumbling from the last and highest step.

Maggie stood, straightened her skirt, and adjusted the ribbon around her waist.

Brendan kissed her cheek. "Maggie, how are you?"

She thrust the telegram forward. "Is it true?"

He glanced at the crowd around them. "We need to go somewhere else to talk. Let's go to Blessed Savior."

Except for asking about Alice Colleen's health, Brendan remained silent as Maggie drove the delivery truck to the church. Once they were within the cool, high-ceilinged walls of his office, he closed the door and sat at the desk across from her. As he lit a cigarette, Maggie knotted her hands in her lap, biting her tongue to keep from blurting out questions.

"Liam sends his love to you, as always," he said.

"Where is he? What happened?"

"You know that Liam chose to represent himself at the court-martial."

"Judah told him to do that," she said. "He said that Liam knew better than anyone what his religious views were. Why didn't it work? Why was he sentenced to twenty-five years?"

"I don't know. I wasn't allowed to sit in on the proceedings." He tapped his cigarette against the marble ashtray on his desk. "Maggie, they offered him a farm furlough first. If he would do farm work, they would let him work off his sentence there. After he'd refused, they offered a him position as a clerk with the rank of Sergeant in the administrative offices in Fort Dodge. They promised that his record would be wiped clean, that it would be a fresh start for him."

"He said no to that?" she cried. "Why would he do that? Why wouldn't he—?"

"They offered Liam more than Sean or Frank or Donnell"—Brendan made the sign of the cross—"or any of the others have gotten for enlisting. And, still, he refused. Now, he'll serve twenty-five years at hard labor at Fort Leavenworth."

Maggie's heart constricted. Liam, whose mind worked with such brilliant clarity, whose head for figures and sums had made him an outstanding accountant, whose quickness with words was his strongest trait—how could he survive the humiliation and strain of hard labor?

"Where is Fort Leavenworth?" she asked weakly.

"Near Kansas City, on the Kansas-Missouri border."

"I'll never get there!"

Brendan reached inside his suit coat. "I have a letter for you. I had to smuggle it out. Liam isn't allowed to send letters."

"There was a letter in the *Denver Post* last week—"

"It was confiscated by the Postmaster General and sent to the newspapers as an example of anti-American thought."

"That was his! They had no right—"

"Maggie, he no longer has rights."

She rubbed a finger across Liam's bold handwriting, swallowing until her throat cleared of tears. "I need to read this somewhere else. I need to be with Alice Colleen when I read it."

"Of course. I'll stop by this evening."

At home, she found her mother sleeping, Alice Colleen in the cradle beside her parents' bed. Maggie gathered the baby in her arms, shushing her so she did not cry. With Alice Colleen in the pram, she walked through the warm afternoon to Berkeley Lake. Under a cottonwood tree that overlooked the lake and the prairie beyond and the newly-bloomed wildflowers, she laid Alice Colleen on a blanket. Alice Colleen gurgled away, bicycling her chubby legs, one fist frequently finding her mouth. Maggie leaned over her, and Alice Colleen made a clumsy swipe at her mother's hair.

"*Críona,*" she whispered. "*Cuisle mo chroí.*"

My heart, the pulse of my heart.

Gathering her courage, she opened the envelope.

June 15, 1918

Fort Dodge, Iowa

My beloved Maggie and Alice Colleen,

I'm sorry I must dispense with the kindness and concerned questions with which letters usually begin, but my letter-writing must be done in a hurry, as I have limited light. I pray that you and Alice Colleen are healthy and lacking for nothing. If you aren't, please talk to Brendan or Judah.

Brendan has probably already told you much of what happened at the sentencing, so I feel that I should tell you what happened during it, when he was not in attendance.

My court-martial before the Mack Board at Fort Dodge was swift and with a foregone conclusion. I argued my innocence by citing the Sixth Commandment and the Bible. Since I was in a room of soldiers who had long ago abandoned any religious training they might have received, I also brought up Rule Thirteen, which states that a man cannot be tried by the military when he has, as I do, a civil case pending, and the fact that I have been held for more than sixty days, while the Army's own regulations state a prisoner cannot be held without court-martial for more than forty-eight days. There were other violations of the Army's rules that I mentioned, but none of it did any good. As you know, I was found guilty of desertion and of distributing propaganda.

Brendan has probably told you of the offers made to me if I would betray my conscience. Don't think that I haven't wept over my decision to refuse them. I would give anything to come home to you and Alice Colleen. But I cannot agree to take part in an armed conflict that is killing thousands every day, and that is so contrary and repugnant in God's eyes. I have been branded a coward, of course, but if I know that you are still with me, faithful and loving as you've always been, I will have the strength to continue. Please write to me, Maggie, and give the letter to Brendan. He will explain to you how it will be delivered to me.

With love of my wife and child, my country, and my God,
Liam

That night, Maggie sits on the outside steps of the Sullivans'
apartment, a half-smoked cigarette in her hand and a bottle of Pa's
home-brewed hooch, which she found in his favorite hiding place
in the storage cellar, beside her. She tips her head, listening for
sounds behind her. She left the windows open in her bedroom so
that she can hear Alice Colleen if she wakes. In her lap lies Liam's
letter. It feels unduly heavy, and she fights the urge to fling it aside
and free herself of the news it contains. But shouldn't she want to
read everything that Liam sends her again and again? If he were in
France, she would rip open the envelope and devour the words of
her soldier husband.

In the incinerator in the back yard, a fire smolders. Earlier, she
had set fire to the evening newspapers, telling her mother that they
hadn't arrived that day. She watched as their headlines—"ARCH
SLACKER DISGRACES STATE OF COLORADO, Refuses to Enter
Army Honorably" and "ANTI-AMERICAN, PRO-GERMAN LIAM
KEOHANE SENTENCED"—shriveled, curled into black ash, and
flaked away in the flames. Tonight, the Berkeley Park neighborhood
is silent, as if everyone is hiding away in their houses, ashamed by
the spectacle made by one of their own.

The breeze blows from the west, and she shivers. She lights
another Lucky Strike, then fingers the bottle, considering taking
another swallow of the horrid stuff. Her stomach rebels at the notion.
She fingers a second envelope that lies in her lap. Just as she is about
to pick it up, someone comes up the street. She makes no effort to
squash the cigarette or hide the bottle that sits at her feet. Whoever it
is, they won't stop to talk. Sullivan's Grocery, once a gathering place
for the community, is now a lonely and isolated place.

But it is Brendan, stopping by as he had promised. "I'm glad
you're not asleep. I'm sorry I'm so late."

"I don't know how I'll sleep," Maggie says. "Ever again."

Brendan comes up the stairs and sits down two below her with his back against the brick wall of the store.

"Why would Liam let them do this to him?" Her voice echoes into the street, like a fox's shriek. "Why is he letting them win?"

Brendan lights a cigarette. "Have you ever heard of moral absolutism? It states that for a person to be good, he has to act as God would have us act, not as laws or morality or our own selfish wishes would have us behave. To act against God's wishes is to engage in and be overtaken by evil. It's essentially black and white."

She closes her eyes. She doesn't want to hear more philosophy, or interpretation of scripture, or theory, or comforting words that do nothing to ease the panic inside her when she lies down in bed at night.

"I can bring a book over to you, if you want to read about it," Brendan offers.

"No," she says immediately. "I don't want to read about it. I don't want to hear about it. Why is it so much more important than Alice Colleen and me? God would have him be a good husband and father. That's black and white to me."

"I think he feels that he is," Brendan says. "By setting this example and following his conscience, he is showing Alice Colleen how to be a good Catholic, a good and moral human being. He's not letting them win. He is winning."

"No, he isn't!" Maggie cries. "Did you see the article in—I don't even remember which newspaper it was—that said that if Liam were to show up in Denver, half the population would be there, too, ready to hang him."

"I saw it."

"How can that be 'winning'?"

"Hear me out," he says. "When we were young, Liam never thought as I did about being cold or hungry or sad. He would have slept on a board or eaten gruel like Oliver Twist. He spent hours considering the best way to honor God, and he argued about every word in the Bible, until once, Father Matthew whacked his hands when he tried to turn the page and show him something." He chuckles. "The intellect, the mind, his faith—they've always carried greater power than the physical for him."

"And, yet, you became the priest."

"Because of his example, Maggie," Brendan says. "Because of the power of his faith. I draw my strength from him."

Maggie inhales from her cigarette. Just as I draw mine from being near him, she thinks. Is it wrong that the physical carries such power for her? That she would rather her husband give in, like all the others, and be where she can see and hear and touch him? Is it wrong that she needs his body to satisfy hers?

"Liam said that I should give you any letters I write to him," she says. "You're sending them to him somehow?"

Brendan hesitates. "Yes."

"How are you doing it?"

"You'll promise not to reveal this to anyone—?"

Her temper flares. "Who would I tell? I'm not exactly invited to join any social clubs any longer."

"Of course, I'm sorry." He glances toward the apartments. "The People's Council has a strong following in Kansas City among the railway workers. Judah put me in touch with someone that he trusts to carry letters to Liam."

"And to carry out the letters that he's written? Even those addressed to the President?"

"Yes."

"Oh, Brendan, no!" she cries. "That will just land him in more trouble—"

"You were right, Maggie," Brendan says. "I can't ignore my brother. I can't put myself ahead of him. I believe in what he's doing. I believe he's right. This war is heinous, it is an abomination against humanity and God. Those caught up in its soul-killing mechanisms aren't living the lives they should as God-fearing and God-loving men. They are living lives that are unnatural and against all that God meant for us—"

He stops, breathing heavily, and Maggie says, "And yet the Church uses the scripture, 'Do not be overcome by evil but overcome evil with good,' to justify the war, while Liam uses it to justify his resistance. The same message, but two different interpretations."

"You have to believe in Liam, Maggie, you have to remain faithful and loving toward him."

"I have his child to raise, Brendan."

Brendan gestures at the bottle and the package of Lucky Strikes. "Those will do you no good."

"Nor will anything else."

"Do you want to pray?"

"No."

Brendan is still for some time, as if he is praying for her. Then, he rises and bids her goodnight. Maggie watches him walk down the street toward the lake, as alone as she is.

Sourness floods her heart: *Take your God and your Bible and everything that the Church has told us that isn't true. Take all your religious scholars and leave me alone. God doesn't love us. He doesn't care what happens to us.*

"Father!" she calls.

Brendan turns toward her.

"I believe in Liam," she says. "I believe in my love for him. But I don't believe in his love for me, and I certainly don't believe in God's love for any of us."

"I'm sorry for you, Maggie," Brendan says. "I will pray for both you and Liam. And for my beloved niece, Alice Colleen. The Heavenly Mother bless her."

He walks into the night. Maggie watches him until he turns the corner and disappears.

To calm herself, she takes the second letter from her lap. Written by Edward W. Bok himself, it is a request from *The Ladies' Home Journal* for another story about Evelyn: "*I would like to see Evelyn and George engage with the patriotic work that so many of our readers have taken upon themselves. I believe the stories that we publish, although fiction, must be reflective of the times in which we live, and just now that is overwhelming support for the war and our soldiers—*"

Maggie swoops up the bottle and cigarettes and goes inside. Creeping along the hallway to her own room, she passes the door of Seaney's room. She turns the doorknob. After she was evicted from the Erwins' house, Ma and Pa had piled Liam's and her possessions in Seaney's room. She looks at the collection—the boxes of books and papers, Liam's clothes, his church shoes set out neatly in front of a standing trunk, as if he'd only just stepped out of them.

At the closet, she pulls out a shirt and holds it against her face. It is white, with thin tan and heavier brown stripes flowing vertically, the collar detached from it now. She remembers sewing it for him— one of the first that she had made—and the care that she had taken with the tiny stitches around the buttonholes. She breathes in, but Liam's scent is gone from it. It smells of the closet now, of the moth balls that Ma put in to protect Seaney's clothes.

She goes to her bedroom and takes paper from the drawer of the vanity. Meeting the reflection of her eyes in the mirror, she imagines herself in an elegantly decorated living room, dressed in a natty silk dress. Turning up the always-lit lamp so that she can write, she begins: *Evelyn wasn't expecting the afternoon to take such a surprising turn. Yet, as she returned home from working at the Women's Red Cross Auxiliary, she discovered George in the living room, dressed in the field uniform of the American Expeditionary Force.*

"I've enlisted," George said . . .

There, it ends. She cannot write another word, she cannot move past that declaration: *I've enlisted.* She hates Evelyn, and what Evelyn has: a perfect home, a beautiful baby, a husband who is what he is supposed to be: a patriot, a soldier, a Sammie, a Doughboy.

She opens the vanity drawer and shoves the page inside, vowing never again to write another word.

TWENTY-FOUR

Nothing prepared Paul for the Front.

Even though he and Kenny had practiced dogfighting, and had flown in strict formation, and had escorted bombers from Issoudun nearly to the coast, nothing came close to resembling the crowded skies over the battlefield. Infantry contact planes, reconnaissance planes, fighters, bombers, and observation planes from both sides vied for territory in the tight space. Agile Nieuports escorted the slow-moving observation balloons, while just as many German Fokkers tried to shoot them down. Both Americans and French flew SPADs and Salmsons, making it difficult to identify squadrons. Shrapnel from the anti-aircraft guns littered the air, breaking through the flimsy fabric of the wings and shredding the fuselage.

Clouds cloaked the battlefield, and rain pierced Paul's regulation layers of silk, leather, and fur clothing. The wind chafed his face with the sensation of a thousand needles, yet he gulped for breathable air. At low altitudes, smoke and poison gas wafted upward from the battlefield and choked him. At altitudes of nearly 20,000 feet, his heart beat irregularly, and his lungs pressed outward, feeling overinflated. A high-pitched squeal filled his ears and did not always abate when he was on the ground.

Paul's old nemesis—air sickness—returned. He had been able to fly brief, controlled training exercises in Cazaux, but now, the sorties lasted up to three hours. After that much time being buffeted and tossed about by the wind and by Kenny's daredevil flying, he often found his goggles shrouded in vomit that had blown back into his face. He struggled to do his job from the second seat of the Salmson. The neatly marked maps that he had pored over for hours in the Observers' Room meant almost nothing. The Front was a mess of debris and broken equipment, and bodies dangling from barbed wire. Paul could not recognize French or German uniforms through the gray sheets of rain. His supplies jumbled together: his pencils and message forms lost, his maps crumpled by the wind, his knife in the wrong pocket, his binoculars at his feet, the two homing pigeons that were used in emergency situations altogether missing from the Salmson.

Paul's first "confirmed kill" came when he and Kenny were assigned to a French squadron in June. They flew in formation, one above another for protection. Almost at once, five Fokkers dove from the air. The French aircraft scattered, drawing off four of the Fokkers, but one plane tailed Kenny. "Plane, four o'clock!" Paul shouted.

Kenny urged the Salmson upward to open sky. Paul lost sight of the enemy plane as it climbed through the cloud, but in the sunlight, the plane reappeared, the German iron cross on its fuselage. "Fokker! Straight on!" he yelled.

A fluffy white cloud floated to their left, disembodied from the great gray mass that hid the ground. Kenny circled around it for protection and came in above and slightly behind the Fokker. With an elegant dip, Kenny swooped down on the Fokker, and Paul opened up with a steady stream of tracer bullets from the rear-mounted Lewis guns. Phosphorescent yellowish streams zagged through the air toward the Fokker. The German pilot jerked his head around in surprise. Paul caught a twist of the pilot's mouth, a vague recognition of fear, before the German plane turned turtle, rolling in the sky once and spinning toward the ground.

Determined to see it through, Kenny dropped below the clouds as the Fokker hit the ground on the German side in a plume of black smoke.

"You got him!" Kenny yelled. "I knew you were a good bet, Reston!"

He wheeled the plane around and beat a hasty retreat to the Allied side of the lines. Once on the ground, he shook Paul's hand over and over and bought drinks for everyone that evening at the tavern. Several officers stopped by to congratulate them on their success.

But later, after the hoopla ended, Paul wrote to Kathleen: *I have taken my first life. I have destroyed an "enemy," who was doing just as I was—trying to stay alive. Kenny laughs it off, telling it as a great adventure. But seeing that German's eyes, his face, was painful for me. I can't help but think, this man has a soul, has a family, has as much or maybe more intelligence and decency than I have. We were equals, except that, at that instant in time, my reflexes were quicker.*

In July, Quentin Roosevelt, the former president's son, was killed. Roosevelt had been an idol to the airmen of the fledgling U.S. Army Air Service. He had long been known as America's greatest pursuit pilot because of his bravery and selflessness in flight.

Paul and Kenny heard the news from Owen, after they came back from an observation run.

"Where did it happen?" Paul asked. "When?"

"On Bastille Day," Owen reported. "He was shot down behind German lines near a place called, um, Chamery or something like that, near the Marne where the worst of the fighting is now. The Germans say they are going to give him a full military funeral out of respect for his father."

Kenny looked at Paul. Paul knew they were both thinking the same thing: *One day, it will be us.* There was no denial in the U.S. Army Air Service; in training, they had been told that the fliers had a ninety-nine percent casualty rate. Nearly eighty-five percent of them were killed— half of those in training—and the rest eventually lost their nerve.

When Paul arrives in Chaumont for a three-day leave of absence, the sight of Kathleen delights him. His heart leaps as he takes in the shape of her face, the way that she moves as if she hates to be still, and her quick, friendly smile. Pride surges through him as her hair attracts the attention of just about every man in the courtyard of the AEF Headquarters. She is dressed in a blue dress with frills on its bodice and a high collar. She looks around the crowded courtyard once before she spies him and takes a skipping step toward him.

He opens his arms to her, emotion dredging in his throat. How desperately he needs to hold her, to see her smile, to hear her voice, to remember the joy of living. He pulls her closer to him.

She runs her hands over his shoulders and down his arms to his hands. "I've missed you so!"

"First Lieutenant Paul Everett Reston of the U.S. Army Air Service, reporting for duty." He kisses her on the lips. "Can you get away?"

"Until 5:30." She raises a basket covered with a cloth. "Mrs. Brently is at a meeting at Headquarters, and Hank has fixed us a picnic lunch."

"Dear Hank. I'll have to say hello to her later. But, for now, let's not waste any time."

"I know just the place."

Hand-in-hand, they hurry through the ornate gates of the AEF compound and into the streets of Chaumont. It's a truly French town—the architecture, the cathedral that rises above all else, the winding streets—but it is bustling with uniformed Americans. Following a swell of sightseers, they reach the three-tiered *Viaduc*.

Kathleen stops. "Here it is!"

Paul takes in the stone behemoth. "What a work of architecture."

"It's the most beautiful structure I've ever seen," Kathleen says. "Apart from the cathedral at Amiens—which we saw together, of course. Oh, and the one at Nice, and—"

"And every other cathedral in France."

She takes his arm. "Come on, the view up above is even better here than the view from the tower at Amiens!"

After showing their identification tags to the American sentry on duty, they climb the steps of the bridge to the walkway. The sun warms the breeze that blows between the arches, but it is chilly in the shadows.

They talk about whatever comes to them, trying to catch up on nearly six months of separation. Mostly, Paul describes his work as an observer.

"Do you like to fly?" she asks.

"It's so beautiful up there, in the clouds, with the sun and wind," he says. "There's so much freedom. You can escape from whatever boundaries and restrictions that you had on the ground. It frees the mind, it frees the soul. There's something called adrenaline that's released in your body. It makes you excited and happy. I think it's what you feel when you ride a horse."

"But if you fall off on horseback, the ground is much closer."

"Then I won't fall."

She opens her mouth to speak, and Paul catches the worry in her expression. She knows, he thinks. Even if she hasn't heard it first-hand from a flier, she will never forget the day that Maurice Bernard burned to death. But that isn't what he wants to talk about. That's what he's come here to forget.

"You know, I miss the ambulance service," he says. "Latour, chumming with the *poilus*, drinking that flat, red wine that we diluted with stagnant water, and smoking that tobacco that made one hallucinate the Second Coming of Christ."

"Why didn't you stay?"

"I couldn't," he says. "It had changed. Everything we'd done for nearly three years was being taken apart by American officers who'd just arrived and had no idea of the conditions in the war zone. It was all so rushed that some of the drivers had never set foot in an auto before."

"I suppose that could be just as dangerous as flying."

"Maybe." He shrugs, unwilling to reveal the statistics about airmen. "I need to feel that I'm contributing to this war, that I'm—in whatever small way—making a difference."

"I wish I could say that I didn't understand," she says. "But I do. We are alike—always trying to do what's right." She stops in the center of the bridge. "Look!" She gestures toward the rolling green landscape of the Suize Valley.

Paul leans up against the railing. "I wish I had my binoculars. Do you have your sketchbook?"

"*Mais bien sûr, Monsieur,*" she says coyly. "The first time I saw this bridge, there were quite a few couples standing in the shadow of the arches, kissing. I thought it was the most romantic place I'd ever seen. I wished you were with me."

"I'm here now."

Paul steps into the shade of an arch and draws her against him. Kathleen kisses him with her lips open and ready. His body fills with warmth—in the palm of his hands, in the depth of his mouth, in the tingle of his arms. Her body lifts against his, tremulous and nervy, desirable and desiring.

She shivers.

"Are you cold?" he whispers.

"A little."

"Come with me to my room."

"Yes," she says. "Let's go."

His room in the boarding house is on the fourth story, far beyond the commotion of the town square and the busy AEF compound. After he retrieves his key from the Concierge, he lets Kathleen in through a rickety back door, and they creep up a little-used staircase. Every time a board creaks beneath their weight, they giggle, as if they are naughty children. By the time they reach the room, Kathleen's hand is over her mouth to quell her laughter.

Inside the room, she exclaims, "There are more squeaks than places to step!" she exclaims.

The billet is simple and neat. The walls are papered in a swirling buttercup yellow pattern, and a rust-colored wool rug lies on the floor. The windows are cloaked with the green wooden shutters that every house in France seems to have, and the feather-filled mattress is neatly made over with a heavy beige coverlet.

"This is nice," Kathleen says.

Paul sets the picnic basket on a chair. "Billets are almost impossible to find here. Fortunately, this one came available at almost the same moment I walked in to ask about it."

He reaches for her hand and twirls her into his arms. With a kiss to her forehead, he holds her close, her head on his shoulder, her hair tickling his cheeks and under his nose.

He smooths it down. "Are you sure? Is this what you want?"

"Yes, oh, yes."

He places his fingers beneath her chin and lifts her face to him. As he kisses her, she opens her lips, and her hands come up on either side of his face. He leads her to the bed, which squeaks under their weight. Kathleen breathes out a nervous snicker.

"Everything in this place needs a good shot of oil," he whispers. "But we're alone, and nothing outside this room exists right now. It's just us."

He trails kisses across her cheek to her jaw below her ear. She smells of rosewater, of something old-fashioned and pure. He unhooks a button on her dress, and she brings up a hand.

"All right?" he asks, unsure if she is trying to help him or stop him.

She nods, and he makes a slow ritual of it—a button undone and a kiss, another button and another kiss, and another—until he uncovers her cotton camisole. He slips the strap from her shoulder and pulls the fabric away.

The scent of roses lingers in the tender spot between her breasts. With his lips, he nuzzles them, one, then the other. He brushes his tongue over the pink tips. She inhales heavily and runs her hands through his hair.

"Take off my shirt," he whispers.

He waits patiently as she fumbles to unbutton his uniform.

"My fingers won't work," she says with a half-laugh. "I'm sorry."

"Let me." Paul finishes the job and pulls his shirt from his shoulders. Kathleen's fingers circle through the hair of his chest. She kisses his neck, her lips sending a thrill through the spot just below his ear. He cups the back of her head and brings her mouth back to his.

Her hands glide over his shoulders, down the muscles of his back and around to his chest. Lying beside her, he urges her leg over his thigh and presses against her. She breathes out an "oh" of desire.

He helps her to shed her petticoat and drawers, then removes his trousers. Leaning over her, he kisses his way down her body— the hollows near her collarbones, the crooks of her elbows, the flesh of her stomach, and the insides of her thighs. She explores his body with her hands, kissing his jaw, his neck, his chest.

His fingers play between her legs, and she rolls toward him, speaking his name, searching for his lips. When he enters her, he feels a slow burn through his abdomen and thighs. He rocks slowly, deliberately, whispering, "Does this feel good? Does this?"

She rasps, "I want—" He thrusts into her with fierce passion. When his body shudders against hers, he calls her name into the tangle of her hair.

They lie motionless in the languid warmth between their bodies. At last, Paul rolls away. "Did you like that?" he whispers.

"Yes." The sound comes out as a breath. "Yes, I did, I did."

"Let me look at you."

"What?"

"Your body. Let me see it."

Instinctively, she crosses one arm over her breasts. "What do you want me to do?"

"Just lie there. I just want to see you."

He lifts away her hand.

"For months, I've dreamed of this," he whispers. "I've imagined you as the woman in the painting *Olympia* by Manet. Have you seen her?"

Kathleen shakes her head.

He kisses her temple. "She is a beautiful woman, lying nude on a bed. She has reddish hair"—he catches a lock of her hair with his fingers—"and she wears a gardenia behind her left ear." He runs a finger around the fold of her ear. "She lies with her shoulders back"—with one finger, he traces a path from one collarbone to the other—"and she is confident and open in her expression. She seems to be saying, 'I am beautiful, I'm desirable, I'm complete in myself, but I'm offering all of it to you.'"

He draws a circle around her breast, spiraling up to the nipple.

She breathes in raggedly. "Is that how you see me?"

"Yes." His fingers trail along the sensitive skin on the side of her ribs, down to her navel, and into the golden-red hair at her thighs. "But you are so much lovelier than I imagined."

His fingers slip inside her, and she responds by arching her back. He kisses her mouth, his tongue meeting hers again and again, until he feels in her kiss that she has lost herself in his touch. She calls, "Paul, Paul—"

He covers her body with his. Straightening his arms, he moves within her, his eyes closed, her hands on his shoulders. His body trembles with pleasure, and she holds on tightly. *I am yours*, he thinks. *I will always be, I never want to be with anyone else.* As his body collapses onto hers, he listens to her breathing, the beat of her heart, the rush of the blood in her veins. He can feel heat from her mouth and neck, from the dampness between her breasts, from the softness between her legs. He can sense the sweetness within her body.

They doze, their arms around one another, their legs still entwined. The sun slants through the slats of the blinds, walking its way across the floor. When the clock beside the bed strikes five, Paul wakes Kathleen with a kiss.

"We have to go back," he says.

Neither of them moves. The seconds tick by on the clock, seeming to grow more frantic as the minutes pass.

"Paul?" she whispers.

"Yes, my love?"

"This is right, isn't it? I know it's sinful, but it isn't bad, is it?"

He moves so that he can see her face. "Why would you ask that?"

Her fingertips play in the hollow of his neck. "Helen says I should behave better," she admits. "She says I need to do what I'm told, and to stop . . ."

"Don't listen to her," Paul says. "Love is the greatest act of hope I can imagine in this world right now. Feeling as I do about you and knowing that you feel the same about me, we can face it all, because nothing will change between us. Love is faith, Kathleen. It's the greatest of human gifts."

"Faith?"

"Just like what you believe in the Church," he says. "Only it's ours, between us, the faith that we have in each other's love. It isn't bad, or wrong, and I'd argue it isn't even a sin."

She kisses him. "After we left Amiens, and I didn't know where you were, I promised myself that, when I saw you again, I would love you the way I want to love you for the rest of my life."

"And that is what we've done today."

"I never want to be without you again," she says.

"We have to go."

"I know," she says. "I know, but—"

By the time they leave, the streets are crowded with American soldiers out for the night, French peddlers with charcoal braziers smoking beneath racks of sausages, and dairy maids carrying pails from the evening milking. Trucks and wagons compete for space in the medieval streets, the drivers honking and the wagoners shouting. At the ornate gates of the AEF compound, the clock reads five twenty-eight. Kathleen glances fearfully at it.

"I have to keep my promise to Hank," she says.

"Can you get away tomorrow? I have three days here."

"I don't know. I'll try—"

"If you can't, I'll come here."

"But—"

"Mrs. Brently can't bar me from the canteen. It would be unpatriotic to deny a hard-working, dutiful flier of the U.S. Army Air Service a respite from the travails of the Front."

"Oh, Paul, I love you so much."

She kisses him goodbye, then hurries toward the gate. He watches her show her identification to the guard and pass through into the compound. She turns and waves at him, and he tips his officer's hat to her, truly the happiest birdman in France.

TWENTY-FIVE

As she sat on the grassy banks of the Suize, Kathleen watched another train trundle across *Le Viaduc*. She had no way to tell whether Paul was on this train, or the previous, or one yet to come. The train station had been a sea of khaki this morning, with entire divisions commandeering train cars. Civilians and individual travelers such as Paul, who was bound for La Ferté, were left to scramble for a seat.

Their farewell had been difficult, even more fraught than their parting in Amiens. Yesterday, as they lay in the bed in Paul's room, Kathleen's head cradled in the hollow of his shoulder, she had confessed her fears. "After what happened to Maurice, that day in Amiens—"

Paul stroked her hair with a gentle hand. "I have thought of him more than once, and yes, there is a possibility it could happen to me. But whatever there is to do over here, it's dangerous. We've always known that."

"Then if love is the same as faith, I'll do as I always have," she had said. "I'll pray for you, for us, for the end of the war, and for peace."

"And I will love you more than I ever have before," he said. "Don't worry, my girl of the Wild West, we'll be together again."

Now, the train passed over the bridge, and a hush spread through the valley. Kathleen returned to the AEF compound. In the canteen, she found Hank in the kitchen, mixing batter for doughnuts. Without greeting her, Hank said, "Mrs. Brently wants to talk to you."

"About what?" Kathleen asked. "Does she know about . . .?"

"I don't know."

She left the canteen for the office shared by Mrs. Brently and two other Red Cross supervisors. Nervously, she tapped on the door. Mrs. Brently, who wore her wimple and uniform, greeted her with a warm smile. "Please sit down, Kathleen."

Kathleen took a seat, her hands clasped in her lap.

Mrs. Brently lifted a page from her desk. "I've received a letter from Captain Decker of the 89th Division. He has asked me to ask you about your relationship with Liam Keohane. Do you know what this is about?"

Kathleen exhaled in relief before telling Mrs. Brently about Liam's refusal to serve in the military. "I've heard from my father that Liam is now in Fort Leavenworth," she said. "He was sentenced to twenty-five years at hard labor."

"Twenty-five years!" Mrs. Brently said. "It's extraordinary that he would choose to go to prison rather than take the chance of being killed in France."

"I don't think he's a coward. If he were just afraid to die, he would have taken one of the jobs the Army offered him. My father says Liam believes in what he's doing with a martyr's passion."

"That helps to explain why he would allow his reputation—and that of his family—to be so damaged in the newspapers. But your family must be feeling some sort of pressure or discomfort because of this—"

"My father didn't say much about that, probably so I wouldn't worry." Kathleen drew in a breath. "I hope this doesn't change my position in the Relief Society."

"Of course it doesn't," Mrs. Brently said. "I've already written to Captain Decker to inform him that you passed through a rigorous selection process before being accepted into our Society and that you have acted in accordance with our expectations. I am hoping that will satisfy him."

"Thank you, oh, thank you."

Mrs. Brently reached into her desk and produced an envelope. "One more thing," she said. "We've heard from Helen."

"I'll take it to Hank right now."

Kathleen rushed back to the canteen, her guilt drowned by relief. She had no intention of fooling Mrs. Brently, but she had no intention of giving up Paul. As soon as she came through the door, Hank asked, "Was it about Paul?"

"No." Kathleen hiccuped out a laugh. "It was . . . oh, it doesn't matter now. But, look what I have."

Hank wiped her floury hands on a towel as Kathleen tore open the envelope and read aloud:

You'll be happy to hear that I am well-settled at Mrs. Ladd's. She has been good enough to let me take a room in her house, so all I have to do is go downstairs in the morning, and I am at work.

I mostly clean up the plaster of Paris and wax that has fallen from the molds and masks, but Mrs. Ladd is teaching me how to fit the masks on the men's faces. So far, she has made 120 masks for the French, and she expects to make many more for both French and Americans before the war ends.

You might remember Henri, the soldier who was being fitted with a mask when we visited. Now that I am here, we have been spending a good deal of time together. He's witty and smart, and he has read nearly everything, and in French, too. He is helping me with my pronunciation. We enjoy each other's company, and I believe that what I feel for him is more than simple affection. Only time will tell what comes of it. I am glad I did not know him before the war, for I might have regretted what has been lost, but now, he seems perfectly normal to me.

Our troops are moving through Paris by the thousands. They parade up and down the Champs Élysées and perform spectacular shows of strength and precision at the Arc de Triomphe, all of them looking very sharp, clean, and strong. Almost everywhere one goes, an American military band serenades them, and the cry of "Vive L'Amérique" fills the air. It breaks my heart to think of what will happen to them in the months to come.

I must go now, for it's time for the dinner and the evening program, which is a piano recital by one of Mrs. Ladd's patients.

Mrs. Ladd herself is singing an aria or two, and I've been asked to read a poem.

Please write to me. I miss you both.

Tout mon amour,

Helen

"Oh!" Hank trilled. "She's in love with Henri!"

Kathleen said nothing. She remembered how Helen had chastised her for wondering how a woman could love a man who had no lips to kiss her or who could not smell her perfume or hair. She felt so different now that she had made love with Paul, but she did not dare to talk to Hank, who had made her feelings clear: "My mother told me that a man won't marry a girl if she has given him . . . well, if she isn't pure on her wedding day, even if he's the man who did it—"

That night, she wrote to Paul: *I think of your shoulders, and the hollow beside the socket where I can lay my head. I think of how warm your lips feel against mine. I think of your hands, and the slight roughness at the end of your fingers. I think of your legs, so strong and sturdy, and the feel of your chest under my palms. I am the most blessed woman in the world to have a man who is as beautiful as you are . . .*

In August, the Graves Family Foundation Relief Society received orders to move to Bar-le-Duc. The two girls loaded their trunks on a truck that joined a convoy of vehicles traveling north.

While Mrs. Brently rode in the cab with the driver, Kathleen and Hank sat on the end of the tarped bed, their legs dangling over the edge. The road was wide and smooth and graveled with white chalk, and the morning sun shone down on them.

"This is different," Hank remarked. "Not a single mud puddle."

Behind them, the military cavalcade stretched over the flat, woodless terrain all the way to the horizon. Kathleen tried to count the tarped trucks, but lost track when the oncoming vehicles blended into the dusty road.

Accompanying the supply vehicles and wagon trains were thousands of soldiers, who marched beside the slow moving vehicles, their steps jaunty and sure.

"Where are you going?" Hank called.

A young man slowed his pace just enough to stay beside them. "We're goin' to take out the Heines."

"Do you know where the 12th Aero Squadron is?" Kathleen asked.

"The what?"

She tried again. "What about the 89th Division?"

"Where are you from?" Hank asked, but the young man said, "I'm gettin' left behind. I have to go!"

In Bar-le-Duc, Kathleen and Hank set up the canteen in a street-side room of a brick convent. The sisters spoke no English, but they were thrilled when Kathleen produced her rosary. They invited her into their chapel to pray, and Kathleen knelt on the stone floor at the back of the Church each evening with four old French women in black as the nuns sang Vespers. After the nuns retreated into silence and sanctity, the canteen rollicked with the antics of American soldiers, and the gramophone's needle scratching out "Turn the Dark Side Inside Out" and "Pack Up Your Troubles in Your Old Kit Bag." Male voices rose in song, and Hank or one of the men pounded out ragtime tunes on an old piano. There was no electricity, so the girls made do with candles placed on the splintery tables. As the rain made a muddy mess of the street outside, they served cocoa and coffee and companionship.

They were in Bar-le-Duc for only a week before Mrs. Brently announced that they were moving again.

"We'll be going to Récicourt," she said. "It is the closest to the Front that any Red Cross canteen unit has gone so far. We will be nearer to the battlefield than we were at Montdidier."

"We haven't even gotten mail here yet!" Kathleen protested.

"I'm aware of that," Mrs. Brently said. "But it will surely catch up with us."

"Why were we asked to go?" Hank asked.

"Because we have been located near the Front before." Mrs. Brently reached out and touched their hands. "We are known and respected for our good work, and it is all because of you."

"And Helen," Hank said.

"And Helen, of course."

"And because of you," Kathleen added.

Mrs. Brently laughed her silvery laugh, which Kathleen had not heard for some time.

This time, the road was neither wide nor smooth. Pitted and broken by shell holes and ruts, it was littered with the great detritus of war—abandoned supplies and rucksacks and trash. Great swaths of coarse camouflage netting stretched on both sides, hiding the travelers from German eyes. Every few yards, a broken-down truck or damaged wagon was being manhandled or drawn by skittish horses into the ditches, to be left behind in the rush to move forward. If a truck couldn't be moved, it was tipped over and rolled out of the way.

Horses were treated no better. If a horse went lame, it was shot. Kathleen hid her face against Hank's shoulder as another horse—a beautiful bay—was led out of the train to be shot and left along the side of the road to rot. "I can't stand this," she said.

"Don't watch," Hank said. "Don't listen."

The woods around them were brilliant with fall colors. The sun skiffed along golden and red leaves, which floated gently to the rich, black earth. A few caught in Kathleen's hair and on her clothes. They were beech leaves, like those from the tree that she and Paul had picnicked beneath near Amiens. She slipped them into her pocket. Later, she would press them between the pages of her Bible.

Récicourt stood only twelve miles from Verdun. The town was deserted, with rubble strewn from one end to the other and the distinct odor of rotting meat in the air. The home in which the Graves Family Foundation Relief Society was to set up its canteen had no windowpanes left, but the roof was intact.

"This will have to do," Mrs. Brently said.

Upstairs, Kathleen and Hank assembled and made up the cots they had hauled with them from Chaumont in one of the bedrooms. Together, they hoisted an empty nickel-plated Fatima cigarette case that Hank had pilfered from the Red Cross up the steps and placed their washbasin and pitcher on it.

"There," Hank said. "Just like home."

Kathleen laughed. "We thought Bar-le-Duc was going to be home, and yet, here we are."

On the first night, it rained, and the roof dripped steadily. Running downstairs in her nightdress, Kathleen gathered up as many pots from the kitchen as she could carry, while Hank stayed behind to shove the cots and their trunks to safety.

On her way back up the stairs, she glimpsed Mrs. Brently in what was once the parlor of the house. She stood with her back to Kathleen, looking out the glassless window. She wore a striped dressing gown, and her hair, usually bound tight, fell to her shoulders in generous waves. In her hand was a cigarette.

Kathleen climbed the stairs as quietly as she could. She had never thought about whether Mrs. Brently was lonely. She had always had Hank and, until recently, Helen, to talk to, but Mrs. Brently seemed to have no close friends except for Lieutenant Colonel Lloyd-Elliot.

After she helped Hank distribute the pans under the leaks, she said, "I'm going downstairs again for a minute."

"Why?" Hank asked.

For some reason, Kathleen did not want to tell Hank that she wanted to speak with Mrs. Brently. "I'll see if I can find more pans."

"I think we've found all the leaks."

"There may be more, if this rain keeps up."

"Well, I'm cold, and my socks got wet. I'm going back to bed."

"I won't be long, and I'll take care of any that I find when I come back."

She grabbed a woolen shawl and tiptoed down the stairs. From the doorway of the parlor, she whispered, "Mrs. Brently."

Mrs. Brently started, but she did not try to hide the cigarette. "Ah, Kathleen."

"I'm sorry, I didn't mean to—"

"Come in. Join me."

Kathleen went to the window. Outside, sentries and MPs patrolled the street.

"Does your roof leak?" Kathleen asked.

Mrs. Brently glanced up the stairs. "I haven't checked in some time. I suppose I should."

She did not move. Kathleen wanted to talk with her, to say: *You know what it is like to be loved by a man. You know how sweet it is. You've been touched and loved in that secret way that makes everything take on a bright sheen. Tell me, is it always this way? Will I always feel as beautiful and perfect as I do now?*

Instead, she said, "Did Helen tell you that she's fallen in love with Henri?"

"Yes, she wrote to me about it. How very brave she is."

"I don't know that I could do it." Kathleen's throat felt raw. "To love a man who has no face, that is."

"It would take a special kind of person," Mrs. Brently agreed. "And Helen is that." She smashed the cigarette beneath one dainty slipper. "I'm aware that you are still receiving mail from Private Reston. Is he well?"

Kathleen's heart clenched at the thought of all she had concealed from Mrs. Brently. "He's no longer a private," she said. "He's a First Lieutenant with the Army Air Service."

"That's quite a jump in rank. Is he a pilot?"

"No, an observer." She relayed the details of Paul's new post. "I worry about him."

"Of course, you do. As I do for Lieutenant Colonel Lloyd-Elliot."

Kathleen held her breath. The last time Kathleen had spoken of Colonel Lloyd-Elliot, Mrs. Brently had scolded her for being too forward.

A creaking sounded in the road outside. Within seconds, it had become the roar of footsteps and rolling wheels. Mrs. Brently stepped forward to lean out the paneless window.

"What is it?" Kathleen asked.

"Troops," Mrs. Brently said. "Only, they are coming from the west, not the south."

"Away from the Front, then."

Kathleen craned her neck. The troops marched silently past the canteen in the heavy rain. Some of the soldiers relied on the arms of their fellow soldiers to stay upright, and others limped along with bandages wrapped around their heads, or with arms in slings, or with a stick of crutch to keep them upright. As the street filled, they came to a jammed-up stop. Some hunched forward, as if this delay was just one of many they had had on their return. A standard that rose into the pouring rain read, "148th Infantry."

At once, Kathleen thought: I have seen this before. I know this.

"Mrs. Brently," she said. "Do you remember—?"

"Our first night in Montdidier. Of course."

It seemed so long ago, although by the calendar, it was not yet a year. That night, she and Mrs. Brently had watched French troops return from the Front. The men had marched in an eerie silence, their faces hollowed out, the horror of what they had just seen and done etched in the flesh. Kathleen had asked, *Why are they so quiet? Why aren't they talking? They seem as if they're dead.*

"But these are Americans," Kathleen whispered.

"Yes, our own." Mrs. Brently touched Kathleen's hand. "I suppose I should go check my room. And we should get some sleep."

Upstairs, the room seemed dry and cozy. Kathleen took the pans to her own room.

Hank stood at the window. "Did you see what's happening below? We saw the 148th as we moved to Bar-le-Duc. They were singing and blowing kisses to us."

"I know."

"I guess there's nothing for it, poor boys." Hank turned away and secured the oilcloth over the window. "What took you so long?"

"Mrs. Brently was downstairs. We looked in her room for leaks. There weren't any."

"That's no surprise," Hank said. "Where she goes, perfection follows."

Only moments after they settled down in their beds, the barrage opened up at the Front. The metal springs of Kathleen's bed twanged, and the pots jumped across the floor, slopping water, as the big guns pounded out an unending concussion. The room lit up with the flares and explosions of the Verey lights, and the smell of phosphorus crept through the air.

"It's Montdidier all over again," Hank said. "Let's hope we aren't losing."

Kathleen did not reply, but she did not sleep, either. The next day, the returning troops had disappeared, and the girls handed out chocolate, milk, cocoa, biscuits and cigarettes to hundreds of fresh and lively soldiers who passed through town, bound for somewhere called St. Mihiel.

TWENTY-SIX

Near Verdun, Captain Black decides that he wants information from the Germans. He calls for a trench raid, and Lieutenant Morgan receives orders to take his best men.

Sean steps forward. "I volunteer."

Around him, no one moves or breathes. They know, he thinks. They all know about Liam. Lieutenant Morgan has said nothing more about the meeting with Major Buell, but the injustice of being questioned about his loyalty to America festers in Sean.

Tony steps forward. "I volunteer, too, sir."

The tension eases in Sean's shoulders. Lieutenant Morgan needs Tony, who is fearless and fast.

"All right, Corporal Sullivan, Corporal Necchi." Quickly, Lieutenant Morgan names the others. Kevin, and Michael Giordano, who is the only other Italian who speaks English well, and Danhour, and Arnie Green, to make a party of seven.

The Lieutenant places Danhour in charge of three of the men.

"You'll be in a flanking party," he instructs. "Your job is to clear the way for me and Corporal Necchi and Corporal Sullivan. The three of us are in charge of bringing back a prisoner." He turns to Sean and Tony. "I will take the prisoner and keep him under my control at all times. If something happens to me, it falls to you, Corporal Necchi, then to you, Corporal Sullivan, if something happens to him."

"Yes, sir," they both reply.

It's the same routine for trench raiding as it is for night patrol: blackening their faces and hands with burnt cork, removing their insignia, stocking up on weapons. They trade their trusty Springfield rifles for a bag of hand grenades. Lieutenant Morgan, Sean and Tony strike out on a course straight through No Man's Land, while the flanking party sweeps forward in an arc. The night closes around them, dark and moonless. They can hear each other moving, but can't see each other. Sean flounders, uncertain if he is still following Lieutenant Morgan or if he's even headed in the right direction.

He finds Tony just as they are about to go under the German wire. He mouths the words: "Where's Lieutenant Morgan?"

Tony nods toward the German trenches, and Sean slithers beneath the wire. The enemy soldiers are sitting in an observation post that allows them a clear view of the American line. They are talking, evidently unafraid. The smell of coffee and cigarette smoke wafts upward from the trench into the nearly still night.

Lieutenant Morgan turns toward Sean and Tony and raises his fingers to count seven. At the Lieutenant's sign, the three Americans drop into the trench, landing with light thuds. Sean follows Lieutenant Morgan toward the observation post, which is a securely boarded notch in the trench, with sandbags on either side of it, and a wall with loopholes for high-powered lenses and machine guns in the front.

The post is guarded by a bored sentry, whose head is tilted to one side as he fiddles with his rifle. Lieutenant Morgan signals to Tony, and Tony slides up to the German, his M1917 knife in his hand. Wrapping his arm around the German's throat, Tony slices with the knife, and the German sinks into the mud without a sound.

Lieutenant Morgan motions for Sean and Tony to take out their automatic pistols. Bullets in the breech, weapons aimed, the three of them step around the corner of the sandbags. Two Germans stand at the wall, looking out across No Man's Land, while the other four crouch on ledges made of sandbags.

"Ergebet euch!" Lieutenant Morgan says in a low voice.

Two of the men at the wall throw up their hands. *"Kamerad!"*

A third scrambles up the sides of the sandbags. Tony lunges, and the German rolls on the floor of the dugout. The other three escape down the trench.

"Damn it!" Lieutenant Morgan covers the two who surrendered in the corner with his pistol. "Go get them."

Sean and Tony slide into the trench, feeling their way through the darkness with their hands against the walls. Hearing movement behind him, Sean whips around, his service pistol in his hand. Kevin, Danhour, and the others in the flanking party slip around the corner of the observation post. With them are the three Germans who escaped. Sean beckons them forward and leads them into the observation post. Tony brings up the rear.

"Kamerad!" one of the Germans speaks to Lieutenant Morgan. *"Wir ergeben uns!"*

"Put them over here," Lieutenant Morgan orders. "Anyone missing?"

"No, sir, we're all here," Danhour says.

"Private Danhour and Private O'Neal, stand guard." Lieutenant Morgan looks over the five prisoners. "You. Come here. *Schnell!"*

With a fearful glance at his fellows, the German comes to stand between Sean and Lieutenant Morgan.

"Private Danhour," Lieutenant Morgan orders. "Dispatch the rest."

Danhour fires his service pistol, and one of the Germans who stands in the corner drops. Sean's entire body reacts to the percussion of the shot: "Sir, they surrendered!"

"Captain Decker said one prisoner," Lieutenant Morgan says.

"But we're to treat prisoners—"

He turns to Sean. "We aren't taking prisoners anymore, Corporal Sullivan. Not after Seicheprey and Cantigny. Not after Belleau Woods. Stand down, *Seaney.*"

Sean steps away, but Tony says, "We're to take them back."

Kevin speaks up as well. "Prisoners are to be—"

"Lieutenant," Danhour says. "They're trying to set the Heines loose on us—"

Lieutenant Morgan says, "You have your orders. All of you, shut up."

Danhour fires again, and again and again, with point-blank efficiency. The bodies slump over in the corner of the dugout, blood seeping from the wounds in the temples. His face pale and drawn, Kevin strips the dead of insignia, while Danhour and some of the others rummage through their packs and pockets, seeking souvenirs.

Sean glances at Tony, but Tony's face shows no emotion. The German prisoner sobs, either thankful that he is still alive or guilty that the others aren't.

"Let's go," Lieutenant Morgan says. "Sullivan, Necchi, see the prisoner over the wall."

Sean and Tony take hold of the German's arms and drag him over the side of the trench as Lieutenant Morgan pokes his pistol into the soldier's back. The German falls into the barbed wire, and Sean grabs for him, hearing the rip of clothing and flesh caught on wire.

They dodge their way through No Man's Land. A barrage has opened up on both sides of the trenches. The sky turns to mud, fouled by dirt thrown up from the bombs. A machine gun opens fire, and the bullets whiz by Sean. He hears someone yelling behind him and throws a look over his shoulder, but sees only silhouettes of men as Verey lights blossom in the sky. The air takes on the oily smell of battle, and Sean runs faster. At the firewall, Lieutenant Morgan hisses out the password, "Detroit," as he and the German disappear into the trench. Tony follows, more or less tumbling down the makeshift steps, while Sean comes third.

The flanking party clamors into the trench a few feet away. As Lieutenant Morgan grabs at the scruff of the German's neck, Danhour rushes forward. "Sir, it's O'Neal."

"What?" Lieutenant Morgan says.

"He went down out there, uh, about fifty feet."

"Was he dead?"

"I don't know. He fell, and I kept going."

Sean's muscles tense: *He yelled. That was what I heard. He called my name.*

"Sir," Sean says. "I'll go find Private O'Neal."

Lieutenant Morgan takes a long, loud breath. "No, I won't lose two men. I'll send out the stretcher-bearers when it's safe enough."

He called my name.

"But, sir, he could still be alive—"

"Corporal Sullivan," Lieutenant Morgan says. "I've given my orders. Corporal Necchi, take the prisoner to Captain Black."

"Yes, sir," Tony says.

At gunpoint, Tony escorts the prisoner down the trench to the communication tunnel. Lieutenant Morgan moves toward the dugout.

He called for me. He trusted me, he knew I would come back.

Sean grabs Danhour by the collar and pins him up against the trench. "Why didn't you stop?" he demands. "Why didn't you bring him back? You can kill in cold blood, but you're too scared to—!"

"You fight for the Germans!" Danhour yells. "Damn Catholics, against decent Christians, trying to make America weak—!"

Lieutenant Morgan jams his arm between them. "Stop it. Private Danhour, go back to the dugout. Corporal Sullivan, get out of here."

Sean twists away. Kevin, Kevin, whose stories about two-headed calves and gruesome farm accidents seemed endless, who never thought to be anything more than he was, who would have lived out his life as a good husband, father, and farmer. Kevin, who has been his friend since Fort Riley.

He announces, "I'm going back out, sir."

Lieutenant Morgan takes a step toward him, his hand on the butt of his service pistol as if he might draw. Sean clenches his jaw and stands his ground.

"If you go, I won't send anyone out to look for you," Lieutenant Morgan threatens. "And I won't alert the sentries. They can shoot you, for all I care."

"Yes, sir."

Sean hefts himself over the trench wall and crawls out into No Man's Land. He tries to remember where he was when he heard Kevin call, but everything is the same, the same earth blown into a thousand shell holes and clods and ditches, just like every other inch of France. The barrage batters the ground, which shifts and mutates beneath him as he bellies under the barbed wire.

"Kevin," he hisses. "Kevin, where are you?"

There is no answer.

He searches the darkness for anything that might move, that might still have a human form to it. All he finds are parts, mangled and sodden in the muddy water. Maybe by daylight, they will find him, but in all likelihood, Kevin is lost, as so many of them are.

He slips over the side of the trench unchallenged by the sentry. He crouches in the mud, his back against the wall. Folding his arms across his knees, he hides his face. The barrage continues, the teeth-jarring concussions slamming the ground again and again. A familiar numbness creeps into his head. As if he no longer exists on this earth, as if what has happened to him—his entire life—has been nothing. His very soul has been pounded away.

When he raises his head, he finds that the sun has risen. As he strikes a match to light a cigarette, someone touches his shoulder.

"Hey." Tony offers him a tin mug of hot coffee. "Here."

They sit in silence, shrouded by smoke and steam. The barrage winds down, but no orders come to move out. For the moment, the war has exhausted itself.

At last, Tony speaks. "You know that prisoner? I took him back to Captain Black, you know. And you know what they did? Fed him, with meat from some French farmer, and gave him coffee with sugar. And all new clothes, with a new coat and gloves. And cigarettes and chocolate bars—when the hell was the last time we got chocolate?"

Sean's sorrow folds over him. "I went back for Kevin."

"What? Morgan let you?"

"He called for me."

"What? Who?"

"Kevin. I heard him call my name."

"Naw, that was just . . . everybody was yelling by then."

"No, he called for me."

Tony says nothing, and Sean opens his mouth to speak again, then closes it.

There isn't anything else to say.

TWENTY-SEVEN

Fort Leavenworth, Kansas
July 4, 1918
Dear Maggie

If you have received this letter, then you will know that Brendan's contact has finally been allowed to visit me and has successfully concealed this in his clothes. I have been trying for five weeks to send a letter to you, my beloved wife.

My introduction to Fort Leavenworth was one I would rather not remember. As I was being led to my cell, I saw a young man lying in another cell in a pool of blood. His face had been battered into an unrecognizable state, and his shirt and coat were soaked through. It wasn't until several days later that I was told that he is Ralph Hunt, who is from a ranch in Colorado. He is a Seventh Day Adventist and a Conscientious Objector on religious grounds, as am I. His brother, Wesley, is also in prison. The day before I arrived, Ralph was beaten into this state of unconsciousness and left to lie overnight with his injuries unattended because he had refused to work in the guardhouse. I discovered later that the guard who ordered the punishment was promoted to Corporal.

I tell you this not to frighten you, dear Maggie, but to share the truth of the treatment of military prisoners who have done nothing but follow their beliefs. At Fort Dodge, I met four men from South Dakota who call themselves Hutterites. According to their traditions, the Hutterites wear clothing of their own making, grow beards, and speak German among themselves. They have as little contact as possible with the world outside their homes. Their community is built on a sharing of property, so that no man becomes rich from the toils of another and no one is left to suffer the degradation of poverty. It is a society much as the People's Council would promote.

Recently I have heard that they have been sent to Alcatraz Island in California to serve a sentence of twenty years at hard labor. There, they have been given nothing but a half-glass of water once a day, no food, and they have been stripped of their clothing and made to sleep on wet stone floors without any covering in the dungeon below the main prison. During the day, their wrists are crossed and chained to the bars far above their heads so that their feet cannot touch the floor.

These things will come to me, I have no doubt. I wish I could see you. I wish I could tell you this with my own lips so that you do not see just the darkness and shadows of this letter, but the righteousness of my stance and the depth of my vision. Man's military nature and the very spirit of militarism take from him what is kind, generous, and caring. Sean, Frank, even Brendan are not evil or bad, but have been caught up in the debasement of the institutions of the government and Church. They have not my contempt or anger, but my prayers.

I remain your loyal and faithful husband, and Alice Colleen's loving and tender father,

Liam

Maggie folded the letter and laid it on the counter at Sullivan's Grocery. The plate glass windows of the store, which were once polished to invisibility by her mother, were now clouded by a summer's worth of dust. The last of Ma's specials painted in tempura and egg were fading in the bright sunlight.

Last night, after she had read Liam's letter for the first time, she had sobbed until every inch of her body ached. How could she live, knowing as she did what was happening to him? When she woke this morning, she wondered why she had not died in her sleep from the grief and heartbreak. Yet her heart kept beating, and she still seemed able to speak and act and walk, as she always had.

I saw a young man lying in another cell in a pool of blood—

Alice Colleen cooed from the basket on the floor where Maggie had left her. Blinking back her tears, she bent toward her daughter. "There's my girl," she said. "There's my one and only."

The baby gave a drooly smile and kicked her legs. Maggie scooped her into her arms and walked up and down the store aisles, showing Alice Colleen the funny labels on the products: the baby chick on Bon Ami; the Indian chief on Calumet baking powder; the baby in a cocoa bean shell on the Hershey's tin. Alice Colleen squirmed and reached for the cans, and Maggie danced her around in a circle.

He was beaten into this state of unconsciousness—

She sat down on the stool behind the counter, Alice Colleen on her lap. She had to do something to stop the voices in her head. Picking up one of the morning newspapers, she paged to the want ads.

"What's in here for Mommy?" she asked, as the baby seized the newsprint. Maggie smoothed it out with her hand and kissed Alice Colleen on the head. Alice Colleen clutched it in her fist again.

But there was—as usual—nothing. A laundress in a private home. Women cooks. Farm hands for Canadian farms. She tried another newspaper, then another. At last, her eyes chanced on an ad for a recorder to work in the Vital Statistics Department of the *Denver City Daily News*. The instructions read: "Ask for Mr. Ledbetter."

Maggie's mind wheeled. Could she do it? How would she do it? Who would keep Alice Colleen? Ma certainly didn't have the strength—

There, they have been given nothing but a half-glass of water once a day, no food, and they have been stripped of their clothing and made to sleep on wet stone floors—

Upstairs, she dressed in her best. Taking Alice Colleen to her mother's room, she said, "I'm going out for a while, Ma. Can you keep her?"

"Sure, I can," Ma said. "Are you goin' to confession?"

"Yes," Maggie lied. "I won't be long."

Her mother stirred as Maggie set the baby on the bed. Ma would read Seaney's letters aloud to her granddaughter to pass the time.

These things will come to me, I have no doubt.

The offices of the *Denver City Daily News* were tucked away in a dingy storefront on Wazee Street amid a slew of factories. The air in the office smelled of tobacco smoke, sweaty armpits, and raw fish. Still, it smelled cleaner than the sooty, oily brown haze outside. Male voices boomed through the room, arguing on telephones or with each other. With some relief, Maggie noted one harried-looking woman at the switchboard.

Mr. Ledbetter, who turned out to be the publisher of the paper, was in his forties, with a full head of heavily pomaded, gray-black hair and a stained olive-colored suit. Deep furrows lined his forehead and mouth, and Maggie wondered if his face perpetually formed into an expression of irritation. After asking her name, which she gave as Mrs. Margaret James, he invited her into his office.

As she sat in the chair in front of his desk, he asked, "What have you written?"

"You may have seen my stories in *The Ladies' Home Journal.* I've written two, now, about a young woman named Evelyn—"

Mr. Ledbetter interrupted. "If you want a job—anywhere—little girly, don't start with lies. I doubt you've written anything more than a very proper, A-plus paper on *A Tale of Two Cities.* Good day, you can see yourself out."

Humiliation pulsed in Maggie's throat. Too indignant to speak, she left the office. At home, she sat with her copies of the magazines spread open on her lap, while Alice Colleen kicked away on a blanket on the floor. Even if she showed Mr. Ledbetter the magazines, she had no proof that she'd written the stories. She heard him call her "little girly" again and again.

The bell in her mother's room tinkled, and Maggie left the baby on the floor while she went to check on her.

"Is the mail here?" Ma asked.

"Not yet. If anything comes from Seaney, I'll bring it in."

She was halfway down the hall when an idea struck her. In her own bedroom, she opened the vanity drawer. As she pulled out papers, she caught the reflection of her face in the mirror. Tomorrow, she would wear make-up—she still had rouge and lipstick somewhere, didn't she?—and marcel her hair. She would look like a woman—like Mrs. James—and not like an eighteen-year-old housewife.

The next morning, she went to the offices of the *Denver City Daily News* again. With a flourish, she laid the letters she had received from Edward W. Bok on Mr. Ledbetter's desk.

He skimmed through them, then leaned back in his chair. "So you're Mrs. James."

Maggie's heart rattled with both anger and hope. "As I told you."

"Why aren't you continuing to write for the magazine?"

"I am," Maggie said. "But it pays only every now and then. I need something more regular."

"But it must pay enough to keep you going for a while—"

"Yes, but—"

"Why not write a novel?" he asked. "That pays well."

"I don't have the time just now," she said. "My husband is away because of the war, and we have a six-month-old baby. My parents own a grocery store, but my father isn't able to manage it on his own without my brother, who is in France, so I'm helping out. My mother has taken to her bed until the war is over. She requires special care."

He looked at the letters again. "Why aren't you writing something for Mr. Bok now?"

"I am," Maggie said. "It's a story close to my own life, about George's enlistment and Evelyn's work with the Red Cross—"

He mulled over the information, and Maggie sweated. The lies she had told! Her latest story about George and Evelyn had gone no farther than the opening paragraph, and she'd had no more letters from Mr. Bok begging her to submit. By now, he had probably forgotten who she was. And to imply that her husband was a soldier! She had to make sure that no one ever knew that her name was not Margaret James, but Maggie Keohane.

Mr. Ledbetter pushed the letters across the desk toward her. "Writing obituaries pays ten cents apiece."

"Ten cents! That's hardly enough to—"

"It's the going rate," he said. "Take it or leave it, Mrs. James."

Maggie swallowed her objections. "How many people die per week?"

"A bit mercenary, aren't you?" He laughed shortly. "About six."

She decided to try one more salvo. "I would need to work from home."

"From home? I can't have that—"

"If I'm paid by the piece, why would I need to be here?"

"If I let you work from home, I'll have reporters who write their stories while lying in bed soaking themselves in bathtub gin served by their favorite doxy." He waited, evidently expecting a response. "You must be made of stronger stuff than your Evelyn, Mrs. James. You didn't even blush."

"I have to be," Maggie said. "With my brother away, and—"

"You told me all that." He waved her aside. "All right, you can have your obits. But you'll have to get the information to and from your home at your own expense."

So, now she would have to spend money for trolley fare, unless she could catch a ride or drive Pa's delivery truck, if there were any gas ration tickets left in the till. Still, it was better than taking in washing or ironing.

She nodded. "I'll take the job.

With a snort of disdain, Mr. Ledbetter said, "I still think you're better off working for Mr. Bok."

"I'll keep that in mind, thank you."

As she left the office, she walked with her chin lifted and her shoulders stiff. As soon as she was out of Mr. Ledbetter's sight, she let all the tension leave her body with one great exhale.

A job! And even if it was writing about dead people for a dime each, it would give her some money of her own. Enough to buy fabric to make church dresses for herself and Alice Colleen and—

At home, she looked through the newspaper ads for a typewriter she could afford. She found one that needed "some repairs" for $5, but it may as well be $500. Fifty people would have to die before she would be able to afford it. While she cooked and cleaned up from dinner, fed Alice Colleen, bathed the baby and put her to bed, filled a bath for Ma with Epsom salts for her aching legs and feet, saw her mother in and out of the copper tub, dumped out the water, and helped Ma into her nightgown and put her to bed, Maggie puzzled over how she would acquire a typewriter. She had typed the stories for *The Ladies' Home Journal* on Brendan's machine at Blessed Savior, but she couldn't do that every day.

By the next morning, she knew the answer.

After breakfast, and after everyone was—once again—fed and settled, she called the office of Judah Rapp. Who better than a lawyer to have a typewriter? Judah offered to pick her up and take her to look at a typewriter that he rarely used.

She waited on the wrought-iron steps outside Sullivan's Grocery until he arrived in his sorry Model T. Driving south, they traveled along Sheridan Avenue past White City, the amusement park. More than once, Ma and Pa had taken Seaney and Maggie there for an afternoon. They had ridden on the miniature train and the watery chutes that spit them out into Lake Rhoda, and at dusk, they'd marveled at the famous Tower of Jewels, which glittered with 5,000 lights. Now, the park was dark and empty, its calliope music silenced and its lights dimmed in order to conserve energy during the war.

"Have you ever been there?" Maggie asked Judah as the white buildings of the park shone in the sun.

He glanced toward the park. "No, but we had Manhattan Beach when I was young."

"Manhattan Beach?"

"The first amusement park west of the Mississippi. They trucked in loads of sand to Sloan's Lake and built it there. It was supposed to be just like Coney Island. But it couldn't compete with White City and Elitch Zoological Gardens."

"I've heard that Elitch Gardens isn't just a zoo anymore. There are rides there, and a theater and a new ballroom, too."

Judah turned the car west on Colfax. Almost at once, the signage on the storefronts changed from plainly marked English to wavering symbols written in thick black strokes.

"What language is that?" she asked.

"Hebrew," Judah said. "Some are written in German or Russian."

"German?"

"Most of the families who came during the gold rush were from eastern Germany."

So, they were Jewish and German! How awful to have so many strikes against you. Despite its proximity to Berkeley Park, she had never been in this part of town, which Seaney called "Jewtown." Others called it Little Jerusalem. In the newspapers, it was called the "West Side."

Judah drove past blocks of stores and markets on Colfax and out into the prairie, where the fields of farmers and ranchers stretched to the foothills. At last, they came to a gate topped by a wooden sign that stretched from one side of the road to the other. On one end of the sign was a message in the same Hebrew script that Maggie had seen along Colfax. The words were translated: "He who saves one life is considered as if he preserved the whole world." In the center, written in English that leaned to the left in the manner of the Hebrew script, the sign announced: "The Sanatorium of the Jewish Consumptives' Relief Society."

"What is this place?" she asked.

"A hospital," Judah said. "Colorado is considered the best place to recover from tuberculosis."

"Is your office here?"

"I have an office here, as well as one that is closer to my home," Judah said. "I help with wills and estates for the patients here. While the sick who go to the National Jewish Hospital—you've seen it, near City Park?—usually recover, those who come here don't."

He followed the road into a maze of neatly aligned white buildings sporting wide, breezy verandahs and large windows. Beyond, the fields were dotted with grazing Holsteins and beef cattle, and carefully planted with orchards of spindly fruit trees. A series of symmetrical lawns and gardens had been carved from the prairie grasses near the buildings, while a large, shaded pavilion stood at the end of a graveled path. White-roofed tents clustered around most of the buildings.

"What are those for?" Maggie asked.

Judah glanced out his window. "They're for our patients. There are over three hundred people here."

"And they live in tents?"

"The tents allow dry air to come into the room. Look over there." He motioned toward a row of beds on one of the verandahs, each one occupied by a man or woman. "It's felt that the fresh air is the best cure for consumption."

"Do they sleep outside at night?"

Judah laughed, the first time she had ever seen him smile. "No, the beds are wheeled inside." He parked the car. "Come with me."

The main building was equipped with sunny rooms filled with bookshelves, pianos, and tables for games, but Judah's office was a forlorn closet near the storage room.

A bantam-sized Corona typewriter sat on the desk. "Will this do?" he asked. "It's portable, so it isn't as heavy as the others."

"It will." Maggie plunked at a few keys. "But don't you need it for your work?"

"I'll have my secretary at my other office type what I need."

As they left the Sanatorium, Maggie marveled again at its existence. How funny that she hadn't known it was so close to her own neighborhood—no more than half a day's walk from it. Even though she and Seaney had played outside as much as the weather allowed, and she and Liam had taken a walk nearly every night, they had never strayed beyond the boundaries of Berkeley Park.

Glancing at Judah, she asked, "Why did you take Liam's case?"

"*Tzedek tzedek tirdof,*" he said.

"What's that?"

"Justice, justice, you shall pursue. It's Deuteronomy 16:20." He glanced at her. "Jews live by the law of *tzedakah,* which is doing good for others, while living by the laws of our Lord."

"But—" She searched for the right words. "Liam's not Jewish—I mean, we aren't—and, sometimes, well, Catholics and Jews don't—"

"Ah, yes. But Liam is part of the People's Council, and so am I. And your Bishop Tihen has given money to the JCRS."

"He has?" Maggie asked. Bishop Tihen was new to Denver, but already, he was known as a far different kind of leader than Bishop Matz had been. "So, is Liam just a charity case?"

"No," Judah said. "Charity suggests that a person gives to another because he has more than others and can afford to give to the poor. I have nothing to give you or Liam in that respect. You're probably as wealthy or poor"—he laughed again—"as I am. But in *tzedakah*, the giver is more blessed than the one who receives the good deed, because he has the opportunity to bring justice and kindness into the world. Working without pay for the patients at the JCRS allows me to help them to leave this world in peace, and for that I am grateful. Liam has given me the chance to fight for freedom of religion and speech. For that, I thank him." He braked the car in front of Sullivan's Grocery. "And I thank you for letting me help you now."

Maggie remembered how Seaney used to call the Jews Christ killers. Yet the Jewish Consumptives' Relief Society, with its dairy and orchards, didn't seem all that different from Mount St. Vincent Orphan Asylum and its farm. *Tzedakah*, charity—call it what you will.

Judah carried the typewriter up the stairs to the Sullivans' apartments and set it up on the table. As he was testing a few of the keys, Ma came from her bedroom, clutching Alice Colleen in her arms. "What's goin' on here?" she asked.

"Mr. Rapp is helping me, Ma," Maggie said. "I've taken a job."

"A job? What kind of—?"

"Good afternoon, Mrs. Sullivan."

Her mother eyed Judah as if she could not believe that a Jew was in her parlor. Maggie looked him over again. His body looked slightly underfed, or perhaps it was just dwarfed by his heavy, black beard, and his baggy black suit with white shirt. His yarmulke perched on the back of his head.

"Would you like to stay for dinner?" Maggie asked.

"Thank you, but no," he said. "I'll be going. But, whatever you need, Mrs. Keohane, I'm happy to help."

Three days later, Maggie carries the finished obituaries to Mr. Ledbetter's office. He sits behind his desk, the odor of boiled egg and cigar emanating from him, and reads through the first.

Maggie silently follows along with him: *The gift of life was stolen from an eighteen-year-old girl in Denver last Thursday. Elvira Mae Dooney went to meet her Maker—*

Mr. Ledbetter lays down the sheets. "You seem to be sufficiently maudlin for this business."

Maggie lets go the breath she has been holding. "Thank you," she says, although she does not know if he is complimenting or criticizing her.

He reads. "'When life's short years are past, No more to weep, no more to part, To meet in Heaven at last—' Did you write this?"

"No, it's from the, uh, the . . . *Blessed Sacrament Book.*"

"A Catholic book?"

"Yes, sir."

He scans the sheet. "Is Elvira a Papist?"

"The funeral was conducted by the Rev. Father Allen, and she was interred at Mt. Olivet."

"It takes one to know one, doesn't it, Mrs. James?" Without waiting for a reply, he continues, "This poem or prayer or whatever you call it is three stanzas long. Obituaries take up advertising space, and a newspaper lives and dies by its advertising revenue. So no poems, Mrs. James. No Bible verses or sweet dedications or anything else that takes more than one hundred words."

"Yes, sir."

He scribbles something on a scrap of paper. "I'll call you when I have more work for you." He hands the paper to her. "See Mr. Ainsley for your pay."

TWENTY-EIGHT

In August, General Pershing decided to amass the largest aviation force ever to engage in one operation. The objective was the St. Mihiel Salient, ten miles south of Verdun, where German-held territory bulged fifteen miles into France along a twenty-five mile stretch of the Front. Pershing designated Colonel William Mitchell as Chief of the Air Service for the first-ever, American-led aerial attack.

For a month, over 1,000 French and American aircraft assembled at French aerodromes: observation and reconnaissance planes, pursuit groups, bombers, and balloon corps. Some of the American fliers had a couple of months of experience at the Front, but most had never been this close before. On the ground, pilots and observers spent their time in classes, studying terrain and strategy, formations and targets. In the crowded Observers' Room in Toul, Paul studied and amended maps of the terrain, trench systems, and barrage fire systems, comparing enemy strong points, calculating routes, and ascertaining distances.

On September 12, the first day of the three day attack, low-hanging clouds grayed the sky, and rain flooded the fields and runways. Paul and Kenny took off at 6:00, as per orders. They flew under the protection of two biplanes from the 1st Aero Squadron. Kenny urged the Salmson upward to an altitude of 9,000 feet, above the clouds, where the sun peeked over the eastern horizon.

For a few precious minutes, Paul enjoyed the sunrise, imagining how he would describe it to Kathleen: the gray of night thinning into a steely blue; the clouds burning yellow, orange, and red as the sun sped upward to its full brilliance. Soon enough, it was full-on daylight.

"Hold on, Reston!" Kenny yelled. "I'm going to chase holes."

He swooped toward spots where the clouds shifted, thinned, or parted. Whenever a break in the cover allowed them to see the ground, Kenny circled, while the escort planes hung back, watching for enemies. Paul alternated between looking through the binoculars and studying his maps. Squinting, he identified Montsec, which was in German-occupied territory, in the distance.

"We have to be close!" he shouted. "Take us down over there."

The three American planes cut through the clouds to 650 feet. Once over the trenches, Paul fired a six-star rocket from his flare gun, then scoured the ground for the fabric communication panels that were supposed to be displayed by the infantry.

"No panels!" he called to Kenny. "They must not be watching!"

"Or they've forgotten what our planes look like again."

Paul readjusted his binoculars. A joke—mostly-true and only half-funny—circulated among the fliers that the infantry cut up the communication panels for blankets and bandages or even as wash rags in the trenches. Worse, the soldiers on the ground hadn't been trained to recognize the insignia of the United States, which had once been a star in a circle, but was now concentric circles of white, red and blue. Moreover, the Army's officers complained that the flares shot by the aerial observers gave away the infantry's position to the Germans. Some of them ordered their men not to answer.

Paul signalled to Kenny to drop in altitude.

"Okay, but I'm not getting any closer to those guns," Kenny shouted.

The escort planes took up positions on either side of the Salmson, while Paul concentrated on finding the American lines. He shot another rocket, but still, there was no response from the infantry. They tried again, without success.

"Let's go home!" he called. "We've been here too long!"

Kenny turned south, but the escort planes waggled their wings to indicate that Kenny should follow them. Together, they flew north over the foremost German trenches.

"Jesus, what are they thinking?" Kenny yelled. "We better beat it!"

They came in over a wide road cut through the gray land. "Troop movement!" Paul called.

Below, a horse-drawn artillery train crawled along the road. For about a mile, the line of draft horses and mules slipped and strained in the mud, one caisson after another forging forward a few feet only to lose momentum behind another that was stuck or disabled. Officers rode alongside the horses, urging the wagon masters, who whipped at the struggling beasts.

"Let's go!" Kenny called. "Get the guns ready!"

The planes from the 1st Aero Squadron took the first pass. Their bullets sent the mired, overloaded horse train into chaos, with one team tangling up with another as men dodged and died beside them. Following behind the others, Kenny shot his single gun from the front, while Paul strafed with the Lewis guns. Close behind the escorts, Kenny looped up into the sky and came around again.

The three American planes flew over the wagon train in the same formation. Smoke obscured the road, but what struck Paul was the horror of it. The masses of dead horseflesh, the ones that clung to life kicking at traces and struggling to escape, men crawling for cover or laid out, their arms thrown to either side as if they were making a plea for mercy, or crumpled in blood-stained heaps.

Kenny made a third pass behind the other planes to catch the last of the stragglers. "Starboard!" he shouted to Paul.

Paul spied a German soldier unhitching a team of unscathed Percherons from a capsized caisson. The soldier ran into the field beside the road, the reins of the balking horses in his hands. As Kenny dropped lower to give Paul a more direct shot, the German seemed to realize the futility of his escape and glanced upward. He had lost his helmet, and his hair was the color of rust. Paul judged his age at no more than sixteen or seventeen.

A boy, a child, not even a man yet, but still, caught up in this landscape of death.

The German boy pressed his face against the noses of the horses as he waited for the bullets that would slaughter the three of them.

Paul fingered the trigger, but did not shoot.

Kenny shouted back. "What's wrong?"

Paul shook his head. "No more."

When they arrived back at the Aerodrome at Toul, Kenny leaped from the plane. As Paul dropped to the ground, Kenny demanded, "What happened back there, Reston? Why didn't you kill him? Hell, I would have done it, but I was out of bullets."

"Let him go home and grow up," Paul said.

"That's claptrap. You should have finished the job. Think about it—there would have been no one left when the Heines came looking for their comrades. Maybe then they'd understand that they shouldn't have made America sore at them." Kenny started to walk away, but swung violently around. "You aren't losing your nerve on me, are you?"

"No," Paul said. "I'm not."

But it grew harder every day. He tried to remind himself of what he had told Kathleen—that their faith in their love for each other would see them through, that they would be together again—but the brutal reality of how many died while serving in the Army Air Service ate away at his confidence.

That day, seven of the eighteen planes sent out from the 12th Aero Squadron had not returned.

The fliers play as hard as they work. On leave in Paris for a few days after the St. Mihiel sortie, Paul, Kenny, Owen, and his observer, Hugh, hit the fashionable Hôtel de Crillon at the end of the Champs Élysées near the Jeu de Paume and the Place de la Concorde. Perhaps because the Crillon sits next to the American Embassy or perhaps because it is the most expensive hotel in Paris, it hosts the crème de la crème: General Pershing, Admiral Sims, Lloyd George, and France's President, Raymond Poincaré. The Yale pilots stay at the cheaper and less sparkling Hôtel des États-Unis.

They seek out entertainment at the Folies Bergère and a music hall called the Casino de Paris. From there, they move on to Harry's

Bar and Ciro's, both known for their warm welcomes toward the American birdmen. It's no secret in Paris that the Air Service pays twenty-five percent more than the Army, and that most of the pilots come from the richest families in America.

As they are leaving Ciro's, a woman in a bedraggled feather stole steps from the shadows and attaches herself to Paul's arm. The restaurant owners aren't the only ones eager to part the boys of the Air Service and their money.

Owen laughs. "Ready to get your Parisian education, Reston?"

"Non, merci, mais non," Paul says to the woman.

"Oh, come on, Paul," Hugh says. "It's our duty to repopulate France the American way."

"You won't get rid of her," Owen says. "It's a two-fisted brawl to get rid of them, and then there's just another one behind that one. This entire city is one big brothel."

"And she's willing to take you with only one wing," Kenny adds.

Paul laughs. Above the left pocket of his uniform is one silver wing attached to an O, the badge of the observer. Only pilots wear the full set of wings.

He waves a dismissal at the woman, and she veers off into the shadows with a hissed, *"Cochon!"*

"Dang, Reston, you've been called a pig." Hugh laughs.

"It's not the last time, I wager," Paul says.

"You forget he talks the language like a true Frenchie," Kenny reminds Hugh. "He could call her a lot worse."

"Then, why didn't you try to talk her down in price?"

Kenny intervenes. "Hey, I heard some of the girls from the YMCA are giving a party at their hotel. I got the address earlier."

"Are they American?"

"No, French."

"What are we waiting for?" Hugh asks.

At a three-story hotel near the corner of Boulevard Raspail and Montparnasse, the party is in full swing. It is an officers-only event: a Major, a Colonel, and four captains from the U.S. Army Air Service are in attendance, as well as the four Lieutenants and a few others. The party is to celebrate the birthday of the Major, who sits on a striped divan beside a giant urn filled with dyed red ostrich feathers. On the sleek coffee table are two bottles of Pol Roger champagne. Already drunk, the Major lists onto the shoulder of a sunny brunette whose thick hair is parted in the middle and pulled into a chignon adorned with flowers. She holds a glass to his lips and coaxes him to drink in a babyish voice: *"Allez, mon Doudou, allez!"*

A phonograph blares from one corner of the apartment, where three couples dance. In another corner, a woman with plaited chestnut-colored hair plays ragtime on the piano with her right hand while an American Captain stands behind her and reaches around to play a sloppy left hand accompaniment. Every time he strikes a chord, he nuzzles her neck. She slaps at him without managing to drive him away.

The Major spends most of his time bragging. "You should have seen it at St. Mihiel. Constant flight—one airplane would touch down and another would take off. Three days of it, in the worst weather we could have imagined. Fog in the valleys and clouds above. But after it was all over, we'd flown more than three thousand sorties, brought down fifty enemy aircraft, bombed the hell out of their trenches, and sent the Germans a message that we are here to stay."

A woman with cropped, silver-blonde hair hands a glass of champagne to Paul, and he accepts it with a *"Merci."*

Kenny watches the girl move away. "What do you think of that one?" he asks Paul. "What do you think of the hair?"

"It's definitely not real."

"What about that one?"

He gestures toward a small, delicate, woman who has black eyes and dark hair. Her face is heart-shaped and her lips pout in a red bow, giving her a more innocent air than the others. She's dressed in a lavender frock with a square neck trimmed with a band of lace. Like Paul and Kenny, she seems to be observing the festivities without taking part. She catches Paul's eye and looks away.

"I call that one," Kenny says. "A regular *fleur-de-lys.*"

"Good luck with the language."

"I don't need it. She'll know what I want. No butting in, Reston, with your smooth Frog talk."

Kenny swallows the last of his drink and wends his way across the room. He and the woman engage in some sort of conversation, with heads nodding and eyes bright. Within minutes, they dance together to a slow and gentle waltz.

The Negro Maître d'Hôtel appears at the door, his threadbare suit neatly pressed and a white bow tie at his neck. He carries a tray of cheeses, sausages, and breads. As he enters the room, the guests grab at it, leaving the tray nearly empty by the time he reaches the coffee table.

The Major rumbles out a request. "Anybody speak French? We need somebody to tell this boy here what we want."

"I do," Paul volunteers.

"Tell him"—the Major showers Paul with boozy breath—"that we want more champagne. Enough to fill the bathtub. Get it?"

"The bathtub?" Paul asks.

"Yeah, the bathtub."

Paul relays the message to the Maître d'Hôtel, whose only response is a flick of his eyebrows. *"Combien de bouteilles s'agit-il, Monsieur?"*

Paul translates. "He wants to know how many bottles you want."

"Hell, I don't know," the Major says.

Others make suggestions. "Twenty bottles," "A hell of a lot," "Enough to get 'D and D,'" which means Drunk and Down. At last, the Major snaps his fingers at the Maître d'Hôtel. "Come on, boy, you figure it out."

"Quinze francs, une bouteille," the Maître d'Hôtel says, stone-faced.

"What's that?" the Major asks.

"Fifteen francs a bottle," Paul says.

Uproar ensues, as the Major and the other officers claim they never have and never will pay that much for wine, especially Frenchie wine.

Paul haggles until the Maître d'Hôtel agrees to twelve francs per bottle.

As they wait for the champagne to arrive, the sunny brunette stands and declares, "When I drink zee champagne, I am wild to dance in zee altoge-zer."

The Major hoots. "The altogether? Do you know what that is?"

Paul leans against the wall, while some of the others take a step backward, evidently unwilling to participate. The dark-haired girl, who has been dancing with Kenny, runs across the room, calling, *"Non, non, Ada, non!"*

"Ferme ta gueule, Mélisande!" Ada snaps as she sways into a Salome-like striptease. The phonograph incongruously blares out "Tiger Rag" as she teasingly unbuttons her blouse. She runs her hands from her waist, over her breasts, and to her shoulders. Someone whistles, and she unbuttons her skirt at the side seam and lets it fall in a puddle on the floor. Now, in ruffled corset, chemise, and drawers, she stretches out her arms and whirls around.

The Major gestures at her black hosiery. "Take them off."

Ada complies, each leg hoisted and a dainty foot planted on the Major's thigh as she unhooks her garters. Mélisande frowns from the corner near the piano.

Ada finishes the show, untying her corset, which flaps to the floor, then shedding chemise and drawers. She sways to a tempo that evidently comes from her own head.

The Major bellows, "She did it!"

A couple of officers slip out of the room, but most stay, laughing at Ada's antics, either nervously or salaciously. Hugh and Owen watch with keen eyes from near the fireplace. Kenny stands stock still, his arms akimbo, while Paul plans an escape through the partygoers to the door.

"J'ai froide!" Ada complains.

"What'd she say, Lieutenant?" The Major asks Paul.

"She's cold, sir," he replies.

"Bring her a blanket!"

Mélisande retrieves a quilt from the bedroom, wrapping it around Ada's shoulders with a firm maiden-aunt-like tug on the front. Without being asked, Hugh stacks wood in the fireplace and tosses in a match.

Paul moves toward the piano, but finds himself next to Mélisande. Kenny is nowhere to be seen.

"She should not have done that," Mélisande says in clear English.

"Do you live here?" Paul asks.

"Oui, avec Ada et Simone."

"How did you learn to speak English so well?"

"My grandmother lives in Virginia, in the United States. I spent summers with her until, until"—she gestures at the room—"this happened."

"The war?"

"Oui."

"Did Lieutenant McKenzie leave?"

"Je ne sais pas," she says indifferently. "You Americans, you come here, and you think we are just to be played with. We are not."

"I'm sorry," Paul says. *"Nous ne sommes pas tous comme ça,"* We are not all like this.

His stomach twists. *But we become like this*, he thinks.

It's because of the cold-blooded nature of what they do. Flying directly into the range of anti-aircraft guns, or striking one-on-one at an enemy plane, or dropping to an altitude where they can see the faces of the men as they strafe them with machine bullets. It demands that emotions, that tenderness and compassion, that any humanity be eliminated, set aside as if it is a bothersome friend. It demands complete control and a deadness of the heart. But everything roars back at some point. It comes out in wanting to dance, to touch, to make love, whether or not the other person understands. He can see it happening here tonight; he fears he will one day see it happen to himself.

Speaking in French so he won't be overheard, he tells Mélisande of strafing the retreating horse-drawn artillery train and of the German soldier who stood in silent resignation with his team of horses. "I didn't shoot them," he concludes.

She speaks in English. "Do you know what the Germans did to Belgium, to where my family lived? They came to us and began to shoot—everyone, anything, even my poor dog that hadn't any quarrel with them at all—and we left on foot, walking for days, with no food, no water, no coats or boots for the cold. I wore heeled, button-up shoes that were meant for a dance floor, and twisted my ankles so often that I had to ride in a wheel barrow. Then the Uhlans came and rode through us, swinging their swords and cutting down whoever they could. My brother, only ten years old, carelessly swerved in front of one of them on a bicycle, and my sister and I were—"

"Bring me some butter!"

Mélisande's words are lost beneath the call from Hugh, who is building a fire for Ada. Either the wood is too green to burn or he is too drunk to do the job properly.

Owen fetches butter from the kitchen, while Mélisande frets. "That is all we have, *c'est tout!* How are we to have more?" She turns on Paul. "See, you should have killed that German. You should kill every one of them. This war must end."

She hurries off, and Paul wonders what he had wanted from her. Had he expected her to applaud his restraint and compliment his soft heart? Had he expected her to respond as Kathleen might—with horror at the carnage, with heartbreak at the needless death of so many humans and animals? Perhaps he's forgotten how to read human nature. Or perhaps this war has made even the most basic sentiment a rare thing.

Mélisande fails to wrestle the chunk of butter from Owen, who holds it high in the air while she stands on tiptoe to try to reach it. "Don't worry, baby, I'll bring you more," Owen promises with a smack to her lips.

He tosses it to Hugh, who rubs it on the wood. When Hugh strikes another match, flames leap upward.

"Voilà!" he says.

At the same time, Ada protests from the divan, *"Non, non! Arrêtez!"*

The Major's hands have slipped beneath the quilt as he cuddles her on his lap. His lips suck at her bare shoulder. Ada clutches the quilt to her breast.

"Sir!" One of the Captains speaks. "Please, sir!"

As Paul reaches the door, the Colonel, who has been quietly courting the peroxide blonde, decides to forgo the champagne and to fill the bathtub with water instead. As Mélisande escorts a sobbing Ada to the bedroom, five of the senior officers pick up the cursing Major and carry him to the bathroom, where they dump him in the cold water: boots, breeches, and all.

TWENTY-NINE

At Récicourt, the barrage never quiets. The earth shakes for miles as the shells plow into the trenches barely seven miles away. Shells fall in town, too, knocking down the few remnants of walls and splintering the shards of glass left in the window panes of the house where the Graves Family Foundation Relief Society lives. Kathleen wears her tin hat all day. Her head aches constantly, but she doesn't know whether it is from the weight of the hat or from the din of the Front, which is ear-splitting even from here. She wonders if she'll ever be able to hear complete silence again.

Outside, the main road through the town is jammed with trucks. Hank keeps a cross-hatched tally of the number of vehicles that fly the Stars and Stripes. She declares that seven hundred trucks pass through Récicourt during the daylight hours.

"That's nearly sixty trucks an hour," she reports.

"And almost as many through the night," Kathleen says.

Hank and Kathleen—and Mrs. Brently, when she has the time—become mourners for the American boys who die at the nearby hospital. They follow the hearses through the surrounding forest to a large clearing that has been consecrated as an American cemetery. As the flag-draped coffin is lowered into the ground, the girls lead the others—a few soldiers, an officer or two—in "The Star-Spangled Banner." Every week, they walk through the cemetery, placing flowers on the graves. Soon, there are too many to tend.

The sky is full at Récicourt. Homing pigeons swoop through the air, released from a camouflaged, wire coop at the other end of town. Hundreds of French and American planes pass overhead.

Kathleen knows that Paul flies in a French Salmson, although she cannot recognize it, but the talk is now of an American plane engine, the Liberty L-12 that is built by the Lincoln Motor Company. When they can, Kathleen and Hank run outside the canteen to watch the squadrons pass. Soldiers pause on the street to watch as well.

"Look, it's the Lafayette Escadrille!" Hank says.

"That's not what it's called now," Kathleen says. "It's the United States Army Air Service."

"United States Army Air Service," Hank repeats. "Oh, I like how that sounds! Do you think Paul is up there?"

Kathleen's heart seizes, as it always does when she hears airplane motors. He could be right above me, she thinks, and he would never know that I'm watching him. The German pilots have parachutes, and only recently, the British have started giving parachutes to their pilots. The French and Americans don't provide them.

Oh, be careful, my love, come back to me.

Every task that Hank and Kathleen have done in the past year is replicated one-thousand fold in Récicourt. They are always rushed, urgent, and frantic to serve the Doughboys who pass through on their way to the Argonne Forest. They make and pour thousands of cups of cocoa in one afternoon. They put together hundreds of sandwiches, only to see them all consumed within an hour. At the nearby field hospital, the girls help with the patients, serving hot soup and water to those who await transport to the base hospitals in the south.

There is no heat in the abandoned house where they are staying. After poking a broomstick up the flue to clear it, Hank discovers it has been cemented closed.

"Maybe the owner of the house was a German sympathizer," Hank says. "I've heard they try to sabotage the French however they can."

"Well, when he comes back, I hope he puts his back out trying to chip it out of there," Kathleen says. "We'll have to rely on our water bottles for warmth."

But in this damp and windowless house, where the kitchen pans overflow with rain water from the leaking ceiling, and sleep is nearly impossible in the noise and light of war, and the cold of another winter seeps in through every nook and cranny, the Spanish flu that has been passed from troops in America to those in France and back to the civilians of America strikes.

First, Hank falls ill, and then Mrs. Brently.

Kathleen does what she can for them. She sits by their beds during the day and reads letters or books to them. Mostly they sleep, but when they awaken, they cough and wheeze. Hank complains of pain in her knees and elbows, while Mrs. Brently mentions nothing about how she feels. Although she rests more peacefully than Hank does, her face and lips blanch to a deathly white and her lustrous blond hair fades to a dull straw color.

Kathleen sends a telegram to Jim advising him of the situation and asking what he wants her to do. With the heavy fighting nearby in the Argonne Forest, she isn't sure that communications are possible. After three days, she still has not received a reply.

Daubing Hank's forehead, she asks, "How are you feeling?"

"Are you there?" Hank asks, as if she can't hear.

"Right beside you."

There is no room in the hospital for flu cases just now; every available bed must be filled by a wounded soldier. Yet, after Dr. Adams from the Evacuation Hospital visits Mrs. Brently and Hank, he insists that both women be moved into the dry, warmer room of the house. Shortly after, two military orderlies arrive to hoist Hank's bed—with her in it—and deliver her across the hall.

Kathleen wanders to her room, which is damp with the rain that falls through the faulty roof. She sits on the bed, looking at the empty space around her. She is alone, without anyone she can depend upon to help her. Alone and in a country where she does not truly speak the language. Alone and caught in a land that is never safe or peaceful.

She lights the lamp and takes from her trunk the box of treasures that Jim sent her from Redlands. The pine cones have grown brittle, and the sap in the branches has dried into a hard resin. The dirt has lost its clean, sandy scent and taken up the leathery smell of the pouch.

Redlands, oh, home. How I wish I were there.

Her head fills with cotton. She's had so little sleep in the past few days that every inch of her skin aches. She feels as if there are weights attached to her wrists and ankles. It is agonizing to move.

Lying down on the bed, she cries herself into a comforting darkness.

As she sleeps, she dreams.

It is the middle of the night, and she's in the hospital ward, carrying a tray. But everything is so jumbled, and nothing is as it should be. She can't find what she is looking for, but she isn't sure what that is. She peers into faces, leaning too close, able to feel her own breath as it touches their skin.

There's the Irish boy whose rosary swarms with lice. "I'll eat French food for the rest of my life if you're not Catholic, too," he had teased, and she had shown him her rosary and said a Hail Mary with him. They had shared stories about their respective parishes, about the priests, about their families, his in Dublin and hers in Denver.

But he wasn't here, was he? Wasn't he in Amiens?

And the German boy, but which one? There have been several now, but she remembers best the one who said "*Danke*" when she offered him water. And she hadn't known how to say God bless you in return.

Gott segne Sie.

She knows how to say it now.

And the men come into the hospital still, with their eyes blistered shut by mustard gas, and arms and legs that are gone. Where do those pieces go? They are caught in the trees, which have human limbs on their stunted trunks rather than green, healthy branches. They are left behind in the trenches or beside a road. They are forgotten amid the wheat fields or dairy pastures. They are piled in one of the outer buildings that the Red Cross canteeners aren't allowed to enter.

And the orderlies draw lots to see who has to bury the amputated parts, in the dark places beyond the cemetery where the flies walk on the soil, digging at what lies just below.

Claim them, she calls. *Oh, come and claim your arms and legs! Take them home, on the ship to America, with you. Don't leave them behind in France! How can you stand to leave such a large part of you, something so precious, behind?*

And Helen has fallen in love with a man who has no face.

I couldn't do that. I couldn't love someone who has no lips, no nose, no cheekbone. I want a man who is whole and healthy—

Paul, whose body is strong and lithe and warm, whose lips taste of tea, whose hands can pleasure with just a touch. Have faith, he had said, just as you do in God, in the Church. Have faith that we will be together again.

But the ambulance drivers won't take the dead away from the hospitals if the bodies are stiff. And horses are shot if they go lame, because the great machinery of war must move forward, onward, grinding up the land beneath it into mud and waste—

And still, we make soup and cocoa and coffee and donuts.

Soup will heal skin flayed by mustard gas.

Cocoa will help that lost leg regrow.

A donut will rebuild your face where your eye socket and cheek bone are now bare, and your jaw has been blown away by a mortar.

Oh, it will, it will, if we only keep doing it. If we only have faith. Cross my heart, hope to die. Stick a needle in my eye.

And that afternoon with Paul, when he had held her so close as the planes fought in the sky, and he had told her of falling through— was it ice?

No, that was Jim, in Central Park. He told of his brother, Stephen, and his sister, and Mrs. Brently lying on the ice, freezing to death, and Jim holding onto the sleigh runner, and the skin tearing from his hands when his father pulled him away. But when Paul falls, he will fall through flaming clouds.

And they sang:

Gee, I'd like to be a monkey in the zoo, You'd never have a bit of work to do.

You've got no one to please, All you do is look for fleas,
Oh, I'd like to be a monkey in the zoo.

A voice cuts through the fog in her head. "Kathleen, what are you doing here?"

Mrs. Brently's face, ghostly and hollowed out, appears before her. Someone must have roused her from her sick bed.

"Kathleen, why are you here?"

"I'm serving cocoa," she says impatiently.

"You need to go back to bed," Mrs. Brently says.

"But they need me."

Mrs. Brently sits beside her. "Who needs you? You are sitting on the floor of the canteen alone in your nightdress and socks. No one else is here—it's the middle of the night." She tugs at the tray in Kathleen's hands. "Give me the tray."

Kathleen clasps it against her breast. "I have to take it to . . . I have to help them . . . I . . ."

Gently, Mrs. Brently wrests the tray from her and sets it to one side.

"You don't need to do this now," she says. "What you need to do is go back to bed."

Paul had said that her body reminded him of . . . what painting was it? Olympia. *The woman with no fear. Olympia, the woman who says, "I offer all this to you."*

But she is afraid of so much, and—

She starts to cry. "He knows what happens—he's seen it. We watched Maurice burn, we saw how fast the plane went up in flames—"

Mrs. Brently shivers with the cold. "Stop, Kathleen. Don't do this."

"Mrs. Brently."

Dr. Adams, who comes from Florida and likes to tease Hank about alligators, speaks.

"This young lady is ill," Mrs. Brently says. "I believe she's also hallucinating."

"Why are you out of bed, Mrs. Brently? You shouldn't—"

"She's in my care. I have a responsibility—"

The voices fade away. *The fighting is done by men,* Kathleen wants to—or does—say. *But we have to fight, too. We have to see what they do to each other, and we have to try to fix it. To be cheery and happy while they lie in their beds with their bodies torn apart and with tubes stuck into their oozing wounds and the smell that made my stomach turn. And we have to wait and hope and pray that they don't die, and Seaney said he wouldn't be killed, and Paul said he wouldn't leave me alone—*

Mrs. Brently's voice fills her ears. "Yes, I believe a sedative would be a good idea."

Moments—or more?—later, she says, "Here, Kathleen, drink this. It's laudanum. Come now, let's go back to bed."

Kathleen lets Mrs. Brently lead her away and tuck her into bed, but the liquid that Dr. Adams gives her makes her dizzy and makes her head hurt even as she sleeps through the next day. That night, she goes downstairs to the canteen again, planning to pass out cigarettes and fix cocoa for the men. There's a sign on the door: CANTEEN CLOSED. QUARANTINE: INFLUENZA. NO ENTRY. It is signed by Major McLaughlin of the American Expeditionary Force.

Kathleen reads it again and again. *Why is the canteen closed? Why is it quarantined? Who is sick?*

Ah, yes, Hank and Mrs. Brently.

But I'm taking care of them.

No, you aren't, you've been sleeping.

Oh, I have to go to them—

But I want to go home. I want to go to Redlands and see Mama and Papa, and to ride Napoli, and to catch the tadpoles in the pond, and to pet the moss that grows between the rocks, and—

At last someone—who?—rouses her and says, "Kathleen, you're very ill, and you need better care than you can get here. We're taking you to Paris."

THIRTY

Mary Jane held the thick doweling of a banner in her gloved hands. The other end was held by Anneka, who struggled to keep her footing as the banner blew backward in the icy, October wind. The two-mile parade route of the Fourth Liberty Loan Drive took the marchers through the sunless, wind-swept canyons between Denver's tallest buildings. Miss Reston, Mrs. Reed, Miss Crawley and a group of about ten women marched just behind them.

Designed by the National Woman's Party, the banner read: DON'T BUY LIBERTY BONDS UNTIL ALL WOMEN ARE AT LIBERTY TO VOTE. It was met by boos, hisses, and catcalls. Mary Jane gritted her chattering teeth and pressed onward. She wasn't sure she believed it was wrong to buy Liberty Bonds. After all, her brother was in France. She glanced toward Anneka, who walked with her chin in the air and her mouth set with the determination of a true believer.

"Unpatriotic!" someone shouted. "Un-American!"

"Put them in jail!"

At last, they came to the Denver Auditorium. No one was allowed inside—all indoor meetings had been banned—so the nearly 10,000 spectators huddled in the cold. Miss Reston and Miss Crawley staked out a spot within sight of the speakers on the stage, who included Governor Gunter, Denver Mayor Mills, and, of course, Mr. Graves. Mary Jane and Anneka rested the poles of the banner on the sidewalk and took up spots on either side of it. As someone coughed behind her, Mary Jane pulled her scarf up over her mouth.

What a mixed up world this was! Although casualty lists from France had started to appear in the newspapers as more American boys fell in battle, they were dwarfed by the obituary lists of local residents. American families had willingly sent their sons and fathers off to war knowing that they might not return, but they hadn't counted on the possibility that their men would come home to find their entire family in America dead from the flu.

So far, no one knew how to quell the tide of illness, although plenty of advice had been offered. Dr. William H. Sharpley, Manager of Health for Denver, suggested that the healthy avoid drinking from cups used by others. The U.S. Surgeon General advised against wearing of tight shoes and gloves and urged folks to remember the three C's: clean mouth, clean heart, and clean clothes. The *Rocky Mountain News* even claimed that the Spanish flu could be avoided if citizens voted for Republican candidates in the upcoming election.

No spitting was allowed, and streetcar windows were to remain open—which made for a cold trip to Graves Oil in the mornings. The police no longer raided the houses of prostitution along Colfax or brought vagrants and loiterers to the jail. Workers at restaurants and soda fountains were now required to wash glasses and utensils in hot, soapy water between customers.

None of it seemed to work. Schools, churches, theaters, and other places of amusement had been shuttered. Businesses were advised to shorten the work day to what was essential, and all were required to lock their doors by 6 p.m., except restaurants, drugstores, and hotels. In the typing pool at Graves Oil, Mavis and Edna had fallen sick, and Miss Crawley had passed on the word that work was now strictly for those who didn't show any signs of illness.

On the stage near the doors of the auditorium, Mr. Graves took the megaphone. "I will be brief," he called. "It's cold, and we are all wishing we were inside, where the fire is burning and the kettle is on, but we must again turn our thoughts and hearts to our boys in France. We know that some of them have made the final sacrifice, but what else have they done? I have here the numbers of prisoners taken by our Doughboys." He pulled a sheet of paper from his pocket. "20,000 German prisoners taken after fighting in Chateau-

Thierry; 50,000 after the Battle of Belleau Woods. It's now said that Germans are giving themselves up without fighting, because they know that Germany has lost, and they would rather be on the side that is right"—he paused for applause and cheering—"the side that is honorable, the side that is kind, the side that believes and trusts in God, the side that is American!"

People burst out in shouts and whistles. Mary Jane looked toward Anneka, who scrutinized Mr. Graves with a somber expression.

"Surely you've seen him before," Mary Jane said. "At his parents' house, at least."

"Oh, yes, I have. But when he talks, he is different somehow."

He certainly was, Mary Jane thought. Even though his breath clouded around his head with every word, his blue eyes radiated warmth. More than one woman in the crowd was transfixed by him.

He continued. "How many of you were in Cheesman Park this weekend? Last Saturday, the first government battle plane ever seen in this state landed on the lawns of Cheesman Park. It came in without a bump or wobble of the wings and touched down on the earth with the same grace as a bird. The pilot was a young man; he could be your son, or yours, or yours. By purchasing Liberty Bonds, you, the people of America, have made it possible for the U.S. to build airplanes that are capable of destroying our enemies! So, let's buy more!"

As the audience roared, Mr. Graves stepped into the crowd with his donation cup, just as he had done so long ago when the war first started. A Four Minute Man bellowed, "How many of you have bought your full quota of Liberty Bonds? If you haven't, you're a pro-German slacker as bad as any other—"

Mr. Graves reached the spot where the members of the National Woman's Party had collected. "Miss Crawley," he acknowledged. "Miss Grayson." His eyes settled on Anneka. "Mrs. Lindstrom, I wouldn't have expected to see you here."

"I am here with the National Woman's Party," Anneka said.

"Well, I trust you'll all be back at your jobs in just a few minutes," he said coolly. "It isn't wise to be out in this cold for long.

Please take care going back. Cover your faces and wash your hands once you're there."

He turned away, and Mary Jane lifted her eyebrows in surprise. "Usually he's delighted to see his employees at these things," she said.

As Anneka's lower lip pressed out in a scowl, Miss Crawley offered, "He doesn't approve of the National Woman's Party. Or of our banner, I would think."

The rally ended, and the women parted, with Miss Reston and some of the others rolling up the banner and taking it with them. Mary Jane and Miss Crawley returned to Graves Oil, while Anneka caught a streetcar to Cheesman Park.

After work, Mary Jane went to Anneka's house. It had started to snow, and the temperature was dropping. She let herself in by the back door, where she could leave her wet boots and coat. She found Mina at the kitchen table. A book of arithmetic sums was open before her, and she had written out a few on a sheet of lined paper, but she was busily coloring in a lopsided star that she had drawn at the top of the page. Her face was drawn up in a thunderous glower.

"Well, hello there," Mary Jane said. "What are you doing in here alone?"

"Mother told me to come in here while she talks to Mr. Yeem."

"Mr. Yeem is here?"

"Yes, but she wouldn't let me see him. She told me to do my studies."

Voices traveled from the other room, the words inaudible through the heavy wooden door of the kitchen. Mary Jane kissed Mina on the head.

"I need to tell her that I'm here," she said. "I don't want to intrude on your mother's privacy."

She opened the kitchen door, but did not let it latch behind her. Quietly, she slipped down the hallway. Her attention was caught by the great coat and hat hanging on the coat rack. They belonged to Jim Graves. She leaned to her right, barely able to see around the corner into the parlor. One red and brown leather cowboy boot came into view as Mr. Graves paced in front of the fireplace.

Mary Jane pulled back quickly.

Mr. Yeem. Of course. Anneka still stumbled over certain sounds, and "j" was pronounced as "y" in Swedish. She would say it softer—perhaps "Yim"—but Mina had picked it up as a child, and the name had become "Yeem."

Mr. Graves' voice floated back to her. "You're putting yourself in jeopardy. The members of the National Woman's Party seek to get assaulted or arrested for the publicity it gives the suffragist cause. Those banners, their marches and protests are meant to provoke, nothing more."

"It is what I believe in," Anneka said forcefully. "So Mina does not have to live as I have had to—"

"What do you mean?" Mr. Graves asked. "If you've ever needed anything, you've only had to ask for it. It's been given to you."

"I don't mean that. I want to be an equal partner to my husband and the father of my children. I want to be as smart as he is, to know how to read and write as he does, and to take care of his home in a good way. I want him to think of me as someone who helps, not as a pet who is to be spoiled."

"I have never disrespected you."

Good Lord, Mary Jane thought, Ross had fallen in love with Jim Graves' mistress. And Mina's beauty and grace, her brilliant eyes and whitish curls, and her sharp intelligence were not just from her mother, but from her father as well.

She started to open the kitchen door to retreat, but the hinge gave a barely audible squeak. She flattened herself against the wall.

"But you want a wife, too," Anneka was saying. "I know that. There is the girl in France, Kathleen."

"Who told you that?" Mr. Graves demanded. "Johanna Crawley? Mary Jane Grayson?"

"It does not matter who told me." Anneka's voice rose. "You've chosen a woman who is younger than me, who is almost the same age as I was when . . . but who has no more money or position than I have. Why, if she is right, wasn't I?"

"It has nothing to do with that. It has to do with—"

"Are you in love with her?" Anneka asked. "Or do you simply want her for a summer, as you did me. I had your child!"

"For God's sake, lower your voice," Mr. Graves snapped. "Where is Mina?"

"In the kitchen. She cannot hear."

Mary Jane eyed the door, which was slightly ajar. She stepped toward it to block the crack with her body.

"You're right," Mr. Graves said. "I'm fond of Miss O'Doherty. I think of her as my equal partner, as you call it, in both temperament and intellect. And the situation—my situation—is different now. I can do as I please."

"You mean that you have the money and position to marry as you please."

"Yes," he said tersely. "And you'll be marrying soon, so you'll have what you want. Isn't that true? You're marrying this man for love and not as a convenience?"

Afraid of what she might hear, Mary Jane covered her mouth with her hand.

"I am in love with him."

"I'm glad that you've found happiness." Mr. Graves' voice grew tender. "Anneka, you can be as free as you like when you're married. You can go to whatever public meetings or marches that you want, but please, don't do anything that attracts attention to you just now. It makes you vulnerable to the clods at the 100% American Club and others like them. It makes me vulnerable as well. That's all I ask."

"Are you afraid you will be asked to leave the Governor's Committee?"

"I will run for political office one day," he said stiffly. "You've always known that."

"And so no one must ever know about Mina," Anneka said. "I just want for Mina to have a real life here, to be a little girl like any other little girl. I want her to think of her mother as someone who does important things, who votes and—"

"Mina has had the chance to be a little girl like any other little girl," Mr. Graves said. "That is exactly what we've done by providing you with what you have."

"But I have to hide her away! I have to pretend—"

"Well, right now, it's better if neither of you goes out. Did you take the streetcar home?"

"Back to your mother's house, yes."

"If you need to go anywhere else, call me. I'll send a car. Please, for Mina's sake. Don't take any chances with her health. Or yours."

"All right." A moment of silence passed. "My friend will be here soon. You should go."

"All right," he said. "Do I have your word that you'll do as I ask?"

"Yes, of course you do, as always."

"Thank you, Anneka."

As soon as she heard Mr. Graves open the front door of the house, Mary Jane rushed through the squeaking kitchen door and sat across from Mina at the table.

"How are your sums coming?" she asked.

Anneka came through the door, her face pale and taut. When she saw Mary Jane, the little color that was left in her cheeks drained.

"How long have you been here?" she asked.

"I'm sorry, Anneka," Mary Jane said. "I started out to tell you I was here, but—"

"Mina," Anneka said. "Would you go fetch my blue shawl from the bedroom? I think it's in one of the drawers. I'm feeling chilly."

Happy to be released from her schoolwork, Mina skipped from the room. Anneka sat down in the chair she had vacated. "She will be gone for a few minutes. My shawl is in the parlor."

Mary Jane said nothing. She had no idea how to start a conversation or whether she even had the right to do so. It was Ross who needed to hear this.

Anneka began. "I agreed to this years ago—the house and the money—because I wanted Mina to be safe. But now, I just want to be married to Ross, to be a real wife, to have a home that is my own."

"Does Ross know about Mina?"

"No, I thought, I hoped . . . oh, I am so tired of this! Will you tell him?"

"I don't know," Mary Jane said. "He has to know the truth. How did—?"

"I met Jim at his parents' house when I was sixteen," she said. "He was only in Denver sometimes, because he was in college somewhere. He seemed like a prince to me, always in and out, to parties at the country club or the Brown Palace. He read most of the time that he was home. One day, when I was cleaning the drawing room, I picked up his book and looked at it. I couldn't read it, of course, because it was in English, but I knew the name, Goethe. Do you know his poem, 'Prometheus'?"

"I haven't read poetry since I left school."

"He came into the room behind me, and he read the poem to me, and we started to talk . . ."

Her voice trailed away, and Mary Jane asked impatiently, "So there never was a Jacob Lindstrom?"

"No, I have never been married," Anneka said. "What do you think Ross will say?"

Mary Jane rubbed at her forehead. Ross wasn't like Matt, who lived strictly by the Bible, but he carried with him their mother's love of propriety. "I don't know," she said.

"I don't want him to stop loving me," Anneka cried. "I don't want him to think I am not in love with him. Oh, God, I could lose everything!"

She crumpled, her arms crossed on the table, her face buried in them. Mary Jane touched Anneka's shoulder. "Don't cry, please, don't cry—"

But everything had changed. All Mary Jane's suspicions, all her doubts about Anneka had been justified.

And now, every time she looked at Mina, she would see Jim Graves in the features of the little girl's face. And she knew she would see him long after Anneka became her sister-in-law and Mina her niece.

THIRTY-ONE

Braving the bitterly cold wind and icy roads, Jim raced across town to the house on Corona Street. Damn Johanna Crawley and Mary Jane Grayson for dragging Anneka into the National Woman's Party. And damn Verner Reed's lovely wife, Mary, whom he had conversed with at more than one social event, and that degenerate Julia Reston, who had come to Denver from Paris with her female, French lover. If they had not felt the need to parade around with their blasted signs on the day of the Liberty Loan Rally a week ago, this would not have happened.

He parked the car in front of Anneka's house and let himself in without knocking. Removing his coat and hat, he walked quietly to Anneka's room. Mina sat next to her mother's bed, reading.

". . . 'pulled their limp bodies to the floor, threw his' . . . I don't know the word."

Anneka mumbled something unintelligible, and Jim stepped around the corner. Mina dropped the book and ran to hug him.

"Mr. Yeem! Mother is sick, so I am reading to her."

Jim sat in the chair. Anneka's honey-colored blond hair had darkened to brown with sweat, and her skin was flushed and waxy. Her forehead radiated heat, and she breathed in tight squeaks, as if her lungs could no longer expand to take in air. Her eyelashes were smeared with mucus.

His fury devolved into panic.

"Mina," he said. "Can you help me? Go and get a pan of water and some clean cloths."

After Mina hurried away, Jim said, "Anneka, Anneka, wake up."

Her eyes rolled open, bloodshot and unfocused. She managed to croak: "Jim."

He took her hand in his. "I came as soon as I could."

"Did your mother call you?"

"Yes."

Her implied accusation hung in the air. Once again, his mother was engineering their relationship.

"I'm sorry," she said.

"You don't need to apologize."

"You said I should not go out, I should not ride on the street cars. You were right."

"I said that far too late for any good to come of it," he said grimly. "Has Mina shown any signs?"

"No, but, oh, Jim, if she does, you must take care of her. You must see that she's made well again—"

"You and I, both, will take care of her. Now, let me take care of you."

She closed her eyes, and Jim thought of a verse from the *Journal of the American Medical Association* that he'd read in the newspaper a few days ago:

O doctor, dear, what shall I do? I think I've got the Spanish flu.

"Well, sir," he answered, "This is true, I don't know any more than you."

Mina came into the room, carrying an overflowing basin. Jim took it from her and set it on the nightstand beside a bottle of mustard pills and a blue glass jar of Vick's VapoRub Salve. When Mina returned with wash rags, he soaked one in the water, squeezed it out, and laid it across Anneka's forehead.

In imitation of Jim, Mina dunked a cloth in the water and pulled it out dripping wet.

"Let me do that, Mina," Jim said. "You should be in the other room."

"I don't want to be out there by myself."

"Watch." He dabbed away sweat from Anneka's neck and chest. "This is what we need to do, gently and lightly. It will make her feel better."

Mina touched Anneka's face a few times with the cloth that Jim gave her.

Anneka's eyes opened, and Mina crowed, "Look, it's working!"

"Is it snowing?" Anneka asked.

"No," Jim said. "It's just a cold wind."

"I wish it would snow. I wish I could see Sweden again, the snow on the lakes, and the trees and birds—"

"There will be snow by the time you're well," Jim said. "You need to sleep, now."

"Mother, I'm here," Mina said. "I'm helping."

Anneka mumbled in Swedish. Mina started to dab Anneka's face again, but Jim whispered, "Mina, come away. Let's let her sleep."

She followed him to the living room, her doll Marta in her arms, and sat on the couch beside him. He put his arm around her and offered her the palm of his right hand. She took it, tracing back and forth over the protruding scar with her index finger.

"What did your mother say to you?" he asked.

"Var en bra tjej, Älskling," Mina said.

"What does that mean?"

"Be a good girl."

"You are a good girl, Mina," Jim said. "But you need to stay out of your mother's room or you might be sick, too. Your mother needs you to stay well so that she doesn't have to worry about you."

"I don't like it when she's sick."

"I don't either," Jim said. "Do you miss school?"

Mina drew a figure eight over the bumpy ridges of his palm. "My teacher died."

The baldness of the comment jolted him. He wondered what Mina understood about death. He considered explaining it to her, but it seemed that Anneka would be a better guide. He would not be able to mention God or mercy with any sincerity, or to imagine anything but the coldness and darkness of death.

"If there's no school, I'll teach you myself," Jim said. "Find a book to read."

Mina hopped off the couch, suddenly animated, and ran down the hallway. She returned with the book she had been reading in Anneka's room. Newly published, the cover read, *Valerie Duval: Somewhere in France* by Martha Trent. The illustration featured a nurse in white dress, apron and wimple. Jim flipped through the pages; it looked too advanced for Mina, and certainly, the sentence he had heard her read suggested it was a better choice for an older girl.

"Who gave you this?" he asked.

"Miss Mary Jane."

Mary Jane Grayson—who had failed in her commitment to the Relief Society and whose unlikely friendship had cost Anneka so dearly.

"How did your mother meet Miss Mary Jane?" he asked.

"She's Mr. Ross' sister."

"Who's Mr. Ross?"

"Mother's feen-cy."

"Fiancé. The man she is going to marry."

"He'll be my father," Mina said. "Miss Mary Jane will be my aunt. And there's Uncle Matt and Uncle Avery, and I will have Grandmother Lanita and Grandfather Amos, too—"

Jim's heart clenched at his parents' refusal to acknowledge Mina. "Have you been to their house?"

"No, but Mother says as soon as Mr. Ross is back from being a soldier in the war, we'll go to see them. He has to go to France on a big ship. He has to wear a uniform."

So, it was Mary Jane Grayson's brother with whom Anneka longed to be an equal partner. How stupid Jim had been to believe that she would want to be coddled, to be given a life of ease that required no participation, to be relieved of responsibility or purpose.

Jim pointed to the illustration on the cover of the book. "I know girls who wear uniforms like this and who are in France now helping the soldiers. My sister is one of them. Has your mother been showing you their letters and pictures in the newspapers?"

Mina nodded. "I like their uniforms."

He entertained her with tales of Ellie's girls in France: making gallons of cocoa or coffee, or putting together music and poetry evenings to entertain the men, or taking concoctions made of oranges, lemons, and syrup to the wounded. As he spoke, the question that Anneka had asked him about Kathleen came into his mind: *Why, if she is right, wasn't I?*

Because you were a fairy tale princess, he thought. A beautiful waif, a vision, something fleeting and rare. You were too precious. I never wanted to see you trapped in the turbulence of marriage, where husband and wife grow too familiar, and love grows stale, or dies. I would not have done that to you.

But Anneka was a woman after all, one who felt jealousy and resentment, one who longed to be bound by matrimony, and motherhood, and earthly desires.

Darkness fell before Dr. Erickson, who had long been the Graves' family physician and privy to their secrets, arrived. Mina had changed into her pajamas and robe. She sat beside Jim on the couch, reading the tale of Valerie Duval to him with a confident and mature ability.

After the doctor examined Anneka, he returned to the parlor. Jim sent Mina and her doll to bed with the promise that he would come and tuck her in.

"Mrs. Lindstrom's case is extremely bad," Dr. Erickson reported.

"Should she be in the hospital?"

"She should, but there are no hospital rooms available just now. We're treating all patients at home."

"Surely there's a private hospital that can take her. You know that the cost needn't be considered—"

"Jim." Dr. Erickson interrupted him. "People are being evicted from their boarding houses and hotel rooms because they're sick and the landlords don't want it to spread to the other guests. They're living in abandoned buildings and alleys because there is nowhere for them to go. There, the sickness just multiplies. You have the best of everything for Mrs. Lindstrom right here, or at your own house, or at your parents' house. There is true suffering out there."

Jim rubbed a hand over his face. "What should I do, then?"

"I'll send over a nurse," Dr. Erickson said. "Not a real nurse, mind you—they are all either sick or busy. But Mayor Mills has recruited some of the teachers who are out of work since the Denver schools closed. They've been trained in the basics of care. Those who are well and who are willing, anyway."

"If that's the best—"

"It is." Dr. Erickson took a film of gauze from his bag. "You shouldn't be here without a mask to cover your face. Your little girl shouldn't either."

"I'll see to it." He exhaled. "Is there any hope for Anneka?"

"I don't know," Dr. Erickson said. "We've had cases where the patient is at death's door one day and back at work the next, and we've had cases where the patient is fit and hardy after recovery and dies in his sleep that night."

After Dr. Erickson left, Jim went to Mina's room. She lay in bed, Valerie Duval still in her hands. As he snugged the blankets around her, he asked, "Would you like to stay at my house?"

"Will Mother go?"

"We'll take her, too."

"All right."

He kissed Mina, checked on Anneka, then settled on the couch in the parlor for the night. He spent his time smoking and drinking what little Anneka had in the house, wishing he had brought along a bottle of his own whiskey or brandy. Twice, he stoked the fire against the chill of the wind. The weather had worsened.

The next morning, he wore the gauze mask into Anneka's room. He laid a hand on her forehead, but it seared yet beneath his palm.

She wheezed out in fear, "Who are you?"

He ripped off the mask, "Anneka, it's me."

"Oh, it's, I don't . . ." She closed her eyes again.

"Anneka, listen to me," he said. "I'm sorry that what we did wasn't what you wanted. I'm sorry I didn't understand what you and Mina need—"

"Where's Mina?"

She had heard nothing of what he said, Jim realized. "She's still sleeping," he said.

"She needs to . . ."

She faded away before she finished the sentence.

Jim let her sleep, with no more attempts at clearing his conscience.

The teacher-turned-nurse arrived in the early afternoon, and Jim went home to clean up, change his clothes, and have rooms prepared for Mina and Anneka. In his study, he found fresh brandy. Harris had an uncanny ability to know when he would come home exhausted and troubled. Beside the brandy decanter were two unopened cables from France.

Worried, Jim slit open the first with his thumb across the envelope. In uneven typeface, it read:

DENVER COLORADO

JIM GRAVES

GRAVES OIL

MRS. BRENTLY AND HARRIET MILLS BOTH SICK WITH SPANISH FLU. PLEASE SEND INSTRUCTIONS.

KATHLEEN

He sat down behind the desk. Not Ellie. Surely, she could not be in the same situation as Anneka—her lungs filled, her throat scratched raw, her brain seared by fever. He ripped open the second telegram, which was from Eleanora: *WE HAVE MOVED BOTH GIRLS TO HOSPITAL IN PARIS. HARRIET'S FLU TURNED TO PNEUMONIA. KATHLEEN HAS NERVOUS CONDITION AS WELL AS FLU. I AM NOT TO BE OUT OF BED YET. PLEASE ADVISE. ELLIE*

Now, it was Kathleen who was lying in a bed somewhere, barely able to breathe and wracked by fever. He recalled how she had looked in Nice—her hair loose and blowing in the sea breeze as she stood beside him on the boardwalk, the glow of the flaming torches behind them, the immensity of the ocean in the darkness beyond. She had been vibrant, luminous.

"Harris?" he called.

The valet appeared at the door of the study. "Yes, sir?"

"Why am I receiving both of these at once? They're dated nearly a week apart."

"Mr. Spratt said that both came to the office today. Evidently, they were held up because there is no one to deliver telegrams in Denver just now."

"When did he bring these over?"

"Not more than half an hour ago."

"Good Lord," Jim muttered. *PLEASE SEND INSTRUCTIONS.* Poor Kathleen—she must think she had been deserted. *PLEASE ADVISE.* Poor Ellie—ill and with no one to turn to. For her to ask for help, the situation must be dire.

"Call for the car," he said to Harris.

Within a few minutes, he was on his way to his parents' home. He bounded up the stone steps, but found no one in the parlor, library or study. At last, he came across a maid dusting an alcove of the sitting room. She told him that his father was at rest and that his mother was upstairs, packing.

"Packing?" Jim asked.

"Yes," said the maid. "For the trip tomorrow."

He climbed the sweeping staircase to the second floor. He found his mother folding garments into a valise while another maid took clothes from the closet.

"Oh, Jim," his mother said. "I'm glad you stopped over." To the maid, she said, "That's all for now. You can go."

As the maid left the room, he said, "I was told that you're leaving. Where are you going?"

"We're going to Inglesfield."

His stomach rose into his throat. Inglesfield—the castle in the mountains that had been built by his grandfather; the location of so many fine parties and holidays in the early years of the privileged and carefree Graves family; the place where Jim's brother, Stephen, and sister, Elizabeth, had drowned, and he and Ellie had nearly lost their lives. Good Lord, his parents had not been to Inglesfield since the accident. The place had all but been forgotten, except for by Jim, who had taken Anneka there for trysts.

Fumbling in his pocket, he pulled out a cigarette. "Has anyone been there to see if it is still inhabitable?"

"We sent Lewis and Mrs. Evers there a week ago to open it up. They've reported back that it's ready."

"But why?"

"It's much safer to be out of the city just now." She caught his expression. "Oh, don't frown that way. The Phipps family is going to Greystone in Bear Creek Canyon until this is over. Uncle Donald and Aunt Minerva left for his father's ranch three days ago, and Samuel plans to spend all his time on the golf course rather than in the office to avoid contact with others. Perhaps you should do the same."

"Why would you go to Inglesfield?" He heard his own voice—a hurt boy's—in his ears. "Surely there's someone you can stay with. Greystone has to have an extra room or a wing, or a guest house or two. Or even my ranch in Durango—"

"And travel all that way on the trains?" His mother closed the valise. "I don't want to stay with anyone for fear they might be carrying it. Your father and I have talked about it. Inglesfield is the best choice. Why are you here?"

"I've received a cable from Ellie," he said, still feeling less than generous. "She's been sick with the flu as well."

His mother crumpled onto the edge of the bed. "Eleanora is sick?"

"She's on the mend, as far as I can gather. I received a cable from Kathleen—Miss O'Doherty—that Ellie and Miss Mills were ill, then another from Ellie herself that the girls were both ill and had been moved to Paris. Ellie says she's weak, but better."

"Oh, Jim, you have to go to Paris," his mother said. "You have to see that she's taken care of—"

"You would send me to France when you won't even ride the train as far as Durango?" he protested. "They are undoubtedly under the care of the Red Cross."

"But how do we know?" she demanded. "You have only the information from the cable, and that isn't enough. You have to go and bring Ellie home!"

Her voice had risen to a near-shriek, and something crept into Jim's head. After Stephen and Elizabeth had died, she had been unable to rise from her bed, and he—a child of eight—had crawled in beside her, begging her, *Mother, don't, please don't cry anymore*—

"You know Anneka is ill," he said. "I can't leave her."

His mother looked up, seemingly surprised. "Mrs. Lindstrom?"

"She's not much better. Dr. Erickson has seen her, and I've hired a nurse of sorts for her—"

"I don't see what else we can do for her."

"I intend to see to her recovery," Jim insisted. "And Mina hasn't caught it yet, but if she does—"

"I've already asked Ethel, who is cook's assistant, to take over food and keep an eye on the little girl. Ethel has already had the flu and, they say, won't catch it again."

"Isn't the staff going with you?"

"No, we're only taking Lewis and Mrs. Evers." His mother relented. "I'll see to Mrs. Lindstrom and the little girl."

"From Inglesfield?" he asked. "How will you do that?"

"We will manage. You must see to Eleanora and her girls."

He said nothing, which aroused his mother's suspicions.

"What is it, Jim?" she asked. "What have you done?"

"I told Mina that I would move both of them to my house."

"Oh, for God's sake," his mother said. "Bring two sick people into your house? What about you?"

"Mina isn't sick—"

"She's been exposed to it through her mother. She could easily infect your entire household."

"I believe it's time to make this right, Mother."

"Make what right?" she asked. "With Mrs. Lindstrom? Haven't we done that?"

"She is Miss Lindstrom, mother."

"Don't be foolish," she snapped. "You need to go to France. This will have to wait."

"I doubt I could even secure passage or permission to go overseas," he said. "The only way I was allowed to go in January was because I had business in London. This time, I don't have—"

"You have to go."

Her statement was flat, final.

"You have never even seen Mina," he flared. "And you barely acknowledge that Anneka exists. Calling her Mrs. Lindstrom, sending Ethel over to see that she is all right. You may not recognize Mina as your grandchild, but you are asking me to choose between my sister and my daughter."

His mother did not retreat. "Between your only sister and a daughter that is not even truly yours."

"Not mine? Whose, then? Do you know something about Anneka that I don't? Was she sleeping with someone else?"

"Don't be vulgar."

He felt the terrible weight of all he had done wrong. Stephen and Elizabeth, his mother and father—he had failed them all in some respect. How could he do that to Anneka? How could he do it to Ellie and Kathleen?

"Please, Jim," his mother said. "Don't let anything happen to my Ellie. Don't let anything happen to my little girl. She's my only—"

Memories of the accident in the lake at Inglesfield came back to him: the pain of warming up again, his ripped and stitched-up hands, the burn of the scar on his face, the guilt that he had lived and Stephen had not.

"I won't even attempt to go to France unless I have a promise that you'll see to Anneka and Mina," he said.

"Yes, I will."

"I'll contact the Red Cross Headquarters and see if I can get permission to travel."

She nodded, her back straight, her pose stately. Jim could see that she was swallowing back tears.

****

His choice grieves him; it burns within him. He knows that it will always haunt him. He stops by Anneka's house on his way to Union Station. As he sits beside her bed, he strokes her hair. Mina stands beside him with a gauze mask over her face.

"I'll be back, Anneka," he says. "If you need anything—anything at all—call my mother's house. Someone will take care of it."

"Are you going because of the girl in France?" she asks.

"I am going for Eleanora. I've taught Mina how to use the telephone so that she can call for help."

"You said we were going to your house to live," Mina says.

"That's what I wanted to do. But I have to go away because my sister is sick. And Miss Edwards"—he names the nurse—"will be here for you."

Mina's eyes—the only visible part of her face—darken with temper and disappointment.

"Promise me you'll call for help if you're scared." He puts a hand on Mina's shoulder. "Even if Marta is scared, you're to use the phone."

"Yes, Mr. Yeem."

He takes Anneka's hands in both of his. "Anneka, when I come back, we will talk about all this."

"About what?" she asks groggily.

He kisses her forehead with a murmured, "My queen," which he had called her long ago, when they had been lovers. He embraces Mina, who is sullen over the broken promise.

Outside, his chauffeur drives Jim and Harris to Union Station and unloads the trunks and valises they will take with them to Paris. Within minutes, Jim is seated in a private state car, a glass of brandy in front of him, headed for Washington, D.C., where he will apply for the necessary papers to travel to France.

THIRTY-TWO

Maggie bowed her head as Brendan said a prayer. Ma, Pa and Uncle Irish stood beside her, huddled against the cold. Last week, Auntie Eileen had caught the Spanish flu, and within three days, it had taken her. Now, she was being laid to rest at Mt. Olivet Cemetery, located on windswept prairie far to the north of Redlands and northwest of Berkeley Park.

Alice Colleen caught the black veil that fringed over Maggie's eyes and tried to stuff it in her mouth. Maggie wrested it from her tiny fist, and Alice Colleen gave an unhappy blat. Maggie kissed her and whispered, "Shhhh, my baby."

Lately, there were funerals every day, and Maggie's job writing obituaries had gone from paying a pittance to a solid week's work. Even better, Mr. Ledbetter had told her to cut the obituaries to fifty words because there were now so many. Maggie was doing less work for more pay than when she started.

Oh, but the reason for it! Even cynical Mr. Ledbetter seemed stricken by the number of deaths in Denver. After eleven people who had attended the Fourth Liberty Loan rally died from flu, all assemblies—either indoor or outdoor—were prohibited by Mayor Mills of Denver. Mass was no longer held at Blessed Savior, which had lost twelve parishioners, including the entire McPherson family.

Poor Auntie Eileen. Maggie wondered if she had ever been happy. Had she ever swooned over Uncle Irish's good looks and smarmy ways? Had she ever eyed Kathleen without a criticism perched on her tongue, ready to fly? Last night, as Maggie had viewed her aunt's body, she had been shocked by the change in her face. The tight skin over Auntie Eileen's cheeks and forehead had relaxed, and her mouth, usually pursed, was at rest. But it wasn't just her aunt's altered looks that had rattled Maggie: it was the uncanny resemblance of Auntie Eileen—a woman for whom nothing had gone as she had imagined it—to Maggie herself.

She blinked to clear the tears from her eyes and looked toward her mother. Poor Ma. As if Seaney's absence weren't enough, now her other half—for isn't that what twins were?—was gone. Standing between Uncle Irish and Pa, she seemed helpless, her tawny hair streaked by gray, her face doughy from lying in bed for so many hours, and her shoulders turned inward. Without Auntie Eileen's emotional starch and vinegar to balance her, she seemed unable to stand upright.

The service ended, and the casket was lowered into the ground. As Brendan and Pa helped Ma to the delivery truck, Maggie walked with Uncle Irish, who took her arm in his and squeezed in close to her. She kissed his cheek in return. His eyes were shot through with red—which Maggie surmised was not from drink alone—and his eyelids were veined with purple.

"This is such a long way for you to visit Auntie Eileen," she said. "Wasn't there somewhere closer to home?"

"There isn't a Catholic Cemetery near us. Only the Masonic Cemetery in Littleton or the Episcopalian one at Bear Cañon."

"I'm sorry, Uncle Irish," she said. "You've done so much for me, isn't there something I can do for you?"

He hesitated. "I haven't told your mother this," he said at last. "And I ask you not to tell her until she is over this latest shock. I received a visit from Jim Graves. Kathleen has the flu."

"Oh, no! Oh, Uncle Irish, I'm so sorry. Is there anything we can do?"

"We can't, but the man himself has left for Washington D.C. in all his pomp and glory to try to get passage to France." The attempt at snideness deflated him, and he continued wearily, "Kathleen doesn't even know about her mother yet. I left it to him to tell her when he arrives. I didn't have the heart to tell her by cable."

"What can I do to help you, then?"

"You have all you can manage here, with your mother and father, and the store, and the baby." He faltered. "I don't know if I have the strength to go on, with Eileen gone, and if Kathleen—"

"She won't," Maggie assured him. "She's young and healthy and—"

"Eileen had never been sick a day in her life—"

"Kathleen never killed herself riding Napoli, and that's as near to a miracle as even a Catholic can get."

Uncle Irish laughed sadly. "You're a godsend, Muffin." He glanced back at Auntie Eileen's grave. "How is your job?"

"I'm one of the busiest in the office just now. Seventy-eight people have died in Denver alone in the past ten days. Over a thousand people are sick with it."

"Make sure you keep Alice Colleen at home," he said. "Have you had any word from Liam?"

She did not reply. For reasons that she couldn't name, she hadn't told her parents about the letter about the Hutterites. Perhaps it was because talking about it made it seem so real. As long as it was only on paper, or only in her mind, there was a chance it was just a story, wasn't there?

"It isn't good." She pulled her hat, which Alice Colleen had slobbered on, from her head. "Sometimes I wonder, sometimes I think—our lives have moved so far apart now, with Liam in Fort Leavenworth, and all that's happened to me. Oh, I know it's wrong to think that way—"

"You don't have to be far apart for that to happen," Uncle Irish said. "Your Auntie Eileen and I moved apart even as we were living in the same house. She always wanted what she never could have. More children, of course—we both wanted that—but she wanted to be thought of as a woman of position and influence, in the Church and in the town. Living so far from town at Redlands was hard on her."

"What should I do, then?"

"Do you still love him?"

"Yes, oh, yes."

"Then, see it through, Muffin. You have this little fairy imp"— he tickled Alice Colleen's cheek and the baby held out her arms for him to take her—"to keep you company, and you have your mother and father and me. And Sean, when he comes home—"

"I doubt he'll forgive Liam for not going to war—"

"Don't worry about it," Uncle Irish said. "Sean's quick to flare, but he burns out pretty quickly, too. When Liam gets out of prison, he'll love you all the more for your faithfulness."

"Thank you, Uncle Irish. I love you."

"Oh, come on, now." He balanced Alice Colleen on his hip. "Your parents are waiting for us."

The following week, Mr. Ledbetter spied Maggie as she returned her completed obituaries to the *Denver City Daily News*. She had driven the delivery truck to the newspaper office. Before she stepped inside, she lifted her scarf and put it over her nose and mouth.

"Mrs. James," he called. "Come into my office."

She steeled herself, fearing that, at last, someone had discovered her true identity. She glanced around warily, but no one in the office paid her any mind. Perhaps Mr. Ledbetter just wanted her to shorten the death notices even more, to something like "Born, Died, Buried."

As she sat down, he said, "You can take off your scarf. I'm not sick."

"But is anyone else?"

He shrugged, and she removed her scarf. Shoving a sheet of paper in front of her, he said, "Read this."

It was a letter addressed to "Miss Delilah." The writer was a young woman who had doubts about the man she was soon to marry. He criticized her constantly, she wrote. He made jokes at her expense in front of others, and teased her publicly about her hair or clothing. One day, he told her that she needed healthier habits and better manners. The letter was signed by "Ruta," but Mr. Ledbetter had scribbled in the margin: "Should she get out the sewing machine or get rid of him?"

"What would you tell her to do?" Mr. Ledbetter asked.

Maggie had no idea what it was all about, but she charged ahead. "He doesn't sound worth her time to me. Doesn't he have more important things to think about? There's a war on. Shouldn't he be serving his country or working with the Red Cross or some other organization? Surely, even a steady job in a factory would allow him a healthy focus for his attention."

Mr. Ledbetter gave a snort. "Go on."

"But, on the other hand, she needs to look into whether there's any merit in his criticism. Maybe her clothes truly are wretched, or ill-fitting, or just old. Then she does need to get out the sewing machine—not for her fiancé's sake, but for her own. As for her habits and manners, well, are they repulsive? Slovenly? Rude? If they're graceful and clean, then, perhaps she does need to get rid of him."

"Spoken like the next Dorothy Dix," Mr. Ledbetter said. "Do you know who she is?"

"Yes, I read her advice column in the . . ."

"In our competitor's newspaper, right?"

"Yes."

"Well, for the past few years, we've had 'Miss Delilah' giving advice to our readers," he said. "Only, Miss Delilah was a sixty-seven-year-old typesetter who thought the world still considered Victorian china painting and tea dances as jaw-dropping entertainment. Never mind that women are close to getting the vote, and that they're working at men's jobs, and are learning how to drive and shoot in case the Germans invade America. He would have told poor Ruta to do everything her boyfriend wanted so she wouldn't lose his love and admiration."

"Miss Delilah is a man?" Maggie asked.

"If women can do men's jobs, why can't men do women's?" Mr. Ledbetter leaned forward. "We need someone who realizes how fast things are changing, how quickly the old morality is disappearing, how this war has created an entirely new society and way of thinking in America. Someone who understands that the Modern Woman doesn't put all her eggs in her boyfriend's or husband's basket, if you know what I mean."

The blood pounded Maggie's ears so loudly that all she could do was nod.

"I want you to take over Miss Delilah's job," Mr. Ledbetter said. "We'll print the letters under a column, 'Mrs. James Speaks'—no, that's too much like 'Dorothy Dix Talks.' I'll come up with something else. I'll use your success with *The Ladies' Home Journal* to sell it."

Her own column! A regular paycheck, an escape from running the store, a respite from Ma's sadness and the misery of Liam's letters.

"What about Miss Delilah?" she asked. "What will happen to him?"

He motioned toward the sheaf of papers in her hand. "Do you have an obituary there for Alvin Davis?"

"Yes, he had the Spanish flu and . . ." Her voice trailed away. "I'm sorry."

"You won't be for long," Mr. Ledbetter said. "I can't pay you more than ten cents per column to start."

"That's what you pay for fifty-word obituaries! This will take thought and time."

"It didn't take you long to tell young Ruta off."

She felt a surge of boldness. "Twenty-five cents per column."

"I can't do that—"

"What were you paying Miss Delilah?"

"Fifteen cents for three responses a day."

"But he had his typesetting job as well," she protested. "Twenty, and I can write as many as I can each day."

"Twenty, and you can write six a day," he snarled. "The column runs in all three editions every day but Sunday, so that's thirty-six a week. Don't write more than two-hundred words per response or I'll throw them away, and you won't get paid."

"All right."

Maggie had no idea whether she had struck a good deal, but seven dollars and twenty cents a week was a fortune! It was almost as much as the ten dollars that Kathleen had made as a typist for Graves Oil. Ma had been so proud of Kathleen's earnings—but this was better, because Maggie wouldn't have to report to an office downtown every morning but Sunday.

"I'll run an introduction tomorrow to tell readers about you," Mr. Ledbetter said. "And before you leave here, write down what you want Ruta to do. I'll use that as a sample of your wisdom. Have your first six responses here by Monday morning, eight o'clock sharp."

"I can still work from home?"

"Would you take the job if I made you come to the office?"

"No, I wouldn't."

Mr. Ledbetter's face grimaced into what Maggie assumed was a smile. "You certainly know your own mind, Mrs. James."

"Oh, there's one more thing."

"What is it?"

"I need a typewriter. I've been borrowing one. I'd like a portable Corona."

The smile disappeared. "You can have Miss Delilah's old Underwood," he growled. "Most of the keys work. The ones that don't, just write in what's missing. I'll have it delivered to your house this afternoon along with the first batch of letters."

That evening, Maggie walks around the dining table, where the thirty-pound Underwood—whose keys are spread so far from one another that only a giant's hands could work it—has supplanted Judah's compact Corona. A stack of letters lies beside the typewriter.

She gathers them up, along with a pencil and a pack of Lucky Strikes, and seeks out the attic, where the millinery shop once was. Leaving the door ajar so she can listen for Alice Colleen, she clears away the dust and odds and ends piled on the vanity and mirror.

The letters are, of course, addressed to Miss Delilah. She scratches out the salutations and prints in neat letters, "Dear Mrs. James," on each one. She flips through them, scribbling her responses. A high school girl wants to quit school to marry her beau (*Absolutely not. You know so little of the world and it barely knows you. Take some time to introduce yourself to it and to learn from it before you marry.*); a woman wonders how to remove a cherry pit stain from her best Sunday blouse (*Try soaking it in vinegar or lemon juice.*); and a man asks whether facial hair is attractive to the opposite sex (*Yes, if it is kept neat and clean and enhances rather than obscures the natural features of the face. No woman wants to feel as if she is kissing a furry critter.*).

"If you want an answer, just ask Mrs. James," she whispers.

The words resonate in her head. On one of the letters, she writes: *Ask Mrs. James*. But it seems plain and uninspiring. In this fast-moving world, a woman is no longer expected to be just a "missus," but a New Woman or a Modern Woman or a Working Woman. But she is none of them. At last, it comes to her. Below *Ask Mrs. James*, she writes, *The Thinking Woman*.

The next Dorothy Dix—isn't that what Mr. Ledbetter said she'd be?

She glances into the mirror:

Dear Mrs. James,

My husband has chosen a path I cannot follow, one that takes him from me. Since we've been separated, I have been thinking a great deal about my own situation. I would dearly love to work and live on my own, in my own house with just my daughter for company. Sometimes the feeling is so strong that I think I will just steal away in the night and forget about my parents and their store and even about him—

She stops herself.

The one problem she can't solve—that she can't even bear to think about—is her own.

THIRTY-THREE

The newest objective of the American Expeditionary Force is another village that is completely destroyed. Once again, Sean's division will risk life and limb to capture homes and barns that are nothing but rubble, trenches that scar the earth, barbed wire that snakes out of the mud, craters and shell holes, dead horse carcasses, broken-down equipment, and trampled wheat fields. But there is something more to it this time: they have been tasked with breaking through the Hindenburg Line.

The place they're invading is the St. Mihiel salient, a ridge that is fully controlled by the Germans, whose trenches and lookouts glare over the plain below. Machine gun nests abound on the slope below the ridge, all entrenched in pockets of bramble and fortified rock. The French have tried for four years to rout the Germans from this spot called the Knoll. The Americans have tried once and failed. And now, the task falls to Sean's division.

He has on him all his usual tools and more. He carries 220 rounds of ammunition and two grenades and water and rations for three days. This time, the Americans also have spades. The short-handled shovels are meant for entrenching, but some of Sean's fellow soldiers have been honing the edges. It's said that the Germans are carrying them now instead of bayonets. One crack on the skull with a spade is so much easier than a thrust with a bayonet. A few nights ago, as they were briefed on their mission, the Americans were shown an assortment of misshapen, creased tin hats. The Captain in charge claimed that it was worse if a man was hit while wearing the hat, because the tin became embedded in his brain. It was much better to suffer a clean, quick hit on your bare skull that killed you immediately.

The morning of the attack dawns: cold, gray, a mist hanging over the ground, the smell of putrefaction trapped against the earth. Sean bows his head as the prayer before battle is read. It comes from Psalm 91:

You shall not fear the terror of the night nor the arrow that flies by day,

Nor the pestilence that roams in darkness, nor the plague that ravages at noon.

Though a thousand fall at your side, ten thousand at your right hand, near you it shall not come.

The orders are to move out from the jump-off trench at a fast, steady pace up the Knoll. They've been warned to be on the lookout for German stragglers who have been left behind after the previous days' fighting. If the enemy soldiers aren't killed during the first advance, they will rise up from shell holes after the American troops have passed and shoot them from behind. It's an old game, but an effective one.

Sean clamors up the steps of the jump-off trench and takes his place, Tony beside him. The spot that belonged to Kevin has been taken by Arnie Green. Lieutenant Morgan blows the whistle and they spill out of the trench behind the rolling barrage.

He has jogged barely ten feet when it begins: one shot rings out, then another, and then a thousand. The slope is steeper than it looks. Each step forward is accompanied by a backward slide through the mud. Machine gun fire rakes through the soldiers. Arnie goes down, falling to his knees on legs that are no longer there. He sinks onto the ground, his clothes blooming with hot blood.

"Get down!" Tony calls, and he and Sean and two others vie for refuge in a shell hole. They pack each other down, elbowing, jostling, sprawling atop one another.

The bullets spray over their heads, stirring up clouds of muck.

"We can't do this," Sean says. "We've lost nearly half our men already. They must have every gun they own up there."

"Where's Sergeant Hicks?" one of the men asks.

"He was shot as we came over the top," the other says.

Sean peers out of the shell hole. Men are still charging forward, but they are cut down almost as soon as they stand.

"They're going to pick us off one by one," he says. "They can see every move we make. We have to take out those machine gun nests. We have to get out of here."

"No way to go but forward," Tony says. "There's others coming up behind us."

As if the same thought has occurred to him, Lieutenant Morgan rises up from the mud a few feet away, his service pistol in hand. "Company C! Follow!" he shouts.

Sean bursts from the shell hole, Tony beside him. Others spring up from nearby craters, and a whistle sounds with a shout to Companies D and E to follow. Sean barrels forward, shooting as he runs. Halfway up the hill, barbed wire tangles in deadly webs. He hacks at the wire with his hatchet.

Beside him, Tony falls. His uniform catches on the barbed wire, and he hangs like a limp scarecrow.

"Tony!" Sean tries to rip the fabric from the snarls.

"Go on, go on," Tony gasps from a bloodied mouth. "Go on!"

Sean follows Lieutenant Morgan, who crests the rise where the machine gun is housed behind a heap of sandbags. Coming face to face with the gunner, the Lieutenant brandishes his pistol. The German gun catches him point blank, and he falls, a mess of blood and flayed flesh.

"No!" someone yells.

The machine gunner twists the gun toward Sean, but before the German can fire, he slumps, a bullet hole through his neck, shot by the man who has come upon the nest just behind Sean.

One of the German soldiers jerks frantically at the dead body of the gunner, trying to pull it out of the way. Sean empties his rifle into him and the others in the nest, his shots echoed by the American standing next to him. The Germans fall in a sorry heap in the cramped nest. One tries desperately to crawl away, but the man beside Sean fires, and his body goes limp.

Out of bullets, Sean pivots and finds himself standing beside Danhour.

"Good God," Sean says, but that's all. They're being targeted from the forward trench now, bullets blazing past their heads. Together, they push forward. Leaping over the lip of the trench, they attack.

The battle is hand-to-hand now, with bayonets and knuckle dusters and axes. Sean and Danhour fight side by side, cleaving and hacking at the Germans, surging in front of other Americans, who pour into the trench. They chase after soldiers who try to escape, cornering those who are too slow, until the Germans throw up their hands and cry, "*Kamerad! Kamerad!*"

"Take prisoners!" One of the company Sergeants who followed Lieutenant Morgan shouts. He climbs over the bloodied and dismembered bodies to stand beside Sean. "Who are you? Which company?"

Danhour salutes. "Private Calvin Danhour, Company C."

"Corporal Sean Sullivan, Company C."

"Jesus, between the two of you, you took out half the Heines in this trench. What made you charge it alone?"

"They shot our Lieutenant." Danhour's face crumples. "He charged 'em with only a pistol, and—"

"I'll see you're commended for this," the Sergeant says. "I'm Sergeant Davis, Company E."

Sean surveys the carnage around him. My God, my God, what had he done? His hands, face, and clothes are stained red by the blood of others, and he reeks of his own sweat and fear. He looks toward Danhour, who leans against the trench wall, equally filthy and still sobbing over the death of Lieutenant Morgan. For the first time, Sean sees him for what he is: not the bully who has bedeviled him, or the coward who let Kevin die alone, but a gawky, awkward boy who'd never traveled outside of his hometown, and who'd known nothing of the world, and who had come to manhood in the most brutal way possible, just as Sean has.

"Where's your Sergeant?" Sergeant Davis asks.

"He's gone, too, and the other Corporal." Sean's chest constricts. How could he have left Tony to be shot up like a rag dangling in the wind? "I need to go back—"

"It looks like you're in charge of Company C for now, Corporal," he says. "And we aren't done. We're going to dig in and hold this salient or go to hell trying."

"Yes, sir," Sean says.

He picks up his rifle and takes up his position at the trench wall. It's all reflex, no thinking, no worrying about whether you come out of it dead or alive. The three companies push the Germans out of the forward trench and take over, planting flags and sentries, aware that the enemy is now just tens of feet from them in the second trench. As night falls, Sean joins the others in clearing the trench—piling both the German and American dead, salvaging weapons and gear, smoking or eating whatever the Germans left behind. He is aware of Danhour moving around him, but he does not speak to him. They act as if they are strangers, just as the new Sergeant and his men are.

Yet he cannot escape the thought: *Danhour saved my life.*

He can think of no reason why Danhour would act as he did, unless it was simply because they were the last two left after so much time together.

But what happened after—

To kill like that, to tear through human flesh without compassion or even a clear reason. He and Danhour had both given into their baser selves, their animal selves, the ones that they've been threatening each other with for the past year and a half. They have always brought out the worst in each other, and now, they have become the worst.

Soulless, heartless, without shame.

He notices that others eye him as they move past. One young soldier approaches him. "They said you and that other guy took out all them Heines by yourself."

"Yeah," Sean says.

"I just got here from Oklahoma, just last week."

"They didn't train you in the Quiet Zone?"

"What's that?"

Sean remembers the months of doing nothing but pretending to be a soldier for some overbearing French or British officer. He has heard that the troops from America now march directly from the port in Bordeaux to the trenches.

"Never mind," he says.

"What you did, well, I wanna do something like that. Tear the Hun bastards apart with my bare hands."

"Sure," Sean says.

He puts as much distance between the kid and himself as he can, which is not far in this overcrowded trench. After a while, he slinks down in a corner and covers himself with a tarp.

He wonders if Danhour feels as ashamed and horrified by their heroic acts as he does.

THIRTY-FOUR

Above the battlefield, it was all nerve: to keep flying when shrapnel ripped holes in the canvas around you; or when the rudder had been shot into a ragged, flopping piece of fabric; or when the choke stuck and the plane stalled over the German lines. It took more nerve to fly the new De Havilland 4 that was manufactured in America and had already won the nickname of "Flaming Coffin" because of the placement of the gas tanks between the first and second seats.

Paul had heard it more than once: *Once you lose your nerve, it is over.*

But Kenny hadn't lost his nerve. He had grown bolder, which seemed even more dangerous to Paul.

More often, they were flying strafing raids. They came in low over the German lines and shot at anything that moved. If Kenny's gun, mounted on the front of the bi-plane, did not finish the job, then Paul's dual Lewis guns, mounted on the rear, did. Their targets were retreating German troops, and Paul had to swallow back his urge to allow them to escape, to return to their mothers and wives and homes. Mélisande's injunction rang in his ears: *You should kill every one of them. This war must end.* And more and more, he heard his instinctive response: *The closer we come to winning this war, the crueler it gets. We kill because we can.*

As the war ground on, a call went out for more night raids. Flying at night was terrifying, for a pilot had to rely on his own instincts and sense of the planes around him. If a tracer bullet struck the plane, a shining green mark betrayed it to the anti-aircraft guns below. More dangerous were the "flaming onions," shot upward from batteries of stationery guns. The flaming onions blossomed in the night sky into a web of viscous green jelly. If an airplane flew through it, the jelly attached itself to the plane's castor-oiled struts, greasy fabric coating, and gas-splattered tanks—anywhere there was oil—and ignited. But Kenny seemed oblivious to the hazard, pushing right through the green goop as Paul beat out the emerging fires.

Bravery, it was called by the United States Army Air Service. Paul called it recklessness.

When he was off-duty, Kenny popped Horlick's Malted Milk Balls into his mouth one after another to settle his stomach. He ate almost nothing, but drank nearly every evening. He was exhausted, but sleep was out of the question. He bragged about his and Paul's kills and how many others he was sure they'd killed, but hadn't been able to confirm. He wanted to be in the air all the time, volunteering for extra duties, as if the air were the only place he understood how to behave.

Recently, Kenny had told Paul that he and Mélisande, the Belgian woman he had met in Paris, were writing to one another. According to Kenny, he had sought her out at the YMCA after the party in the hotel. They had walked around Paris for most of the day, ending their evening on one of the pleasure boats on the Seine, which cruised from the Eiffel Tower to Notre Dame while they necked in a quiet corner.

Privately, Paul wondered whether Mélisande would consent to that, but he had seen the letters from her to Kenny. Kenny bragged about his relationship with the girl to everyone, to anyone, in a way that Paul—who rarely discussed Kathleen—mistrusted. He thought of them both as damaged, broken. If anything, the war needed to end for Kenny and for Mélisande so that they could both reclaim normal lives.

On a cold day in October, Paul heard someone calling him from behind as he walked from the hangar to the Mess.

"Monsieur Reston?"

He turned and saw Jean Latour, who had been his partner for more than two years in the ambulance service. "Lieutenant Latour," he said. "I'm pleased to see you."

"Moi aussi, Monsieur, moi aussi." Jean heartily shook his hand. "Are you here at the Aerodrome now?"

"I'm with the 12ᵗʰ Aero Squadron."

"Zut alors, un pilote."

"Non, non, pas du tout. Je suis un observateur."

"Ah, oui, bien." Jean continued in English, "And the young woman *de la Croix Rouge*—"

"Kathleen," Paul said. "I saw her recently in Chaumont."

"That is a great joy," Jean declared. *"Elle est très jolie."*

"Would you join me for a drink?" Paul offered.

"Oui, s'il vous plaît."

While sharing a bottle of wine in a nearby café, the two talked of their time together in the Norton-Harjes Ambulance Corps. They spoke of Kathleen and of Jean's continued work with the ambulance service. "They are all *les filles* driving the ambulances, now that *les Américains sont*—"

"Have vanished?" Paul supplied.

"Oui," he said. "But the French girls are all very pretty, but from the good families, so they are all very—"

His English failed again, and Paul said, "Chaste and refined?"

"Oui, comme Mademoiselle Kathleen."

Paul only smiled, but it was enough for Jean to intuit that their relationship had changed.

"L'amour est l'emblème de l'éternité," Jean said gravely. *"Il confond toute la notion de temps, efface toute la mémoire d'un commencement, toute la crainte d'une extrémité."*

Love is the emblem of eternity; it confounds all notion of time, effaces all memory of a beginning, all fear of an end.

"One of the great French writers, I presume?" Paul asked.

"Bah, *non*," Jean said. "Madame de Staël."

Paul laughed, and the two shared stories late into the evening.

As they were parting, Paul said, "You know what I'm doing is far more dangerous than the ambulance service."

Latour shrugged. *"C'est la guerre."*

And Paul had started to laugh. That phrase, which had been used so much that it didn't even mean anything anymore—just like this war—summed it up perfectly.

Without conferring with Paul, Kenny signs up to go after an observation balloon. Missions against observation balloons are flown only by volunteers, for the chances of coming home are minimal. The balloon is behind the German lines near Malancourt, with a strategic view of the French and American trenches. Although the lumbering balloons, which rise only to an altitude of a mile or so, are called "easy meat," they are well-protected by batteries of guns that send out barrages of shrapnel and explosives.

"Let's take out this gas bag," Kenny says to Paul as they are loading the D.H. 4. "I want a balloon on my record."

"You're sure?" Paul asks. "You're steady enough for this?"

"What the hell, Reston? You scared?" Kenny tests the elevator pulleys. "You know, you could have stayed in the ambulance service and never crossed the lines."

Paul says nothing more.

The D.H. 4 flies as part of a three-aircraft escort for four Sopwith Camel bombers, their machine guns loaded with tracer bullets. After take-off, they gain as much altitude as they can, leveling off at 7,000 feet and curving into Malancourt. They drop in formation toward the gray, floating sausage.

The first barrage from the anti-aircraft guns explodes just under the wing, and shrapnel bites into the fuselage. Paul's left leg stings, and something warm seeps onto his pants.

"You okay?" Kenny yells.

"Keep going!"

On the ground, the German work party strains at the winches, trying to bring in the balloon. The American bombers make a second pass, as Paul strafes the soldiers on the ground with his Lewis guns. The balloon is only about 500 feet in the air when a bomb connects and it blows, the hydrogen flaming upward. The observers in the basket leap from the fiery hulk. Shreds of burning material plummet with them. One parachute is caught up in the fire, and the German struggles to rip off his harness.

"We got it!" Kenny shouts.

"Fokkers, seven o'clock!" Paul yells.

Four German planes come in on the tail of the D.H. 4. Kenny climbs upward, trying to outrun them. Paul shoots his Lewis gun at the German aircraft. To his left, one of the American escort planes turns turtle and spirals downward. The other American veers off, pulling two of the Fokkers away.

A Rumpler joins the two remaining Fokkers. The D.H. 4 sputters as its engines overheat in stiff headwind. Kenny works the throttle, restarting the engines with a rough grind. The Germans swarm, one ahead of the D.H. 4, and the others to the left. As Paul mans the gun, he puts his weight on his right leg, ignoring the sticky warmth in his left. As he swings the gun around toward the Rumpler, his back sears with pain.

His right arm hangs loose and disconnected. He flails about—falling, twisting, his knees buckling and his arms and chest jouncing against the frame of the fuselage.

A Fokker dives, bringing Kenny and the German pilot face to face. Paul yells, "Shoot! Shoot!" But Kenny panics and jerks the D.H. 4 upward.

"No!" Paul yells. "We don't have the power!"

The German fires, and the D.H. 4 rolls upside down and then starts to twist. Paul clings to the fuselage as blood rushes to his head.

"Kenny, pull up!" he shouts, but Kenny's head lolls to one's side. "Pull up!"

The ground spins upward, and the smoke from the flaming balloon envelops the plane in a dense haze. The pain in Paul's head escalates, as if his brain were exploding. His vision goes black just as the ground snags the D.H. 4.

THIRTY-FIVE

Outside Bethany Swedish Evangelical Lutheran Church on 32nd Avenue, Mary Jane listened to the pastor's words echo against the red brick walls of the building. She had had a terrible headache since last night, and now, the sky was too bright, and the distances between things too far. All the same, she had dressed, eaten what little she could, and boarded the nearly-empty street car far from her home and Graves Oil in order to attend the funeral of Anneka Lindstrom.

Poor Anneka. She had suffered so in the last days of her life. Her fever never broke, and the congestion in her lungs kept building until she could breathe only in short gasps. Dr. Erickson had written four prescriptions and supplied a respirator to Miss Edwards, but nothing helped.

And now this funeral outside a church that looked more like a school. No steeple, no stained glass, no cross above its double-arched doors. There were few mourners here—Mary Jane, Miss Edwards and Mina, two young women who were most likely maids in the home of Mr. and Mrs. Arthur Graves, and an older man who might be a butler.

But no one from the Graves family.

No one, but especially, not him.

Mary Jane bowed her head for the Lord's Prayer. Afterward, the attendees filed past the closed coffin. At Miss Edwards' urging, Mina laid a rose on it.

Mary Jane approached Miss Edwards. Upon seeing her, Mina ran to her and hugged her legs. "Miss Mary Jane!"

"Mina, oh, Mina!" Mary Jane said. "I'm so glad to see you. And you didn't catch the sickness, did you?"

Miss Edwards answered. "We've been able to keep her healthy by keeping her out of her mother's bedroom."

Mary Jane's heart twisted. When Miss Edwards came to stay, she had posted the quarantine placard with the word "SICKNESS" on the front door. No one was to enter the domicile as long as the placard was posted. Mary Jane had stopped visiting, but now she felt a twinge of guilt. Had Mina been kept away from her mother in the last days of her life? If so, it must have broken Anneka's heart.

"What will happen now?" Mary Jane asked Miss Edwards.

"I'll be staying at her home with her until another situation can be found. I'll be going back to work soon."

"To work?"

"I'm a teacher. I only volunteered as a nurse during the worst of the epidemic."

"Have you contacted the Graves family?"

"I believe that Dr. Erickson has."

Mary Jane knelt down to Mina's level. "I'll come and visit you," she promised. "We'll stay friends, and I'll bring you a new book to read."

Mina wrapped her arms around Mary Jane's neck. "Mr. Yeem said Mother and I could live with him."

"He did? Oh, that's good news! I'm sure he'll come for you as soon as he can, and I promise I'll come see you at his big house."

"He has a big house?" Mina asked.

"Bigger than this church!" Mary Jane enthused. "You will love living there."

"We should go," Miss Edwards said. "We're to follow the hearse to the cemetery."

Mary Jane hugged Mina one more time. After the hearse rolled down the street, with Mina and Miss Edwards in a Model T behind it, Mary Jane covered her face with her scarf and caught the streetcar back to work.

At Graves Oil, she started down to the basement typing pool, but her perception failed, and she could no longer see the next step. She grabbed onto the handrail as her feet slipped out from under her. Her head swirled, and she couldn't right herself. She clung to the rail, sprawled over the steps, until Miss Crawley came out for lunch and found her.

Even though she has taken Pleasant Purgative Pellets and gargled twice a day with foul-tasting Listerine, Mary Jane catches the Spanish Influenza. For a week, she lies in her bed, her entire body pulsing with pain, barely able to lift her head as her mother feeds her ice cream and cold coffee. When her fever rises, her mother rubs shards of ice against her lips. When Mary Jane's eyes crust shut with mucus, her mother washes them clean with a solution of boric acid.

After a week, she recovers, but both her brothers, Avery and Matt, have the flu, and her father struggles to keep the quarry open and operating. As soon as she can, Mary Jane takes the street car to Anneka's house. The quarantine placard still hangs on the door. She knocks, but no one answers. Next door, at the house of Mrs. Stroop, the babysitter, Mary Jane finds another placard reading, "SICKNESS."

She goes to the neighbors who live on the other side of Anneka's house. A middle-aged woman with a scarf wrapped around her hair answers the door. Mary Jane asks about what has happened to the neighbors in the next two houses.

"I think they all caught the flu," the woman says. "I think some of them died."

"Some of them?" Mary Jane asks. "What about the little girl?"

"The little girl? I don't remember seeing her after her mother died. Maybe she went to live with relatives, or maybe she died, too."

Mary Jane walks back to the street car. Her head feels too heavy to hold upright, and her joints ache with fatigue. She goes to Graves Oil and works for most of the afternoon. But at the end of the day, she makes the trip up to Mr. Graves' office.

Inside, she finds a male secretary whose name plaque reads, Joel Spratt.

"May I speak to Mr. Graves?" she asks.

"He isn't here," Mr. Spratt says. "Is this a complaint about someone in the company? If so, you should take it up with—"

"No, it isn't. It's about . . . a friend of his."

"A friend that the two of you have in common?"

"Yes."

His lips turn down in disdain. "What's this friend's name?"

She tries a different approach. "I'm one of the girls from the Relief Society."

"You're the one who came home," Mr. Spratt says flatly.

"Yes, but I—"

"If this is about the Relief Society, you should know that he is on his way to France now."

"To France. Oh, no! Why is he going to France?"

Mr. Spratt frowns at her reaction. "I'm afraid I can't say. Now, what is it you want?"

Mary Jane panics. If Mr. Graves has already taken Mina to his house, then there is no need to divulge the secret of his relationship with Anneka. But if he hasn't—

"When did he leave?"

Mr. Spratt's expression is one of outrage, but he deigns to answer. "Three weeks ago."

Three weeks. Before Anneka died. So, unless one of his servants or employees has done so, he hasn't taken Mina to live with him.

She speaks again. "If I could just send him a letter or telegram—"

"Mr. Graves has left me in charge of his correspondence, Miss Grayson. Any letters that pass to or from him go through me."

"You read them all?"

Mr. Spratt's eyes narrow. "Why, yes, I do. It is my job."

Mary Jane retreats. "Thank you," she says. "I'll speak with him when he returns. When is that?"

"I have no idea."

She turns away, and goes downstairs to the typing room in the basement. After work, she approaches Miss Crawley and explains the situation.

"I can try to send a telegram," Miss Crawley says. "But I, too, have to seek the approval of Mr. Spratt, and he can be difficult."

"Would you?"

Miss Crawley places her hand on Mary Jane's. "I will see what I can do. You go home and rest."

That night, Mary Jane writes to Kathleen: *Please tell Mr. Graves that Mrs. Anneka Lindstrom has passed away from the flu. She is a friend of his who lives here in Denver. I am not sure who has taken over the care of her daughter, Mina. If he knows where she's living, would you please ask him to send the address to me? I promised Mina I would visit her.*

She addresses the letter to the Red Cross in Paris, which has been the contact point for the Graves Family Foundation Relief Society since it arrived in France.

That done, she writes to Ross:

I write to you with sad news. Anneka caught the flu and passed away. I'm sorry to tell you this in a letter, but I don't know when I will see you again.

My heart is broken. I was not with Anneka because the house had been placarded by the Health Department, and I'm not sure where Mina was at the time. Anneka loved you, and she loved darling Mina with all her heart. She wanted so badly to learn English and American ways so that she could be a good wife to you. I can't tell you how many hours we spent reading or looking at magazines or talking about the "girl things" that Avery always teases me about. I loved her as the great friend and sister that you hoped she would be to me.

As for Mina, there is some troubling news. Anneka told you that her father died in Sweden, but this isn't true. Mina is the daughter of my employer, Jim Graves. It is a long story, and I will tell you when I see you again. While Anneka was sick, Mr. Graves told Mina that she could come and live with him, but he is currently in France.

I feel an obligation to Anneka to make sure that Mina is safe. I am going to try to find her and bring her to our house to live until Mr. Graves is back in the country. Please write to Mom and Dad and tell them about your connection to Anneka. I think they'll be much more willing to take her in if they know how much her mother meant to you. Right now, poor little Mina has no family.

Please write back as soon as you can.

With love,

M.J.

She crumples the letter and rewrites it, then tears that one in half, and writes another. But regardless of how many attempts she makes, the news is dire, tragic, and hopeless. She considers allowing Ross the bliss of ignorance, but she knows that, eventually, when his letters to Anneka go unanswered or returned, he will write to his sister for an explanation.

As the clerk at the Post Office affixes the proper postage to the letters, Mary Jane asks, "How long will it take these to get to France?"

"Right now, I can't say," he says. "Plan on a month, more depending on how many more clerks catch flu. We were already short-handed because of the draft. Now, it's whoever shows up to work. We don't know if we will have one or five come in to work."

"But this is urgent—"

She grabs the counter to keep from falling on the floor.

"You don't have flu, do you?" the postal clerk demands. ""If you're sick and don't stay away from public places, you're no better than a Hun."

"I'm just over it."

"It can come back, you know." He returns the letters to her. "Here, you're just sending germs through the mail. Go home and stay there."

"You can't do that," she protests. "The Post Office has promised to stay open—"

A sheet of blackness spreads before her eyes.

The next time she wakes, she is in a hospital bed.

THIRTY-SIX

It is *déjà vu*—a French expression that has recently come into fashion. Sitting next to the sick bed of a young woman, feeding her the pulp of oranges, smoothing her forehead with a rag dipped in cold water from a basin, supporting her shoulders and back every time she coughs, struggling to keep up with the French doctor whom only Eleanora can understand well.

Jim stands, massages his stiff back, and looks out the window to the Parisian street below. Behind him, Kathleen lies tucked beneath bleached, white sheets by a nurse who speaks only French. Except for the flame of her hair and a crescent of pink lower lip, she is invisible. She sleeps most of the day and through the night, helped by laudanum into a stupor from which Jim has not yet seen her escape.

It isn't the flu—at least, not at this point. Her heart beats strongly into the doctor's stethoscope; her lungs are clear. All the same, Monsieur Remillard shakes his head morbidly after he examines her, although he never explains what brings him to such despair. He is old—ancient, in fact—and Jim imagines that he has been shaking his head since the days of the Napoleonic Empire. But he is one of the few civilian doctors left in Paris.

Monsieur Remillard calls Kathleen's condition *la dépression nerveuse*, although Ellie has suggested shell shock. The old man only shakes his head and says, "*Non, non, pas une femme.*"

Not a woman.

And yet, here they are. When he arrived in Paris, Jim found that Ellie had rented a third floor suite of rooms in a quiet hotel on the Rue Rennequin near the Arc de Triomphe. She had also contracted for the services of a night nurse and Monsieur Remillard for Kathleen. Harriet Mills—Hank—had died only two days before.

He held his sister as she wept.

"I never thought it would come to this! We started with such hope—"

"Shh, shh, I'm here now. Together we'll figure it out."

"How can we figure this out? Hank is dead."

"I don't know," he admitted. "We'll do what we can for her family. Have you sent a telegram?"

Ellie nodded. "Yesterday."

"I'll arrange the services for her, then. Don't worry about it."

He should be in Denver, he had realized, offering consolation to Harriet Mills' family, and to the employees of Graves Oil, and to the city that has followed the adventures of the Graves Family Foundation Relief Society for more than a year. As soon as he could, he sent a cable requesting that Miss Crawley and Mr. Hobart take on the burden of visiting the Mills family. The weight of being unable to achieve that task himself had left him, once more, feeling torn and desperate—as worried as he had felt in leaving Anneka behind, as guilty as he had felt for breaking his promise to Mina that he would care for them.

His first glimpse of Kathleen came as she lay in her darkened bedroom off the main parlor. She woke when he touched her hand, but it took some time before her eyes settled on him.

"Am I home?" she asked. "Am I in Colorado?"

"You're in Paris," Jim said.

She dozed off again, then opened her eyes. "Why are you here?" she asked. "Did you come for another meeting?"

"No, I came for you, and for Miss Mills and Mrs. Brently."

He had worried that she would ask about their fates, and that he would be forced to choose whether to tell her the bad news or to wait until she was in better health, but she said, "You sent me dirt."

Jim thought he might have misunderstood. "I'm sorry?"

She made a noise that might have been a laugh, but the weakness in her lungs quickly silenced her. "You sent me dirt," she repeated. "Hank said, 'All that money, and he sends you dirt.'"

He recalled the package of souvenirs from Redlands that he had sent her shortly after his visit to Nice. "What did you say?" he asked.

"I didn't say anything," she said. "But I thought, He knows. He knows what I think about." Then, entirely lucid, she spoke directly to him. "You know what I love."

Jim had marveled at how she had changed.

Eleanora has also changed.

One afternoon, she announces that she is expecting a visitor. Her sickness-and-worry-worn face acquires some color, and she dresses in her best afternoon tea gown. When Thomas Lloyd-Elliot arrives, she dances into his arms for an embrace and kiss. Cleanly shaven and in uniform, he is as tall and dashing as a newly promoted Colonel of the British Expeditionary Force should be. He shakes Jim's hand with a palm calloused from his hours on horseback.

They sit on the couch, while the French maid fetches tea. Colonel Lloyd-Elliot relates the news that Austria and Bulgaria have surrendered, requesting a different peace settlement than what will be offered to Germany.

"We need Germany to agree to unconditional surrender," Thomas says. "If we allow Germany to keep any sort of dignity or military power, we will have to fight this war all over again. Even your General Pershing agrees."

"But Germany might be befriended by more undesirable countries, such as Japan, if the Allied nations treat her too harshly," Jim warns.

"Germany has lost nothing but her blood in this war," Thomas argues. "All the fighting has been done in the territory of other nations—France and Belgium. And nothing has stopped the brutality of its soldiers. My men speak of seeing the British wounded piled in heaps by the Germans at Ypres, who then tossed a grenade into their midst. Or Canadian officers crucified in their own trenches—"

Ellie interjects. "Thomas—"

"My apologies," he says. "I'm sorry, Eleanora, Jim. I think it will be a long while before I'll be able to speak without bitterness about what has happened. The number of British dead in this war is more than a million and twice that number wounded—"

"Where have you been recently?" Ellie changes the subject. "In the end, we were moving so quickly and so often that the mail became confused. I haven't received anything in weeks."

"I've been mostly in Picardy again. I'm only here for a day and a half, then I'll be back to Amiens." He takes from the his jacket pocket a stack of postcards. "I have pictures of how the place looks now."

Ellie sifts slowly through the cards, studying them for a long time before she tearfully hands them to Jim. He looks at a picture of a bombed-out shell of a building identified as the Hôtel de Ville in Montdidier. Another is of barely standing walls and a pile of rubble behind a wrought-iron fence with the note, "L'Église de Saint Sepulchre, Montdidier." A third shows the intersection of two dirt roads in Montdidier. Every structure on every corner is reduced to a pile of wood and dust. Only a single sign remains: "Au Train." Perhaps the most heart-wrenching sight is of the Cathedral at Amiens. Its great columns stand naked and bare like the ribs of the skeleton. The façade of the great tympanum of the West Entrance is disconnected from the rest of the building by a complete collapse of the walls.

"The French had constructed walls of sandbags in the nave and transept with the hopes of stabilizing the columns and keeping the roof from falling," Thomas explains. "But nothing could stand the barrage of thousands of shells."

Jim lays the photos aside. Even though he has never visited either town, he recognizes that the scope of the destruction is immense.

"It makes me so sad," Ellie says. "Such a beautiful town and city, such a beautiful landscape—oh, and for all those people to lose their homes. What about the chateau where we stayed in Amiens?"

"It, too, is gone."

"We loved those places. Kathleen, Helen, Hank—"

The doorbell rings, and Ellie looks toward Jim. "Are we expecting Monsieur Remillard?"

"I don't believe so."

Harris comes from the back of the parlor to answer the door. Without closing it, he brings a telegram to Jim.

"What is it?" Ellie asks.

"Most likely business." He tears open the envelope and pulls the out the yellow sheet. The cable, from his mother, reads:

MRS. LINDSTROM HAS DIED. DAUGHTER NOW WITH NEIGHBOR. I WILL CHECK ON HER AS I CAN.

He reels, the ground unsteady beneath his feet. But Anneka had been feeling better. Her fever had broken, and she had responded to his words. And poor Mina, who did not understand her teacher's death—

"Jim, is something wrong?" Ellie asks. "Mother and Father— they're all right?"

"Yes, it isn't that. It's . . . it isn't—"

"Do you wish to make a reply?" Harris asks.

"Yes." On the form, Jim writes: *Make sure Mina is well. Take her with you. I will arrange permanent care when I am home again.*

Harris carries the telegram to the messenger.

Jim sits down, but the conversation—which has now moved on to the tenuous chances of the League of Nations—annoys him. He rises almost immediately. "I'm sorry, please excuse me."

In his bedroom suite, he stands near the window and lights a cigarette. What had gone wrong? Had Dr. Erickson neglected to visit her? Had the teacher-turned-nurse, Miss Edwards, failed to care for her? He had promised Mina that it would be all right.

He stubs out the cigarette in a crystal ashtray and goes to Kathleen's room. She sleeps soundly, as if she is catching up on the rest that has been denied to her for the past year. He sits in the chair beside her bed, trying to calm the rising panic.

I came here for you, he thinks. You might have died—as Hank did—and I could not have borne that. And Ellie, darling Ellie, as well. I promised Mother I would bring her home safely, and I will.

Pain stabs through him, constricting his lungs, wrenching his stomach. He lowers his chin to his chest, the familiar darkness in his soul just at bay, an animal about to pounce.

Ellie comes into the room. "What was the telegram about?"

"Has your Colonel gone?"

"Yes, he left."

Jim lets the words float through the room before he answers, "Anneka has passed away."

"Oh, I'm so sorry, Jim. And the little girl?"

"She's with a neighbor, according to Mother. I sent instructions for her care." A sudden rage erupts in him. "And she is not the 'little girl.' Her name is Mina."

"Wasn't Anneka intending to be married? Wasn't it all nearly resolved?"

He does not answer, but walks to the window.

"What will you do, Jim? Certainly you can't claim her."

"I won't let her go to an orphanage. And why shouldn't I take care of her? Men have done it before and maintained respectability."

"Not those who intend to be governor at some point in their careers," Ellie says. "And not those with our mother. I know you developed a soft spot for the little . . . Mina. Mother wrote to me that you were seeing rather more of Mrs. Lindstrom than she liked. But it will never cease to be a troubling situation."

"Damn it, Ellie, at some point, I have to take responsibility."

She motions toward Kathleen. "What about her?"

"Isn't she in love with the ambulance driver?"

"As far as I know. But, if you were to pursue her, how would you explain Mina? Kathleen is as devout as she was when she left Denver."

"If she is true to her faith, then she wouldn't deny charity and kindness for Mina."

"But if she's true to her heart, she will," Ellie replies. "No woman wants a reminder of the one who came before." She pauses. "It seems that we have—once again—lost more than one person for whom we cared. Just as when we . . ."

She does not finish the sentence, and Jim says, *"Déjà vu."*

"Pardon?"

"Surely you've heard that expression."

"Of course. But when we were children, our parents shielded us from much of the grief and sadness. Now, there is no one to do that."

"I have a dilemma," he admits. "Kathleen's mother passed away."

"Oh, no, why didn't you tell me?"

"It happened just as I was preparing to come here. I spoke to her father, but I really couldn't offer to help him."

"Please, Jim, don't tell her until she is well. And I want to be with her when you tell her."

"All right."

She starts for the door, but stops before she reaches it. "What do you think of Thomas?"

"Your Colonel? I think he's pompous, irascible, vain—a typical Brit."

She laughs. "He is all that."

"But he makes you happy. I can see that."

"Thank you."

"For?"

"For coming here and taking charge. For seeing things through eyes that haven't spent the last year witnessing the death of nearly every living thing in nearly every way it could happen. For being able to use the word, 'happy.'" She breathes in. "Listen to me, anyone who heard me would think I was at the end of my rope."

"Nonsense, you're your mother's daughter. If the rope runs out, you'll simply braid a new one from your own hair. Or, more likely, from someone else's."

She trills a laugh, but quickly sobers. "I'm sorry about Anneka. I know that you cared for her deeply when you were younger. I wish that it would have been easier for you."

He makes no response, and Ellie leaves. Easier, he thinks. How much easier could it have been? Perhaps if it had not been so easy, he would have done what was right for Anneka and Mina.

He looks back to Kathleen. "Wake up," he whispers. "Wake up. Come back from wherever you have gone and realize that a new life awaits you."

Kathleen's eyelids flutter, as if she has heard.

THIRTY-SEVEN

The Hindenburg Line was broken, and the American Expeditionary Force pushed northward, over ground that had been in German hands for years. To ensure victory, the generals of the AEF ordered the American troops to press on, to fight for untenable goals, to engage in battles that would leave thousands dead with no military gain. In a spectacular exhibition of waste, barrages lasted for days, the number of shells exceeding what had ever been launched before. Wave after wave of American soldiers charged over the top, heedless of the guns pointed their way, and fell to their deaths in the last hours of the war.

When the Armistice came at last, Sean was somewhere north of Verdun. As usual, he was lying in a hole in the mud in a place that would smell of death for the next hundred years.

The artillery put up a heavy barrage until 10:59 in the morning. Then came a roar that Sean did not immediately recognize: silence. The men looked at one another—was it real? Could they trust it? If they stood at full height or moved unexpectedly or let go a fart or burp or snore into the stillness, would the war start up again?

Then, the artillery men and the machine gunners began to cheer and sing, and the infantry soon joined them. Within hours, the division band assembled in front of the forward trench to play "Yankee Doodle" to the defeated Germans. Soldiers dashed about waving the Stars and Stripes and the French Tricolor. Men howled and hooted and cried. Reporters and photographers appeared from out of nowhere to catch trenchful after trenchful of American soldiers throwing down their guns and chucking their tin hats and gas masks in the air.

In the reformed Company C, where he knew almost no one, Sean celebrated with his fellow soldiers. He had been promoted to Sergeant, while Danhour was now a Corporal. Danhour had been shipped off to another company, for which Sean was grateful. He never wanted to be reminded of the day of the attack at St. Mihiel again.

On the night of November 11, the ragged, shell-pocked hills around Verdun flickered with open campfires and the sparks of cigarettes. American soldiers set off Verey lights one after another in a blinding fireworks display. Extra powder and explosives burned on immense, popping bonfires. Some soldiers threw their weapons and packs into the fires until the officers halted them.

There was food, too, from the captured German trenches: barrels of sauerkraut and kegs of beer and the delicious yellow cakes that everyone talked about but no one knew the German word for. Yet, everywhere, reminders of the war seeped into the celebration: intestines wrapped around the one remaining branch of a shattered tree; a leg with its genitals still attached to it and displayed openly on the ground, which evoked equal parts laughter and horror from the rowdy soldiers; a spiked German helmet with the scalp still inside.

For the next week, Sean and most of the one million soldiers of the American Expeditionary Force marched twenty kilometers— or about twelve miles—a day to the area around Chaumont. When the troops arrived in Esnouveaux to await orders, Sean applied for leave and went to Chaumont. There, he learned that Kathleen hadn't been at the canteen at AEF Headquarters—which had already been cleaned out and shut down by the Red Cross—for several weeks. No one he talked to had any idea what had become of the Graves Family Foundation Relief Society.

In Rimaucourt, Sean searched through a mile long stretch of look-alike barracks at AEF Base Hospital #238. He found Tony lying in a bed set only inches from others in one of the long, lightless wards. An oozing gash ran up his left arm, and his leg was trussed up in a plaster and a sling and hung from the ceiling by a rope on a pulley.

"I see they're trying to keep you from deserting," Sean said.

Tony laughed weakly. His face was drawn and thin, perhaps from the injury and the pain, or perhaps from the morphine. Still, his first words were: "You cheated me out of a medal, you son-of-a-bitch."

Sean motioned toward the sling. "At least you kept your leg."

Tony paled, but said calmly, "Naw, the bullet just hit the bone and gave it a good crack. They say I won't have no trouble walking again someday. Thing is, they didn't take out the bullet."

"A souvenir from France."

"Hey, they said I'm a Sergeant now, just like you," Tony said. "But now, the damn war's over."

"Sergeant Necchi, huh?" Sean asked. "Maybe they'll let you be an American now."

"Ha," Tony said. "So, tell me what happened to you. Everybody's talking about the crazy American soldiers who 'snapped'—they use that word to say it—and killed a whole trench of Germans—"

"We didn't kill a whole trench—"

"How the hell did you end up with Danhour?"

Sean looked up at a nurse who had come onto the ward. "He saved my life," he said at last. "He shot the machine gunner just as he was about to get his sights on me."

"He's a good shot, lucky for you," Tony agreed. "They said in the newspaper report that because of you two, they could take the hill."

"I don't know. I don't think that's true."

"You don't know?" Tony laughed. "I bet you was just trying to kill Danhour and the Germans just got in the way."

Sean laughed, even though his stomach twisted. Should he tell Tony that he could not stand himself now? That he was praying every night for forgiveness for his actions? Or that he was praying even harder to forget it all? Worse, he wondered if he would always be like that.

Better to have died in a splash of mud and guts than to live his life as a savage.

"Your *mamma* will be so proud," Tony said. "Did they put it in the newspapers? Did they send it to Colorado?"

"Yeah," Sean said. He and Danhour had posed for the newspaper reporters, and one reporter had promised to see that the story made it to the Denver papers. Sean had silently wondered if his actions would bump Liam off the front page.

"What's wrong?" Tony asked. "You don't wanna go home?"

"I want to go home," Sean said. "I never want to see this place again."

"Yeah, me neither. You going back to Colorado?

"Yes. What about you? Are you going back to Brooklyn?"

"Yeah, I guess. I don't know. My brothers—they got wives and kids, I'm gonna be behind them. They tell me, *'Sei brutto e stupido.'*"

"What's that?"

"You are ugly and stupid." Tony shrugged. "I tell them, I know, I know, but so are you. We all got the same blood, the same *madre e padre*, the same faces and brains, and you two got wives. So I can, too."

Sean laughed. "What about going to Montana to find your father?"

"Naw," Tony said. "He never wrote or nothing."

Sean watched the nurse again. After all they had done, shouldn't he and Tony have more to talk about? But, when the memories were of nothing but slaughter and death, who would want to talk about them?

Sean offered his hand. "Well, I guess this is it. I'm catching a train north in a couple of hours."

"That's lucky," Tony said. "I don't know when I'm gonna get out of here."

They told each other goodbye—exchanging addresses, promising to write, shaking hands, wishing each other well—and Sean rejoined his unit, where he found himself alone once again.

THIRTY-EIGHT

Maggie woke with a start. A bell was ringing—not the telephone or the buzzer of the door. No, bells were ringing, loudly and wildly, every church within a hundred miles overtaken by some insane Quasimodo. On the street, an automobile raced by, honking its horn, invading this quiet corner of Berkeley Park.

Alice Colleen began to cry, jarred awake by the noise. Maggie put on her robe, gathered up the baby, and went to the parlor. At almost the same time, her mother and father came from their room. Ma's hair was pulled into a thick braid at the nape of her neck, while Pa wore nothing but his union suit.

"What's happening?" Maggie asked. "What time is it?"

"Two o'clock," Pa said.

She opened the outside door and stepped into the cold November night. Lights were coming on in the houses up and down the block, and she could hear voices and—strangely enough at this hour of the morning—music. Straining, she detected the melody of "The Star Spangled Banner." She turned to her mother and said, "It's the Armistice! It has to be!"

Her father answered. "They said 'twas over the other day. What's to keep this from bein' false, too?"

Maggie didn't reply. A few days ago, Americans had grown so hysterical over a report that Germany had surrendered that violence had broken out in Chicago and some of the other large cities. The police had used their night sticks to quell the crowd, with several injuries reported.

"I could go downtown and find out," she offered.

"You aren't goin' anywhere," her mother said. "Especially where there might be riots."

"But, Ma, don't you want to know? Seaney could be home soon."

Her mother fretted, slower to make decisions now that Auntie Eileen was gone. But Maggie's mind raced. Seaney would be home. Seaney, who would know what to do to save the store. Seaney, who would be able to charm Ma out of bed and back into making hats and attending Church and balancing the till. Seaney, who had always been able to manage Pa and his drunkenness. Everything would be as it had been before.

"I'll go to the newspaper office," Maggie said. "It will be safe there, and Mr. Ledbetter will know."

"Promise you'll come right back to tell us," Ma said. "We've waited so long for it."

"I will."

By the time Maggie had dressed, fed Alice Colleen, brewed tea for her parents, and managed to start the cantankerous and always-low-on-gas delivery truck, it was nearly three in the morning. Even in the darkness, the streets near downtown roiled with pedestrians and horseback riders, who shouted and cheered as the truck rolled past. As she stopped to let a wagon cross in front of her, someone fiddled with the rear of the truck.

She leaned out the window. "What are you doing?"

"Put her in gear and see."

Maggie heard the clatter of a tin can tail behind her as she inched the truck forward. Around her, people cheered and clapped. She drove on, the cans bouncing and clanging along the street, Harbinger of the Armistice.

At the newspaper office, every reporter that Maggie had ever seen there bustled around, shouting on phones or pounding away with two fingers on the typewriters. Maggie found Mr. Ledbetter on the phone in his private office.

He cranked it viciously. "About time you got here."

"Is it true?" she asked. "Is it really over?"

"The Armistice was signed at 11:00 a.m. yesterday French time," he snapped. "No column today, Mrs. James, but I want three-hundred words with advice for women about when their soldiers return from war. Mothers, lovers, wives, all of them. You know, what to do to make him feel the hero when he comes home—"

She stopped listening. If the war was over, if the soldiers were coming home, surely there was no longer any reason for Liam to be in prison.

With a flood of elation, she asked Mr. Ledbetter, "Do you have any family members in France?"

"Two sons," he said flatly. "One will stay there, buried somewhere near St. Quentin."

"I'm sorry," Maggie said.

"Go write your article."

In the newsroom, she gave up on trying to snatch a seat at a typewriter and settled for a beat-up black-topped desk in the corner. Liam, home again, and she, his loving wife and mother of his children. Why, this might be the last column she ever wrote before she became Maggie Keohane again. Happily, she typed: *Remember that he has not seen you, his beloved wife, mother or sister, for a long time. Wear your best clothes and take time to wash your hair. He has not seen a house with plush sofas and warm fireplaces for many months, so clean the house to spotless perfection, nor has he eaten anything but "canned bill" for some time, so cook his favorite meal with vegetables that you have harvested from your Liberty garden. Tell him how proud you are of him for being a Sammie. Show him how thankful you are to have him home on American soil by offering a prayer. Most of all, be a good sport and listen when he tells you his stories about his days in France—*

After Mr. Ledbetter approved the article with a grunt, Maggie went to gather her things. As she slipped her arms inside her coat, someone said, "This just came across the wire. Another hero story, but this one is local. A Sergeant from Denver, Sean Sullivan. He and a foot soldier from Texas killed ten Boche and captured twenty-one on their own in a trench. Do we run it or save it?"

Maggie hurried across the room. "May I see that?"

The copywriter handed it to her, and she read it quickly. Seaney—a hero! It was reported that he and the other man, Calvin Danhour of Mustang, Texas, had received the Distinguished Service Cross for their bravery. More importantly, though, he was alive just a few days ago. And now, it was over and he was no longer in danger. Ma would be so relieved.

"You know him?" the copywriter asked.

Maggie glanced up to find every eye in the newsroom turned in her direction. If she admitted that she knew Seaney, they would know her maiden name was Sullivan. How long would it be before someone discovered that her married name was not James, but Keohane?

"No," she said. "I thought I . . . but I was wrong."

The copywriter turned away dismissively, and the newsroom cranked into gear again.

Outside, the sun had crested the prairie to the east of Denver. Although she intended to go directly home and tell her mother the good news, Maggie was drawn into the crowd that flowed up 17th Street toward the Capitol Building. People darted down the street, racing in front of cars and bicyclists. Girls in feather boas danced the French cancan before a terrified horse and rider. A strident orchestra of gray-haired veterans dressed in ragged Grand Army of the Republic uniforms careened around the corner of Colfax, playing "The Battle Hymn of the Republic."

The mass of humanity swept Maggie down the street. Body pressed against body, a wave of faces, an entanglement of arms and legs. People banged on dishpans, metal rims from automobile tires, or leather drums. Whistles and bugles pierced through the shouting and singing. Paper streamers flew through the air, and someone handed Maggie a hat of silver foil. She placed it on her head and tied the ribbon around her chin. The mob washed onto the Capitol lawns and the grassy lot across Lincoln Street. A man mounted a platform, dragging an effigy of the Kaiser behind him. "We burn him at midnight!" he shouted again and again, a refrain in the chaos. "Be here at midnight for a Kaiser roast and an American toast!"

A boy charged through the crowd. "The public meeting ban's been lifted!" he called. "The theaters are open tonight! Everyone come! The theaters are open!"

People cheered, and the boy announced, "Tonight, at the Broadway Theater, Theda Bara in *Salome!* See the great Biblical story as you've never seen it before! Tonight, at the Broadway—!"

A woman beside Maggie said, "Is your husband coming home?"

"Yes, I hope so."

"That is good news, such good news," the woman said. "It's so nice to see people out again! It's so nice to be well and at peace!"

All at once, Maggie had to know. She worked her way back through the crowd to where she had parked the delivery truck. Inching out of downtown, she drove to Blessed Savior. The bells pealed as she walked up the steps of the Church, and she imagined the ringers pulled off their feet by the vehemence of the clanging.

Inside, she knocked on the open door of Brendan's office.

"You've heard the news," he said.

The words rushed from her. "Liam will come home, now, won't he?"

"Maggie," Brendan said. "Maggie, don't . . . I've already talked to Judah. It will have to go through the courts again. His sentence won't end because the war's over. He'll have to serve it out or seek a new trial. And when he's out, there are the charges here in Denver—"

"But why?" she cried. "What reason do they have for holding him now? What sense does it make to keep him in prison?"

"It's the law."

"But the Sedition Acts aren't even needed anymore. Surely there's something we can do."

Brendan hesitated before he took an envelope from the drawer of his desk. "I think you need to know the truth," he said. "I've been . . . well, I wanted to wait until I knew you were strong enough, what with your aunt's illness and passing and the uncertainty of Seaney's fate—"

"You kept a letter from Liam from me?"

"It isn't addressed to you."

He handed it to her, and Maggie read:

Dear Brendan,

I have been moved to what is called "the Hole," which is a dungeon beneath Fort Leavenworth, a place of no light and no warmth. I and the others who are here—all Conscientious Objectors—are given just bread and water to eat, the portions easily consumed by a single swallow. Our cages, for that is the only way to describe them, perch directly above the sewer, so that the most abominable of smells and gases reach us night and day.

It is a terrible place. During the short time I've been here, four prisoners have hanged themselves, using their sheets and clothing to accomplish the evil deed, and many have become insane, raving and screaming at all hours. Some have been taken to the "hospital," from which they've never returned. Even more have died, uncared for, of influenza.

During the day, my jailers strip my body of clothing, shackle my wrists to the bars of my cell so that my feet barely touch the ground, beat me with blackjacks, and splash buckets of cold water over me. Bedbugs fall from the ceiling and crawl up from the floor. I can smash some of them between the bars of the cells and my manacles, but they feast on me throughout the day and night, and my skin swells and itches from the bites.

But in my solitude, I remember Ephesians: "Be strengthened in the Lord, and in the might of His power." Why should I, a Christian, a Catholic, doubt His mercy? The power of God is invincible. With it, we have all. Without it, we have nothing. To forget Christ and his suffering for us is to go against ourselves and our very humanity.

I thank God for my faith, for nothing else can restrain me from despair. Nothing else can keep me from thinking of how I miss Maggie, and our dear daughter, and the love that we shared. Nothing else can keep me from mourning how you, dear brother, and I were always both solace and strength for each other, and how much I long to speak to you.

I must go now. Give my love to Maggie and Alice Colleen and see that our daughter is raised as an obedient and loving child in the faith and the Church of her father.

With love in Jesus Christ,

Liam

P.S. Do you remember the story of Ralph Hunt, the young Seventh Day Adventist from Colorado who was beaten nearly to death? I must report to you that he has now been committed to the State Insane Asylum in Pueblo. It is said that the wounds and injuries that Ralph received from his beatings and other mistreatment at the hands of the military have left him, ironically, physically unfit for service in the U.S. Army.

She laid the letter in her lap. My God, my God. Wasn't this agony just as bitter as the sorrow of a wife who'd lost her husband on the battlefields of France? Even if he returned to her without a leg or arm, wouldn't it have been better that he come home gravely wounded after fighting for his country rather than being tortured by it?

"You can see why I've been hesitant to let you see this," Brendan said.

She looked at the letter again, but could see nothing but the most terrible of the words. She mused, "See that Alice Colleen is 'raised as an obedient and loving child.' It sounds as if he's never coming home. It's as if he's become—"

"A martyr for his faith?"

"Did you suggest that to him?" she demanded. "Did you write that to him? He's not in his right mind, he's been deprived of—"

"No, I didn't suggest it, but it seems to me that's what he is saying."

"It's simply because he's been alone for so long. If he were to come home, he'd be—"

What would he be?

"Liam is living according to God's plan for him, Maggie," Brendan said. "I think you must accept it."

The bells pounded in the steeple, still ringing without any sort of pattern. All at once, it was just noise, without meaning or coherence. Maggie rubbed at her forehead. She had been up half the night, she hadn't eaten since dinner, and she couldn't bear the brilliance of the day. She did not want to witness the beaming faces of those who expected their sons or husbands to come marching triumphantly home.

"I have to lead the Mass," Brendan said. "Father Devlin's still weak from the flu. Would you like to attend?"

"No, I need to go home and tell Ma about Seaney."

"Seaney? Has something happened to him?"

"He killed a bunch of Germans and was given a medal—or something, I didn't read it that closely. It will be in the *Denver City Daily News* this afternoon."

"Thank God he's not injured," Brendan said. "You've heard about Frank MacMahon? He was killed in the Argonne Forest last week."

"Oh, no, he's Liam's best friend. And Ma will be so upset—"

"I'll stop by and see her later."

As he left the office, Maggie looked up at the crucifix on the wall. Seaney, a hero, with a medal on his chest and a new rank to show off and every newspaperman in Denver awaiting his return. And Liam, a martyr to his faith and a prisoner of his own stubbornness and every newspaper in the nation condemning him. And she— Margaret Mary Sullivan, Maggie Keohane, Mrs. Margaret James— what was she? Who was she?

THIRTY-NINE

Coming out of darkness, Kathleen opens her eyes to see a man by the window, his body a blank form in the dim light, his face featureless. He jiggles a decanter, and the stopper clinks against the glass. She closes her eyes again: *Please let it be Paul, please, let it be him.*

But it isn't, as she already knows. She has awakened often to this sound in this daintily decorated room in Paris, and Jim has always been there. Again and again, he has urged, "Drink this. Drink as much as you can. It's lemon water. It will give you strength."

She remembers little of the influenza that nearly took her life. A fever of 105 degrees for nine days; sleeping almost continually only to awaken to a heavy dull ache through her entire body; crying out as they—who? nurses and doctors?—moved her from lying flat in the bed to a semi-sitting position against a mountain of down pillows; and seeking within herself a comforting blankness, where there was no war, or death, or sickness, or willful thought. Where there was nothing.

Except for a trio of golden-haired cherubs. Painted in a circular recess at the center of the room's ceiling, they tumble in naughty nakedness through a china blue sky. One dives headfirst, his face tilted upward, and his back, bottom, and baby feet drawn in chubby perfection. The wings on his shoulders are cerulean, and his hands spread greedily toward the arc of the circle, grasping for life. The second cherub faces the floor, his arms spread out to fly, his face more contemplative than his brother's. The third looks gleefully over his shoulder, as smiling and sweet as America's Gerber baby. His wings are snow white.

When Kathleen closes her eyes, the three angels await her in the darkness. When she awakens, she looks upward to reassure herself that she is still living, she is still breathing.

"Did I wake you?" Jim appears in the weak circle cast by the lamp.

"I don't think so." Kathleen checks to see that the cherubs cavort still, playful and daring.

"How do you feel?" He places a cool palm on her forehead. "You have no fever. It doesn't appear that the flu will strike again or turn to something more serious."

He takes his hand away, and she feels the dread of coming awake, of coming back to herself and to the knowledge that her mother is dead in Colorado, that Hank has died in France.

Although she remembers Mrs. Brently telling her about Hank, only words come back to her now: Récicourt, leaky roof, pneumonia, doctor, train to Paris, too late, too late, too late.

And now, Hank has been laid to rest in Suresnes, on the slope of Mont Valérien—places her parents and brother and sisters will never be able to visit or even to pronounce.

"Who took over our canteen?" Kathleen had asked.

"I don't know," Mrs. Brently said. "Surely someone came along or, since it was nearly on the Front, perhaps they moved it back to Bar-le-Duc or some other town."

"But the Red Cross was already short-handed, with so many Americans arriving," Kathleen had protested. "Thousands of them coming from home each day—"

"Kathleen, don't worry about it," Mrs. Brently had said. "We've been relieved of our assignments by Mrs. Vanderbilt until we are recovered and can make decisions as to what is best for us. There is talk that the war can't last much longer. And Jim has come all this way to help us, at terrible cost to himself—"

"Oh, I'm sorry!" Kathleen had said. "I sent a cable asking him what I should do. I didn't know he would come here. I'll repay him from my salary when—"

"That isn't what I mean," Mrs. Brently said. "The money is of no consequence. I meant that he left behind personal business that should have been attended to before he came. But he came because you and I both asked him, and I thank God that he was here to see Hank properly cared for."

"But she's dead, Mrs. Brently, and I loved her so—"

"We all did, Kathleen." Mrs. Brently cleared her throat. "There is something more that you should know. The flu has run rampant in America, too, and Denver is no exception. I'm afraid your mother caught it and, sadly, succumbed to it."

Kathleen had struggled to understand the words. "Mama? No, she is never sick, and Papa hasn't written anything—"

"It happened just before Jim left Denver. I believe the service was to be at Mt. Olivet."

"No," Kathleen said again. "Not Mama. Not—"

She had dissolved into sobs, and Mrs. Brently had taken her hand in both of hers. "I'm so very sorry."

"I never loved my mother as I should have," Kathleen confessed. "I always wanted to be with Papa, to be outside or in the fields with him, or to walk with him beside the creek. I thought that cooking and cleaning were the worst jobs, and I hated it when she said I should become a secretary. I didn't want to—"

"Shhh, I'm sure she realized that you were just young. I'm sure she knew you loved her. You mustn't upset yourself so. I'll call the nurse."

And then it was the same thing over again—a dose of laudanum to calm her, and the darkness, and the cherubs beckoning to her, promising that she would feel no sadness.

Now, Jim asks, "Would you like to look out the window? It's snowing."

He helps her to swing her legs out of the bed, stand, and walk. She leans heavily on his arm—an old, broken woman. Every muscle in her body feels shrunken, deflated. Jim props several pillows on the chair, then lowers her into it. As he opens the curtains, even the pale light of the Parisian winter is too bright for her eyes. She shades them with one hand.

"Sorry!" He closes the blinds halfway.

"No, please open it."

In the early hours of the morning, everything is in motion. Wagons and pushcarts jolt up and down the street. French women, dressed in the usual black, hurry along arm in arm. A faint buzz emanates from them.

"What's happening?" Kathleen asks. "Everything is so stirred up out there."

"It's the rumor that the war could end at any moment," Jim says. "You can feel it when you step outside like a draft of warm air in the cold."

"We should pray that it will." Kathleen speaks before she recalls his lack of belief. "I will, anyway."

He kisses the top of her head. "I'll leave you in charge of it, and if your God answers you, I'll be sure to give you and Him full credit."

A visitor comes for Kathleen on a dreary afternoon filled with clouds and rain. Mrs. Brently and Jim have gone out, and Kathleen is alone in the suite. She sits in the chair in her bedroom next to the window, watching the movement on the street outside, when Harris, who is acting as both valet and butler, steps into the room to announce that Lieutenant Latour has arrived.

"Latour?" Kathleen asks. "Oh, show him in, please!"

Her heart beats faster. He has surely been sent by Paul. As Latour, who is as short and portly as Kathleen remembers, enters the room, she says with delight, *"Oh, Monsieur Latour, je suis très heureux de vous voir!"*

"Le plaisir est à moi." Latour continues in English. "But, *Mademoiselle*, I hear you have been sick?"

"Oui, la grippe."

"Quelle domage." He shakes his head. "But you are better now?"

"Oui, merci." Kathleen says. "What brings you here? How did you know where to find me?"

"La Croix Rouge. I am here only for a day before I go to Belgium."

"I'm so glad you came to see me."

"But, *Mademoiselle,* the news I bring . . . it is not good."

Kathleen knows immediately, she knows without a doubt. Paul is dead.

Latour tells her of Paul's last mission to destroy the observation balloon.

"The *avion* went beyond German lines," Latour says in heavily accented English. "It is struck by bullets from the German guns, and flies down, down, and down to—" He puffs out air in the sound of an explosion.

"Did it catch on fire?"

"Je ne sais pas."

Oh, no, it couldn't have, she thinks, not like we saw in Amiens. Poor Maurice—nothing left of him but blackened bones. And now Paul—

Her tears drip from her chin.

"Je suis désolé, Mademoiselle Kathleen," Latour says. "I know Monsieur Reston was very in love, we talked about it, that he would go to Colo—, Colo—"

"Colorado—"

"—*oui*, with you to live. He was very happy to go."

She says nothing, unable to speak for the pain that jags through her body.

"He asks me when we meet for the last time in Issoudun to give these back to you if he, if he, if something happens to him." Latour produces a packet of papers folded neatly and tied with string, and a roll of thick paper. "These are *les lettres* and some of the, um, *les croquis*—"

"My sketches." Her words are barely audible.

"Oui, he wants them to come back to you." Latour clutches the packet to his chest. "To keep them *pour éternité* and to think of him."

He offers the letters and sketches to her, and she takes them in hands that lift with a dead weight. She has no control over her own actions—she reacts, but does not respond; she answers, but does not express; she breathes, but does not live.

Latour hands her an envelope. "This, he was to send to you," he says. "But . . . *non*, he does not. Anything, *Mademoiselle Kathleen*, that you want while you are *ici*, anything, I will do."

"*Merci, Monsieur Latour. Au revoir.*"

He kisses her hand, then leaves the room.

For some time, she sits without moving as wave after wave of tears breaks from her. Why, why? Jim had said that the Armistice was likely to be called at any moment, so why was Paul flying over the German lines? What would it have gained?

She hugs the letters against her breast. To think that she will never see his light eyes again, or his smile, as crooked as it was wide, or hear him speak to her as he did the afternoon in Chaumont, or to feel his hands against her skin.

Desperate, she opens the unsent letter from him. After the initial greeting, she reads:

I know now how you feel when you ride your horse at a gallop through open fields. When I am in a plane, I give my body over to the air currents and forward movement and just ride with it. The wind is both blistering and cold against my face, and I have the sense that I possess some sort of singular freedom. I'm lifted away from the earth and from myself, and yet, every part of me is still attached to the earth by the forces of air and gravity.

One afternoon, Kenny and I flew out over the ocean near Bordeaux. It's a different sensation to be enveloped by both sky and sea, a mingling of the horizon and color and light until it gives the perception that it is all one. I felt at peace, as if I had, at last, accomplished something in my life.

When we are home again, I plan to learn to fly. Then, I will take you up in an airplane, and we'll soar over those Rocky Mountains that you love so much, and over your home at Redlands—

She folds the letter without finishing it, unable to bear one more utterance of hope and joy. She undoes the string that ties the sketches together, and the stiff papers fall in blossom-like curves on the bed. Immediately, she sees the one that she drew of Paul after he gave her the colored pencils. He stands at a crenellation of the Medieval tower near Amiens, his back to her.

Sobs wrench up from her breast, painful and loud, echoing through the room. Later—she doesn't know how long—Mrs. Brently rushes into the room and embraces her.

"I'm so sorry," Mrs. Brently says. "Harris told me about Lieutenant Reston. Shh, shh, oh, I'm so sorry—"

After some time, Mrs. Brently suggests a dose of laudanum, and Kathleen nods her head. She does not even glance toward the ceiling and the friendly cherubs before she closes her eyes. What is left for her but that dark, silent limbo between living and only existing?

She does not know how long it is until Jim comes into her room. It could be hours, or days, or weeks. She isn't able to recollect or mark time just now. Everything is a blur—from the morning when the nurse wakes her, takes her temperature and listens to her lungs, gives her the juice of an orange and a hard-boiled egg for breakfast, and helps her to change her underclothing, to the evenings, when a similar ritual takes place in preparation for the night. She is without strength or volition.

Jim sits in the chair beside her bed. "I hear you've had more bad news. If there's anything Eleanora or I can do, let us know."

Kathleen manages through tears, "Thank you."

He takes his time before speaking again. "When someone leaves this world . . . when they go, even if it's someone that you would see only occasionally, or perhaps not at all, you can feel the void that they have left. You can feel the absence of their existence. It isn't just thoughts of what might have been or a conversation that never was, but the loss of the intelligence, the beauty and grace that was only within them. Their departure leaves gaps in you, black voids in your heart and mind where that person used to be."

Pain wells up in Kathleen's throat. Jim speaks, undoubtedly, of his sister and brother, lost in the lake in Colorado. At last, she chokes out, "Does it . . . do you ever stop missing them?"

"No," he says. "Of course you don't spend your life in constant pain, but there are times when it comes back and is unbearable. You think you will die of the sorrow."

"What do you do then?"

He strokes a lock of hair from her forehead. "Nothing in this world stops because of grief, as much as we might wish it would."

"Is that how it is for you? With the memories of your brother and sister?"

"And others."

"Who?" She asks before she thinks. "I'm sorry, it isn't my concern—"

He leans back in his chair. "I've come to tell you that we will be sailing from Bordeaux on the *S.S. Lorraine* on the second of December. I've booked first class tickets. I thought it might ease your mind some to know that we're going home."

"But we can't go home! We need to go back to—"

"Kathleen," he says gently. "Neither you nor my sister is fit to continue your work. Eleanora has secured a release from the Red Cross for our Relief Society."

"It shouldn't end this way! There are soldiers who need us—"

"And they will be helped by someone else. You need rest and recovery. The doctor has ordered it."

Kathleen feels as if something precious has been stripped from her. She wants to be there at the end, when the final moments of the war play out. She wants—she needs—the sense of a task completed and done well.

"What are you thinking?" Jim asks.

"This past year . . ." She starts again. "This time in France has been the one time in my life that I'll ever be more than I could be. I could be truly kind and good in everything I did. It was easy—there was almost never any question about what needed to be done. If there had been no war, I would . . ."

She trails off, uncertain of what she wants to say.

"But the war is horrible." She chokes, tears coming rapidly. "And it shouldn't have happened, I don't know what I'm saying—"

"It's all right," he says. "You need time before you think about the quiet of everyday living."

"But that's just it. I don't know what everyday living is anymore. I don't know if I remember how to get up in the morning and go to work with people who don't know what it was like over here. I don't know if I can go back to listening to Mavis talk about movies or Annabel sighing over how handsome—" She stops before she names him. "I'm sorry. I didn't mean to imply that those who didn't come to France weren't doing their duty—"

"I'm long past being bothered by such insinuations."

"I should be so happy to be going home."

He lets the words fall in the room before he speaks. "You needn't fear going home because of me. I won't ask you again to be my wife. It isn't a wise prospect for either of us just now. Perhaps it never was. The next time we speak of matrimony—if we ever do—it will have to be at your bidding."

Kathleen closes her eyes against tears.

"That said," he continues, "I will tell you that nothing has changed. I still feel that you are, in every way, my equal. I don't believe that you were more than you could be in this past year. I'm not even sure what that means. And I don't believe this is—was—the one time in your life that you could do good in the world. It was just a beginning." He squeezes her hand and rises from the chair. "Rest now, Miss O'Doherty. You'll need to be strong enough to travel soon."

Mrs. Brently brings the next visitor to Kathleen. Entering the bedroom, she says, "Look who has come to see you."

Helen stands at the door. She wears a plain black dress with white collar and cuff, looking very much like a native Frenchwoman.

"Helen, oh, Helen!" Kathleen opens her arms.

Helen rushes across the room and embraces Kathleen. "I'm so glad to see you!" she says. "I've missed you so much!"

"Helen is going to stay with us for a few days," Mrs. Brently says. "Mrs. Ladd has been so kind as to spare her so that we can enjoy her company."

The maid serves tea and cakes, and the three reminisce about their time together. The conversation settles onto the final days at Récicourt.

"There was an American general who told me we needed to leave immediately," Mrs. Brently recounts. "He said that women shouldn't be so close to the Front."

"I didn't know that," Kathleen says.

"I decided it would be best to keep that to myself. I told him we wouldn't leave until I heard from Mrs. Vanderbilt or one of her assistants."

Helen laughs. "Oh, Mrs. Brently, you are a tiger!"

Her composure slips. "But now, I wish we had left. If we hadn't been in such damp and drafty quarters, perhaps we all wouldn't have caught the flu—"

"There were thousands of American soldiers quarantined for it near Chaumont," Helen says. "There still are. I don't think you could have avoided it no matter where you were assigned."

Mrs. Brently smiles wanly. "Perhaps you're right." Rising from her chair, she says, "I have some correspondence to write. I'll leave the two of you to catch up. It's so good to have you back again, Helen."

She leaves the room, with both Helen and Kathleen watching. As the door closes behind her, Helen says, "She is a truly great lady."

"Yes, she is." Kathleen pauses before she broaches the next topic. "Were you there when Hank—?"

"No," Helen says. "You and Mrs. Brently were both ill, and no one told me—"

"Then, she was alone, and in a foreign country. Oh, Helen, we helped so many, we watched so many soldiers die, and we were there, we were beside them. Yet, we weren't there for the people we loved."

"But maybe there was someone like us—someone who sat with Hank—who didn't even know her, but cared for her all the same." Helen draws in a breath. "I'm sorry about Paul."

Tears flow down Kathleen's cheeks. She cannot stop them. They will drown her, Helen, the entire room. "Oh, Helen, what will I do? What will I do?"

With a soft handkerchief, Helen wipes them away. "I'm so sorry. Kathleen, I know we didn't always get along, and I know that I never understood how deeply you felt about Paul, but—"

"It doesn't matter now. Hank, Paul—we have lost so much—"

"I wrote to Hank's parents," Helen says. "I filled my letter with as many stories as I could remember about her." She falters. "Some of the words in the letter were smeared because I was crying."

"I'm so glad you wrote to them. I haven't been able to . . ." The words fade away. "You've heard we're going home?"

"Mrs. Brently told me."

"Are you going, too?"

"I'm staying here. My parents have given their permission, and Mrs. Ladd has arranged for me to stay on as her assistant."

"I'm so glad," Kathleen says. "You'll do so much good there. Are you and Henri planning to get married?"

"He hasn't asked, and I don't believe he will," Helen says. "He feels too self-conscious about his face. If we marry, it will be because I've asked him."

"Will you?"

Helen smiles secretively. "It's early still—we've only known each other for a few months—but I think there might come a time when I do."

"Paul and I knew almost at once. I think we were in love before we even knew each other's names. I knew when I saw his eyes—"

"Oh, Kathleen." Helen takes Kathleen's hand in both of hers. "I'm so sorry for you. But . . . I don't know if I should say this, but Mr. Graves is a gentleman, as good as his sister is, and . . ."

Kathleen says nothing.

Helen presses on. "I've always known he was in love with you. From the time we were getting ready to come to France. He would walk into the room, and both of you would act in a silly, sort of flighty way." She laughs sheepishly. "I guess it was just flirting, but I was always jealous because he talked to you more than he did to any of us. And then we all knew it in Nice, and Hank and I started hoping you'd come around to loving him. He's so good-looking and so nice, and he's funny, too. I know you'd be happy with him. And Kathleen, you'd be so rich. You'd never have to work again."

"I wouldn't marry anyone for that!"

"Well—" Helen's voice rises. "If he were penniless, it would be all right to ask how you would manage to live. Why isn't it all right to do the opposite? To point out that you would live well?"

Kathleen relents. "I'm sorry. It is nice to live this way."

"We're both so lucky to know the Graves family. If you don't, um, marry him, will you go back to working at Graves Oil?"

"I don't know. I suppose that will be my only choice."

As she speaks, she feels detached, deadened. She can't imagine how she will return to Colorado and take up her old life. It is too far behind her now; she isn't the same person she once was.

"You'll make the right choice, I know you will," Helen says. "And when you do, you'll feel it, just as I have, deep down in here"— she taps the center of her breast—"and you'll be happy again."

Kathleen twines her fingers through Helen's. "Where are you sleeping?"

"I'll be in the room that's just next door, where the nurse has been staying. Mrs. Brently told me they don't think you need her any longer—and, anyway, you'll have me."

"Wake up, oh, wake up!"

Sloughing off the darkness, Kathleen finds Helen at her bedside, with a single candle in her hand. Outside, bells clang and a rumbling rises from the street below.

"It's over!" Helen cries. "At 11:00 this morning, it will all be over! The Germans agreed to the Armistice at midnight, and all hostilities will cease at 11:00. Oh, Kathleen, you have to get out of bed! You have to come and see!"

Kathleen goes to the window. The Rue Rennequin is alight with torches and lamps and candelabra, and the gas street lamps flicker wanly after months of being dark. Swarms of people shout and sing and make noise on any kind of surface imaginable. Fireworks flare in front of the church at the end of the block, while the bells toll a wild rhythm. Someone plays on a mouth harp, another on a concertina. At nearly every window, someone leans over the sill to wave the French flag. Across the way, children dump huge handfuls of shredded newspaper from a second story window onto the crowd below.

Helen laughs. "They're saying that everyone should come out in uniform to the Champs Élysées at dawn. You have to get dressed!"

"What about you?"

"I left my uniform behind at Mrs. Ladd's—"

"You can borrow my extra, and you can wear Hank's cloak."

"It would be too long."

"But it would be as if a part of her were with us, and we could honor her—"

Helen's eyes shine. "I'll go ask Mrs. Brently for it."

"And don't forget the fox collar and muff. Hank loved them so."

After the girls dress, they join Jim and Mrs. Brently in the dining room for a fully-cooked breakfast and hot tea. Mrs. Brently wears her uniform and a newly starched wimple, while Jim has donned a crisply-tailored suit and immaculately pressed shirt. On his feet are cowboy boots of red, white, and blue.

The doorbell rings, and Harris opens it. Henri steps inside, dressed in his sky blue uniform with its array of medals dangling from the chest. He wears the mask that Mrs. Ladd shaped for him. Held on by eyeglasses, it gives him a nose where there is only a stump, and his lack of lips is hidden by a bushy mustache.

Helen runs to him. *"Oh, Henri, c'est finie! La guerre est finie!"*

He wraps his arms around her. *"Oui, mon amour."*

Kathleen catches Mrs. Brently's eye and smiles at her.

Jim addresses Kathleen. "If you feel ill or weak at all, Miss O'Doherty, just let me know and I'll spirit you out of the crowd to a place of safety. I've been threatened—or, rather, commissioned—by my sister to make sure you are comfortable at all times."

Mrs. Brently laughs, but says, "Indeed, that's so."

As the sun rises on Paris, they join the revelers in the street. It takes them nearly an hour to crawl the four blocks from the hotel to the Place de L'Étoile and the Arc de Triomphe. Kathleen clings to Jim's arm. She worries less about her health than she does about becoming separated and lost in the immense number of people.

At the Place de L'Étoile, celebrants surge toward the Arc from every spoke of the side streets. More than one impromptu band bounces out a tune, and people sing whatever comes into their heads. Some dance, and others cling to the walls of the Arc and weep. After a while, the throng begins to wend its way down the Champs in the direction of the Place de la Concorde. Jim shouts over the din, "Should we join them?"

There is almost no forward movement. As the cold fog of the Parisian night lifts, Kathleen sees that an ocean of people sways along the Champs Élysées from the Arc to the Place de la Concorde: a sea of Frenchmen in blue; Americans in their overseas caps; British still wearing their tin helmets; Aussies in their brown slouch hats with the left side looped up; Sepoys in their turbans; French officers in their scarlet uniforms and billed hats; civilians in bowlers or fedoras, women in veiled mourning or wide-brimmed felt. Here and there, the flags of the French, British and Americans float above the crowd, carried along to the sound of cheers.

When it becomes apparent that no one will reach the Place de la Concorde for hours, French soldiers clear spots on the sidewalk to set up regimental bands. An American military band takes over a low, concrete barrier near one of the street lamps in the center of the Champs Élysées and begins crashing out, "Over There," as the spectators applaud and shout, "*Vive l'Amérique!*"

A French soldier points at Kathleen. "*Ici! La Croix Rouge!*"

"What is it?" Jim asks.

"They want us to come up and, I believe, take a bow," Mrs. Brently says.

"Should we?" Helen asks, her eyes alight.

"We should."

The three women are passed hand over hand to the stage as the band members scoot aside to make room for them. A French soldier leaps onto the stage with them, carrying both the American and the French flags. He beckons for one of the uniformed band members to take the American flag and to stand just to the right and slightly behind the women. He strikes an identical pose to the left with the French flag. "Zee Star-Span-gel Ban-neer!'" he calls to the band. *"Oui, La Marseilles!"*

The band launches into "The Star-Spangled Banner," and Kathleen and Helen and Mrs. Brently place their hands over their hearts and sing. Kathleen's lungs sting, but she pushes out the notes as strongly as she can. For Paul, she thinks, for Hank, for Seaney and his fellow soldiers, for all of them. From the corner of her eye, she can see the American Doughboy standing perfectly still, saluting, the Stars and Stripes hanging with dignity from the long pole in his hands.

After the anthem ends, the band plays the "Marseilles." The entire street fills with music, and Kathleen lets the tears fall from her eyes as she joins in to honor the French. Once the anthem ends, a great cheer erupts: "Hurrah for the Red Cross! *Vive la Croix Rouge!"*

Suddenly someone calls out, *"Écoutez! Écoutez! Silence, s'il vous plaît! Silence!"*

The message echoes, repeated again and again, and the thousands gathered in the street obey with remarkable rapidity. For a full minute, no one speaks; no one moves. Standing on the stage, Kathleen hardly dares to breathe. Then, the clocks chime eleven, and the bells of the churches clamor again, more joyfully than they had before. The whole city swells with sound, as if a great dam has been released.

"C'est finie! Dieu merci! La guerre est finie! Grâce à Dieu!"

"It's over! Thank God! The war is over! Praise God!"

Kathleen spies Jim and Henri in the crowd. Jim talks with— or more likely, shouts at—Henri, and Kathleen wonders at their conversation. Either Jim must be speaking in French, which he claims he doesn't know, or Helen has taught Henri to speak English. Or perhaps it doesn't matter. Jim laughs at something that Henri says, and Kathleen's heart tightens.

Jim looks up at her, and his expression changes from an easy smile to solemn assessment. She hears his words: *Of course you don't spend your life in constant pain, but there are times when it comes back and is unbearable. You think you will die of the sorrow.* Just as she had so long ago in New York, she senses the darkness in him that he keeps at bay through furious living. Only now, she possesses a well of loss and grief deep in her own soul. Now, she knows it, too.

But there will be time for grief later. Today, there is hope as the War to End All Wars ends. Today is the day that good has defeated evil, that kindness has won out over cruelty, and mercy over injustice. It is a time to celebrate not only the Armistice, but a return to living.

Mrs. Brently says, "Let's move on," and the three women work their way back to Jim and Henri.

Jim greets them. "That was a lovely tableau."

Helen laughs as she links arms with Kathleen. "I didn't think I would make such a spectacle of myself until my wedding day. Did you?"

"Shall we go?" Jim offers his left arm to Kathleen. She takes it, and in a flush of affection squeezes it. In reply, Jim brings his elbow in, snugging her hand against his body. Henri and Helen join arms, and Mrs. Brently takes Jim's other arm.

Together, they join the procession along the Champs Élysées, the celebration of victory a glorious wind at their backs.

The adventure has only begun!
Follow Kathleen, Sean, and Maggie as the White Winter Trilogy continues.

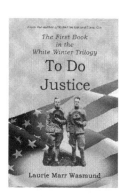

To Do Justice

Three young Irish-Americans encounter the turmoil of a world at war and embark on a journey that will forever change their lives, their country, and the world.

To Love Kindness

In spring, 1918, the Americans mount their greatest battles against the Germans. For Kathleen, Sean, and Maggie, each passing day threatens to take from them the things they love most.

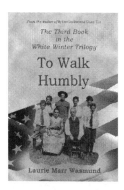

To Walk Humbly

The war is over, yet in Colorado, a more daunting foe has awakened: the Ku Klux Klan. A new battle begins for Kathleen, Sean, and Maggie—one in which the stakes are even higher.

If you enjoyed
To Do Justice and *To Love Kindness,*
read *To Walk Humbly,* the final
book in the White Winter Trilogy!

You can contact me at
lost.ranch.books@gmail.com.

Help others enjoy this book, too!

Share it with others!
Pass on your copy to friends and acquaintances.

Recommend it!
Please help other readers find this book by recommending
it to your friends, book groups, libraries, and discussion
boards. If your book group is in the Rocky Mountain
region, contact me at **lost.ranch.books@gmail.com** to
discuss the possibility of an author visit!

Review it!
Please tell other readers why you liked this book by
reviewing it at Amazon or Goodreads. If you write a review,
send me an email at **lost.ranch.books@gmail.com** so
that I can thank you with a personal reply.

Visit lostranchbooks.com
for more information.

AUTHOR'S NOTE

In addition to those that I used for *To Do Justice*, I consulted the following sources for this book: *Canteening Under Two Flags: Letters of Doris Kellogg* by Doris Kellogg; *Canteening Overseas, 1917-1919* by Marian Baldwin; *The Millionaires' Unit* by Marc Wortman; and *The U.S. Air Service in World War I, Volumes I-IV,* compiled and edited by Maurer Maurer. For Liam's story, I read *Benjamin Salmon's Book,* which has been published online by the ACLU, and *Unsung Hero of the Great War* by Torin R.T. Finney. My research on Woman's Suffrage comes from two sources: *The History of Woman Suffrage, Volume VI, 1900-1920,* edited by Ida Husted Harper, and *The Grounding of Modern Feminism* by Nancy F. Cott. The treatment of German-Americans during the war is discussed by Lyle W. Dorsett in his article, "The Ordeal of Colorado's Germans during World War 1." Once again, the Colorado Historic Newspaper Collection, which is available online, supplied a snapshot of events and attitudes in Colorado during the war years. See my website, lostranchbooks.com, for a full list of resources used to write this book and the others in the trilogy.

Countless readers have given me advice and help in writing this book. I wish to thank all of them for their encouragement. I would especially like to thank the following: C.J. Prince, Karen Steinberg, Jesse Kuiken, Jordana Pilmanis, and Tom Reeves. My sincerest appreciation goes to Linda Burnside and Cynthia Norrgran, who read early drafts of the full manuscript for me, and to Mark Putch, whose sharp-eyed criticism is always welcome. I must also thank my sister, Carol Bryant, for her enthusiasm and diligence in editing the manuscript.

My husband, Bill Wasmund, served as a source for the technical vocabulary of flight during the early years of the U.S. Air Force. The French dialogue in the book derives from my own knowledge of French and from translations found on the web. Any errors in theology, military history, or the language are mine alone.

Once again, my deepest indebtedness is to Bill, whose generous and constant support allows me to write. Thank you, my love.

Made in the USA
San Bernardino, CA
26 January 2020